The Temptation of
Elminster

Ed Greenwood

THE TEMPTATION OF
ELMINSTER

Cover art by Todd Lockwood
First Printing: December 1998
First Paperback Edition: November 1999
Library of Congress Catalog Card Number: 97-62384

9 8 7 6 5 4 3 2 1

ISBN: 0-7869-1427-0
T21427-620

U.S., CANADA,
ASIA, PACIFIC, & LATIN AMERICA
Wizards of the Coast, Inc.
P.O. Box 707
Renton, WA 98057-0707
800-324-6496

EUROPEAN HEADQUARTERS
Wizards of the Coast, Belgium
P.B. 2031
2600 Berchem
Belgium
+32-70-23-32-77

Visit our website at **www.tsr.com**

Novels by Ed Greenwood

Elminster: The Making of a Mage
Elminster in Myth Drannor
The Temptation of Elminster

Spellfire

Crown of Fire

Stormlight

<u>*The Shadow of the Avatar Trilogy*</u>
Shadows of Doom
Cloak of Shadows
All Shadows Fled

Cormyr: A Novel
Ed Greenwood & Jeff Grubb

Silverfall: Stories of the Seven Sisters
August 1999

To
Steve & Jenny Helleiner

Great friends, good people,
champions of gaming
and the gamers who play.
Let all your triumphs together
not be in Another World.

The realm of Galadorna lay east of Delthuntle.
Its capital, Nethrar, survives as present-day Nethra.

The events of Part I span about five years,
beginning in the Year of the Missing Blade (759 DR).

The events of Part II span sixteen or seventeen days
in the Year of the Awakening Wyrm (767 DR).

Prologue

There is a time in the unfolding history of the mighty Old Mage of Shadowdale that some sages call "the years when Elminster lay dead." I wasn't there to see any corpse, so I prefer to call them "the Silent Years." I've been vilified and derided as the worst sort of fantasizing idiot for that stance, but my critics and I agree on one thing: whatever Elminster did during those years, all we know of it is—nothing at all.

Antarn the Sage
from **The High History of
Faerûnian Archmages Mighty**
published circa The Year of the Staff

The sword flashed down to deal death. The roszel bush made no defense beyond emitting a solid sort of thunking noise as tempered steel sliced through it. Thorny boughs fell away with dry cracklings, a booted foot slipped, and there was a heavy crash, followed, as three adventurers caught their breath in unison, by a tense silence.

"Amandarn?" one of them asked when she could hold her tongue no more, her voice sharp with apprehension. "Amandarn?"

The name echoed back to her from the walls of the ruin—walls that seemed somehow watchful . . . and waiting.

The three waded forward through loose rubble, weapons ready, eyes darting this way and that for the telltale dark ribbon of a snake.

"Amandarn?" came the cry again, lower and more tremulous. A trap could be anywhere, or a lurking beast, and—

"Gods curse these stones and thorns . . . and crazed Netherese builders, too!" a voice more exasperated than pain-wracked snarled from somewhere ahead, somewhere slightly muffled, where the ground gave way into darkness.

"To say nothing of even crazier thieves!" the woman who'd called so anxiously boomed out a reply, her voice loud and warm with relief.

"Wealth redistributors, Nuressa, if you *please,*" Amandarn replied in aggrieved tones, as stones shifted and rattled around his clawing hands. "The term 'thief' is such a vulgar, career-limiting word."

"Like the word 'idiot'?" a third voice asked gruffly. "Or 'hero'?" Its gruffness lay like a mock growl atop tones of liquid velvet.

"Iyriklaunavan," Nuressa said severely, "we've had this talk already, haven't we? Insults and provocative comments are for when we're lazing by a fire, safe at home, *not* in the middle of some deadly sorcerer's tomb with unknown Netherese spells and guardian ghosts bristling all around us."

"I thought I heard something odd," a deep, raw fourth voice added with a chuckle. "Ghosts bristle far more noisily than they did in my father's day, I must say."

"Hmmph," Nuressa replied tartly, reaching one long, bronzed and muscled arm down into the gloom to haul the still struggling Amandarn to his feet. The point of the gigantic war sword in her other hand didn't waver or droop for an instant. "Over-clever dwarves, I've heard," she added as she more or less plucked the wealth redistributor into the air like a rather slim pack-sack, "die just as easily."

"Where do you hear these things?" Iyriklaunavan asked, in light, sardonic tones of mock envy. "I must go drinking there."

"*Iyrik,*" Nuressa growled warningly, as she set the thief down.

"Say," Amandarn commented excitedly, waving one black-gloved hand for silence. "That has a ring to it! We could call ourselves . . . The Over-clever Dwarf!"

"We *could,*" Nuressa said witheringly, grounding her sword and crossing her forearms on its quillons. It was obvious anything lurking in this crypt—or mausoleum, or whatever it was yawning dark and menacingly just ahead of them—wasn't asleep or unwarned anymore. The need for haste was past and the chance for stealth gone forever. The brawny warrior woman squinted up at the sun, judging how much of the day was left. She was hot in her armor . . . really hot, for the first time since before last harvest.

It was an unexpectedly warm day in Mirtul, the Year of the Missing Blade, and the four adventurers scrambling in the sea of broken, stony rubble were sweating under their shared coating of thick dust.

The shortest, stoutest one chuckled merrily and said in his raw, broken trumpet of a voice, "I can hardly elude my born duty to be the dwarf—so that leaves it to ye three to be 'over-clever.' Even with the triple muster, I'm not before-all-the-gods sure you've wits enough—"

"That'll do," the elf standing beside him said, his tones as gruff as any dwarf could manage. "It's not a name I'm in overmuch favor of, anyway. I don't want a joke name. How can we feel proud—"

"Strut around, you mean," the dwarf murmured.

"—wearing a jest we're sure to become heartily sick of after a month, at most. Why not something exotic, something . . ." He waved his hand as if willing inspiration to burst forth. A moment later, obligingly, it did. "Something like the Steel Rose."

There was a moment of considering silence, which Iyriklaunavan could count as something of a victory, before Folossan chuckled again and asked, "You want me to forge some flowers for us to wear? Belt buckles? Codpieces?"

Amandarn stopped rubbing his bruises long enough to ask witheringly, "Do you have to make a joke of everything, Lossum? I like that name."

The woman who towered over them all in her blackened armor said slowly, "But I don't know that I do, Sir Thief. I was called something similar when I was a slave, thanks to the whippings my disobedience brought me. A 'steel rose' is a welt raised by a steel-barbed whip."

The merry dwarf shrugged. "That makes it a bad name for a brace of bold and menacing adventurers?" he asked.

Amandarn snorted at that description.

Nuressa's mouth tightened into a thin line that the others had learned to respect. "A slaver who makes steel roses is deemed careless with a whip or unable to control his temper. Such a welt lowers the value of a slave. Good slavers have other ways of causing pain without leaving marks. So you'll be saying we're careless and unable to control ourselves."

"Seems even more fitting, then, to me," the dwarf told the nearest stone pillar, then jumped back with a strangled oath as it cracked across and a great shard of stone tumbled down at him, crashing through a sudden flurry of tensely raised weapons.

Dust swirled in the silence, but nothing else moved. After what seemed like a long time, Nuressa lowered her blade and muttered, "We've wasted quite enough time on one more silly argument about what to call ourselves. Let it be spoken of *later*. Amandarn, you were finding us a safe way into yon . . ."

"Waiting tomb," Folossan murmured smoothly, grinning sheepishly under the sudden weight of the three dark, annoyed glares.

In near silence the thief moved forward, hands spread for balance, his soft-soled boots gripping the loose stones. Perhaps a dozen strides ahead lay a dark and gaping opening in the side of a broken-spired bulk of stone that had once been the heart of a mighty palace but now stood like a forlorn and forgotten cottage amid leaning pillars and heaps of fern-girt rubble.

Iyriklaunavan took a few steps forward to better watch Amandarn's slow and careful advance. As the slim, almost child-sized thief came to a halt just outside the ruined walls to peer warily ahead, the maroon-robed elf whispered, "I have a bad feeling about this. . . ."

Folossan waved a dismissive hand and said, "You have a bad feeling about everything, O gruffest of elves."

Nuressa jostled both of them into silence as Amandarn suddenly broke his immobility, gliding forward and out of sight.

They waited. And waited. Iyriklaunavan cleared his throat as quietly as he could, but the sound in his throat still seemed startlingly loud even to him. An eerie, waiting stillness seemed to hang over the ruins. A bird crossed the distant sky without calling, the beats of its wings seeming to measure a time that had grown too long.

Something had happened to Amandarn.

A very quiet doom? They'd heard nothing . . . and as the tense breaths of time dragged on, heard more of it.

Nuressa found herself walking slowly toward the hole where Amandarn had gone, her boots crunching on the shifting stones where the thief had walked with no more noise than a falling leaf. She shrugged and hefted the war sword in her hands. Skulking was for others.

She was almost in under the shadow of the walls when something moved in the waiting darkness ahead

of her. Nuressa swept her blade up and back, ready to
cut down viciously, but the face grinning at her out of
the gloom belonged to Amandarn.

"I knew you were annoyed with me," the thief said,
eyeing her raised steel, "but I'm quite short enough
already, thank you."

He jerked his thumb at the darkness behind him.
"It's a tomb, all right," he said, "old and crawling with
runes. They probably say something along the lines of
'Zurmapyxapetyl, a mage of Netheril, sleeps here,' but
reading Old High Netherese, or whatever it's properly
called, is more Iyrik's skill than mine."

"Any guardians?" Nuressa asked, not taking her eyes
off the darkness beyond Amandarn for an instant.

"None that I saw, but a glowblade's pretty dim. . . ."

"Safe to throw in a torch?"

The thief shrugged. "Should be. Everything's made
of stone."

Wordlessly Nuressa extended an open, gauntleted
hand behind her. After a few scrambling minutes,
Folossan put a lit torch into it. The warrior looked at
him, dipped her jaw in wordless thanks, and threw.

Flames *whup-whup-whupped* into the darkness. The
torchlight guttered when it landed, then recovered and
danced brightly once more. Nuressa stepped forward to
fill the opening with her body, barring the way, and
asked simply, "Traps?"

"None near the entrance," Amandarn replied, "and
this place doesn't *feel* like we'll find any. Yet . . . I don't
like those runes. You can hide anything in runes."

"True enough," the dwarf agreed in a low voice.
"Are you satisfied, Nessa? Are you going to stand
aside and let us in or play at being a closed door until
nightfall?"

The armored woman gave him a withering look, then
silently stood aside and gestured grandly at him to proceed.

Folossan put his head down and scuttled past, not
quite daring to whoop. The normally gloomy-looking

Iyriklaunavan was hard on his heels, trotting forward with fluid grace and maroon robes held high to avoid tripping. It would not do to tumble and fall helplessly into a tomb where just about any sort of snake or other foe might be lurking.

Amandarn wasn't far behind. In exasperated silence Nuressa watched them storm past and shook her head. Did they think this was some sort of pleasure outing?

She followed more cautiously, looking for doors that might be shut to imprison them, traps Amandarn might have missed, even some sort of lurking foes, hitherto unnoticed. . . .

"Gods on their glittering thrones!" Folossan gasped, somewhere ahead. He made of the curse a slow, measured bricklaying of awe, building a wall of utter astonishment that seemed to echo around the dark tomb chamber for just an instant before something swallowed it.

Nuressa shouldered her way out of the sunlight, war sword ready. Trust them to cry no warning to tell her what peril awaited.

The chamber was high and dusty and dark, the torch dying a slow, sullen death at its heart. There was a space that bore some sort of circular design in the floor tiles, framed by four smooth, dark stone pillars that soared from the pave to the lofty, unseen ceiling.

Away beyond those ever feebler flames rose dark steps crowned by what could only be the casket of someone great and important—or a true giant, so large was the massive black stone, blotched with deep emerald green, its curves aglitter with golden runes that flashed in time with the pulsing, fading light of the torch. Two empty braziers taller than she was flanked this dais, and over it hung the dusty-shrouded ends of what looked like a curtain of mail but could, under the dust, be almost anything that would drape like fabric, hanging motionless from the distant, scarcely seen ceiling.

It was not the tomb that the gruff elf mage, the awed dwarf, and the boyish thief were staring at. It was something else, rather nearer than that, and above them. Nuressa shot a hard glance up at it, then all around the tomb chamber, seeking some other entrance or waiting peril. None offered itself to the tip of her gleaming blade, so she grounded it and joined in the general staring.

High above them, starting perhaps fifty feet up in the air, hung what might be a scarecrow, and might have once been a man. Two worn bootheels they could see, standing on emptiness, and above that a man-sized bulk of gray dust so thick it looked like fur, joined to the ceiling and walls by lazy, dusty arcs of cobwebs that must be as thick as ropes.

"That was a man, once, I think," Iyriklaunavan murmured, voicing what they were all thinking.

"Aye, so, but what's holding him up there?" Folossan asked. "Surely not those webs . . . but I can see naught else."

"So it's magic," Nuressa said reluctantly, and they all nodded in slow and solemn agreement.

"Someone who died in a trap or spell duel," Amandarn said quietly, "or a guardian, who's been waiting all these years, undead or asleep, for the likes of us to intrude?"

"We can't afford to gamble," the elf told him gruffly. "He could well be a mage, and he's above us, where none can hide from him. Stand back, all."

The adventuring band that had no name moved in four different directions, each member taking his own path backward across the ever more dimly lit room. Folossan was fumbling in his voluminous shoulder bags for another torch as Iyriklaunavan raised his hands to cup empty air, murmured something, then spread his hands apart.

Between those hands something shivered and glimmered for a tumbling instant before it flashed, so bright as to sear the watching eye, and leaped through the dark emptiness like a sizzling blade. The spell clove air and all as it smote whatever hung so high above, bringing down a heavy rain of choking dust.

Clods of gray fur fell like snow melting from high branches, pattering down on all sides as the four adventurers coughed and wiped at their eyes and noses, shaking their heads and staggering back.

Something flickered nearby, in several places. Struggling to clear the dust from watering eyes and see, the four adventurers could not help but notice two things through the swirling dust: the booted feet above were still exactly where they had been, and the flickerings were pulsing radiances playing rapidly up and down the four stone pillars.

"He moves!" Iyriklaunavan shouted suddenly, pointing upward. "He moves! I'll . . ."

The rest of his words were lost in a sudden grinding, rumbling noise that shook the floor tiles under their boots. The light dancing down the pillars suddenly flashed into brightness, gleaming back from four tensely raised weapons. Stone facings on all of the pillars slid down into the floor, leaving behind openings that stretched the height of the pillars.

Something filled those openings, dimly seen as the radiances died away, leaving only the ruby embers of the torch on the floor. Folossan dived for that torch, blowing hard on it and coughing in the swirling dust with each breath he took. He thrust a fresh torch against the old one and blew on where they met.

The others were peering suspiciously at what filled the floor-to-ceiling channels in the pillars. It was something pale and glistening that writhed in the channels like maggots crawling over a corpse. Pearly white here, dun-hued there, like rice glistening under a clear sauce but expanding outward, as if flexing and stretching after a long confinement.

The new torch flared, and in the newly leaping light Nuressa saw enough to be certain. "Lossum—*get out of there!*" she shouted. "All of you! Back—out of this place—*now!*"

She had distinctly seen pale flesh peel and wrinkle back to unhood a green-gray eye . . . and there was another, and a third. These were forests of eyestalks!

And the only creatures she knew of that had many eyes on stalks were beholders, the deadly eye tyrants of legend. The others knew the same tales and were sprinting through the settling dust toward her now, all thoughts of tomb plunder and laden sacks of treasure forgotten.

Behind the hurrying adventurers, as Nuressa watched, eyes winked and came to life and began to focus.

"*Hurry!*" she bellowed, drawing in enough dust to make her next words a croak. "Hurry . . . or die!"

A glow suddenly encircled one eye, then another— and burst into beams of golden light that stabbed out through the dust, parting it like smoke, to scorch the heels of hurrying Folossan and the wall beside Iyriklaunavan. Amandarn darted past Nuressa, stinking of fear, and the warrior woman pressed herself against the wall so as not to block the passage of her other two desperately hurrying companions. The elf then the dwarf clattered past, cursing in continuous babblings, but Nuressa kept her eyes on the pillars. Four columns of awake and alert eyes were peering her way now, radiances growing around many of them.

"Gods," she gasped, in utter terror. Oh let them be fixed here, unable to follow. . . .

A ruby beam of light from one eye stabbed at Nuressa and she ducked away, sparks erupting along the edge of her war sword. Sudden heat seared her palm. As a dozen golden beams lanced through the dust at her, she threw the blade over her head, back behind her out of the chamber. She wheeled in the same motion to flee headlong after it, diving for safety as something burst near her left ear with a sound like rolling thunder. Stones began to fall in a hard and heavy rain.

*　　*　　*　　*　　*

It feels odd, to stand on air, neither solid like stone, nor the slight yielding of turf under one's boots. In dry and dusty darkness . . . where by Mystra's sweet kisses was he?

Memory flowed around him like a river, cloaking him against madness for so long that it would not answer his bidding now. There was a tingling in his limbs. Great power had struck him, forcefully, only moments ago. A spell must have been hurled his way . . . so a foe must be near.

His eyes, so long dry and frozen in place, would not turn in their sockets, so he had to turn his head. His neck proved to be stiff and set in its pose, so he turned his shoulders, wheeling his whole body, as the walls drifted slowly past, and dust fell away from him in wisps and ropes and huge clods.

The walls drifting . . . he was sinking, settling down through the air, released from . . . what?

Something had trapped him here, despite his clever walking on air to avoid traps and guardian spells. Something had seized on the magic holding him aloft and gripped it as if in manacles, holding him immobile in the darkness.

A very long time must have passed.

Yet something had shattered the spell trap, awakening him. He wasn't alone, and he was descending whether he wanted to or not, heading toward . . . what?

He strained to see and found eyes looking back at him from all sides. Malevolent eyes, set in columns of pale eyestalks that danced and swayed with slow grace as they followed his fall, radiances growing around them.

Some strange sort of beholder? No, some of the stalks were darker, or stouter, or larger all around than others . . . these were beholder eyestalks, all right, but they'd come from many different beholders. Those radiances, of course, could only mean him harm.

He still felt oddly . . . detached. Not real, not *here*, but still afloat in the rush of memories that named him

. . . Elminster, the Chosen One—or at least *a* Chosen—
of Mystra, the dark-eyed lady of all magic. Ah, the
warmth and sheer *power* of the silver fire that flowed
through her and out of her, pouring from her mouth,
locked onto his, to snarl and sear and burn its agoniz-
ing, exhilarating way through every inch of him, leaking out nose and ears and his very fingertips.

Light flared and flashed, and Elminster felt new
agony. His dry throat struggled to roar, his hands
clawed uncontrollably at the air, and his guts seemed
afire and yet light and free.

He looked down and found silver fire raging and
sputtering around him, spilling restlessly out of his
stomach along with something pale, bloody, and ropy
that must be his own innards. Fresh fire flashed, and
a searing pain and sizzle marked the loss of his hair
and the tip of an ear along the right side of his head.

Anger seized him, and without thinking Elminster
lashed out, raking the air with silver fire that shattered
and scattered a score of reaching magical beams on its
way to claw at struggling eyestalks.

Eyes melted away, winking and weeping and thrashing with futile radiances sparking and flickering around
them. El wasted no time watching their destruction, but
turned to point at another pillar and sear its column of
eyestalks from top to bottom.

He knew not what magics preserved all these severed
eyestalks, but Mystra's flames could rend all Art, and flesh
both alive and undead. Elminster turned to scorch another column of angry eyes. He was still sinking, his guts
sagging out in front of him, and with each bolt of silver
fire something beyond the pillars glowed in answer. Eye-
born beams of deadly magic were stabbing at him in
earnest now, failing before the divine fire of Mystra. The
angry crackle and the surflike rising and falling roar of
much unleashed magic was howling about the chamber
like a full-throated winter storm, shaking the wizard's
long-unused limbs.

A last column of eyes darkened and died, to droop and dangle floorward, weeping dark sludge that mirrored Elminster's own tile-drenching flow of vital fluids. He clawed at his own innards, tucking them back inside himself with hands that blazed with silver flames, and was still about it, feeling sick and weak despite the roused, surging divine power, when his boot heels found something solid at last. He stumbled, all balance gone, staggered, and almost fell before he got his feet planted firmly. Dust swirled up anew around him, crackling angrily as it met surging silver fire. Beyond the pillars, runes graven on the steps and casket of what must be a tomb flashed and crackled with flames of their own, mirroring every roar of Mystra's fire.

Gasping as agony caught at him, El bent his efforts to healing the great wound in his middle, ignoring the last few flickering eyes. The flowing silver fire would, he hoped, catch and rend their spells before he was harmed. His blood had fallen in a dark rain on the tiles during his descent, and he felt emptied and torn. The last mage of Athalantar snarled in wordless anger and determination.

He had to get himself whole and out of this place before the stored silver fire faded and failed him, retreating to coil warmly around his heart and rebuild itself. Whatever had entrapped him before could well do so again if he tarried, and his present agony had been caused by only one eyestalk attack. He turned slowly, bent over with silver flames licking between trembling fingers, and held his guts in place as he moved haltingly toward the place where dim daylight was coming from.

Eyestalks flashed forth fresh beams of ravening magic to scorch floor tiles inches behind Elminster's shuffling boots. Sealing the last of his great wound, he slashed behind him with a sheet of silver flame, shielding himself from more attacks.

Behind him, unseen, the surviving eyestalks all went limp and dark in the same instant. In the next breath, the runes on the tomb acquired a steady, strengthening glow. Small radiances winked amid the metallic curtain above it, climbing and descending like curious but excited spiders, flaring forth ever stronger.

Elminster found his way out into the waiting light, half expecting arrows or blades to bite at him while he was still blinking at the dazzling brightness of full daylight. Instead, he found only four frightened faces staring at him over a distant remnant of wall.

He tried to call to them, but all that emerged was a dry, strangled snarl. El coughed, gargled, and tried again, managing a sort of sob.

The elf behind the wall lifted a hand as if to cast a spell, but the dwarf and the human male flanking him struck that hand aside. A furious argument and struggle followed.

El fixed his eyes on the fourth adventurer—a woman watching him warily over the crazed and crumbling edge of a great sword that had been struck by lightning or something of the sort not very long ago—and managed to ask, "What . . . *year* . . . is this?"

"Year of the Missing Blade, in early Mirtul," she called back, then, seeing his weary lack of comprehension, added, "In Dalereckoning, 'tis seven hundred and fifty-nine."

El nodded and waved his thanks, on his stumbling way to lean against a nearby pillar and shake his head.

He'd been exploring this tomb—a century ago?—seeking to learn how the mightiest archwizards of Netheril had faced death. Some insidious magical trap had ensnared him so cleverly that he'd never even noticed his fall into stasis. For years, it seemed, he'd hung frozen near the ceiling. Elminster the Mighty, Chosen of Mystra, Armathor of Myth Drannor, and Prince of Athalantar stood in midair, a handy anchor for spiderwebs, acquiring a thick cloak of dust and cobwebs.

Careless idiot. Would that ever change, the hawk-nosed mage wondered briefly, if he lived to be a thousand years old or more?

Perhaps not. Ah, well, at least he *knew* he was an idiot. Most wizards never even make it that far. El drew in a deep breath, dodged behind the pillar as he saw the elf glaring at him and raising his hands again, and sorted through his memories. These were the spells—and *that* one would serve. He had a world to see anew, and decades of lost history to catch up on.

"Mystra, forgive me," he said aloud, calling up the spell.

There came no answer, but the spell worked as it was supposed to, plucking him up into a brief maelstrom of blue mists and silver bubbles that would whisk him elsewhere.

Abruptly, the figure behind the pillar was gone.

"I could have had him!" Iyriklaunavan cursed. "Just a few moments longer, and—"

"You could've had us killed in a spell duel, right here," Amandarn hissed. "Shouldn't we be getting away from here? That man was freed from how we found him, those eyes sprouted from the pillars . . . what *else* is waking up, in there?"

Folossan rolled his eyes and said, "Am I hearing rightly? A thief, walking away from treasure?"

The wealth redistributor eyed him coldly. "Try saying it thus," he replied. " 'Hurrying away from likely death, in the interests of staying alive.' "

The dwarf looked up at the silent warrior woman beside him.

"Nessa?"

She let out a deep, regretful sigh, then said briskly, "We run, away, as swift as we can on these loose stones. Come—*now.*" She turned, a hulking figure in blackened armor, and began to shoulder her way around pillars and stub-ends of fallen walls.

"We're barely twenty paces from the strongest magic

I've seen in decades," the elf mage protested, waving a hand at the darkness.

Nuressa turned, hands on hips, and said tartly, "Hear my prediction: it's not only the strongest magic you've seen—it's the strongest you'll *ever* see, Iyrik, if you tarry here much longer. Let's get gone before dark . . . and while we still can."

She turned away once more. Folossan and Amandarn cast regretful glances at the hall they'd fled from, but they followed.

The elf in maroon robes cursed, took one longing step around the end of the wall as if to return to the tomb, then turned to follow his companions. A few paces later he stopped and looked back.

He sighed and went on his way, never seeing what came out of the tomb to follow him.

*   *   *   *   *

The second torch died down. In the near total darkness that followed, the runes on the steps of the tomb blazed like so many altar candles. From somewhere there came a rhythmic thudding, as if from an unseen, distant drum. The lights winking and playing in the curtain above the dark stone casket began to race about, washing down over the stone tomb as showers of sparks that sank into the runes they touched and caused little flames to flare up briefly from the stone. A mist or wispy smoke came with them, and a faint echo that might have been an exultant chant mingled briefly with the thudding.

The runes flared into blazing brilliance, faded, flashed almost blinding-bright—then abruptly went out, leaving all in darkness and silence.

The embers of the torch gave just enough light, had anyone been in the tomb, to see the massive lid of the casket hovering just above its sides. Through the gap between them, something emerged from the tomb and swirled around the room.

It was more a wind than a body, more a shadow than a presence. Like a chill, chiming whirlwind it gathered itself and drifted purposefully toward where the sunlight beckoned. Living things that had been in the tomb not long ago still walked . . . for a little while yet.

PART I

THE LADY OF SHADOWS

One

A FIRE AT MIDNIGHT

Azuth remains a mysterious figure—sometimes benevolent, sometimes ruthless, sometimes eager to reveal all, sometimes deliberately cryptic. In other words, a typical mage.

Antarn the Sage
from **The High History of
Faerûnian Archmages Mighty**
published circa The Year of the Staff

"Tempus preserve us!"

"Save the prayers, fool, and *run!* Tempus'll honor your *bones* if you don't hurry!"

Pots clanged together wildly as Larando cast them aside, rucksack and all, and sprinted away through the knee-deep ferns. A low branch took his helm off, and he didn't even pause to try to grab at it.

Panting, the priest of Tempus followed, sweat dripping from his stubbled chin. Ardelnar Trethtran was exhausted, his lungs and thighs aching from all the running—but he dared not collapse yet. The tumbled

towers of Myth Drannor were still all around them . . .
and so were the lurking fiends.

Deep, harsh laughter rolled out of the trees to Ardelnar's left—followed by a charging trio of barbazu, their
beards dripping blood. They were naked, their scaled
hides glistening with the gore of victims as well as the
usual slime. Broad shoulders rippled, and batlike ears
and long, lashing tails bobbed exultantly as they came
bounding along like playful orcs, black eyes snapping
with glee. They flung away the bloody limbs of some
unfortunate adventurer they'd torn apart and swarmed
after Larando, shouting exultant jests and boasts in a
language Ardelnar was glad he couldn't understand.
They waved their heavy, saw-toothed blades like toys
as they hooted and snorted and hacked, and it took
them only a few moments to draw blood. Larando
screamed as one frantically flailing arm went flying
away from him, severed cleanly by a shrewd strike.

The competing bearded fiend wasn't so deft; the warrior's other arm was left dangling from his shoulder,
attached to his body by a few strips of bloody flesh.
When Larando moaned and collapsed, two of the fiends
used their saw-toothed blades to lift him in an impro-
vised cradle, and run along with him so the third barbazu could have some sport involving the warrior's
innards and carving openings to allow them to briefly
see the wider world.

Larando's head was lolling despite the brutal slaps
being dealt him, as Ardelnar fled in a different direction.
The priest's last glimpse of his friend was of a beautiful
winged woman—no, a fiend, an erinyes—swooping
down out of the trees with a sickle in her hands.

Giant gray-feathered wings beat above a slender
body that was shapely and pale wherever cruel barbed
armor didn't cover it. Scowling black brows arched with
glee, a pert mouth parted as the she-fiend's tongue
licked her lips in anticipation, and she sliced, twisted,
and flew on, waving a bloody trophy. Behind her, gore

spattered all over the barbazu as they howled their disappointment, a headless corpse thrashing and convulsing in their midst.

"Tempus forgive my fear, I pray," Ardelnar managed to stammer through white and trembling lips, as he fought down nausea and ran on. It had been a mistake to come here, a mistake that looked very much like it was going to cost all of them their lives.

The City of Song was no open treasure pit, but the hunting ground of fiends. These malevolent creatures would hide, letting adventurers venture freely into their midst to wander the very ruins of the riven city. Then they'd trap the intruders and take cruel sport in slaying them as a sort of hunt-and-run game.

Tales of such cruelty were told in taverns where adventurers gather. That was why three famous and very independent companies of adventurers had uneasily joined in a pact and gone into Myth Drannor together. Surely seven mages, two of them archwizards of note, could handle a few bat-winged . . .

Most of those mages had been torn apart already or left to stumble around with eyes and tongues plucked out, for the fiends to tease at leisure later. When the rest of us are dead, Ardelnar thought grimly as he tripped over a fallen statuette, hopped a few awkward steps to keep his footing, and found himself stumbling through the shattered, overgrown remnants of a garden fountain.

Oh, they'd found treasure. His belt pouch was bulging right now with a generous double handful of gems—sapphires and a few rubies—torn from the chest of a mummified elf corpse as its preservative magics faded with a few last glows and sighs. There'd even been a lone erinyes in that crypt; they'd slain her—it— with confidence. With her wings hacked off in a shower of bloody feathers, she'd not lasted long against the blades of a dozen adventurers, for all her hissing and spitting. Ardelnar could still see the spurt of blood from a mouth beautiful enough to kiss, and her blood smoking as it ran along her dusky limbs.

Not long after that, the jaws of the trap had closed, with gloating fiends strolling out of every ruin, glade, and thicket on all sides. The adventurers had broken and fled in all directions to the tune of cold, cruel laughter . . . and the slaughter had begun.

Back in the here and now, he was seeing the erinyes again. Four of them swooping past, gliding low. Ardelnar ducked involuntarily, but found himself ignored as they banked off to his right, giggling like temple-maids—nude, beautiful, and deadly. They'd have passed for dusky-skinned women of the Tashalar without those great gray-feathered wings. They were after the mage he'd been hoping would get them both out of this fiend-haunted ruin. Klargathan Srior was a tall, spade-bearded southerner who seemed the most capable of all the mages, as well as the most arrogant.

All that hauteur was gone now, as the mage ran wearily along on Ardelnar's right, hairy legs stained with blood where he'd gashed himself while slicing off his own robes so he could flee faster. Gold earrings bobbed amid rivers of sweat, and a steady stream of mumbled curses marked the mage's flight for his life. The erinyes glided in, veering apart to come at Klargathan from different directions, razor-sharp daggers in their hands. Sport was in their laughter and their cruel eyes, not outright murder.

Gasping, the mage stopped and took his stand. "Priest!" he bellowed, as a baton from his belt grew of its own accord into a staff. "Aid me, for the love of Tempus!"

Ardelnar almost ran on, leaving the man's death to buy himself a few more breaths of flight, but he stood no chance in this deep and endless wood without Klargathan's spells, and they both knew it. They also both knew that this cold realization carried more weight than the command to serve in the name of the

Foehammer. The shame of that was like a cold worm crawling in Ardelnar's heart. Not that there was time to brood or fashion denials.

He swallowed in mid-stride, then almost fell as he wheeled around without slowing and ran to the mage, stumbling over bones half-glimpsed amid the forest plants, old bones—human bones. He had a momentary glimpse of a skull rolling away from his foot, jawless and unable to grin.

Klargathan was whirling his staff over his head with desperate energy, trying to smash aside the gliding erinyes without having one of them slash open his face or pluck the weapon from his hands. They were circling him like sharks, reaching out with their blades to cut at his clothing. One shoulder was already bared—and wet with blood from the dagger cut that had left it so.

Through the desperate chaos of thudding staff and flapping wings, the mage's eyes caught those of the priest. "I need . . ." the southerner gasped, "some time!"

Ardelnar nodded to show he understood and plucked off his own helm to smash at one wing of an erinyes. She flapped aside and he brought his warhammer up from his belt into her beautiful face, hard. Blood sprayed and the fiend squalled. Then she was past them, flying blindly into a tumble along the ground and into a waiting tree, while her three companions descended on Ardelnar in a shrieking, clawing cloud. He jammed the helm over the face of one and ducked under her gliding body so close that her breasts grazed his shoulder, using her as cover against the blades of the others. They struck at both her and the priest, not caring who they cut open, and as Ardelnar ducked away and rolled to his feet to avoid being caught between those last two screaming, spitting she-fiends, he heard Klargathan stammering out an incantation, ignoring the gurgling erinyes who plowed into the ground beside him, her side slashed open and black, smoking blood fountaining forth.

The last two she-fiends soared up into the air to gain height enough to dive back down on this unexpectedly tough pair of humans, and Ardelnar snatched a quick glance back at the overgrown, ruined towers of Myth Drannor. More fiends were coming. Barbazu and barb-covered hamatula, far too many to outfight or outrun, loped along with tails lashing and blood-hunger in their faces. This fern-covered ground would be his grave.

"Tempus, let this last battle be to your glory!" he cried aloud, holding up his bloodied hammer. "Make me worthy of your service, swift in my striking, alert in my fighting, agile and deft!"

One of the erinyes tapped his hammer aside with her dagger, and leaned in to snicker as she swooped past his ear, "My, my—anything else?"

Her voice was low, and lush, full of lusty promise. Its mockery enraged Ardelnar more than anything else ever had in all his life. He bounded after her, almost leaving himself open to easy slaughter at the hands of the other erinyes, but instead she became the first victim of Klargathan's spell.

Black, slimy coils of what looked like a giant serpent or eel erupted from the ferns not far away, spiraling upward with incredible speed. Now they seemed more like taproots, or the boughs of a tree sprouting from nothing to full vigor in mere seconds.

One bough encircled the throat of the erinyes as she turned leisurely to slice at Ardelnar, and another looped about her ankle. The force of her frantic wing beats swung her around to where the black tree was already entwined around both of the previously grounded erinyes. Their bodies were visibly shriveling, sucked dry of blood and innards with the same unnerving speed as everything else this spell-tree did.

Still trying to fly, the snared she-fiend crashed into a tangle of thickening trunks. Her head was driven off, dangling to one side, and thereafter she moved no more.

"By the Lord of Battles, what a spell!" Ardelnar gasped, watching tendrils swarm over the body of the erinyes with that same lightning speed. More were waving in the air above them, encircling the fourth she-fiend. Despite her frightened, wildly slashing struggles, the tendrils caught at her wings, pulled, and slowly dragged her down. The priest of Tempus laughed and waved his hammer at the mage in salute.

Klargathan gave him a lopsided grin. "It won't be enough," he said sadly, "and I haven't another like that. We're going to die for the sake of a few gems and elven gewgaws."

The running fiends were almost upon them now. Ardelnar turned to flee, but the southerner shook his head. "I'm not running," he said. "At least my tree keeps them from taking us from the rear."

A sudden hope lit his features and he added, "Have you any sapphires?"

Ardelnar tore open his pouch and emptied it into the mage's hand. "There must be a dozen there," he said eagerly, no longer caring a whit when Klargathan raked through them and dumped everything that wasn't a sapphire onto the ground.

The southerner swept one arm around the priest and hugged him fiercely. "We're still going to die here," he said, bestowing a firm kiss on the startled priest's lips, "but at least we'll turn a few fiends to smoking bones around us." He grinned at Ardelnar's expression, and added, "The kiss is for my wife; tell Tempus to deliver it to her for me, if you've time left for another prayer. Hold them off again, please."

He crouched down without another word, and Ardelnar hefted his warhammer in one hand and unhooked his small belt-mace to hold ready in the other, taking a stance in front of the mage as ever-thickening black tendrils curled around and over them like a cupping hand.

The tree shivered under the blows of many barbazu blades even as it grew, and gargoyle-like spinagons,

folding their wings and barbed tails flat, scuttled in
along the tunnel-like opening in its branches to face the
priest, who found fresh happiness—no, *satisfaction*—
welling through him. He was going to die here, but die
well. Let it befall so.

"Thank you, Tempus," he said, blowing Klargathan's
kiss to the air for the god of war to take on. "Let this
my last worship please thee."

His warhammer swept up and crashed down.
Spinagon claws raked his arm, and he smashed them
aside with his mace, being driven back by the sheer
force of five charging fiends. "Hurry, mage!" he snarled,
struggling to keep from being buried under clawing
limbs.

"I have," Klargathan replied calmly, nudging Ardelnar with one knee as he hurled a sapphire down the
tunnel of tendrils, and the world exploded in lightning.

From one gem to another held in the mage's cupped
hand the lightning bolts blazed, crackling and rebounding in arcs that raced back and forth rather than striking once. Though every hair on both their bodies stood
on end, neither the mage nor the priest took harm from
the spell.

The biting, clawing fiend wrapped around Ardelnar
was protected from the lightning, too, but Klargathan
stepped forward and thrust a silver-bladed dagger hilt-
deep into one of its eyes, then pulled it out and drove
it into the other. It collapsed, slithering down Ardelnar's
legs as the two adventurers watched fiends—even one
of the tall barb-covered, point-headed hamatulas, its
bristling shoulders shedding tendrils with every
spasm—dance in the thrall of the lightning. Flesh darkened and eyes sizzled as the bolts flashed back and
forth.

Then, as abruptly as it had erupted, the spell ended,
leaving Klargathan shaking his hand and blowing on
his smoking palm. "Good, large gems," he said with a
tight grin, "and we've more to use yet."

"Do we run?" Ardelnar asked, eyeing a pair of erinyes who glared down at him as they swept past overhead, "or bide here?"

The next group of winged she-fiends was struggling under the weight of a broken-off elven statue larger than any of them. They let it go with deft precision. Good Myth Drannan stone crashed through tangled tree limbs, its fall numbing both men despite their dives for safety. They scrambled up to find the falling statuary had left an opening to the sky that spinagons were already circling, aloft, massing to dive into.

The southerner shrugged. "It's death either way," he said. "Moving gives both sides more fun, but tarrying here wins us more time, and we can shed more of their blood before we go down. Not quite the way I'd planned to dance in the ruins of Myth Drannor, but it'll have to do."

Ardelnar's answering laughter was a little wild. "Let's move," he suggested. "I don't want to wind up half crushed under a stone block, with them tormenting my extremities while I die slowly."

Klargathan grinned and clapped the priest on the shoulder. "So be it!" he said and shoved, hard. As the startled Ardelnar crashed headfirst into black tendrils that at least didn't claw at him, half a dozen spinagons slammed down into the space where he'd been standing, their cruel forks stabbing deep into the suddenly vacated ground, too deep to tear free in haste.

"Run!" the mage shouted, pointing up the tunnel. Ardelnar obeyed, steadying himself with his mace against the trampled ground as he stumbled over a forest root, then rushing headlong away from the conjured tree. Behind him raced the mage, a sapphire clenched in his hand and his head cocked to look back as he ran.

When the outstretched claws of the hard-flying, foremost pursuing spinagon were almost touching him, Klargathan held up the gem and said one soft word. Lightning erupted from it right down the fiend's throat.

Its struggling gray gargoyle body burst apart in the roar of bolts lashing into it from both in front and behind—for the mage had left another gem on the ground by the fallen statue, where the fiends had swooped down. As the dark, blood-wet tatters fell away behind the rushing men, Ardelnar saw the rest of the spinagons tumbling and shuddering in the grip of those snarling bolts. He followed the mage around a huge duskwood tree, onto a game trail that led more or less in the direction they wanted to go: away from the ruins, in any direction, downright swiftly.

Ardelnar saw the mage toss down another gem as they sprinted on, dodging around standing trees and leaping over fallen ones, out among the barbazu now, in the deep and endless forest now reclaiming the riven city of Myth Drannor.

In the distance they saw another fleeing adventurer cut down. Then a barbed tail swept down out of dark branches overhead to send Klargathan sprawling, and the two men were too busy for any more sightseeing.

The first lash of the cornugon's whip snapped the warhammer from Ardelnar's numbed fingers, and the second laid his shoulder open to the bone, clear through the pauldron and mail shirt that should have protected it. The priest tumbled helplessly away, thrashing in his agony. This was a good thing. It took him well clear of the first howling bolt of lightning.

The bolt crashed into the huge, scale-covered cornugon and toppled it, roaring, right into the pit-of-spikes trap on the trail that it had been guarding. Impaled, it roared more desperately, its cry high and sharp, until a bleeding Klargathan leaped in on top of it, and drove his silver-bladed dagger into another pair of fiend eyes. Those sightless orbs wept streams of smoke as the mage scrambled back out of the thrashing tangle of shuddering bat-wings, long claws, and flailing tail in the pit, and shook the moaning Ardelnar to his feet.

"We'd better run beside the trail, not on it," Klargathan gasped. "I don't suppose you brought any healing-quaffs along? You need one about now."

"My thanks for confirming what a mess I must be," the priest grunted, reeling. "I'm afraid I wasn't the one carrying the potions, but if you'll guard me for a few breaths . . ."

The mage's baton became a staff again, and he stood guard, watching his last fading lightning bolts snap back and forth along the now empty trail as Ardelnar healed himself.

As they stumbled on, the priest felt weak and sick. Ahead, a steep hill rose, forcing them to run around it or try to climb its tree-girt slopes and somehow stay ahead of fiends who could fly. It was no surprise when Klargathan headed around the hill, panting raggedly now. Ardelnar followed, wondering just how long they'd be able to outrun half the vacationing occupants of the Lower Planes.

They came out into a clearing caused by the crashing fall of a shadowtop tree, and Ardelnar had his answer. Unfortunately, it was a very final one.

Klargathan went down under the claws of half a dozen pouncing cornugons. He hurled a handful of gems into the air with his last breath and died in the wild hail of lightning bolts that followed, sending his slayers tumbling away in all directions. The priest saw that, and managed one last, exultant shout. As fiend-talons burst through his chest and his own hot blood welled up to choke him, Ardelnar was briefly glad he'd healed himself before this final fray. It seemed somehow . . . tidy.

* * * * *

His last prayer to Mystra had been answered by a silence as deafening as all the previous ones. A year passed since he'd awakened in a tomb full of malevolent eyes with no words from the goddess Elminster so loved. He'd wept, on his knees, before wearily wrapping his cloak around himself and seeking despondent, lonely slumber out under a sky of rushing, tattered clouds, on a deserted hill out in the rolling wilderlands. He was dozing when the sign had come to him. Unbidden, a scene had swum into his drowsy mind, of him standing on a hilltop he knew . . . and did not know.

It was Halidae's Height, a forest-covered hilltop south and a little west of Myth Drannor that he'd stood on a time or two before, usually with a laughing elf lass on his arm and a warm, star-filled night stretching out before them. In the scene that had come to him there were no elf maidens. Moreover, something had toppled more than one tree on the Height and lit fires here and there, marring it from what he remembered.

He knew he'd journey thence without delay, come morning. He had to know what Mystra desired him to do—and this at least was *something*. For the thousandth time El lamented Mystra's silence and wondered what he'd done to earn it. Surely not getting caught in a trap for a few generations because he'd followed her dictates to seek out ever more magic, in old places and hidden ones.

Yet he retained his powers, some even more vigorous than before—so there must be a Mystra, with her own powers intact and the governance of magic still in her hands. Why was she silent, keeping her face hidden from him?

And just who was he to question what she might do, or not do?

A man, challenging the gods as other men did—and with about as much success. El fell asleep thinking of stars moving about in the heavens as part of a gigantic chess game played among the gods. The last thing he remembered was seeing the sudden, tremulous trail of a shooting star—probably a real one, not a dream's whim—dying, off to the east.

*   *   *   *   *

Halidae's Height was as scarred as the vision had shown him. He teleported in to stand beside a duskwood tree that didn't seem to have changed one whit between his memory and the vision. A gentle breeze was blowing, and he was alone on the hilltop. Elminster had barely glanced over its ravaged slope and started to swing his gaze toward Myth Drannor, knowing, by now, the sadness he'd see, when the breeze brought cries to his ears. Shouts of battle.

He sprang to the edge of the Height, where in happier days one could look out and down over the city. Tiny figures were leaping and dying in the thinned-out forest below. Humans and—fiends, monsters from the Lower Planes—were running about, the humans fleeing. Winged she-fiends were swooping here and there. Lightning bolts suddenly stabbed out in all directions from one knot of creatures, in a deadly star of death that sent fiends staggering and screaming. Other devils were slaying humans down there, disemboweling one last adventurer as he watched. Just in case any of the fleeing men escaped, a door in the air—a magical gate—had opened at the foot of the Height, and a steady stream of fiends was pouring forth from it.

El stared at the gate grimly, and raised his hands. "Gates," he told the air softly, "I can handle." He worked a magic that Mystra herself had given him and sent it splashing down on the maw that was still releasing hordes of fiends.

It washed over the gate with a menacing crackle of spell energy, and there were screams and roars from the fiends emerging from it. Yet when the raging fires of the spell fell away, long moments later, the gate stood unchanged.

Elminster gaped at it. How could—?

A moment later, he had an answer . . . of sorts. The last flickering, floating motes of light caused by his spell brightened, rose up to face him, and shaped themselves into letters in one of the elder elvish tongues he'd learned to read in Myth Drannor; it was a language only he and several hundred elf elders could read. Floating in the air, the letters spelled out a blunt message: "Leave alone."

As El stared at them in utter bewilderment, they fell into shapeless tatters of light then faded away, trailing down into wisps of smoke to join the chaos and death below. Fiends looked up, snarling. This could only be from Mystra . . . couldn't it?

Well, if not her, who else?

The last prince of Athalantar looked down at the fiends capering in the ruins of Myth Drannor and asked the world bitterly, "What good is it to be a mage, if ye don't use thy power to do good, by shaping the world around ye?"

The answer came from the air behind Elminster: "What good can it be, save by blind mischance, if you try but lack eyes and wits powerful enough to see the shape you're sculpting?"

The voice was low and calm but filled with a musical hum of raw power that he'd only ever heard before when Mystra spoke. It sounded male and somehow both familiar and wholly new and strange.

Elminster spun around. He stood alone; the Height was empty but for a few trees and the wind stirring them.

He stared hard at the empty air, but it stayed empty.

"Who are ye, who answer me? Reveal thyself," he demanded. "Philosophy comes hard when the lectures are delivered by phantoms."

The empty air chuckled. Suddenly it held two glimmering points of light, miniature stars that circled each other lazily, then whirled around with racing speed and burst into a blinding cascade of starry motes of light.

When the flood of brightness fell away, Elminster beheld a robed man standing behind it. He was white-bearded and black-browed, and his calm eyes shone very blue before they filled with all the colors of the rushing rainbow. As Elminster watched, the man's eyes darkened to black shot through with tiny, slowly moving stars.

"Impressive," Elminster granted amiably. "And ye are . . . ?"

The chuckle came again. "I meant it not as a show, nor yet as a herald's cry of my identity . . . but since we seem to be speaking suchwise, why don't you have a guess?"

El looked the man up and down. Old, ancient even, and yet spry, perhaps as young as some fifty-odd winters. White-haired, save for the brows, forearms, and chest, where the hair was black. He was empty-handed, with no rings in evidence, wearing simple, spare robes with flared sleeves and no belt or purse; bare feet below—feet that could afford to be bare, because they hovered a few inches off the ground, never quite touching.

Elminster looked up from them to the wise face of their owner, and said softly, "Azuth."

"The same," the man replied, and though he did not smile, El thought he seemed somehow pleased.

Elminster took a step forward, and said, "Forgive my boldness, High One, if ye will . . . but I serve Mystra in a manner both close and personal—"

"You are the dearest of her Chosen, yes," Azuth said with a smile. "She speaks often of you and of the joy you've brought her in the times she's spent playing at being mortal."

The prince of Athalantar felt joy and a vast relief. In his sigh of contentment and relaxation he almost stepped backward off the Height. At that moment a barbed whip arced around at his face, from the air off to his left, and something unseen took him around the shoulders as he swayed on the edge of oblivion then snatched him forward, away from the cornugon an instant before its reaching talons could thrust into Elminster's eyes. He found himself skimming across the scorched stones of the hilltop, Azuth receding before him so they always faced each other from the same distance.

"M-my thanks," El stammered, as they came to a gentle halt. He felt himself lowered into a comfortable, lounging position, lying on yielding but somehow solid air. Azuth was also sitting on nothing, facing him, across a fire that suddenly sprang out of nowhere. Flames danced up from air a handspan above the unmarked rock of the Height. El looked at it, then around at a sky now full of bat-winged, scaled, hissing fiends, clawing at the air with widening, many-toothed smiles as they dived nearer.

"I don't wish to seem ungrateful or critical, High One," he said, "but yon fiends can't fail but notice this light, and we'll have them visiting."

Azuth smiled, and for an instant his arms seemed to flow with slowly marching lights, winking and sparkling. "No," he replied in the calm, musical voice that was at once splendid and laced with excitement—and at the same time soothing and reassuring. "This Height, henceforth, is shielded against fiends—of all kinds—so long as my power endures. Now hearken, for there are things you should know."

Elminster nodded, bright-eyed in his eagerness. His manner brought the ghost of a smile to the lips of the Lord of Spells, who caused both of their hands to be suddenly full of goblets of wine that smoked and glowed. The god began to speak.

Over Azuth's left shoulder, a hulking red monster of a fiend flapped huge wings in a booming clap of fury, clawed at air that seemed to resist it, and burst into flames. With fire raging up and down its limbs, it gibbered, fangs spraying green spittle, and a flash of unleashed magic burst from its taloned hands and crawled across an unseen barrier for long moments before rebounding with a flash and roar that plucked the pit fiend from its clawing perch on empty air, sending it tumbling away through the air like a tattered leaf.

The god ignored this, as well as the wails and moans of watching, circling fiends that followed, as he addressed Elminster like a gentle teacher, speaking at ease in a quiet place. "All who work magic serve Mystra whether they will or no," he said. "She is of the Weave, and every use of it strengthens her, reveres her, and exalts her. You and I both know a little of what is left of her mortal side. We've seen traces of the feelings and memories and thoughts she clings to in desperation from time to time, when the wild exultation of power coursing through the Weave—that is the Weave—threatens to overwhelm her sentience entirely. No entity, mortal or divine, can last in her position forever. There will be other Mystras, in time to come."

A hand that trailed tiny stars pointed to Elminster, then back at Azuth's own chest. "We are her treasures, lad—we are what she holds most dear, the rocks she can cling to in the storms of wild Art. She needs us to be strong, far stronger than most mortals . . . tempered tools for her use. Being bound to us by love and linked to us to preserve her very humanity, she finds it hard to be harsh to us—to do the tempering that must be done. She began the tempering of you long ago; you are her 'pet project,' if you will, just as the Magisters are mine. She creates her Chosen and her Magisters, but she gives the training of them to others, chiefly me, once she grows to love them too much or needs them to be distant from her. The Magisters must needs be distant, that creativity in Art be untrammeled. You, she has grown to love too much."

Elminster blushed and ran a finger around the rim of his goblet. Fiends clawed the air in the distance as he looked down—and was abashed as he might not have been at another time—to find the vessel full of wine again after he had drunk deep.

Azuth watched him with a smile and said gently, "You are now wanting to hear much more of how the Lady of Mysteries feels for you, and not daring to ask. Moreover, you are also dying to know more about what 'Magisters' are and can find tongue to say nothing for fear of deflecting me from whatever wonders I was going to reveal if left to speak freely. Wherefore you are riven and will remember but poorly what follows . . . unless I set you at ease."

Elminster found himself wanting to laugh, perhaps cry, and grope for words all at once. He managed a nod almost desperately, and Azuth chuckled once more. Behind him, the air roiled with sudden raging green fire that came out of nowhere, and from its heart boiled two pit fiends, reaching out mighty-thewed and sharp-clawed limbs to clutch at the Lord of Spells . . . limbs that caught fire for all of the time it took Elminster to gasp in alarm before they met with some invisible force that melted them away, boiling off flesh and gore like black smoke. The screams were incredible, but Azuth's gentle, kindly voice cut through them like lantern light stabbing into darkness.

"Mystra loves you as no other," the god told the mage, "but she loves many, including myself and others neither of us know about, some in ways that would astonish or even disgust you. Be content with knowing that among all who share her love, you are the bright spirit and youth she cherishes, and I am the old wise teacher. None of us is better than the other, and she needs us all. Let jealousy of other Chosen—of other mages of any race, station, or outlook—never taint your soul."

Elminster's goblet was full again. He nodded his understanding to the god through its wisps of smoke, as a score of winged she-fiends stabbed at the god with lances that blazed with red flame—and the air, with a silent lack of fuss, ate both weapons and fire.

One of the dusky-skinned fiend-women strayed a little too close to Azuth in her boldness and lost a wing to hungry empty air in a single blurred instant. Shrieking and sobbing, she tumbled away, falling to death below—a death that came rather more swiftly than the waiting ground, as other erinyes, eyes blazing with bloodlust, swooped on her and drove their lances home. Transfixed, the stricken erinyes stiffened, spurted blood in several directions, and fell like a stone.

Ignoring all of this, the god spoke serenely on. "Magisters are wizards who achieve a measure of special recognition—powers, of course, as we spell hurlers measure things—in the eyes of Mystra, by being 'the best' of her mortal worshipers in terms of magical might. Most achieve the title by defeating the incumbent Magister and lose it by the same means—a process often fatal."

As cornugons and pit fiends raged around the Height, watching their spells claw vainly at the god's unseen barrier, Azuth sipped from his own goblet and continued, "Our Lady and I are working to change the nature of the Magister right now—though not overmuch—to make the Magisters less killers-of-rivals and more creators of new spells and ways of employing magic. Only one wizard is the Magister at a time. By serving themselves, they serve to proliferate and develop magic . . . and there is no greater way to serve Mystra. The purpose of her clergy is more to order and instruct, so that novices of the Art don't destroy themselves and Toril many times over before they've mastered basic understandings of magic . . . but were this task not governing them, the priests of Mystra would bend their talents more to what we now leave to the Magister."

Azuth leaned forward, the fire brighter now, and said through the flames, "You serve Mystra differently. She watches you and learns the human side of magic in all its hues from your experiences and the doings of those you meet—foes and friends alike. Yet the time has come for you to change, and grow, to serve as she'll need you to, in the centuries ahead."

"Centuries?" Elminster murmured and discovered suddenly that he needed the contents of his goblet rather urgently. "Watches me?"

Azuth smiled. "Indiscretions with alluring ladies and all. Set all thoughts of that aside—she needs the entertainment 'you just being you' affords her more than she needs someone playacting to impress her. Now attend my words, Elminster Aumar. You are to learn and grow by using as little magic as possible in the year ahead. Use what is needful and no more."

Elminster sputtered over his goblet, opened his mouth to protest—and met Azuth's kindly, knowing, almost mocking gaze. He drew in a deep breath, smiled, and sat back without saying anything.

Azuth smiled at that, and added, "Moreover, you are not to have any deliberate contact with your own pet project, the Harpers, until Mystra advises you otherwise. They must learn to work and think for themselves, not forever looking over their shoulders for praise and guidance from Elminster."

It was Elminster's turn to smile ruefully. "Hard lessons in independent achievements and self-reliance for us all, eh?" he ventured.

"Precisely," the Lord of Spells agreed. "As for me, I shall be learning to guide and minister to the mages of all Toril without Mystra to call upon, for a time."

"She's—'going away'?" El's tone made it clear that he didn't believe a goddess truly could withdraw from contact with her world, her worshipers, and her work.

Azuth's smile deepened. "An inevitable task confronts her," he said, "that she dare not put off longer; contingencies that must be determined and ordered, for the good and stability of the Weave. Neither of us may hear from her or see any manifestation of her presence or powers for some time to come."

" 'Dare not'? Does Mystra serve the commands of something higher, or do ye speak of what the Weave requires?"

"The Weave by its very nature places constant demands on those attuned to it and who truly care for it . . . and the nature of all life and stability on this world it dominates. It is a delight and a craft—and something of a game—to anticipate the needs of the Weave, to address those needs, and to make the Weave something greater than it was when you found it."

"I don't believe ye quite revealed the nature of the Lady's 'inevitable task,' or whom—if anything—she answers to and obeys," Elminster said with a smile of his own.

Azuth's own smile broadened. "No, I don't believe I did," he replied softly, merriment dancing in his eyes as he raised his goblet to his lips.

Elminster found himself sinking gently and being brought upright, to stand on the stony ground once more with a landing as soft as a feather landing on velvet. Once, long ago, in Hastarl, the young thief Elminster had spent several minutes watching a scrap of pigeon-down floating down onto a cushion, ever so *slowly* . . . and he still judged those minutes well spent.

Azuth was standing, too, bare feet treading an inch or so of air. It seemed their converse was at an end. Though he hadn't even looked at the raging fiends, they were suddenly tumbling away in all directions, wreathed in white flames, their bodies dwindling in struggling silence as they went. The siege of the Height, it seemed, was at an end.

The High One didn't seem to step forward, but he was suddenly nearer to Elminster. "We may not respond, but call upon us. Look to see us not, but have faith. We do see you."

He reached out a hand; wonderingly, Elminster extended his own.

The god's hand felt like a man's . . . warm and solid, gripping firmly.

A moment later, Elminster roared—or tried to; the breath had been shocked right out of his lungs. Silver fire was surging through him, laced with a peculiarly vivid deep blue streak that must be Azuth's own essence or signature. El saw it clearly as jets of flame burst forth from his own nose, mouth, and ears.

It was surging through him, burning everything it found, wrenching him in spasms of utter agony as organs were consumed, blood blazed away, and skin popped as the flesh beneath boiled away . . . through swimming eyes, Elminster saw Azuth become an upright spindle of flame—a spindle that seemed somehow to watch him closely as it swooped nearer and murmured (despite its lack of any mouth El could see), "The fire cleanses and heals. Awaken stronger, most precious of men."

The spindle whirled nearer, touching the nimbus of magical fire around Elminster, fed by the silver jets still erupting from him—and the world suddenly leaped aloft with a silver-throated roar, whirling Elminster up into ecstasy and ragged ruin, torn apart into dark droplets spewed into a looping river of gold . . . gold too bright to look upon, outshining the sun.

The last Prince of Athalantar lay sprawled on the stones, senseless, with silver fires raging around him and two goblets floating nearby, a cruising spindle of flame between them. The flames touched the goblet Elminster had held, and it jumped a little and vanished into the conflagration, spewing forth fat golden sparks some moments later.

Then the spindle of flame touched the flames raging around Elminster. They rushed into it, and the reinforced, towering Azuth-flames collapsed with a roar that shook all Halidae's Height, washing over Elminster—who convulsed, but did not awaken—then gathered themselves. With sinuous grace and suddenly leisurely speed, the flames rose into a column and flowed up over the edge of Azuth's floating goblet into the steaming wine there. Length after length of roaring flame followed behind, vanishing into the liquid.

In the end, all that was left was that goblet, wisps of wine rising off its brimful contents like smoke whipped by a breeze.

It was the first thing Elminster saw—and drank—the next morning.

The goblet vanished into the air during his last swallow, leaving nothing behind. Elminster smiled at where it had been, got up, and left the Height with a lighter heart and a body that felt new and young again. He stopped at the first still pool of water he came across to peer down to look at his reflection and be sure that it was his. It was, hawk nose and all. He grimaced at his reflection, and it made the face it was supposed to make back at him. Thank Mystra.

Two

DOOM RIDES A DAPPLE GRAY

*And in the days when Mystra revealed herself not, and
magic was left to grow as this mage or that saw best or
could accomplish, the Chosen called Elminster was left
alone in the world—that the world might teach him
humility, and more things besides.*

Antarn the Sage
from **The High History of
Faerûnian Archmages Mighty**
published circa The Year of the Staff

When chill ruled mornings, mists lay heavy among
the trees. Few folk of the Starn ever ventured this far
into Howling Ghost Wood, so the pickings were plenti-
ful—and Immeira had never seen any howling ghosts.
Her sack was already half-full of nuts, berries, and
alphran leaves. Soon the moontouch blooms would
sprout in handfuls among the trees, followed by fiddle-
heads and butter cones . . . and to think some folk—even
some Starneir—claimed that only a hunter who could
bring down a stag a tenday could live off the woods.

Immeira rubbed an itch on her cheek thoughtfully, and looked back to where the trees thinned. Over the fields beyond them, down in the vale where Gar's Road crossed the Larrauden, stood Buckralam's Starn.

"Forty cottages full of nosy old women who weave cloaks all day while their sheep wander untended," the bard Talost had once described it. Longtime Starneir were still angry over those words and could be counted on to provide a few new and even more colorfully twisted misfortunes the gods could—and should—visit on the over-critical bard, forthwith. As far as Immeira could tell, Talost had got it about right, but she had already learned, and learned well, that truth wasn't necessarily highly prized around the Starn.

Her father had disappeared while adventuring. He was part of a proper chartered adventuring band who called themselves Taver's Talons after the brawling, always guffawing old warrior Taver who led them with the sun shining back off his bald pate. In Immeira's memory Taver still sat his saddle, bright and bluff, but folk said he was bones and dust these eight years gone. None could tell his bones from those of the next six—her father among them—who'd fallen to the dragon's jaws that day.

The Starn had talked of Taver's Talons for eight winters now, and some of them swore the Talons were fiends in human form, hiding here to better corrupt the women of passing caravans and spread their dark seed over all Faerûn. Others were just as insistent that the Talons had been bandits all along, just lurking hereabouts until they could learn all about Starneir and the forest trails so as to found a bandit realm back in the real woods, not so far off. Some called this kingdom Talontar—to others it was Darkride—but no one knew just where its borders started or who dwelt there or why they'd never come down on the Starn with ready bows and hungry knives in the years since the Talons had fallen or stolen away or committed whatever great crime kept them now in hiding.

Yes, truth was something a wagging tongue or two could change overnight in the Starn. The only exception to that, so far as Immeira could see, was the truth that lurked in the sharp and ready blades of the Iron Fox and his men.

They'd come out of the east on Gar's Road some six springs ago. A handful of hardened mercenaries with cold steel in their hands and a world-weary, merciless set to their colder eyes. The leader was a tall, fat man whose helm peaked with an iron fox head; even his men called him only "the Iron Fox." He rode into the court-yard of the little Shrine of the Sheaf, ordered the feeble old priest Rarendon out into the spring snows at sword point, and taken the place as his home.

Henceforth, he told the silent villagers at the Trough and Plough that evening, services to Chauntea would be held out in the open fields, as was proper. Former keeps were better suited to the purpose they'd been built for: housing men of action such as he and his men, who henceforth would dwell in the Starn and defend it, to the betterment of all.

A little after highsun the next day, a crudely lettered scroll of laws was tacked upon the door of the Trough. It was distressingly short, proclaiming the Iron Fox the sole judge, lawmaker, and authority in Fox's Starn. That very night, a few who'd dared disagree with specific laws, or disapprove of the entire affair, were left sprawled in their blood on the road or on their own steps—or simply disappeared. A few of the best-looking young Starneir ladies were taken from their homes to Fox Tower and installed in scanty gowns there, a cart of stonemasons arrived a tenday later to rebuild it into a fortress, and talk about the hidden evil of the Starn's only heroes, Taver's Talons, began.

Kindly, confused old Rarendon was taken into the old stables behind the mill, where the dwarven mill-wright allowed orphans of the Starn—including Immeira—to live. In the month that followed, several able-bodied farmers whose lands lay close about Fox Tower died right after planting was done, when their farmhouses mysteriously caught fire by night, their doors were propped shut from outside, and their windows overlooked by hitherto undetected brigands equipped with crossbows of the same sort used by the Fox's men. Two gossipy old Starneir women and blind old Adreim the Carver were flogged in the Market for minor transgressions against the laws. The folk of the Starn started to get used to ever-present patrols of hard-eyed swordsmen, the seizure of not quite half of all the harvests they brought in, and living in fear.

They made their silent, feeble protests. "Fox's Starn" remained Buckralam's Starn in the mouths of one and all, and the Fox's men seemed to ride about in a perpetually silent, nearly deserted valley. Wherever they went, children and goodwives melted away into the woods, leaving toys discarded and pots unwatched, whilst the farmers of the Starn were always in the farthest, muddiest back hollows of their fields, too hard at work to even look up when a plate-armored shadow fell across them.

Like many girls of the Starn on the budding verge of womanhood, Immeira became another sort of shadow—one that lurked in drab old men's clothes and kept to the woods by day, sleeping in barn lofts and on low roofs by night. They'd seen into the eyes of their gowned older sisters, seen their scars and manacles too, and had no desire to join a dance of warmth, good food and ready drink that cost them their freedom and handed them brutality, servility, and pain. Immeira had a figure to equal many of the Fox's "playpretties" now and took care to wear bulky old leather vests and shapeless tunics, keep her hair wild and unkempt—and keep herself hidden in forest gloom or night dark. Even more than the sullen boys of the valley, the she-shadows of the Starn dreamed of the Talons riding up the road someday soon, with bright, bared swords at the ready, to carve the Iron Fox into flight.

Once or twice a tenday Immeira stole through the pheasant-haunted eastern ridges of Howling Ghost Wood to where the Gar's Road topped Hurtle Tor and descended into the Realm of the Iron Fox. The Fox's cruel warriors kept a patrol there to keep watch over who came to the Starn and to exact a toll from peddlers and wagon trains too weary or undermanned to refuse to pay.

Sometimes Immeira kept them occupied by making animal crashings in the underbrush and stealing any crossbow quarrels they were foolish enough to loose into the trees, but more often she simply hunkered down in silence and watched the antics on the road. Word must be getting around the lands beyond the valley. Fewer and fewer peddlers were taking Gar's Road. The Starn hadn't seen anything that could be called a caravan since the season after the coming of the Iron Fox.

This morning there had been a rime of ice along the banks of the Larrauden and frost had touched white sparkles onto many a fallen leaf. Immeira had to keep rubbing her bare fingertips to keep warm, knowing her lips must be blue, but the damp of the slow-warming day kept her footsteps in the forest near-silent, so she was thankful. Once she'd startled a hare into full crashing flight through the trees, but for the most part she moved through the mists like a drifting shadow, dipping gentle fingers to pluck up what food she needed. A little hollow she'd used before afforded her a dirt couch from which to watch the Foxling road patrol with ease. Propped up against a mossy bank with the comforting weight of the tree limb she kept ready there, in case she ever needed a club, ready in her hands, she'd even begun to doze when it happened.

There was a sudden stir among the six black-armored men, a jingling of mail that marked swords sliding out and their owners hurrying back into the roadside trees, to crouch ready while fellow Foxlings swung into their saddles to block the road.

Someone was coming—someone they expected to have either trouble or a bit of fun with. Immeira rubbed her eyes and sat up with quickening interest.

A moment later, a lone man on a dapple gray horse topped the rise, a long sword swaying at his hip as his mount walked unhurriedly down into the valley. He was young and somehow both gentle and hard of face, with a hawklike nose, and black hair pulled back into a shoulder tail. He saw the waiting men, swords and all, but neither hesitated nor checked his mount. Unconcernedly it plodded onward with its rider empty-handed and almost jaunty, humming a tune Immeira did not know.

"Halt!" one of the Foxlings barked. "You stand upon the very threshold of the Realm of the Iron Fox!"

"Wherefore I must—what?" the newcomer inquired with a raised eyebrow, reaching to take up a rolled cloak from his saddle. "Abandon hope? Yield up some toll? Join the local nunnery?"

"Show a lot less smart-jaws first!" the Foxling snarled. "Oh, you'll pay a toll, too—*after* you're done begging our forgiveness . . . and mewling over the loss of your sword hand."

The newcomer raised his brows and brought his mount to a halt. "A rather steep price to cross a threshold," he said. "Don't we get to fight each other first?"

Immeira rubbed her eyes again, in wonder. There was a general roar of rage from the Foxlings, and they surged forward, those afoot springing from the trees. The newcomer backed his horse, and a small knife flashed in his hand. He threw the cloak he'd taken from his saddle into the faces of the oncoming riders, turned the dapple gray, and rode down one of the men on foot, the horse kicking viciously. Its rider kicked at another Foxling to keep him clear, snatched something from his saddle, slashed at it, and threw it at the man. A spurt of sand marked where it burst in the Foxling's face.

Then the newcomer was behind the line of Foxlings. One horse had bolted, throwing its rider. The other two were tangled amid the reason for its flight: the length of barbed chain that had been inside the cloak.

The newcomer leaned back with a matching length of chain in his hand to lash one of the mounted Foxlings across the throat. The man toppled from his saddle without a sound, and the Foxling next to him suddenly sprouted the newcomer's little knife in his eye.

Suddenly riderless, one mount reared and the other jostled it, trampling two fallen Foxlings under its hooves. Another knife flashed into the throat of the Foxling who'd taken the sand in his face. As he fell, another bag of sand wobbled harmlessly past the shoulder of one of the two Foxlings who were left.

Used to bullying frightened men, their faces were white and their steps uncertain. As they advanced slowly on the hawk-nosed man, he plucked another knife from a saddle side sheath and gave them a welcoming smile.

At that, one of the Foxlings moaned in terror and fled. The other listened to booted feet crashing away into the trees, looked into the blue-gray eyes of the man who'd so swiftly and easily slain his fellows, then hurled his sword at that coldly smiling face, wheeled round, and ran.

A bag of sand took the Foxling on the side of the head after he'd managed only a few scrambling strides, and he fell heavily on the road. The dapple gray surged forward to dance on his fallen form, as its owner turned in his saddle, sighed, and leaped for the trees, abandoning Gar's Road to the dead and dying.

The hawk-nosed man ran lightly, another knife in his hand, on the trail of the Foxling who'd fled. It wouldn't be wise to let one foe go free to warn others of his arrival—not if a fifth of what he'd heard of these vicious warriors of the Fox was true.

It wasn't hard to mark where the fleeing man had gone; panting and crashing in plenty were going on among the dancing tree branches up ahead, as the dark-mailed man struggled up a ridge.

A moment later the running man slipped into some sort of hole or gully with a startled yell.

Immeira's scream matched it, as the Foxling warrior suddenly plunged down into her hiding place. She snatched up her tree limb as the sweating man crashed down atop her, struck the side of his helm so hard the wood broke, and somehow got out from under his trembling weight.

She needed only a moment to plant the battered toe of her boot on a projecting tree root and boost herself out, but desperately strong fingers grabbed her before she got that moment, and dragged her back down. She kicked out with her feet and flailed about with her elbows as the man beneath her grunted and snarled half-coherent curses. Then she swung around to claw at his face. Immeira got a momentary glimpse of one furious eye amid grizzled cheeks before a fist out of nowhere crashed into her temple, sending her reeling back against the forest dirt with sun glare and shadows swirling in her eyes.

Immeira was dimly aware of an armored bulk moving toward her. She kicked out and in the same motion rolled over to claw at roots and moss and try to get out of the pit again. One surge, another, and she was on her knees in the forest moss at the lip of the hollow, rising. She came to a quivering halt, with a grip as crushing and cruel as iron around her ankle, dragging her back.

Steel flashed past her head, and the grip was suddenly gone.

Immeira sprawled on her face in damp dead leaves, as a wet gurgling sound slid back down into the hollow behind her. A long sword dark with fresh blood was wiped on the moss to one side of her, and a surprisingly gentle voice said, "Good lady, will ye tarry here by yon duskwood? I have need of thy aid, but urgent battle yet to attend to."

"I—I—yes," Immeira managed to say, shuddering, and a moment later gentle but firm fingers were opening her moss-smeared right hand, laying the hilt of a dagger in her palm, and closing her fingers around it. Immeira stared down at it, a little dazed, as sudden silence descended on this corner of the forest again.

The hawk-nosed man was gone, trotting lightly back through the trees toward the road. Immeira stared after him, licked suddenly dry lips, and could not help but glance back into the hollow.

The Foxling was a huddled heap, his throat drenched crimson with blood, and she suddenly felt very sick.

Retching into the leaves and ferns, Immeira never saw the newcomer busily rolling over bodies, making sure of death and plucking forth weapons. She was waiting by the duskwood when he came back through the trees bearing a large bundle whose innards clashed steel upon steel from time to time as he moved. The stranger gave her a grin. "Well met," he said politely, sketching a courtly bow.

Immeira stared at him, then snorted with sudden, helpless mirth. She found herself trying to manage a low curtsy in return, despite her old breeches and flopping boots, and fell over in the moss. They hooted with laughter together, and a strong arm righted Immeira, leaving her staring into the eyes of the hawk-nosed warrior.

"I—" Immeira began hesitantly.

The newcomer gave her an easy grin, patted her arm reassuringly, and said, "Call me Wanlorn. I've come hunting foxes . . . *Iron* Foxes. What's thy name?"

"Immeira," she replied, looking down at the dagger he'd given her, then back up at him, scarcely able to believe that the salvation she'd watched for all these years had come to the Starn so quickly and so capably deadly.

"Is it safe to tarry here—not long—and talk?" he asked.

"It is," Immeira granted, then summoned up her wits and will enough to ask a question of her own.

"Are you alone?" she asked, studying the man's face. It was not so young as it had first appeared, and "Wanlorn" was an old folk name for "wanderer searching for something." How could one man—even one so skilled at arms as this one—defeat, or even escape alive, from all the men who raised blades for the Fox?

As if he'd read her mind, the hawk-nosed man took Immeira gently by her upper arms and said urgently, "I am indeed alone—wherefore I need thy help, lass. Not to fight Foxlings with tree limbs . . . or even daggers, but to tell me: do the folk of the Starn wish to be rid of the Iron Fox?"

"Yes," Immeira said, a little bewildered by how fast Faerûn had been turned upside down in front of her eyes. "By the *gods*, yes."

"And how many blades answer the Fox's call? Both ready-armed, like these, and others who may hurl spells or be able to fire a crossbow or hold loyal in some other wise . . . tell me, please."

Immeira found herself spilling out all she knew and could remember or guess about the Iron Fox and his forces. The newcomer's dancing eyes and ready grin never failed, even when she told him that those who wore the dark mail and the fox head badge numbered a dozen more than the six he'd slain, and that no man remained in the Starn with brawn or courage enough to back a lone newcomer against the Iron Fox. Nor could she trust anyone beyond herself to aid him, for fear of tales being carried back by those among the she-shadows who might well, after a hard winter, want to win warmth and fine clothes and good food enough to betray someone they scarcely knew.

His grin broadened when she told him that as far as she'd heard no sorcerer or even priest dwelt in Fox

Tower or anywhere near the Starn and that the Fox commanded no magic himself.

Immeira told Wanlorn, or whatever his name truly was, where the guards were posted and how soon the six men would be missed. The half dozen Foxlings were lying in the trees with their helms tossed into the Larrauden and their mounts—plus one unfamiliar dapple gray horse—tethered nearby. She told him as much as she knew—of how the Iron Fox spent his evenings; where his four hunting dogs and the crossbows, lanterns, and horses at Fox Tower were kept; and of life in the Starn both these days and before the fall of the Talons—until she was quite weary of answering questions.

Wanlorn asked her if there were any haystacks in the Starn that could be approached unseen from these woods and that would escape being disturbed by farmers in the next day or two. She told him of three such, and he asked her to guide him to the best of them as stealthily as possible, to hide his bundle of seized weapons.

"What then?" she asked quietly.

" 'Twould be safest, Immeira," Wanlorn said directly, his eyes very steady on hers, "if ye then went to wherever ye're supposed to dwell—not out in the woods where angry armed men with hunting dogs may search—and never went near this hollow or the haystack again until the Fox is gone from the Starn, whatever befalls me."

"And if I refuse?" she almost whispered.

He smiled thinly and said, "I'm no tyrant. In the Faerûn I want to see, lads and lasses should be free to walk and speak as they please. Yet, if ye follow me or step forth to aid me, I cannot protect thee . . . for I am alone in this, with no god to work miracles when battle turns against me."

"Oh, no?" Immeira asked, lifting a hand that trembled rather less than she'd feared it would, to indicate where the Foxling patrol had barred the road. "Was that not a miracle?"

"No," Wanlorn replied, smiling. "Miracles mostly grow when deeds are told of, through years of retelling. If ye speak too freely, it may become a miracle yet"

Who *was* this man, and why had he come here?

Immeira met those calm blue-gray eyes for a moment—just now, they seemed rather more blue than her mind told her they were—and asked simply, "Who are you, really? And why . . . why do you want to face death here? What does the Starn matter to you? Or seek you revenge on the Iron Fox?"

Wanlorn shook his head slightly. "I first heard of him less than a tenday ago. I do as my heart leads me to do, wherefore I am here. I wander to learn and to make the Realms be more as I desire them to be. Unless the Starn proves to be my grave, I cannot stay here but must needs wander onward. I am a man, thrust onto this road by my birth and . . . choices I have made." He fell silent, and as her brows rose and she parted her lips to ask or say more he raised a hand as if to still her and added, "Take me as ye find me."

Immeira held his gaze in silence for a handful of very long moments, then replied, "So then I shall, crazy man—and feel honored to have met you. Come, the haystack awaits."

She turned her back on him—she trusted no other man to so turn her gaze from him, especially one who stood close and armed behind her—and led the way along trails only she and the beasts who'd made them knew. He followed, clanking slightly.

* * * * *

It would be *so* easy to clear the feast hall of Fox Tower with a fireball and strike down the few stray Foxling

armsmen with lesser magics, but that was just the temptation Elminster was here to resist. It had been a long
summer since he'd talked with a god on a hilltop, but the
habit of calling on spells to answer every need or whim,
without thinking, was slowly crumbling. Slowly.

The cruelty and butchery of these men of the fox
head were so freely and so often practiced that he need
not worry about slaying them out of hand. If he could.

One man, fighting fairly and in the open, would have
little chance against such dark battle dogs as these.

Hmmm, yes, he thought, those dogs . . .

It was a little shy of highsun now, and the lass
Immeira was still at his shoulder. She was a skulking
shadow with no less than a dozen daggers strapped and
laced all about her and his heavy chain in her hands.
Surely the men he'd slain this morn would be found in
a very short time, and warning horns would blow. At
just about that time a trio of Foxlings would arrive from
Fox Tower to relieve this guard post, here at the opposite end of the valley from where he'd met with such a
warm and bloody morning reception.

"Relieve" . . . an apt choice of word, that. One of the
bored Foxlings who'd been sitting in the roadside shade
across the way was now up on his feet, unlacing his codpiece as he headed across the hot, dusty road to this
side to answer a call of nature.

This time nature was going to have a little extra to
say to him.

Elminster rose out of the shrubbery with unhurried
grace and threw one of his knives the moment the man
stopped and took up a stance. He cursed soundlessly
and hauled out another blade, knowing he'd misjudged
his throw. The Foxling lifted his head in sudden alarm
as the first knife flashed past—and the second missed
the eye it had been meant for, sinking hilt-deep in the
man's cheek instead.

As a thick, wet scream arose, El snatched the chain
out of Immeira's grasp and sprinted at the man, knowing

he hadn't enough time to manage this but had no choice but to try it anyway.

The man was flailing his way blindly back toward the road that both of his fellow Foxlings were crossing now, heading in the direction of the sounds of his distress with drawn swords and wary frowns.

They slowed as they moved out of the bright sun into the dappled shade of the trees, not wanting to be struck down by a ready foe. The two stopped as their fellow Foxling staggered into view. El, running hard, came up right behind him, using his lurching body as a shield as he swung the chain out over it, hard, smashing a sword arm down, then rushing to close with its stunned owner and drive a knife at the man's face.

The man sprang away before El could strike, shaking his numbed arm and shattered fingers. The last prince of Athalantar saw the angry face of the other Foxling glaring at him across the man he'd first wounded, so he threw his knife hard into it.

The man went down with a yell, more startled than hurt, and El brought the chain up to smash the man he'd disarmed across the face. Blood flew, a head lolled loosely, and the man went down—followed by Elminster, who had to hurl himself into the dirt to avoid the desperate swings of a broadsword wielded by the man he'd first injured at this guard post.

The man had torn El's dagger free and was spitting blood, half-blinded by the tears of pain streaming down his face, but he could see enough to know his danger and mark his foe.

El rolled, trying to get away from the sword that kept slashing at him. As he wallowed in the dust with his assailant staggering and hacking after him, he wondered when the third Foxling would reach him. He knew he'd have to use one of his spells then, Mystra or no Mystra, or die.

The man overbalanced after a particularly vicious swing and stumbled. El put his shoulder into the dirt and spun around, kicking out with both feet. That cursedly persistent sword clanged and bounced by his ear as its owner fell heavily, grunting as the wind was driven from him. El kept spinning, bringing his feet under him and running four paces away before he dared turn to look at his foes. Where was that third Foxling?

Lying still and silent on the road, it seemed, with a white-faced, panting Immeira rising from beside him, bloody dagger in hand. Her eyes met El's through the dust, and she tried to smile . . . not very successfully.

El gave her a wave, then pounced on the man who had chased him with the sword. He stabbed down thrice with his own dagger, and when he looked up again, El saw that both he and Immeira were dusty, sweating, panting, and alive. They traded true smiles this time.

"Lass, lass," El chided her, as they swung each other into an exultant embrace, "I *can't* protect ye!"

Immeira kissed his cheek, then pushed him away, making a face at him through her wild-tangled hair and the Foxling blood spattered across her face. "That's fair enough," she told him. "I can't protect *you,* either!"

El grinned at her and shook his head. He strode to the shade where the three Foxlings had been sitting and chuckled in satisfaction.

"What, Wanlorn?" Immeira asked. "What is it?"

Elminster held up a crossbow and said, "I'd hoped they'd have one of these. Light armor, no lances or horses . . . it stands to reason they'd have something to use against, say, three armsmen guarding a caravan. Here, lass—help me with the windlass. We mayn't have much time."

Immeira ducked past him to scoop up a sling bag bulging with crossbow quarrels. "We don't," she said shortly. "Their relief is riding out here. I just saw them top the last rise . . . the one by Thaermon's farm. They'll be on us in—"

"Then get my chain and take it back the other side of the road," El hissed, cranking the windlass for all he was worth. "Haste, now!"

. The Starneir lass showed a little haste, moving with speed and grace despite the heavy, awkward weight of the bloody chain. El crossed the road in a half-crouch right behind her, the bow just about ready.

He had one hand in the sling bag for a quarrel, with Immeira coming to an awkward halt to let him get one out, when the first rider bobbed up over a crest in the road and saw the bodies. The man shouted and hauled on the reins, bringing his horse to a snorting, almost rearing halt. His two companions drew up beside him, and they gaped in unison at the sprawled Foxlings and the trees so close and so innocent on either side of them.

"Drop the chain and *run*," El murmured in Immeira's ear. "Drop this bag soon and go anywhere to avoid being caught. If we lose sight of each other, look for me in that grove west of the haystack. Go!"

Without waiting for her reply, Elminster stepped calmly into the road and shot the most capable-looking Foxling through the throat. Then he sprinted back to the trees, tossing down the bow, and snatched up the chain from where Immeira had let it fall. There was no sign of her but branches dancing in the dim forest distance.

He took two running strides into the woods, then crouched down to listen. He heard the expected curses, but also fear in the furious voices, and hooves pawing as horses were turned.

A moment later, the horn calls Immeira had told him to expect rang out over the valley, fast and strident. The other dead patrol had been discovered. The bugling went on for a long time, and El used the din to cover a quick sprint through the trees beside the road, heading back the way these two horsemen would have to come. Any hopes of felling another on the way past were dashed, however, when they burst past him at a gallop, eager to return to Fox Tower before any more crossbow quarrels came calling.

The riderless mount followed them, depriving El of any chance to rummage in its saddlebag. He stared after it, shrugged, and scurried to retrieve the quarrel from the dead Foxling's throat, then the man's weapons, the crossbow, and its bag of quarrels. Luckily this man's fall had swept his night cloak from its perch on his saddle; it served admirably to bundle everything up in. El's chain, hooked to itself, wrapped the bundle as if it had been made to do so.

The bundle was heavy, but Immeira was waiting for him several trees away to take the crossbow and gaze at him as if he was some great hero.

Elminster hoped she was wrong. In his experience, all the great heroes very soon became dead heroes.

*   *   *   *   *

The feast hall in Fox Tower had been in an uproar, but frightened and angry men cannot snap and snarl at each other endlessly without breaking into a brawl or falling into tense, waiting silence.

The silence now hung as heavy as a cloak under the flickering candle wheels. Their hanging chains cast long shadows down the stone walls as the Iron Fox—a great bulk of a man, more like a rotund bear than a fox—and his eight remaining warriors hunkered down over a roast that seemed suddenly tasteless, and drank wine as if they all wanted to drown in it. Servants hardly dared approach the table for fear of being run through, and many a sudden glance was shot up at the dark, empty minstrels' gallery. The ladies waited behind closed doors in the bedchambers beyond, dismissed from the board at the first news. They were all dreading the humor that might govern their men when those who wore the fox head at last came to bed.

Nine men brooded over the long table as the candles guttered lower. The possible identity and allegiance of the lone, briefly glimpsed crossbowman had been endlessly debated, the decision long since made to lock the tower gates, maintain vigilant watch, and sally forth in armed force in the morning. Doors were barred from within, locks checked, and keys retrieved onto this very table. Now all that was left was the waiting, the wondering who this unseen foe was, and the rising fear.

An elbow toppled a goblet, and half a dozen men sprang up shouting, blades half drawn, before the disgusted Iron Fox shouted them to a halt. Men glared around at each other, black murder in their eyes, then slowly sat down again.

Fearful heads drew back from the kitchen doors before someone might see them and go for a whip. The kitchen had grown cold and quiet, but the three serving maids dared not leave.

The last time a lass had dared slip away early she'd been hunted up and down the tower and whipped until long after her clothes had fallen away and the bloody skin beneath was in danger of following it. The Iron Fox had ordered that her bloody footprints not be scrubbed away from the passage floors, so as to serve as ever-present reminders of the reward awaiting laxity and disobedience.

The serving maids cowered sleepily on a bench just inside the kitchen door, more terrified than the men in the hall. The warriors feared the unknown and what might be lurking nearby in night-shrouded Starn, but the servants knew exactly what danger awaited them in the next room and knew they were locked in with it. There'd be a lot of slapping and screaming behind those bed-chamber doors soon, if they were any judge, and—

With a sudden loud rattle of chain, one of the candle wheels plunged from its customary height toward the table below. Foxlings boiled up, shouting, their swords flashing into their hands. One of them sprinted across the room with a curse, followed by another. They were through an archway and gone before the Iron Fox's shouted commands could be heard.

The ruler of the Starn had a huge, rough slab of a face, decorated with stubble, a thick and bristling mustache, and eyes as cold and cruel as all bleak midwinter. The body below it, sweating in full armor even to gorget and gauntlets, was no smaller or more dainty. The curved metal plates held in the quivering breasts and belly that would otherwise have shaken and rippled like a pale and obscene sea of flesh as their host rose to his feet and leveled a long and ruthless finger at the rest of the Foxlings. "The next man to leave this room without my leave had best keep going, right off my land and into exile! D'you know how stupid it is to rush off like that, whe—"

He jerked his head around at the high, shrill scream that interrupted him from the passage whence the two men had gone. That hall led to pantries and the back rooms of the tower . . . including Beldrum's Room, a name left over from a long-dead Chauntean priest, where tables were stored and the chains that held the candle wheels were spiked. A room, it seemed, that was suddenly held by foes. The Iron Fox snatched up his helm from the table before him and jammed it down onto his head.

His men followed suit and clustered in close about him to hear his orders. "Durlim and Aawlynson—to the gallery. Shout down that it's clear when you get there. Gondeglus, Tarthane, and Rhen—stand here with me. One of you look under the table; then we'll turn our backs to it and keep watch. Llander, guard yon passage door. When the gallery is secure, all four of us will join you, and we five will scour Beldrum's Room."

The Iron Fox fell silent, and silence followed his orders. His men seemed to be waiting to hear more. Sudden rage almost choked him. Was he leading *sheep?*

"*Move,* you whoresons!" he thundered. "Get gone about it! Movemovemove, *move!*"

Silence held for a fleeting moment after the echo of his shout died away. Then everyone moved at once.

Gondeglus groaned and reeled backward, followed by Aawlynson, the hissing of the crossbow bolts that had slain them loud in the echoing room. Then it was Rhen's turn to sprout a quarrel in the face and fall. None of them had helms with snout-visors in the southern style. The Iron Fox was wise enough to raise his old and heavy broadsword up in front of his face before he scuttled sideways, turned, and peered up at the gallery.

He was in time to get a glimpse of a black-haired, hawk-nosed man bobbing up from behind the gallery rail with a loaded and ready crossbow in his hands. This time his target was Durlim, but the tall veteran ducked and slapped at the air with his gauntlet, and the quarrel rang off his rerebrace and shattered harmlessly against the far wall.

There were screams of fear from the kitchen, but the Fox didn't have time to see if they heralded an intruder there or just fear at what was happening out here. No matter; the gallery held a known foe, who must have run out of ready-loaded crossbows and be scuttling for cover by now.

"Llander! Tarthane! Up those stairs," the Iron Fox bellowed, brandishing his blade. "Now!"

His most loyal warriors were both noticeably hesitant to obey, but they mounted the stairs as instructed. The Fox took care to back himself in under the edge of the gallery as he watched them ascend, under the guise of ordering Durlim to get down the passage to the bottom of the back stairs to the gallery, in real haste.

He lumbered after Durlim as far as the archway that led into the passage, and crouched there, peering up at the gallery.

Llander and Tarthane were up there, moving cautiously forward.

"Well?" he bellowed. "What news?"

It was then that the tapestry fell on Llander. Tarthane stumbled back to avoid his friend's wild sword thrusts, then lunged, striking past the chaos of heavy cloth with his black war blade, hoping to stab whoever was beyond it and swarming all over the shrouded Llander.

That someone was already flat on the floor, tugging at the runner-rug under all their feet. Tarthane, already off-balance, flailed about, made a grab for the railing to keep upright missed his hold, and toppled over with a crash. The hawk-nosed man bounced up from behind the rolled tapestry and drove a dagger into Tarthane's face.

Llander's sword burst blindly out of the tapestry to stab at the man, who jabbed his dagger through the fabric in response, then vaulted over the railing to land lightly in the feast hall, give the Iron Fox a cheery wave, and race away toward the front of the tower.

Enraged, the Iron Fox gave roaring chase, then stopped two strides short of leaving the hall and put up his blade. No . . . he'd be running alone into a part of the keep he'd sent his men away from, an area offering all too many places where a man with a knife could get above an armored foe and leap down. No, it was time to see if Llander was still alive and go find Durlim, and the three of them could find some defensible room to hold against leaping madmen with knives.

He lumbered back across the feast hall, slashing backhanded behind him twice on the way, and mounted the stairs where Tarthane lay crumpled and the tapestry was rippling slowly and wearily.

"Llander?" he called, hoping not to get a sword thrust in the face. "Llander?"

He heard a small sound behind him and lashed out viciously with his blade, hacking so hard that the steel rang off the stone wall with numbing force, shedding a few tinkling shards of metal in its wake.

He was rewarded with a gasp. When he turned to see who it was, the Iron Fox found himself face to face not with a hawk-nosed man or a bleeding corpse but with a young lass he'd seen a time or two before about the

Starn. She was three safe steps down the stair, beyond his sword tip, and looked very stern, a hand at her throat. As the Fox gazed at her, still startled to see this wench here in his locked and barred tower, she brought her hand slowly and deliberately down, and the front of her gown open with it.

His eyes followed her movement until the halberd smashing into his ankles from above sent him cannoning helplessly down the stairs. He screamed out a curse as he swung his blade around to hack away this latest attack. The Fox found himself once more nose to nose with the grinning, hawk-nosed man. A slim dagger driven by a slender but firm arm plunged into the Iron Fox's right eye, and Faerûn whirled away from him forever.

Breathing heavily, Immeira sprang away from the huge armored carcass and let it clang and slither a little way down the stair, gauntlets clutching vainly at empty air.

Then she looked quickly away and up at the man who was smiling down at her. "Wanlorn," she moaned, and found herself trembling—a moment before she burst into tears. "Wanlorn, we've done it!"

"Nay, lass," said the soothing voice that went with the arms that held her then. "We've but done the easiest part. Now the hard and true work begins. Ye've slain a few rats, is all . . . the house they infested must still be set in order."

He plucked the fouled and dripping dagger from her hands and tossed it away; she heard it ring against the floor tiles below.

"The Realm of the Iron Fox is broken, but Buckralam's Starn must be made to live again."

"How?" she moaned into his chest. "Guide me. You said you would not stay. . . ."

"I cannot, lass—not more than a season. 'Twould be better for thee if I left this night."

Her arms tightened around him like a vise.

"No!"

"Easy, lass," he said. "I'll stay long enough to see you take old Rarendon—and whichever of the orphans and farmers ye can trust as an escort on the road—to Saern Hill. I'll write ye a note to give to a man there, a horse breeder named Nantlin; ask him if his harp sounds as sweet as ever, and he'll know who the note is really from. He'll bring folk to dwell here and women and men of honor and ready blades to keep laws all Starneir approve of, to make the Starn strong again. There is a doom laid upon me though, lass . . . I must be gone before he or any of his folk come into the valley."

Immeira stared up at him, her face drenched with tears. She could see plain sorrow in his eyes and tight-set lips, reaching up two timid fingers to trace the set of his jaw.

"Will you tell me your true name, before you go?"

"Immeira," he said solemnly, "I will."

"Good," she said almost fiercely, reaching up her hands to his neck, "for I'll not give myself to a name-less man."

*   *   *   *   *

A smile that did not belong to Immeira swam through his dreams and sent Elminster into sudden, coldly sweating wakefulness. "Mystra," he breathed into the darkness, staring up at the cracked stone ceiling of the best bedchamber in Fox Tower. "Lady, have I pleased thee at last?"

Only silence followed—but in it, sudden fire appeared, racing across the ceiling, shaping letters that read: "Serve the one called Dasumia."

Then they were gone, and Elminster was blinking up at darkness. He felt very alone—until he heard the soft whisper against his throat.

"Elminster?" Immeira asked, sounding awed and frightened. "What was that? Do you serve the gods?"

Elminster reached up his hand to touch her face, feeling suddenly close to tears. "We all do, lass," he said huskily. "We all do, if we but know it."

Three

A FEAST IN FELMOREL

If human, dragon, orc, and elf can in peace sit down anywhere together in these Realms, it must be at a good feast. The trick is to keep them from feasting on each other.

Selbryn the Sage
from **Musings From A Lonely Tower In Athkatla**
published in The Year of the Worm

"And just who," the shortest and loudest of the three gate guards asked with deceptive cheerfulness, "are you?"

The hawk-nosed, neat-bearded man he was staring coldly at—who was standing out in the pelting spring rain, on foot and muddy-booted, yet somehow dry above the tops of his high and well-worn boots—matched the guard's bright, false smile and replied, "A man whom the Lord Esbre will be very sorry to have missed at his table, if ye turn me away."

"A man who has magic and thinks himself clever enough to avoid answering a demand for his name," the guard captain said flatly, crossing his arms across his chest so that the fingers of one hand rested on the high-pommeled dagger sheathed at the right front of his belt, and the fingers of the other could stroke the mace couched in a sling-sheath on the left front. The other two guards also dropped their hands ever so casually to the waiting hilts of their weapons.

The man out in the rain smiled easily and added, "Wanlorn is my name, and Athalantar my country."

The captain snorted, "Never heard of it, and every third brigand calls himself Wanlorn."

"Good," the man said brightly, "that's settled, then."

He strode forward with such calm confidence that he was among the guards before two hard shoves—from gauntlets coming at him from quite different directions—brought him to an abrupt halt.

"Just where d'you think you're going?" the captain snarled, reaching out his hand to add his own shove to Wanlorn's welcome.

The bearded man smiled broadly, seized that hand, and shook it in a warrior's salute. "In to see Lord Esbre Felmorel," he said, "and share some private converse with him, good lad, whilst I partake of one of his superb feasts. Ye may announce me."

"And then again," the captain hissed, leaning forward to glare at the stranger nose-to-nose, "I may not." Blazing green eyes stared into merry blue-gray ones for a long moment, then the captain added shortly, "Go away. Get gone from my gate, or I'll run you through. I don't let rude brigands—or clever-tongued beggars—"

The bearded man smiled and leaned forward to land a resounding kiss on the guard's menacing mouth.

"Ye're as striking as they said ye'd be," the stranger said almost fondly. "Old Glavyn's a fire-lord when he's angry, they said. Get him to spit and snarl and run ye away from his gate—oh, he's a proper little dragon!"

One of the other guards sniggered, and Guard Captain Glavyn abandoned blinking, startled, at the stranger to whirl around with a snarl and thrust his glare down the throat of a more familiar foe. "Do we find something *amusing*, Feiryn? Something that so overwhelms our manhood and training that we must abandon our superiors and fellows in the face of danger whilst we indulge ourselves in a wholly inappropriate and insultingly demeaning display of *mirth*?"

The guard blanched, and a satisfied Glavyn whirled back to fix the hawk-nosed stranger with a look that promised swift and waiting death hovering only inches away. "As for you, goodman . . . if you *ever* dare to—to *violate* my person again, my sword shall be swift and sure in my hand, and not all the gods in this world or the next shall be enough to save you!"

"Ah, Glavyn, Glavyn," the bearded stranger said admiringly, "what flow! What style! Splendid words, stirringly delivered. I'll tell Esbr—the Lord so, when I sit down to dine with him." He clapped the captain on one shoulder and slipped past him in the same movement.

The guard captain exploded into red rage and snatched out his weapons to . . . or, rather, tried to. Somehow, strain and struggle as he might, he couldn't make either mace or dagger budge, or uncross his arms to reach for the short sword slung across his back or his other dagger beside it. He couldn't move his arms at all. Glavyn drew in breath for what would have been a hoarse, incoherent scream, but for—

"My lords, what is all this tumult?" The low, musical voice of the Lady Nasmaerae cut through Glavyn's gathering wind and the rising alarm of his fellow guards like a sword blade sliding through silk. Four men moved in silence to place themselves where they could best—that is, without obstruction—stare at her.

Slender she was, in a gown of green whose tight, pointed sleeves almost hid her fingers but left supple shoulders bare. A stomacher of intricate worked silver caught the gleam of the dying day, even through the rain and mist, as she turned away slightly in the darkness and worked some small cantrip that made the candelabra in her hand burst into warm flame.

By its leaping light eyes that were dark pools grew even larger, and indigo in hue—indigo with flecks of gold. Lady Nasmaerae's mouth and manner seemed all chaste innocence, but those eyes promised old wisdom, dark sensuality, and a smoldering hunger.

A smile rose behind her eyes as she measured her effect on the men at the gate, and she added almost lightly, "Who are we, on a night such as this, to keep a lone traveler standing in the wet? Come in, sir, and be welcome. Castle Felmorel stands open to ye."

The hawk-nosed stranger bowed his head and smiled. "Lady," he said, "ye do me great honor by thy generosity to a stranger—outpouring, as it is, of a trusting and loving manner that thy gate-guards would do well to emulate. Wanlorn of Athalantar am I, and I accept thy hospitality, swearing unreservedly that I mean no harm to ye or to anyone who dwells within, nor to any design or chattel of Felmorel. Folk in the lands around spoke volubly of thy beauty, but I see their words were poor, tattered things compared to the stirring and sublime vision that is—ye."

Nasmaerae dimpled. Still wearing that amused smile, she turned her head and said, "Listen well, Glavyn. *This* is how the racing tongue encompasseth true flattery. Idle and empty it may be—but oh, so pretty."

The guard captain, red-faced and still trembling as he fought with his immobile arms while trying not to appear to be doing so, glowered past her shoulder and said nothing.

The Lady Nasmaerae turned her back on him in a smooth lilt that wasn't quite a flounce and offered her arm to Wanlorn. He took it with a bow and in the same motion he assumed the lofty bearing of the candelabra, their fingers brushing each other for a moment—or perhaps just a lingering instant longer.

As they swept away out of sight down a dark-paneled inner passage, the guards could have collectively sworn that the flames of that bobbing candelabra *winked*. That was when Glavyn found that he could suddenly move his arms again.

One might have expected him to draw forth the weapons he'd so striven to loose these past few breaths—but instead, the captain poured all his energy into a vigorous, snarling-swift, prolonged use of his tongue.

By the time he was finally forced to draw breath, the two guards under his command were regarding him with respect and amazement. Glavyn turned away quickly, so they wouldn't see him blush.

*   *   *   *   *

The arms of Felmorel featured at their heart a mantimera rampant, and although no one living had ever seen such an ungainly and dangerous beast (sporting, as it did, three bearded heads and three spike-bristling tails at opposing ends of its bat-winged body), the Lord of Felmorel was known, both affectionately and by those who spoke in fear, as "the Mantimera."

As jovial and as watchfully deadly in manner as his heraldic namesake was reputed to be, Esbre Felmorel greeted his unexpected guest with an easy affability, praising him for a timely arrival to provide light converse whilst his other two guests this night were still a-robing in their apartments. The Lord then offered the obviously weary Wanlorn the immediate hospitality of a suite of rooms for rest and refreshment, but the hawk-nosed man deferred his acceptance until after the feast was done, saying it would be poor repayment of warm generosity to deprive his host of a chance to share that very converse.

The Lady Nasmaerae assumed a couch that was obviously her customary seat with a liquid grace that both men paused to watch. She smiled and silently cupped a fluted elven glass of iced wine beside her cheek, content to listen as the customary opening courtesies were exchanged between the two men, down the long and well-laden, otherwise empty candlelit feasting table.

"Though 'twould be considered overbold in many a hall to ask so bluntly," the Mantimera rumbled, "I would know something out of sheer curiosity, and so will ask: what brings you hither, from a land so distant that I confess I've not heard of it, to seek out one castle in the rain?"

Wanlorn smiled. "Lord Esbre, I am as direct a man as thyself, given my druthers. I am happy to state plainly that I am traveling Faerûn in this Year of Laughter to learn more of it, under holy direction in this task, and am at present seeking news or word of someone I know only as 'Dasumia.' Have ye, perchance, a Dasumia in Felmorel, or perhaps a ready supply of Dasumias in the vicinity?"

The Mantimera frowned slightly in concentration, then said, "I fear not, so far as my knowledge carries me, and must needs cry nay to both your queries. Nasmaerae?"

The Lady Felmorel shook her head slightly. "I have never heard that name." She turned her gaze to meet Wanlorn's eyes directly and asked, "Is this a matter touching on the magic you so ably demonstrated at our gates—or something you'd rather keep private?"

"I know not what it touches on," their guest replied. "As we speak, 'Dasumia' is a mystery to me."

"Perhaps our other guests—one deeply versed in matters magical, and both of them widely traveled—can offer you words to light the dark corners of your mystery," Lord Esbre offered, sliding a decanter closer to Wanlorn. "I've found, down the years, that many useful points of lore lie like gems gleaming in forgotten cellars in the minds of those who sup at my board—gems they're as surprised to recall and bring to light once more as we are that they possess such specific and rare riches."

A fanfare sounded faintly down distant passages, and the Mantimera glanced at servants deftly dragging open a pair of tall, ebon-hued doors with heavy, gilded handles. "Here they both come now," he said, dipping a whellusk, half-shell and all, into a bowl of spiced softcheese. "Pray eat, good sir. We hold to no formality of serving nor waiting on others here. All I ask of my guests is good speech and attentive listening. Drink up!"

Side by side, and striding in careful step—for all the world as if neither wanted the other to enter the hall either first or last—two tall men came into the room then. One was as broad shouldered as a bull, and wore a high-prowed golden belt that reached almost to his bulging breast. Thin purple silk covered his mighty musculature above it and flowed down corded and hairy arms to where gilded bracers encircled forearms larger than the thighs of most men. Both belt and bracers displayed smooth-worked scenes of men wrestling with lions—as did the massive golden codpiece beneath the man's belt. "Ho, Mantimera," he boomed. "Have you more of that venison with the sauce that melts in my memory yet? I starve!"

"No doubt," Lord Felmorel chuckled. "That venison need not live only in memory longer; but lift the dome off yonder great platter, and 'tis thine. Wanlorn of Athalantar, be known to Barundryn Harbright, a warrior and explorer of renown."

Harbright shot a look at the hawk-nosed man without pausing in his determined striding to the indicated platter, and gave a sort of grunt, more noncommittal acknowledgment than welcome or greeting. Wanlorn nodded back, his eyes already turning to the other man, who stood over the table like a cold and dark pillar of

fell sorcery. The hawk-nosed guest didn't need the Mantimera's introduction to know that this was a wizard
almost as powerful as he was haughty. His eyes held
cold sneering as they met Wanlorn's but seemed to
acquire a flicker of respect—or was it fear?—as they
turned to regard the Lady Nasmaerae.

"Lord Thessamel Arunder, called by some the Lord of
Spells," the Mantimera announced. Was his tone just a
trifle less enthusiastic than it had been for the warrior?

The archwizard gave Wanlorn a cold nod that was
more dismissal than greeting and seated himself with
a grand gesture that managed to ostentatiously display
the many strangely shaped, glittering rings on his fingers to everyone in the vicinity. To underscore their
moment, various of the rings winked in a random scattering of varicolored flashes and glows.

As he looked at the food before him, a brief memory
came to Wanlorn of the jaws of wolves snapping in his
face, in the deep snows outside the Starn in the hard
winter just past. He almost smiled as he put that bloody
remembrance from his mind—hunger, it had been
simple hunger for those howling beasts; no better and
no worse than what had hold of him now—and applied
his own gaze to the peppered lizard soup and crusty
three-serpent pie within reach. As he cut into the lat-
ter and sniffed appreciatively at the savory steam
whirling up, Wanlorn knew Arunder had darted a
glance his way, to see if this stranger-guest was suffi-
ciently impressed with the show of power. He also knew
that the mage must be sitting back now and taking up
a glass of wine to hide a mage-sized state of irritation.

Yet he only had to look at himself in a seeing-glass
to know that power and accomplishment of Art lures
many wizards into childlike petulance, as they expect
the world to dance to their whim and are most selfish-
ly annoyed whenever it doesn't. He was Arunder's current source of annoyance; the wizard would lash out at
him soon.

All too soon. "You say you hail from Athalantar, good
sir—ah, *Wanlorn*. I'd have thought few of your age
would proclaim themselves stock of that failed land,"
the wizard purred, as the warrior Harbright returned
to the board bearing a silver platter as broad as his own
chest, which fairly groaned under the weight of near a
whole roast boar and several dozen spitted fowl, and
enthroned himself with the creak of a settling chair and
the clatter of shaking decanters. "Where have you dwelt
more recently, and what brings you hence, cloaked in
secrets and unheralded, to a house so full of riches, if I
may ask? Should our hosts be locking away their gem
coffers?"

"I've wandered these fair realms for some decades
now," Wanlorn replied brightly, seeming not to notice
Arunder's sarcasm or unveiled insinuations, "seeking
knowledge. I'd hoped that Myth Drannor would teach
me much—but it gave me only a lesson in the primal
necessity of outrunning fiends. I've poked here and
peered there but learned little more than a few secrets
about Dasumia."

"Have you so? Seek you lore about magic, then—or
is your quest for mere treasure?"

At that last word, the warrior Harbright glanced up
from his noisy and nonstop biting and swallowing for a
moment, fixing Wanlorn with one level eye to listen to
whatever response might be coming.

"Lore is what I chase," Wanlorn said, and the warrior gave a disgusted grunt and resumed eating. "Lore
about Dasumia—but instead I seem to find a fair bit
about the Art. I suppose its power drives those who can
write to set down details of it. As to treasure . . . one
can't eat coins. I've enough of them for my needs; alone
and afoot, how would I carry more?"

"Use a few of them to buy a horse," Harbright grunted,
spraying an arc of table with small morsels of herbed
boar. "Gods above—*walking* around the kingdoms! I'd
grow old even before my feet wore off at the ankles!"

"Tell me," Lord Felmorel addressed Wanlorn, leaning forward, "how much did you see of the fabled City of Song? Most who even glimpse the ruins are torn apart before they can win clear."

"Or did you just wander about in the woods near where you *imagine* Myth Drannor to be?" Arunder asked silkily, plucking up a decanter to refill his glass.

"The fiends must have been busy hounding someone else," the hawk-nosed man told the Mantimera, "because I spent most of a day clambering through overgrown, largely empty buildings without seeing anything alive that was larger than a squirrel. Beautiful arched windows, curving balconies . . . it must have been very grand. Now there's not much lying about waiting to be carried off. I saw no wineglasses still on tables or books propped open where someone was interrupted in their reading, as the minstrels would have us all believe. No doubt the city was sacked after it fell. Yet I saw, and remember, some sigils and writings. Now if I could just determine what they *mean*. . . ."

"You saw *no* fiends?" Arunder was derisive—but also visibly eager to hear Wanlorn's reply. The hawk-nosed man smiled.

"No, sir mage, they guard the city yet. 'Twill probably be years, if ever, before folk can walk into the ruins without having to worry about anything more dangerous than a stirge, say, or an owlbear."

Lord Felmorel shook his head. "All that power," he murmured, "and yet they fell. All that beauty swept away, the people dead or scattered . . . once lost, it can never be restored again. Not the way it was."

Wanlorn nodded. "Even if the fiends were banished by nightfall," he said, "the place rebuilt in a tenday, and a citizenry of comparable wit and accomplishments assembled the day after, we'd not have the City of Beauty back again. That shared excitement, drive, and the freedom to experiment and freely reason and indulge in whimsy that's founded on the sure knowledge of

one's own invulnerability won't be there. One would
have a players' stage pretending to be the City of Song,
not Myth Drannor once more."

The Mantimera nodded and said, "I've long heard
the tales of the fall, and have even faced a fell fiend—
not there—and lived to tell the tale. Even divided by
their various selfish interests and rivalries, I can scarce
believe that so grand and powerful a folk fell as completely and utterly as they did."

"Myth Drannor *had* to fall," Barundryn Harbright
rumbled, spreading one massive hand as if holding an
invisible skull out over the table for their inspection.
"They got above themselves, you see, chasing godhood
again . . . like those Netherese. The gods see to it that
such dreams end bloodily, or there'd be more gods than
we could all remember, and none of 'em with might
enough to answer a single prayer. 'Sobvious; so why do
all these mages keep making this same mistake?"

The wizard Arunder favored him with a slim, superior smile and said, "Possibly because they don't have
you on hand to correct their every little straying from
the One True Path."

The warrior's face lit up. "Oh, you've heard of it?" he
asked. "The One True Path, aye."

The mage's jaw dropped open. He'd been joking, but
by all the gods, this lummox seemed serious.

"There aren't many of us thus far," Harbright continued enthusiastically, waving a whole, gravy-dripping
pheasant for emphasis, "but already we wield power in
a dozen towns. We need a realm, next, and—"

"So do we all. I'd like several," Arunder said mockingly, swiftly recovered from his astonishment. "Get me
one with lots of towering castles, will you?"

Harbright gave him a level look. "The problem with
over- clever mages," he growled to the table at large, "is
their unfamiliarity with *work*—not to mention getting
along with all sorts of folk and knowing how to saddle a
horse or put a heel back on a boot or even how to kill

and cook a chicken. They seldom know how to hold their drink down, or how to woo a wench, or grow turnips . . . but they *always* know how to tell other folk what to do, even about turnip-growing or wringing a chicken's neck!"

Large, hairy, blunt-fingered hands waved about alarmingly, and Arunder shrank away, covering his obvious fear by reaching for a distant decanter. Wanlorn obligingly moved it nearer to the mage but was ignored rather than thanked.

Their host cut into the uncomfortable moment by asking, "Yet, my lords, True Paths or the natures of wizards aside, what see you ahead for all who dwell in this heart of far-sprawling Faerûn? If Myth Drannor the Mighty can be swept away, what can we hold to in the years to come?"

"Lord Felmorel," the wizard Arunder replied hastily, "there has been much converse on this matter among mages and others, but little agreement. Each proposal attracts those who hate and fear it, as well as those who support it. Some have spoken of a council of wizards ruling a land—"

"Ha! A fine tyranny and mess *that'd* be!" Harbright snorted.

"—while others see a bright future in alliances with dragons, so that each human realm is a dragon's domain, with—"

"Everyone as the dragon's slaves and ultimately, its dinner," Harbright told his almost-empty platter.

"—agreements in place to bind both wyrm and people against hostilities practiced on each other."

"As the dragon swept down, its jaws gaping open to swallow, the knight stared into his doom, shouting vainly, 'Our agreement protects me! You can't—' for almost the space of three breaths before the dragon gulped him up and flew away," Harbright said sarcastically. "The surviving folk gathered there solemnly agreed that the dragon had broken the agreement, and the proposal was made that someone should travel to the dragon's

lair to inform the wyrm that it had unlawfully devoured
the knight. Strangely, no one volunteered."

Silence fell. The hulking warrior thrust his jaw forward
and shot the wizard a dark and level gaze, as if daring him
to speak, but Thessamel Arunder seemed to have acquired
a sudden and abiding interest in peppered lizard soup.

Wanlorn looked up at his host, aware of the Lady
Felmorel's continuing and attentive regard, and said,
"For my part, Lord, I believe another such shining city
will be a long time in coming. Small realms, defended
against orcs and brigands more than aught else, will
rise as they have always done, standing amid lawless
and perilous wilderlands. The bards will keep the hope
of Myth Drannor bright while the city is lost to us, now
and in foreseeable time to come."

"And this wisdom, young Wanlorn, was written on
the walls of the ruined City of Song?" Arunder asked
lightly, emboldened to speak once more, but carefully
not looking in Harbright's direction. "Or did the gods
tell you this, perhaps, in a dream?"

"Sarcasm and derision seems to run away with the
tongues of wizards all too often these days," Wanlorn
observed in casual tones, addressing Barundryn Harbright. "Have you noticed this, too?"

The warrior grinned, more at the wizard than at the
hawk-nosed man, and growled, "I have. A disease of the
wits, I think." He waved a quail-lined spit like a scepter
and added, "They're all so busy being clever that they
never notice when it strikes them personally."

In unspoken unison both Harbright and Wanlorn
turned their heads to look hard at the wizard. Arunder
opened his mouth with a sneer to say something
scathing, seemed to forget what it was, opened his
mouth again to say something else, then instead put a
glass of wine up to it and drank rather a large amount
in a sputteringly short time.

As he choked, burbled, and wheezed, the warrior
reached out one shovel-sized hand to slam him solidly

between the shoulder-blades. As the mage reeled in his seat, Harbright inquired, "Recovered, are you—in your own small way?"

Into the dangerous silence that followed, as the wizard Arunder struggled for breath and the Lady Nasmaerae lifted a hand both swift and graceful to cover her mouth, Lord Esbre Felmorel said smoothly, "I fear you may have the right of it, good sir Wanlorn. Small holds and fortified towns standing alone are the way of things hereabouts, and things look to stay that way in the years ahead—unless something befalls the Lady of Shadows."

"The Lady—?"

"A fell sorceress," the warrior put in, raising grim eyes to meet those of the hawk-nosed man.

Lord Esbre nodded. "Bluntly put, but yes: the Lady of Shadows is someone we fear and either obey or avoid, whenever possible. None know where she dwells, but she seeks to enforce her will—if not to rule outright—in the lands immediately east of us. She's known to be . . . cruel."

Noticing that the wizard seemed to have recovered, Lord Esbre sought to restore the man's temper by deferring to him with some joviality. "You are our expert on things sorcerous, Lord Arunder—pray unfold for us whatever of import you know about the Lady of Shadows."

It was time for fresh astonishment at Lord Esbre's feast table. Lord Thessamel Arunder stared down at his plate and muttered, "There's no—I have nothing to add on this subject. No."

The tall candles on the feast table danced and flickered in the heart of utter silence for a long time after that.

*   *   *   *   *

A dozen candles flickered at the far end of the bedchamber like the tongues of hungry dragon hatchlings.

The room was small and high-ceilinged, its walls shrouded in old but still grand tapestries that Elminster was sure hid more than a few secret ways and spy holes. He smiled thinly at the serenity awaiting him, as he strode past the curtained and canopied bed to the nearest flame.

"Wanlorn am I," he told it gently, "and am not. By this seeming, in your service, hear me I pray, O Mystra of the Mysteries, O Lady most precious, O Weaving Flame." He passed two fingers through the flame, and its orange glow became a deep, thrilling blue. Satisfied, he bent forward over it until it almost seemed as if he'd draw the blue flame into his mouth, and whispered, "Hear me, Mystra, I pray, and watch over me in my time of need. *Shammarastra ululumae paerovevim driios.*"

All of the candles suddenly dimmed, sank, guttered, then in unison rose again with renewed vigor, building like spears of the sun to a brighter, warmer radiance than had been in the room before.

As warm firelight danced on his cheek, Elminster's eyes rolled up in his head. He swayed, then fell heavily to his knees, slumping forward into a crawling posture that became a face first slide onto the floor. Lying senseless among the candles, he never saw the flame spit a circle of blue motes that swirled in a circle around him and faded to invisibility, leaving the candle flame its customary amber-white in their wake.

$$* \quad * \quad * \quad * \quad *$$

In a chamber that was not far away, yet hidden down dark ways of spell-guarded stone, flames of the same blue were coiling and writhing inches above a floor they didn't scorch, tracing a sigil both intricate and subtly changing as it slowly rotated above the glass-smooth stones. They licked and caressed the ankles of their creator, who danced barefoot in their midst as they rose and fell around her knees. Her white silk night-gown shimmered above the flames as she wove a spell that slowly brought their hue up into her eyes. It spilled out into the air before her face like strange tears as the Lady Nasmaerae whirled and chanted.

The room was bare and dark save for the spell she wove, but it brightened just a trifle when the flames rose into an upright oval that suddenly held the slack face of the hawk-nosed Wanlorn, sprawled on the stones of his bedchamber amid a dozen dancing candles.

The Lady of Felmorel beheld that image and sang something softly that brought the half-lidded eyes of the sleeping man closer, to almost fill the scene between the racing flames. "*Ooundreth,*" she chanted then. "*Ooundreth mararae!*"

She spread her hands above the flames and waited for them to well up to lick her palms, bringing with them what she so craved: that dark rush of wit and raw thought she'd drunk so many times before, memories and knowledge stolen from a sleeping mind. What secrets did this Wanlorn hold?

"Give me," she moaned, for the flood was long in coming. "Give . . . me . . ."

Power such as she'd never tasted before suddenly surged through the flames, setting her limbs to trembling and every last hair on her body to standing stiffly out from her crawling, tingling flesh. She struggled to breathe against the sudden tension hanging in her body and the room around her, heavy and somehow *aware*.

Still the dark flood did not come. Who *was* this Wanlorn?

The image in the loop of flame before her was still two half-open, slumberous eyes—but now something was changing in those encircling flames. Tongues of silver fire were leaping among the blue, only a few at first, but faster and more often, now washing over the entire scene for a moment, now blazing up brighter as the wondering dancer watched.

Suddenly the silver flames overwhelmed the blue, and two cold eyes that were not Wanlorn's opened in their midst. Black they were, shot through with twinkling stars, but the flames that swam from them like tears were the same rich blue as were spilling from Nasmaerae's own.

"Azuth am I," a voice that was both musical and terrible rang out of the depths of her mind. "Cease this prying—forever. If you heed not, the means of prying shall be taken from you."

The Lady of Castle Felmorel screamed then—as loud and as long as she knew how, as blue flames whirled her off her feet and held her captive and struggling, upright in their grip. Nasmaerae was lost in fear and horror and self-loathing, as the blue flames of her own thought-stealing spell were hurled forcibly back through her.

She shuddered under their onslaught, fell silent as she writhed in helpless and spasmodic collapse, then howled with a quite different tone, like a lost and wandering thing. All the brightness had gone out of her eyes, and she was drooling, a steady stream plunging from the corner of her twisted mouth.

The eyes that swam with stars regarded the broken woman for several grim moments, then spat forth fresh blue flames to enshroud her in a racing inferno that raged for only moments.

When it receded, the barefoot woman was standing on the stone floor of the spell chamber, her fiery weavings shattered and gone. Her nightgown was plastered to her body with her own sweat, and her hands shook uncontrollably, but the desolate eyes that stared down at them were her own.

"You are Nasmaerae once more, your mind restored. You may consider this no mercy, daughter of Avarae. I've broken all of your bindings—including, of course, the one that holds your Lord in thrall. Consequences will soon be upon you; 'twould be best to prepare yourself."

The sorceress stared into those floating, starry eyes in helpless horror. They looked back at her sternly and steadily even as they began to fade away, dwindling swiftly to nothingness. All of the magical light in the chamber faded and failed with them, leaving only emptiness behind.

Nasmaerae knelt alone in the darkness for a long time, sobbing slightly. Then she arose and padded like a wan-eyed ghost along unseen ways she knew well, feeling turns and archways with her fingertips, seeking the sliding panel that opened into the back of the wardrobe in her own bedchamber.

Thrusting through half-cloaks and gowns, she drew in a deep, tremulous breath, let it out in a sigh, and laid her fingers on her most private of coffers, on the high, hidden shelf right where she'd left it.

The maids had left a single hooded lamp lit on the marble-topped side table; the needle-slim dagger caught and flashed back its faint light as she drew it forth, looked at it almost casually for a moment, then turned it in her hand to menace her own breast.

"Esbre," she told the darkness in a whisper, as she drew back her hand for the stroke that would take her own life, "I'll miss you. Forgive me."

"I already have," said a voice like cold stone, close by her ear. A familiar arm lashed out across her chest to intercept the wrist that held the dagger.

Nasmaerae gave a little startled scream and struggled wildly for a moment, but Lord Esbre's hairy hand was as immovable as iron, yet as gentle as velvet as it encircled her wrist.

His other hand plucked the dagger out of her grasp and threw it away. It flashed across the room to be caught deftly by one of the dozen or so guards who were melting out from behind every tapestry and screen in the room now, unhooding lanterns, lighting torches in wall sconces, and moving grimly to bar any move she might make toward the door or to the wardrobe behind her.

Nasmaerae stared into the eyes of her lord, still too shocked and dazed to speak, wondering when the storm of fury would come. The Mantimera's eyes blazed through a mist of tears, burning into her, but his lips moved slowly and precisely as he asked in tones of quiet puzzlement, "Self-slaying is the answer to misguided sorcery? You had a *good* reason for placing me in a spell-thrall?"

Nasmaerae opened her mouth to plead, to spill forth desperate lies, to protest that her deeds had been misunderstood, but all that came out was a torrent of tears. She threw herself against him and tried to go to her knees, but a strong hand on her hip held her upright. When she could form words through the sobs, it was to beg his forgiveness and offer herself for any punishment he deemed fitting, and to—

He stilled her words with a firm finger laid across her lips and said grimly, "We'll speak no more of what you have done. You shall never enthrall me or anyone else again."

"I—believe me, my Lord, I would never—"

"You *can't,* whatever you may come to desire. This I know. So that others may also know it, you shall try to place me in thrall again—now."

Nasmaerae stared at him. "I—no! No, Esbre, I dare not! I—"

"Lady," the Mantimera told her grimly, "I am uttering a command, not affording you a choice." He made a gesture involving three of his fingers; all around her, swords grated out of scabbards.

The Lady Felmorel darted glances about. She was ringed with drawn steel, the sharp, dark points of well-used war swords menacing her on all sides. She saw a white-faced Glavyn above one of them, trusty old Errart staring grimly at her over another. Then she whirled away, hiding her face in her hands.

"I—I . . . *Esbre!*" she sobbed. "My magic will be shorn from me if I—"

"Your life shall be shorn from you if you do not. Death or obedience, Lady. The same choice warriors who serve me have, every day. It comes not so hard to them."

The Lady Nasmaerae groaned. Slowly her hands fell from her face and she straightened, breathing heavily, her eyes elsewhere. She threw back her head to look at the ceiling and said in a small voice, "I'll need more room. Someone pluck away this rug, lest it be scorched." She walked deliberately onto the point of someone's sword until they gave way before her and she could get off the soft, luxurious rug, then turned to face back into the ring and said softly, "I'll need a knife."

"No," Esbre snapped.

"The spell requires it, Lord," she told the ceiling. "Wield it yourself, if it gives you comfort—but obey me utterly when I begin the casting, lest we both be doomed."

"Proceed," he said, his voice cold stone again.

Nasmaerae strode away from him until she stood in the center of the ring of blades once more, then turned and faced him. "Glavyn," she said, "bring my lord's chamber pot hence. If it be empty, report so back to us."

The guard stared at her, unmoving—but spun from his place and hastened to the door at a curt nod from Lord Felmorel.

While they waited, Nasmaerae calmly tore the soaked nightgown from her body and flung it away, standing nude before them all. She stood flatfooted, neither covering herself modestly nor adopting her usual sensual poses, and licked her lips more than once, looking only at her lord.

"Punish me," she said suddenly, "in any other way but this. The Art means all to me, Esbre, every—"

"Be still," he almost whispered, but she shrank back as if he'd snapped a lash across her lips and said no more.

The door opened; Glavyn returned bearing an earthen pot. Lord Felmorel took it from him, motioned him back

into his place in the line, and said to his men, "I trust
you all. If you see aught that offers ill to Felmorel,
strike accordingly—both of us, if need be." Bearing a
small belt knife and the pot, he stepped forward.

"I love you, Esbre," the Lady Nasmaerae whispered,
and went to her knees.

He stared at her stonily and said only, "Proceed."

She drew in a deep, shuddering breath and said,
"Place the pot so that I can reach within." When he did
so, she dipped one hand in and brought it out with a
palmful of his urine. Letting her cupped hand rest on
the floor, she held out her other hand and said, "Cut
my palm—not deeply, but draw blood."

Grimly Lord Felmorel did as he was bid, and she
said, "Now withdraw—pot, knife, and all."

As he retreated, the guards grew tense, waiting to
leap forward with their steel at the slightest sign from
Lord Esbre. As her own dark blood filled her palm, Nasmaerae looked around the ring. Their faces told her just
how deeply she was feared and hated. She bit her lip
and shook her head slightly.

Then she drew in another deep breath, and with it
seemed to gain courage. "I'll begin," she announced, and
without pause slipped into a chant that swiftly rose in
urgency and seemed fashioned around his name. The
words were thick and yet somehow slithering, like
aroused serpents. As they came faster and faster, small
wisps of smoke issued from between her lips.

Suddenly—very suddenly—she clapped her hands
together so that blood and urine mixed, and cried out
a phrase that seemed to echo and smite the ears of the
men in the chamber like thunderclaps. A white flame
flared between her cupped palms, and she lifted her
head to look at her lord—only to scream, raw and horrified and desperate, and try to fling herself to her feet
and away.

The star-swirling eyes of Azuth, cold and remorse-
less, were staring at her out of Lord Felmorel's face, and

that musical, terrible voice of doom sounded again, telling her, "All magic has its price."

None of the guards heard those five words or saw anything but grim pity in their Lord's face, as the Mantimera held up a hand to stay their blades. The Lady Felmorel had fallen to the floor, her face a mask of despair and her eyes unseeing, dying wisps of smoke rising from her trembling limbs—limbs that withered before their eyes, then were restored to lush vitality, only to wither again in racing waves. All the while, as her body convulsed, rebuilt itself, and shriveled again, her screaming went on, rising and falling in a broken paean of pain and terror.

The guards stared down at her writhing body in shocked silence until the Mantimera spoke again.

"My lady will be abed for some days," he said grimly. "Leave me with her, all of you—but summon her maids-of-chamber hence to see to her needs. Azuth is merciful and shall be worshiped in this house henceforth."

* * * * *

Somewhere a woman was twisting on a bare stone floor, with leveled swords all around her in a ring and her bare body withering in waves as she wailed . . . elsewhere motes of light, like stars in a night sky, were whirling in darkness with a cold chiming sound . . . there followed a confusing, falling instant of mages casting spells and becoming skeletons in their robes as they did so, before Elminster saw himself standing in darkness, moonlight falling around him. He was poised before a castle whose front gate was fashioned in the shape of a giant spiderweb. It was a place he knew he'd never been, or seen before. His hands were raised in the weaving of a spell that took shape an instant later and spell blasted apart the gate in a burst of brilliance. The light whirled away to become the teeth of a laughing mouth that whispered, "Seek me in shadows."

The words were mocking, the voice feminine, and Elminster found himself sitting bolt upright at the foot of his unused bed, cold sweat plastering his clothing to him.

"Mystra has guided me," he murmured. "I'll tarry no longer here, but go out to seek and challenge this Lady of Shadows." He smiled and added, "Or my name isn't Wanlorn."

He'd never unpacked the worn saddlebag that carried his gear. It was the work of moments to make sure no helpful servant had removed anything for washing and he was out the door, striding briskly as if guests always went for late night walks around Castle Felmorel. Skulking is for thieves.

He nodded pleasantly to the one servant he did meet, but he never saw the impassive face of Barundryn Harbright watching him from the depths of a dark corner, with the faintest of satisfied nods. Nor did he see the moving shadow that slipped out from under the staircase he descended to follow him, bearing its own bundle of belongings.

Only a single aged servant was watching the closed castle gate. El peered all around to make sure guards weren't hiding anywhere. Seeing none, he hefted the doused brass lantern he'd borrowed from a hallway moments ago, swung it carefully, and let go.

The lamp plunged to the cobbles well behind the old man, with a crash like the landing of a toppling suit of armor. The man shouted in fear and banged his shin on a door frame trying to get to his pike.

When he reached the shattered lantern, limping and cursing, to menace it with a wobbling pike, El had slipped out the porter's door in the gate, just one more shadow in this wet spring night.

Another shadow followed, conjuring a drift of mist to roll before it in case this wandering Wanlorn looked back for pursuit. The briefest of flashes marked the casting of the shadow's spell—but the servant with the pike was too far away to notice or to have identified the face so fleetingly illuminated. Thessamel Arunder, the Lord of Spells, had also felt the need to suddenly and quietly take his leave of Castle Felmorel in the middle of the night.

The lantern was a bewilderment, the limp painful, and the pike too long and heavy; old Bretchimus was some time getting back to his post. He never felt or heard the chill, chiming whirlwind that was more a wind than a body, more a shadow than a presence, and that, drifting purposefully, became the third shadow that evening to pass out the porter's door. Perhaps it was just as well. As he leaned the pike back against the wall, its head fell off. It was an old pike and had seen enough excitement for one evening.

* * * * *

Torntlar's Farm covered six hills and took a lot of hoeing. Dawn saw Habaertus Ilynker rubbing his aching back and digging into the stony soil of the last hill—the one that adjoined the wolf-prowled wood that stretched all the way to Felmorel. As he did every morning, Habaertus glanced toward Castle Felmorel, though it was too far away to really see, and nodded a greeting to his older brother Bretchimus.

"Yourn the lucky one," he told his absent brother, as he did each morning. "Dwellin' yon, with that vast wine cellar an' that slinking silkhips Lady orderin' y'about, an' all."

He spat on his hands and picked up his hoe once more in time to see a few stray twinklings in the air that told him something strange was arriving. Or rather, passing him by. An unseen, chiming presence swept out of the trees and across the field, swirling like a mist or shadow, yet curiously elusive—for no shadow could be seen if one stared right at it.

Habaertus watched it start to snake past, pursed his lips, then, overcome by curiosity, took a swipe at it with his hoe.

The reaction was immediate. A sparkling occurred in the air where the blade of the hoe had passed through the wind, loud chiming sounded on all sides, then the shadowy wind overwhelmed Habaertus, howling around him like a hound closing on a kill. He hadn't even time for a grunt of astonishment.

As a wind-scoured skeleton collapsed into dust, the whirlwind roused itself with another little chorus of chimings and moved on across Torntlar's Farm. In its wake a battered hoe thumped to the earth beside two empty boots. One of them promptly fell over, and all that was left of Habaertus Ilynker fell out and drifted away.

Four

STAG HORNS AND SHADOWS

I wonder: do monsters look different from inside?
Citta Hothemer
from **Musings Of A Shameless Noble**
published in The Year of the Prince

The farmer's eyes were dark with suspicion and sunken with weariness. The fork in his hands, however, pointed very steadily toward Wanlorn's eyes and moved whenever the lone traveler did, to keep that menace on target.

When the farmer finally broke the long, sharp silence that had followed the traveler's question, it was to say, "Yuh can find the Lady of Shadows somewhere over the next hill," a sentence the speaker ended by spitting pointedly into the dirt between them. "Her lands begin there, leastways. I don't want to know why yuh'd *want* to meet her—an' I don't want yuh standing here on *my* land much longer, either. Get yuh boots yonder, and yuh in 'em!"

A feint with the fork underscored the man's words. Wanlorn raised an eyebrow, replied, "Have my thanks," in dry tones, and with neither haste nor delay got his boots yonder.

He did not have to look back to know the farmer was watching him all the way over the crest of the hill; he could feel the man's eyes drilling into his back like two drawn daggers. He made a point of not looking back as he went over the ridge—and in lawless country, no sensible traveler stands long atop any height, visible from afar. Eyes alert enough to be watching for strangers are seldom friendly ones.

As he trotted down the bracken-cloaked hillside that was his first taste of the Lands of the Lady, he briefly considered becoming a falcon or perhaps a prowling beast . . . but no, if this Lady of Shadows was alert and watchful, betraying his magical abilities at the outset would be the height of foolishness.

Not that the man who was Wanlorn, but who'd walked longer under the name of Elminster, cared over-much about being thought a fool. It was a little late for that he thought wryly, considering the road he'd chosen in life—with his stealthy departure from Castle Felmorel not all that many steps behind him. Mystra was forging him into a weapon, or at least a tool . . . and in all the forging he'd seen, those rains of hammer blows looked to be a little hard on the weapon.

And who was it long ago who'd said, "The task forges the worker"?

It would be so much easier to just do as he pleased, using magic for personal gain and having no care for the consequences or the fates of others. He could have happily ruled the land of his birth, mouthing—as more than one mage he'd met with did—the occasional empty prayer to a goddess of magic who meant nothing to him.

There was that one thing his choice had given him: long life. Long enough to outlive every last friend and neighbor of his youth, every colleague of his early adventures and magical workings and revelry in Myth Drannor . . .

and every friend and lover, one after another, of that wondrous city, too.

Elminster's lips twisted in bitterness as remembered faces and laughter and caresses rushed past his mind's regard, one after gods-be-cursed another . . . and the plans with them, the dreams excitedly discussed and well intended, that blow and dwindle away like morning mist in bright sunlight and come to nothing in the end.

So much had come to nothing in the end. . . .

Like the village in front of him, it seemed. Roofs fallen in and overgrown gardens and paths greeted him, with here and there a blackened chimney stabbing up at the sky like a dark and battered dagger to mark where a cottage had stood before fire came, or a vine-choked hump that was once a fieldstone wall or hedgerow between fields. Something that might have been a wolf or may have been another sort of large-jawed hunting beast slunk out of one ruined house as Elminster approached. Otherwise the village of Hammershaws seemed utterly deserted. Was this what Lord Esbre had meant by the Lady of Shadows seeking to "enforce her will" on these lands? Was every such place ahead of him going to be deserted?

What had happened to all the folk who dwelt here?

A few strides later brought him a grim answer. Something dull and yellow-gray cracked under his boots. Not a stone after all, but a piece of skull . . . well, several pieces, now. He turned his head and walked grimly on.

Another stride, another cracking sound; a long bone, this time. And another, a fourth . . . he was walking on the dead. Human bones, gnawed and scattered, were strewn everywhere in Hammershaws. What he'd thought was a collapsed railing on a little log bridge across the meandering creek was actually a tangle of skeletons, their arms dangling down almost to the water. El peered, saw at least eight skulls, sighed, and trudged on, looking this way and that among leaning carts and yard-gates fast vanishing under the brambles and creeping tallgrass that had already reclaimed the yards beyond them.

None but the dead dwelt in Hammershaws now. El poked into one cottage, just to see if anything of interest survived, and was rewarded with a brief glimpse of a slumped human skeleton on a stone chair. The supple mottled coils of an awakened snake glided between the bones as the serpent spiraled up to coil at the top of the chair. It was seeking height to better strike at this over-bold intruder. As its hiss rose loud in that ravaged room, Elminster decided not to stay and learn the quality of the serpent's range and aim.

The road beyond Hammershaws looked as overgrown as the village. A lone vulture circled high in the sky, watching the human intruder traverse a fading way across the rolling lands to Drinden.

A mill and busy market town, was Drinden, if the memories of still-vigorous old men could be trusted. Yet this once bustling hamlet proved now to be another ruin, as deserted as the first village had been. El stood at its central crossroads and looked grimly up at a sky that had slowly gone gray with tattered, smoke-like storm clouds. Then he shrugged and walked on. So long as one's paper and components stay dry, what matter a little rain?

Yet no rain came as El took the northwestern way, up a steep slope that skirted a stunted wood that had once been an orchard. The sky started to turn milky-white, but the land remained deserted.

He'd been told the Lady of Shadows rode or walked the land in the company of dark knights he'd do well to fear, with their ready blades and eager treacheries and vicious disregard for surrenders or agreements. Yet as he walked on into the heart of the domain of the Lady of Shadows, he seemed utterly alone in a deserted realm. No hoofbeats or trumpets sounded, and no hooves came thundering down into the road bearing folk to challenge one man walking along with a saddlebag slung over his shoulder.

It was growing late and the skies had just cleared to reveal a glorious sunset like melted coins glimmering in an amber sky as Elminster reached the valley that held the town of Tresset's Ringyl, once and perhaps still home to the Lady of Shadows. He found that it, too, was a deserted, beast-roamed ruin.

Forty or more buildings, at his first glance from the heights, still stood amid the trees that in the end would tear them all apart. Sitting amidst the clustered ruins were the crumbling walls of a castle whose soaring battlements probably afforded something winged and dangerous with a lair. El peered at it as the amber sky became a ruby sea, and the stars began to show overhead.

The long-dead Tresset had been a very successful brigand who'd tried his hand at ruling and built a slender-spired castle—the Ringyl—here to anchor his tiny realm. Tressardon had fallen within days of his death.

Elminster's lips twisted wryly. 'Twould be an act of supremely arrogant self-importance to try to read lesson or message for himself out of such local history. Moreover, from here at least he could see no spiderweb gate like the one in his dream set into the walls of the ruined castle. It could take days to explore all of what was left of the town—assuming, of course, that nothing lived here that would want to eat him or drive him away sooner than that—and nothing he could see but the Ringyl itself stood tall or grand enough to possibly incorporate the gate in his dream. Or at least, he reminded himself with a sigh, so it looked from here.

He'd time for just one foray before true nightfall, by which time it'd probably be most prudent to be elsewhere . . . perhaps on one of those grassy hilltops in the distance, beyond the shattered and overgrown town. A wise man would be setting up camp thereon right now, not scrambling down a slope of loose stones—and more human bones—for a quick peer around before full night came down. But then Elminster Aumar had no intention of becoming a wise man for some centuries yet. . . .

The shadows were already long and purple by the time Elminster reached the valley floor. Thigh-high grass cloaked what had once been the main road through the town, and El waded calmly into it. Dark, gaping houses stood like graying giants' skulls on either side as he walked quietly forward, sweeping the grass side to side with a staff he'd cut earlier to discourage snakes from striking and to uncover any obstacles before his feet or shins made their own, more painful discoveries.

Night was coming down fast as Elminster walked through the heart of deserted Ringyl. A tense, heavy silence seemed to live at its heart, a hanging, waiting stillness that swallowed echoes like heavy fog. El tapped on a stone experimentally but firmly with his staff. He could hear the grating thud of each strike, but no answering echo came from the walls now close around.

Twice he saw movement out of the corner of his eye, but when he whirled he was facing nothing but trees and crumbling stone walls.

Something watchful dwelt or lurked here, he was sure. Twilight was stealing into the gaps between the roofless buildings now, and into the tangles where trees, vines, and thorn bushes all grew thickly entwined. El moved along more briskly, looking only for walls lofty enough to hold the spiderweb gates of his dream. He found nothing so tall . . . except the Ringyl itself.

Gnawed bones, most brown and brittle enough to crack and crumble underfoot, were strewn in plenty along the grass-choked street. Human bones, of course. They grew in abundance to form almost a carpet in front of the riven walls of the castle. Cautiously Elminster forged ahead, turning over bones with his staff and sending more than one rock viper into a swift, ribbonlike retreat. Darkness was closing down around him now, but he had to look through one of these gaps in the wall, to see if . . .

Whatever had torn entire sections of wall as thick as a cottage and as tall as twenty men was still inside, waiting.

Well, perhaps one need not be *quite* so dramatic. El smiled thinly. It's a weakness of archmages to think the fate of Toril rests in their palm or on their every movement and pronouncement. A spiderweb-shaped gate would be sufficient unto his present needs.

He was looking into a chapel or at least a high-ceilinged hall, its vaulted ceiling intact and painted to look like many trees with gilded fruit on their branches though strips of that limning were hanging down in tongues of ruin. All this stood over a once polished floor in which wavy bands of malachite were interwoven between bands of quartz or marble—a floor now mantled in dust, fallen stone rubble, birds' nests and the tiny bones of their perished makers, and less identifiable debris.

It was very dark in the hall. El thought it prudent not to conjure any light, but he could hardly miss seeing the huge oval of black stone facing him in the far wall. Sparkling white quartz had been set into that wall to form a circle of many stars—fourteen or a dozen irregularly shaped twinklings, none of them the long-spindled star of Mystra—and in the center of that circle a carving as broad as Elminster's outstretched arms stood out from the wall: a sculpted pair of feminine lips.

They were closed, slightly curved in a secret smile, and El had a gnawing feeling that he'd seen them, or something very like them, before. Perhaps this was a speaking mouth, an enchanted oracle that could tell him more—if he could unlock its words at all, or understand a message not meant for him. Perhaps it was something less friendly than that.

Well, such investigations could wait until the full light of morning. It was time, and past time, to leave

Tresset's Ringyl and its watchful shadows. El backed out of the gaping ruin, saw nothing lunging at him out of the darkness, and with more haste than dignity headed for the hills.

The heights on the far side of the Ringyl weren't yet touched by moonlight, but the glittering stars cast enough light to make their grassy flanks seem to glow. El looked back several times on his determined march up out of the town, but nothing seemed to stir or follow him, and the many eyes that peered at him out of the darkness were no larger than those of rats.

Perhaps he would have time to win some sort of slumber, after all. The hilltop he chose was small and bare of all but the ever-present long grass. He walked it in a smallish ring, then opened his pack, took out a cloth scrip full of daggers that glowed a brief, vivid stormy blue when unwrapped—radiance that prompt-ly seemed to leak out of them, dripping and dancing to the ground—and retraced his steps around the ring. He drove a dagger hilt-deep into the soil at intervals and muttered something that sounded suspiciously like an old and rather bawdy dance rhyme. When the ring was complete, the Athalantan turned back along it and drove a second ring of daggers in, angling each of these additional blades into the turf on the inside of the ring, so that its blade touched the vertical steel of an already-buried dagger. He held out his hand, palm downward and fingers spread, said a single, soft word over them, wrapped his cloak around himself, and went to bed.

*   *   *   *   *

"What, pray tell, are you reading?"

The balding, bearded mage set aside a goblet whose contents frothed and bubbled, looked up unhurriedly

over his spectacles, elevated one eyebrow at a fashion-
ably slow pace, and replied, "A play . . . of sorts."

The younger wizard standing over him—more splen-
didly dressed and still possessing some of his own
hair—blinked. "A 'play,' Baerast? And 'of sorts'? Not an
obscure spellbook or one of Nabraether's meaty
grimoires?"

Tabarast of the Three Sung Curses peered up over
his spectacles again, more severely this time. "Let there
be no impediment to your dawning understanding,
dearest Droon," he said. "I am currently immersed in a
play, to whit 'The Stormy Knight, Or, The Brazen
Butcherer.' A work of some energy."

"And more spilled blood," Beldrune of the Bent Finger replied, sweeping aside an untidy stack of books
that had almost buried a high-backed chair and planting himself firmly in it before it even had time to
wheeze at its sudden freedom. The crash of tomes that
followed was impressive in both room-shaking solidity
and in the amount of dust it raised. It almost drowned
out the two smaller thunderings that followed, the first
occasioned by the clearance of the footstool of its own
tower of tomes by means of a hearty two-footed kick,
and the second caused by the collapse of both back legs
of the old chair.

As Beldrune abruptly settled lower amid scattered
literature, Tabarast laid a dust-warding hand over the
open top of his goblet and asked through the roiling
cloud of dancing motes, "Are you *quite* finished? I begin
to weary of this nuisance."

Beldrune made a sound that some folk would have
deemed rude and others might judge impressive and by
way of elaborating on this reply uttered the words, "My
dear fellow, is this—this burgeoning panoply of literary
chaos *my* achievement? I think not. There's not a chair
or table left on this entire floor that isn't guarding its
own ever-growing fortress of magical knowledge at your
behest, and—"

Tabarast made a sound like a serpent's skull being crushed under an eager boot heel. "*My* behest? Do you now deny the parcenary of this disarray around us? I can confute any claims to the contrary, if you've a day or two to spare."

"Meaning my wits are that slow, or words so slow and laborious to come to your lips that—*atch,* never mind. I came not to bandy bright phrases all evening but to banish a little lonely befuddlement by talking a while."

"A prolusion I've heard before," Tabarast observed dryly. "Have a drink."

He pulled on the lever that made the familiar cabinet rise from the floorboards to stand between them and listened to Beldrune pounce on its contents from the far side with an absence of continued speech that meant young Droon must be *very* thirsty.

"All right . . . have two," he amended his offer.

The sounds of swallowing continued. Tabarast opened his mouth to say something, remembered that a certain topic was by mutual agreement forbidden, and shut it again. Then another thought came to him.

"Have you ever read 'The Stormy Knight?' " he asked the cabinet, judging Beldrune's head to be inside it.

The younger wizard raised his head from clinkings and uncorkings and gurglings, looking hurt. "Have I not?" he asked, then cleared his throat and recited,

"What knight is that
"who yonder comes riding
"bright-arrayed in armor of gold
"his sash the dripping blood of his foes?"

There was a pause, then, "I did it in Ambrara, once."

"*You* were the Stormy Knight?" Tabarast asked in open disbelief, his small round spectacles sliding down his nose in search of unknown destinations.

"Second Undergardener," Beldrune snapped, looking even more hurt. "We all have to start somewhere."

Taking a large and dusty bottle firmly in one fist, he plucked its cork and hurled the stopper back over his shoulder where it hit the Snoring Shield of Antalassiter with a bright *ping*, glanced off the Lost Hunting Horn of the Mavran Maidens, and fell somewhere behind the man-high, dust-covered mound of scrolls and books that Tabarast considered his "Urgent Reading of the Moment." He drained the contents of the bottle in one long and loud swallowing that left him gasping, with tears trailing down his face, and in urgent need of something that tasted better.

A knowing Tabarast silently handed him the bowl of roast halavan nuts. Beldrune dug in with both hands until the bowl was empty, then smiled apologetically, burped, and took his worry stone from its drawstring pouch. Thumbing its smooth, familiar curves seemed to calm him.

Settling back in his chair, he added, "I've always preferred 'Broderick Betrayed, Or, The Wizard Woeful.' "

"This would be my turn," the older mage replied with a dignified nod, and in the manner of an actor on center stage threw out his hand and grandly declaimed:

"That so fat and grasping a man
"Should have the very stars bright in his hands
"To blind us all with their shining
"Blotting out his faults in plenty.

"His huge and howling ghost
"Doth prowl the world entire
"but loves and lingers most
"upon this very same and lonesome spot
"Where gods loved, men killed, and careless elves
     forgot."

"Well," Beldrune said after a little silence, "not to deny your impressive performance—your usual paraph, and then some!—but it seems we've returned again to the subject we agreed was forbidden: the One Who Walks, and just what Mystra meant by creating a Chosen One as her most esteemed mortal servant."

Tabarast shrugged, his long and slender fingers tracing the wisps of his own beard thoughtfully. "Men collect what is forbidden," he said. "Always have, always will."

"And mages more so," Beldrune agreed. "What does that tell us about those who follow our profession, I wonder?"

The older mage snorted. "That no shortage of witty fools has yet fallen over Faerûn."

"Hah!" Beldrune leaned forward, stroking one splendid silk lapel eagerly between forefinger and thumb, the worry stone momentarily forgotten. "Then you grant that Our Lady will take more than one Chosen? At last?"

"I grant no such thing," Tabarast replied rather testily. "I can see a succession of Chosen, one raised after another falls, but I've yet been shown no evidence of the dozen or more you champion, still less of this Bright Company of star-harnessing, mountain-splitting archwizards some of the more romantic mages keep babbling about. They'll be begging Holy Mystra to issue merit badges next."

The younger mage ran one hand through his wavy brown hair, utterly ruining the styling the tower's maid-of-chamber had struggled to achieve, and said, "I quite agree with you that such things are ridiculous— and yet could they not be used as a mark of accomplishment? Meet a mage and see seven stars and a scroll on his sash, and you know where he stands?"

"I know how much time he's willing to waste on impressing folk and sewing little gewgaws onto his undergarments, more like," Tabarast replied sourly. "Just how many upstart magelings would add a few unearned stars to grant themselves rank and hauteur accruing to power and accomplishments they do not in fact possess? Every third one who knows how to sew, that's how many! If we must talk about this—this young elf-loving jackanapes, who seems to have been a prince and the slayer of the mighty Ilhundyl and the bed mate of half a hundred slim elf lasses besides, the object of our discourse shall not be his latest conquest or idle utterance, but his import to us all. I care not which boot he puts on first of mornings, what hue of cloak he favors, or whether he prefers to kiss elf lips or human ones—have we understanding and agreement?"

"Of course," Beldrune replied, spreading his hands. "But why such heat? His achievements—as a Chosen One favored by the goddess Herself, mind—do nothing to belittle yours."

Tabarast thumbed his spectacles back up to the bridge of his nose and muttered, "I grow no younger. I've not the years left to encompass what that youn—but enough; I'll say no more. I beg leave to impart to you, my young friend, things about this One Who Walks of rather more importance to us both. The priests of the Mantle, for ins—"

"The priests of the which?"

"The Mantle . . . Mystra's Mantle, the temple to Our Lady in Haramettur. I don't suppose you've ever been therein."

Beldrune shook his head. "I try to avoid temples to Holy Mystra," he said. "The priests tend to be nose-in-the-air sorts who want to charge me coffers full of gold for casting—badly—what I can do myself with a few coppers of oddments."

Tabarast flapped a dismissive hand and replied, "Indeed, indeed, all too often . . . and I've my own quarrel with their snobbery—pimply younglings sneering down their noses at such as myself because we wear real, every-day, food-stained robes, and not silks and sashes and golden cross-garters, like rakes gone to town of an ardent evening. If they truly served wizards and not just awestruck young lasses who 'think they might have felt Mystra's kiss, awakening at midnight this tenday last,' they'd know all *true* mages look like rag heaps, not fashion-pretty popinjays!"

Beldrune looked hurt—again—and gestured down the front of his scarlet silk tunic. The gesture made it ripple glassily in the lamplight, its cloth-of-gold dragons gleaming, the glittering emeralds that served them as eyes a-winking, and the fine wire wrought into spirals that passed for their tongues bobbing. "And what am I? No true mage, I suppose?"

Tabarast passed a weary hand over his eyes. "Nay, nay, good Droon—present company excepted, of course. Your bright plumage doth so outshine mine aged eyes that I overlook it as a matter of course. Let us have no quarrel over your learning or able mastery of realm-shaking magics; you *are*, before all the gods, a 'true mage,' whatever by Mystra's gentle whispers *that* is. Let us by more heroic efforts resist the temptation to drift away into other matters, and—if discuss the forbidden we must—speak plainly. To whit: the priests of the Mantle say that the One Who Walks is free to act on his own; that is, to make just as bad a hash of things as you and I are free to do . . . moreover, that it is holy Mystra's will that he be left to blunder and choose and hurl recklessness on his own, to 'become what it is needful he become.' They want us all to pretend we don't know who or what he is, if we should meet with him."

Beldrune rested his chin on one hand, a fresh and smoking goblet raised in the other. "Just what is it that they say he must become?" he asked.

"That's where their usefulness ends," Tabarast snorted. "When one asks, they go to their knees and groan about 'not being worthy to know,' and 'the aims of the divine are beyond the comprehension of all mortals'—which tells me right there that *they* haven't figured it out yet—then they rush into an almost puppy-panting whirl of 'oh, but he's important! The signs! The signs!' "

Beldrune sipped deeply from his goblet, swallowed, and asked, "What signs?"

Tabarast resumed the ringing voice of doom that he'd used to delivered the lines from Broderick, and intoned: "In this Year of Laughter, the Blazing Hand of Sorcery ascends the starry night cloak, for the first time in centuries! Nine black tressym landed upon the sleeping princess Sharandra of the South and delivered themselves of four kittens each upon her very bosom! (Don't ask me how she slept through *that* or what she thought of the mess when she did wake!) The Walking Tower of Warglend has moved for the first time in a thousand years, taking itself from Tower Tor to the midst of a nearby lake! A talking frog has been found in Candlekeep, wherein also six pages in as many books have gone blank, and two books appeared that have never been seen by any Faerûnian scholar before! The Well of the Bonedance in Maraeda's run dry! The skeleton of the lich Buardrim has been seen dancing in—ah, *bah!* Enough! They can keep it up for hours!"

"Gullet Well's gone dry?"

Tabarast favored Beldrune with a look. "Yes," he said mildly. "Gullet Well *has* gone dry—for whatever real reason. I saw the dead horses to prove it. So there you have it. Tell me, good Droon, you get out and about more than I do, and hear more of the gossip—however paltry or deliberately fabricated it may be—among our fellow workers-of-Art. How say the mages about this One Who Walks? What do the trendy wizards think?"

It was Beldrune's turn to snort. "Trendy wizards *don't* think," he retorted, "or they'd take care never to be caught up in any trend. But as to what's being said . . . of him, less than nothing. What our colleagues seem to have heard out of whatever the priests have proclaimed can be boiled down to great secret excitement and preening over the chance to be named a Chosen of Mystra—and thereby get all sorts of special powers and inside knowledge. They seem to view it as the most exclusive club yet, and that someone is certain to privately contact them to join, any day now. If Mystra is selecting mortal mages to be Her personal servants, endowing them with spells mighty enough to shatter mountains and read minds, each and every mage wants to get into this oh-so-exclusive group without appearing in the slightest to be interested in such status."

Tabarast raised an eyebrow. "I see. How do you know I'm already not a Chosen and reading your mind even now?"

Beldrune gave his friend a wry smile. "If you were reading my mind, Baerast," he said, "you'd be trying to smite me down, right now—and blushing to boot!"

Tabarast lifted the other eyebrow to join the first. "Oh? Should I bother to venture further queries?" he asked. "I suspect not, but I'd like to be prepared if your incipient anger bids fair to goad you into muscular and daring feats that I must needs resist . . . You *do* feel incipient anger, don't you?"

"No; not a moment of it," Beldrune replied cheerfully. "Though I could probably work up to it, if you continue to guard that jar of halavan nuts so closely. Pass it over."

Tabarast did so, freely giving his colleague a sour look along with it and saying, "I value these nuts highly; one might even say they are precious to me. Conduct thy depredations accordingly."

The younger wizard smiled wryly. "All mages, I daresay, conduct their depredations while considering—if they take time to consider at all—what they're about to seize or destroy to be precious. Don't you?"

Tabarast looked thoughtful. "Yes," he murmured. "Yes, I do." He lifted an eyebrow. "How many of us, I wonder, fall so into exultation at our own power that we try to seize or destroy everything we deem precious?"

Beldrune scooped up a handful of nuts. "Most of us would consider a Chosen precious, would we not?" he asked.

Tabarast nodded. "The One Who Walks is going to have an interesting career in time soon to come," he predicted softly, his face very far from a smile. "Pour me something."

Beldrune did.

*   *   *   *   *

Lightning rose and snapped out, splitting the night with a bright flash of fury. El blinked and sat up. Blue arcs of deadly magic were leaping and crackling from dagger to dagger around his ring, and in the night beyond something was thrashing wetly—something that was being avoided by a score or more slinking, prowling things that looked like ragged shadows, but moved like hunting cats. Elminster came fully awake fast, peering all around and counting. The thrashing hadn't ended, and anything that could survive such a lash of lightning was something to be respected. Respected twenty-fold, it seemed.

He folded his cloak, slung it through the straps of the saddlebag in case hasty flight should be necessary, and stood up. The prowling shadows were moving around his roused ring from right to left, quickening their pace for a charge to come. Something was urging or goading them; something El could feel as a tension in the air, a growing, heavy, and fell presence with the force and fury of a hailstorm about to break. Shaking his hands and wriggling his fingers to leave them loose and ready for frantic casting to come, he peered into the night, trying to see his foe.

He could *feel* when he was facing it, its unseen gaze transfixing him like two hot sword tips, but he could see nothing but roiling darkness.

Perhaps the thing was cloaked in a wall of these prowling shadows. It might be best to conjure a high, glowing sphere of the sort folk called a "witchlight," just to see what he faced. Yet he had only one such spell. If his foe dashed it to darkness, El would be blinking and blinded for too long a time to keep his life against a concerted attack from many prowling things.

Should he—then it came. The shadows swerved and moved in at him on all sides in a soundless charge of rippling darkness.

His wards crackled and spat blue-white, leaping death into the night. Shadows stiffened, reared, and danced in agony amid racing, darting lightning. El spun around to make sure his ring had held in all places against this initial charge.

It had, but the shadow beasts weren't drawing back. Weeping as they perished, dwindling like smoke before the fury of the lightning crawling through them, they clawed and convulsed and tried to hurl themselves past the barrier. El watched and waited, as his lightning flickered and grew dim, dying with the creatures it was slaying. By the Lady, there were a lot of them.

It would not be long now before the spell failed utterly and he'd stand alone against the onslaught. He had one teleport spell that could snatch him from this peril, aye, but only to a place back along his wanderings, leaving these Lands of the Lady in front of him once more; and who knew how much a foe who was expecting him could muster for his second visit?

Here and there, as dying shadows roiled away into smoke, his spell was being brought to collapse: the daggers were rising from the ground, their cracklings and radiances fading, to leap at shadows. They would fly hungrily, points first, at anything outside the ring; he'd best stay where he was and hope they'd reap a good crop of shadow beasts before his unseen foe tried something else. Such as a spell of its own.

Green, many-clawed lightning was born in the night—in the hand of something manlike, bare-bodied, and stag-headed that juggled its conjuration in wickedly long fingers for a moment beside its hip, then hurled it at Elminster.

Snarling and expanding as it came, that ball of spell lightning burst through the last tatters of his ring shield without pause and rushed hungrily at the Athalantan, who was already muttering a swift phrase and angling his hand up, palm slanted out, in a curious gesture.

Lightning struck and rebounded, springing away as if it'd been struck, to go howling back the way it'd come. El could see red eyes watching him intently now and felt the weight of a mirthless smile that he could not see, as the figure simply stood and let the lightning flow back into it to be swallowed up as if it'd never been.

Elminster's raised, warding hand flickered with a radiance of its own, then was itself again. His spell still lurked, though, awaiting another attack . . . or two, if this stagheaded foe struck swiftly.

The last few slinking shadows rushed to the stagheaded being and seemed to flow up and *into* it. El used its moment of immobility to launch an attack of his own, tossing a dagger into the air that his Art made into thirty-three blades. He swept them all, whirling and darting, down upon his foe.

Antlers dipped swiftly as the figure of shadows ducked away, emitting what might have been a low growl or might have been an incantation. The thing stiffened and sent out a high, shrill cry that might have been a human woman taking a blade in the back (for Elminster had heard such a sound before, in the city of Hastarl, several centuries ago), as blades bit deep. There was a flash of unleashed magic, motes of light raining to the ground like water dashing off a warrior's shield in a heavy rain, and the whirling, stabbing blades were abruptly gone.

El pressed his advantage; winning this spell duel was certainly needful if he wanted to keep his life—no mage bent on capture hurls lightning—and it would be the act of a fool to stand idly awaiting the next spell Silent Antlers here wanted to bury him with.

He smiled thinly as his fingers traced an intricate pattern, their tips glowing as the casting concluded.

Many, many of the things he'd done since that day when a mage-ridden dragon had pounced on Heldon and torn his life asunder could be viewed as acts of a fool.

"I'm a fool goaded by fools, it seems," he told his half-seen assailant pleasantly. "Do you attack all who pass this way, or is this a personal favor?"

His only answer was a loud hiss. He thought it ended with the stag-headed being spitting at him, but he couldn't be certain. His spell took effect then, with a roar that drowned out all other sounds for a time.

Blue flames blossomed around those night-black, spiderlike fingers and on the antlers beyond. The screams came in earnest this time.

El risked time enough to look all around, in case a lurking shadow was on the prowl—and so, glancing back over his own shoulder, he escaped being blinded when a counterspell set the night aflame.

It consumed his wardings in an instant, sending him staggering back among the smoke of shattered spells. Heat blistered his left cheek, and he heard hair sizzle as tears washed the sight from his left eye.

Softly and carefully through the pain, Elminster said the waiting word that awakened the final effect of the spell he'd already cast—and the blue flames cloaking the extremities of his foe blazed up in an exact echo of those that had just struck him.

The shriek that split the night was raw and awkward, born of real agony. El caught a brief glimpse of antlers thrashing back and forth before the flames died and heard harsh gasping receding eastward, amid the swish and crackle of grasses being trampled.

Something large fell in the grass, at least twice. When silence came at last El glided three quick steps to the west and crouched, listening intently to the night.

Nothing. He could hear the long grass stirring in the breeze, and the faint cry of some small wild creature dying in the jaws of another, far off to the south.

At length, El wearily drew the last enchanted dagger he owned—one that did nothing more than glow upon command—and threw it in the direction the sounds had gone, to strike and there illuminate the night.

He took care not to approach its glow too closely and to keep bent low over the grass . . . but nothing moved, and no spell or prowling shadow came leaping out of the night. When he looked where the dagger's light reached, all that could be seen was a broken trail leading a little way to a confused heap of crumbling and smoking bones, or antlers . . . or perhaps just branches. Something collapsed into ash as he drew nearer; something that had looked very much like a long, slim-fingered hand.

* * * * *

Dangling strips of paint quivered, fell, and were followed enthusiastically by the vaulted ceiling itself, leaping to the floor below with a deafening, dust-hurling crash. In its wake, the entire Ringyl shook.

Flung stones were still pattering down nearby buildings and crashing through bushes when the hall where an Athalantan had earlier seen stars rocked, groaned, and began to break apart. Gilded fruit shattered as the wall they were painted on burst asunder, splitting a dark oval and spitting sparkling stars into the night.

Sculpted stone lips quivered as if hesitant to speak, seemed to smile even more for an instant, then broke into many fragments as the widening crack reached them and spat stony pieces out to roll and crash across the trembling hall. The lips toppled, sighed into oblivion, and left a gaping hole in the wall where they'd been.

Echoes of the earth's fury that had caused this cleaving rolled on . . . and out of the hole in the wall, framed by a few surviving stars, something long and black and massive slid into view.

With a growing, grating roar, it canted over on the stony rubble and rattled out into the room: a black catafalque whose upthrust electrum arms held aloft a coffin and several scepters for a few impressive moments before toppling over on its side and crashing into and through the floor.

Shards of floor tile leaped into the air, chased by crawling purple lightning that spat out of the riven coffin. Electrum arms, smashed and twisted in the fall, melted as shattered scepters in their grasp died amid their own small and roiling magical blazes. One arm spat a scepter intact out onto the dust-choked pave an instant before failing protective magics flickered the length of the coffin, hung silent and grappling in the air for a long, tense time of silence, then collapsed in a small but sharp explosion that transformed coffin, catafalque, and all into dark dust and hurled it in all directions.

Amid the tumult, the scepter on the floor gave its own small sigh and collapsed into a neat outline of gently winking dust.

Silence fell in earnest upon the riven hall, and all was still save for the dust drifting down.

Not long afterward, the starlight grew stronger over Tresset's Ringyl, until a mote of blue-white radiance could clearly be seen drifting down out of the starry sky—descending smoothly, like a very large, bright, and purposeful will-o'-wisp, into the heart of the riven hall.

The light came to a smooth stop a handspan or so away from the floor and hung for a moment above the dust that had been the scepter—dust that winked and flickered like blown coals beneath its nearness.

There was a flash, a faint sound like bells struck at random, very far off, and the dust was a scepter once more—smooth and new-lustrous, glimmering with stored power.

A long-fingered, feminine hand suddenly appeared out of empty air, as if through a parted curtain, to grasp the scepter and take it up.

It flashed once like a winking star as it rose. As if in answer the hand grew an ivory-hued arm, the arm a bare shoulder that turned, allowing a glossy flood of dark hair to cascade over it, and rose into a neck, ear, line of jaw—then a beautiful, fine-boned face. Cold was her visage, serene and proud, as she turned dark eyes to look around at the ruined hall.

The scattered quartz stars glowed as if in greeting as the rest of the body grew or faded into view, turning with fearless, unconcerned grace to survey the shattered hall. A beautiful, dark-eyed sorceress held up her scepter like a warrior brandishing a blade in victory and smiled.

The scepter flashed and was gone, the sorceress with it, leaving sudden darkness behind, and only three glows flickering in that gloom: the scattered quartz stars. As the lengthening moments passed, those faint fires faded and went out, one by one, until lifeless darkness reigned in Tresset's Ringyl once more.

*   *   *   *   *

"Holy Lady," Elminster said to the stars, on his knees in what had once been his ring of daggers, with the sweat of spell battle still glistening on him, "I have come here, and fought—perhaps slain—at thy bidding. Guide me, I pray."

A gentle breeze rose and stirred the grasses. El watched it, wondering if it was a sign, or some evil thing his words had awakened, or simply uncaring wind, and continued, "I have dared to touch ye, and long to do so again. I have sworn to serve thee and will so, if ye will still have me—but show me, I pray, what I am to do in these haunted lands . . . for I would fain not blunder about, doing harm in ignorance. I have a horror of not knowing."

The response was immediate. Something blue-white seemed to snap and whirl behind his eyes, unfolding to reveal a scene in its smoky rifts: Elminster, here and now, rising from his knees to take up pack and cloak and walk away north and east, briskly and with some urgency . . . a scene that whirled away to become daylight, falling upon an old, squat, untidy stone tower that seemed more cone or mound than lofty cylinder. A large archway held an old, stout wooden door that offered entrance with no moat or defenses to be seen—and that arch displayed a sequence of relief-sculpted phases of the moon. Elminster had never seen it before, but the vision was clear enough. Even as it faded, he was leaning down to take up his belongings and begin his walk.

No more visions came to him. He nodded, spoke his thanks to the night, and set off.

*   *   *   *   *

Not three hills had the last prince of Athalantar put at his back when a chill, chiming wind whirled and danced through the Ringyl, like a flying snake of frost, and climbed the grassy slopes to where Elminster's ring had been.

It recoiled from that place, a startled wisp of cold starlight arching and twisting in the night air, then slowly advanced to trace the outline of the wards that were now gone. Completing the circle, the wind leaped into its center rather hesitantly, danced and swirled for a time over the spot where Elminster had knelt to pray, then, very slowly, drifted off along the way El's feet had taken him. It rose and flickered once as it went, almost as if looking around. Hungrily.

Five

ONE MORNING AT MOONSHORN

A mage can visit worlds and times in plenty by opening the right books. Unfortunately, they usually open the tomes full of spells instead, to find ready weapons to beat their own world and time into submission.

Claddart of Candlekeep
from **Things I Have Observed**
published circa The Year of the Wave

Out of the dawn mists it rose, dark and old and misshapen, more like a gigantic, many-fissured tree stump than a tower. The sleepless and stumbling man silently cursed Mystra's dictate to use no needless magic for perhaps the hundredth time and winced at the blisters his boots were giving him. It had been a long and weary way hence from the lands of the Lady of Shadows.

Aye, this was it: Moonshorn Tower, just as Her vision had shown him: relief-carved phases of the moon proceeded around the worn stone arch that framed its massive black, many-strapped and bolted door.

As he approached, that door opened and a yawning man stepped out, shuffled a short distance away from the tower, and emptied a chamber pot into a ditch or cesspit somewhere in the tall grass. As the pot-emptier straightened, El saw that the man was of middling years and possessed of raven-dark hair, good looks framed by razor-edged sideburns, one normal—and deep brown—eye, and one eye that blazed like a distant star, white and glowing.

He saw Elminster and stiffened in wary surprise for a moment before striding back to bar passage through the open door. "Well met," he said, in carefully neutral tones. "Be it known that I am Mardasper, guardian of this shrine of Holy Mystra. Have you business here, traveler?"

Elminster was too tired to indulge in witty repartee, but he noted with some satisfaction that the state of the morning sunlight touching the tower matched the vision granted to him last night . . . or early this morn . . . or whenever. "I do," he replied simply.

"You venerate Holy Mystra, Lady of All Mysteries?"

Elminster smiled at the thought of how shocked this Mardasper would be if he knew just how intimately a certain falling-down-exhausted mage had venerated Mystra. "I do," he said again.

Mardasper gave him a hard look, that blazing eye stabbing out at the hawk-nosed Athalantan, and moved his hands in a tiny gesture that El knew to be a truth-sensing spell.

"All who enter here," the guardian said, gesturing with the chamber pot as if it was a scepter of office, "must obey me utterly and work no magic unbidden. Anyone who takes or damages even the smallest thing from within these walls forfeits his life, or at the least his freedom. You may rest within and take water from the fount, but no food or anything else is provided—and you must surrender to me your name and all written magic and enchanted items you carry, no matter how small or benign. They will be returned upon your departure."

"I agree to all this," El told him. "My name is Elminster Aumar. Here's my spellbook and the sole item of magic I yet carry: a dagger that can be made to glow as one desires, bright or dim. It can also purify water and edibles it touches and is guarded against rusting; I know of no other powers."

"This is all?" the fire-eyed guardian demanded, staring intently into Elminster's face as he accepted the book and the sheathed dagger. "And 'Elminster' is your true and usual name?"

"This is all, and aye, Elminster I am called," the Athalantan replied.

Mardasper gestured that he should enter, and they passed into a small chamber, dark after the bright sunlight, that held a lectern and much dust. The guardian wrote down Elminster's name and the date in a ledger as large as some doors El had seen, and waved at one of three closed doors behind the lectern.

"That stair leads to the upper levels, wherein are kept the writings you doubtless seek."

El inclined his head and replied wearily, "Have my thanks."

Writings I doubtless seek? he thought. Well, perhaps so. . . .

He turned, his hand upon the pull-ring of the door, and asked, "Why else would a mage come to Moonshorn Tower?"

Mardasper's head snapped up from the ledger, and his good eye blinked in surprise. The other one, El noticed, never closed.

"I know not," the guardian said, sounding almost embarrassed. "There's nothing else here."

"Why came ye here?" El asked gently.

The guardian locked eyes with him in silence for a time, then replied, "If my stewardship here is faithful and diligent for four years—two being already behind me—the priests of Mystra have promised to end the spell upon me that I cannot break." He pointed at his staring eye and added pointedly, "How I came to have this is a private matter. Ask no more on this, lest your welcome run out."

El nodded and opened the door. Probing magics sang and snarled around him for a moment. Then the darkness inside the door became a shrinking, receding web that melted away to reveal a smooth-worn, plain stone stair leading up. As the last prince of Athalantar set his hand upon its rail, an eye seemed to appear in the smooth stone just above his hand and wink at him . . . but perhaps it was just his over-weary imagination. He went on up the stair.

*   *   *   *   *

"To work!" The balding, bearded mage in the stained and patched robe threw up the shutter and set its support bar firmly in the socket, letting sunlight spill into the room.

"Aye, Baerast," the younger wizard agreed, wrapping his hands in a cloth to keep dust from them before he caught up the next support bar, "to work it is. We've much to do, to be sure."

Tabarast of the Three Sung Curses peered over his spectacles a trifle severely and said, "The last time you made such enthusiastic utterance, dearest Droon, you spent the entire day with some Netherese chiming-ball *child's* toy, trying to make it roll by itself!"

"As it was meant to do," Beldrune of the Bent Finger replied, looking hurt. "Is that not why we labor here thus, Baerast? Is restoring and making sense of the scraps of elder magic not an exalted calling? Doth not Holy Mystra Herself smile betimes upon us?"

"Yes, yes, and aye besides," Tabarast said dismissively, waving away the argument like three-day-old feast table scraps. "Though I doubt overmuch if she was

impressed by a failed effort to resurrect a toy." He hefted the last support bar. "Yet, passing on from that trifle,
let us recollect together."

He thrust the last bar into its socket, settled it with
a slap, and turned to the vast and uneven table that
filled most of the room, in several places almost touching the massive and crammed bookshelves ranked
along the walls.

Sixty or more untidy piles of tomes rose here and
there from a carpet of scrolls, scraps of old parchment,
and more recent notes that completely covered the
table; in places the writings were three layers deep. The
papers were held flat by a motley assortment of gems,
ornate and aged rings, scraps of intricate wire or
wrought metal that had once been parts of larger items,
candle-topped skulls, and stranger things.

The two mages thrust out their hands above the pages
and moved them in slow circles, as if a tingling in their
fingertips would locate a passage they were seeking.
Tabarast said slowly, "Cordorlar, writing in the failing days
of Netheril . . . the dragonsblood experiments . . ." His hand
shot out to grasp a particular parchment. "Here!"

Beldrune, frowning, said, "I was tracing a triple-
delayed-blast fireball magic some loosejaw named Olbert
claimed to have made by combining earlier magics from
Lhabbartan, Iliymbrim Sharnult, and—and . . . *agghh,*
the name's gone now." He looked up. "So tell me: *what*
dragonsblood experiments? Stirring the stuff into
potions? Drinking it? Setting it aflame?"

"Introducing it into one's own blood in hopes that it
would bring a human wizard longevity, increased vigor,
the same immunity to certain perils that some dragons
enjoy, or even full-blown draconic powers," Tabarast
replied. "Various mages of the time claimed to have
enjoyed successes in all of those areas. Not that any of
them survived or left later evidence we've found yet, to
bear out any such claims." He sighed. "We've *got* to get
into Candlekeep."

Beldrune smote his forehead and said, "That again? Baerast, I agree, wholeheartedly and with every waking scrap of my brain. We do indeed have to be able to look at the tomes in Candlekeep—but we need to do so freely, whenever thoughts take us hence, not in a single or skulking visit. I somehow doubt they'll accept us as the new co-Keepers of Candlekeep if we march in there and demand such access."

It was Tabarast's turn to frown. "True, true," he said with a sigh. "Wherefore we've got to make the most of these salvaged scraps and forgotten oddments."

He sighed again. "No matter how untruthful and incomplete they may be."

He poked at one yellowing parchment with an almost accusatory forefinger, adding, "This worthy claimant boasts of *eating* an entire dragon, platter by platter. It took him a season, he says, and he hired the greatest cooks of the time to make it palatable fare by trading them its bones and scales. I began to doubt him when he said it was his *third* such dragon, and that he preferred red dragon meat to the flesh of blue dragons."

Beldrune smiled. "Ah, Baerast," he said. "Still clinging to this romantic delusion that folk who go to the trouble of writing are superior sorts who always set down the truth? Some folk lie even to their own diaries."

He waved at the ceiling and walls around them and added, "When all this was new, do you think the Netherese who dwelt or worked here were the great paragons some sages claim them to be—wiser than we, more mighty in all ways than the folk of today, and able to work almost any magic with a snap of the fingers? Not a bit of it! They were like us—a few bright minds, a lot of lazy-wits, and a few dark and devious twisters of truth who worked on folk around them to make others do as they desired. Sound familiar?"

Tabarast plucked up a falcon's head carved from a single palm-sized emerald an age ago and stroked its curved beak absently.

"I grant your point, Droon, yet I ask myself: what follows? Are we doomed to wallow in distortions and untruths as the years pass, with but seventeen spells to show for it—*seventeen?*"

Beldrune spread his hands. "That's seventeen more magics than some mages craft in a lifetime of working the Art," he reminded his colleague mildly. "And we share a task both of us love—and, moreover, are granted the occasional *personal* reward from Herself, remember?"

"How do we know She sends those dream-visions?" Tabarast said in a low voice. "How do we really know?"

Moonshorn Tower shook all around them for the briefest of instants, with a deep rumbling sound; somewhere a stack of books collapsed with a crash.

Beldrune smiled crookedly and said, "That's good enough for me. What do you want Her to do, Baerast? Dole out a spell a night, written across our brains in letters of everlasting fire?"

Tabarast snorted. "There's no need to be ridiculous, Droon." Then he smiled almost wistfully, and added, "Letters of fire would be nice, though, just once."

"Old cynic," the younger mage responded with an air of offended pomposity, "I am *never* ridiculous. I merely afford a degree of jollity that has never failed to please even more discerning audiences than yourself, or should I say *especially* more discerning audiences than yourself."

Tabarast mumbled something, then added more loudly, "This is why we accomplish so little, as the hours and days pass unheeded. Clever words, *clever words* we catch and hurl like small boys at skulltoss, and the work advances but little."

Beldrune gestured at the table. "So take up some new scrap, and let's begin," he challenged. "Today we'll work together rather than pursuing separate ends and see if the Lady smiles on us. Do start, old friend, and I shall keep us to the matter at hand. In this my vigilance shall be steadfast, but as nothing to my wroth."

"Isn't that 'wrath,' m'boy?" Tabarast asked, his hand hovering once more above the table.

"Lesser beings, dearest mage of my regard, may well indulge in wrath—I feel wroth," Beldrune replied loftily, then added with a snarl, "Now take up a paper, and let's be about it!"

Tabarast blinked in astonishment and took up a paper. "—'That so surpasseth all mine previous . . . other mages decry such . . . Yet will I prevail, the truth being my guide and guardian,' methinks, methinks, methinks, ho ho hum . . . Hmmm. Someone writing in the South, before Myth Drannor but probably not all that long before, about a spell to put a mage's wits and all in the body of a beast, to make it prowl at his bidding for a night, or stay longer or forever within it should his own body be threatened or lost."

"Good, good," Beldrune responded. "Could it be Alavaernith, in the early days of working on his 'Three-cats' spell? Or is it too effusive for that?"

"I suspect someone other than Alavaernith," Tabarast said slowly. "He was never so open with his secrets as this. . . ."

Neither of them noticed a red-eyed, hawk-nosed man step into the room and lean for a moment against the door sill with an air of utter weariness, looking around at everything as he listened to them.

"And does he say anything useful?" Beldrune pressed. "Or can we cast this aside on the heap in the barrel?"

Tabarast peered at the page, turned it over to make sure the back was blank, held it to the light seeking oddities in (or hidden under) the writing, and finally handed it to his colleague with a sound that was half sigh and half snort. "Nothing useful, beyond telling us what someone was working on or had thought of back then. . . ."

The hawk-nosed man stepped forward to peer at the gilt-lettered spines of tomes wedged tightly into the nearest bookshelf, then looked over at the table and carefully turned over a twisted, crumpled cage of wrought metal that had probably once held the shape of a globe. Examining it carefully, the stranger set it softly back down and peered at the writings beneath it.

"Now, *this* one," Tabarast said slowly, bent over the other side of the table, "is rather more interesting. No, we shan't be hurling this into the barrel quite so quickly." He held it up under his nose as he straightened, then paused as Elminster's boot made a slight sound and the dark-haired mage asked, "How goes it, Mardasper? Keeping an *eye* on things, as usual, hmmm?"

When there was no reply, he turned, and both mages stared across the room at the newcomer—who gave them a polite nod and smile, looked for a moment at an old and brittle scroll on the table, then stepped sideways, seeking more interesting writings.

Tabarast and Beldrune frowned at the stranger in unison, then turned their backs, drew in side by side, and continued their investigations in muttered tones.

El gave their eloquent backs and shoulders a wry, exhausted smile, then shrugged and peered at another parchment. It was something about crafting a spike-studded torture coffin so that folk latched into it were teleported elsewhere rather than suffering impalement, and it was written with that squaring of the letters that marked its origin as the south shore of the Sea of Fallen Stars. The glint of metallic inks shone back at him, and the page had reached that soft brown state just before crumbling begins . . . as old as he was, or older. El looked at the next page, sliding aside a Netherese ocular to do it.

He gave the beautiful item a second glance. The enchantments that would affix it over a wearer's eye were gone, but the gem would still, by the looks of it, afford vision of heat, and even through wood or stone a handspan thick or less. With the curled filigree around it, it looked like a giant, elegant tear that would glisten endlessly on a lady's cheek.

What a lot of work. Crafting far in excess of its usefulness, done for the sheer joy of mastering the Art and
creating something that would last . . . and there must
be a thousand times a thousand such items, scattered
all over a world so rich in natural magic that all of them
could be said to be frivolities.

And was Elminster Aumar, in truth, one more frivolity?

Perhaps, and perhaps he was destined to leave
behind little more than these endless dusty scraps of
parchment, the confused and unfinished ideas of centuries . . . yet that flow of mistakes and vain strivings
and occasional triumphs or destructive disasters *was*
the Art, with Mystra the gatekeeper of the Weave from
which it all came and to which it all returned.

Enough. He was standing in a parchment-littered room
in Moonshorn Tower, here and now, and the flow of magics or the very nature of Art were alike in their irrelevance.
His world was a place of hunger, and thirst, feeling cold
or hot—or feeling so gods-spitting tired that he could
barely keep his eyes open an instant longer.

Wait! There—he'd seen *that* writing before. The fine,
flowing hand of Elenshaer, who'd been so good at crafting new and unusual wardings in Myth Drannor—until
he'd been torn apart by a Phaerimm he'd rashly caged
in too-feeble spells to do a little experimentation . . . a
victim, some would say, of that arrogant assumption of
elven superiority and of the ethical right to transform,
mutilate, or tamper with "lesser beings," even if they're
not truly lesser beings, that afflicts so many of his race.
An unfortunate moment of misjudgment and another
of carelessness, others would term it. And who was to
say which view was right or if any of it truly mattered?
Seeing the slender elf laughing and gesturing, fluted
wineglass in hand, in his memory of a terrace that no
longer stood, amid folk who no longer lived, El slid aside
other writings to expose all of Elenshaer's missive.

It was a spell, of sorts. Or rather, the beginnings of a
"hook" of Art that would allow an additional power to be

added to an existing ward by the casting of another spell into the invisible hook—which would then draw the spell into the weaving of the ward and permit the caster to govern and adjust its effects. Elminster read the spell over silently until it approached its ending and stopped.

Elenshaer had followed a common elf mages' practice. He'd set down the crowning part of the casting on another paper, kept elsewhere. His abode would have held thousands of such papers, with Elenshaer's memory as the only link of what paper went with which. There'd even been a rogue mage in the City of Song, Twillist, who'd sought power by pilfering such "ends" of spells, trading them to young apprentices and others eager for more knowledge and power in exchange for lesser, but whole, magics.

The missing ending was almost obvious to a mage who'd had a hand in crafting mythals and studied with Cormanthan elves. A summation or linking bridge, probably "*Tanaethaert shurruna rae*," a shaping gesture—thus—mirrored immediately and incorporated into the incantation with the utterance of "*Rahrada*," then the declaration that would make the hook recede into the ward-weave and give its caster control of the spell effects it brought with it: "*Dannaras ouuhilim rabreivra, tonneth ootaha la, tabras torren ouliirym torrin, dalarabban yultah.*" A concluding gesture—thus—and it would be done.

He'd spoken those words aloud, though near-soundlessly, and was startled when something spun into being in the air before him, a little more than the length of his hand above Elenshaer's incomplete spell. A little glowing construction hung in the air above the page: lines of fire looping into a tiny knot that began to rotate as he watched it, to spin endlessly and silently.

Sigh. If there was such a thing as a needless magic, this was it. Unthinkingly he'd broken Mystra's decree, after enduring so much discomfort and danger to keep it. Gods *blast!*

As if that silent, savage thought had been a cue, the hook he'd created commenced to spit tiny sparks at the parchment beneath it. Oh, that was all he needed! In a room such as this, with dry and dusty paper inches deep on everything. . . .

His hands were already darting to shield the thickly strewn parchments against the sparks . . . too late. They landed, hopped, and—

Formed glowing words that were overlaying Elenshaer's writing as they advanced before his astonished eyes, leaving no smoke or sign of conflagration in their wake.

Leave. Now. Seek the Riven Stone.

The message flashed once, as if to make sure that he read it, blazed brightly, then slowly began to fade away.

El read them one more time and swallowed. He could barely stand, but the command couldn't be much clearer; he must leave this place without delay. He raised his head and looked regretfully around at all the lore he'd not be able to poke around in, now. No more sparks fell from the tiny whirling hook, and the two old wizards were still hunched against him on the far side of the room, mumbling secrets to each other so he'd not hear.

He looked down at the letters of magical flame again, found them just fading into invisibility, and watched until they were quite gone. Then he gave the room a deep, soundless sigh, followed it with a rueful grin, and crept out as softly as the thief in Hastarl he'd once been.

*   *   *   *   *

After the fourth page of unrelated lore, Tabarast murmured, "Will you look behind us and see where this stranger has got to? If he's wandered back to the door, or out of it, this guarding of tongues shall cease forthwith. I feel like a guilty servant gossiping in an outhouse."

"How can we discuss things if we can't speak freely?" Beldrune agreed, performing an elaborately casual glance back over his shoulder at the littered table. Then he swung right around, and said, "Baerast, he's gone."

Something in the younger mage's tone made Tabarast's head snap up. He turned around, too, to stare across the room where they'd labored for so long, and find it empty of strange mages, but now home to—

"The sign!" Beldrune gasped, voice unsteady in awe. "The sign! A Chosen was here among us!"

"After all these years," Tabarast murmured huskily, almost dazed. In an instant his life and his faith and all Toril around him had changed. "Who can it have been? That beak-nosed youngster? We must follow him!"

Slowly, as if they dared not disturb it, the two old mages advanced around the table. By unspoken agreement they walked in opposite directions, to come upon the spinning sigil from different directions—as if it might escape if they didn't pounce.

The little whirling knot of blazing lines was still there when they met in front of it to gape at it in awe. "It matches the vision completely," Tabarast murmured, as if there'd been some possibility of a mistake or counterfeit. "There can be no doubt."

He looked around the room at their piled, cluttered years of work. "I'm going to miss all of this," he said slowly.

"I'm not!" Beldrune replied, almost bowling the older mage over in his rush for the door. "Adventure—at last!"

Tabarast blinked at his fast-receding colleague and said, "Droon? Are you mad? This is exciting, yes, but our road's just beginning—it'll be a hard fall for you soon, if you're dancing this high in glee right now."

"The Dark Gods take your gloom, Baerast—we're going *adventuring!*" Beldrune shouted back up the stairway.

Tabarast winced and started descending steps, a sour expression settling onto his face. "You've never been on an adventure before, have you?"

*   *   *   *   *

Years of travel had made the hard-packed mud lane between Aerhiot's Field and Salopar's Field sink down into its own ditch, until now the tangled hedges almost met overhead, as disturbed birds and squirrels fretted and darted along in the perpetual gloom whenever anyone ventured along the lane.

The oxen were used to it, and so was Nuglar. He trudged along half asleep with his goad-stick in the crook of his arm, not expecting to have to use it, while the three massive beasts ambled along ahead of him, also half-asleep, hardly bothering to switch their tails against the biting buzzflies.

Something chimed nearby. Nuglar lifted one heavy eyelid and turned his head to see what could be making the sound . . . a wandering lamb, perhaps, collared with one of those tiny toy bells the priests of the Mother hung down their aspergilla? Several younglings?

He could see nothing but a sort of white, sparkling mist in the air, whirling tongues of it that trailed the chiming. It was all around him now, loud and somehow cruel, settling around him like a cold shawl . . . and around the oxen. One of them sobbed in sudden alarm as the chiming mist became a howling, tightening whirlwind encircling it.

Nuglar shouted, or thought he did, and stretched out a hand to that ox's rump—only to feel a deathly, searing chill, numbing in an instant like icy winter water. He drew back his arm.

It was a stump, blood streaming from where his hand should have been. He opened his mouth to scream, and a wisp of that deadly whirlwind spun out of nowhere to plunge down his throat.

Less than a breath later, Nuglar's jawbone dropped away from a wavering, wind-scoured skull—an instant before his skeleton collapsed into whirling dust, whipped together into crumbling oblivion with the three oxen.

With a loud, triumphant chorus of chiming, like many exultant bells being rung together, a larger, brighter whirlwind rose out of the lane and poured itself across Aerhiot's Field, leaving the muddy lane empty of all but a stout, well-worn goad-stick. It danced in the air in the whirling wake of the chiming mist for an eerie moment, then fell to the mud for other frightened farmers to find later.

A long time passed in the gloomy lane before squirrels meekly scampered and the birds dared to sing again.

*   *   *   *   *

The Riven Stone must be a place, or more likely a landmark—a rock cloven by a spring or winter ice. A feature he'd never heard of, but then there was a lot of Faerûn he knew nothing about, yet.

Was Mystra going to make him walk over every stride of it?

Almost reeling in exhaustion, Elminster trudged up a grassy slope, trying to keep in sight of the road that had brought him to the Tower . . . and was now taking him on away from it. Leaving the tower had been a matter of flat urgency, aye, but the Lady—or Azuth, speaking for her—knew he'd have to search for the Riven Stone. Well, then, he couldn't be expected to find it immediately.

That was good, because he could barely find the strength to put one foot in front of another any longer.

El took another two clumsy steps, found himself sliding back down the slope to the roadside, stumbled, and a short rushing while later, fetched up hard against a duskwood tree.

It felt good to lean against the comforting bulk of the tree, when he was so gods-forsaken *weary* . . . bark burned against his cheek, and El caught himself halfway along a sliding fall. Sprawling a-snore in the road wouldn't be a wise thing, in this land of daggers ready for unprotected throats.

There was no branch handy to cling to, to climb the tree or even keep himself on his feet . . . and speaking of that, his knees were starting to buckle . . . ah, but wait. What had the Srinshee taught him about a tree-shaping spell? Some simple change in the incantation of one of the spells he was carrying; Thoaloat's Variant, aye, that's what it had been called. "Doabro Thoaloat was a wily old goat"—and that little rhyme brought back the memory he needed: the change was *thus*.

It was possible that Elminster snored gently twice or thrice during the incantation, but the duskwood that appeared an instant later, leaning against an identical duskwood that had been there rather longer, preferred deep silence to snoring, and so peace fell by the roadside.

*   *   *   *   *

When he was in the steward's chamber, the wards always warned him. They almost blazed in great measure of approaching magic, this time, so Mardasper was through the door and standing behind his lectern with the diadem on his head, its eyepiece over his accursed eye, and the Lady Scepter on his head before the door opened—without any knock—and an elf mage stepped within, cloak swirling around him, and the gems set into the staff of living wood in his hand winking on and off in an ever-changing display. The elf met the steward's eye, let go of the staff—it hung upright in the air, its lights continuing to wink and twinkle—and watched for Mardasper's reaction with the faintest of sneers playing about his thin lips.

The steward took care not to look impressed or even interested and managed to add a faint air of dismissal to his visual examination of the newcomer. With elves, status and control were always issues. Push-push-shove, disdain, sniff, sneer . . . well, not this day, by Holy Mystra! He looked young, but Mardasper knew that even without spells to alter the body or appearance, one of the Fair Folk could look this green and vigorous for centuries. He looked haughty—but then they all did, didn't they?

"Well met," he said, in carefully neutral tones. "Be it known that I am Mardasper, guardian of this shrine of Holy Mystra. Have you business here, traveler?"

"I do," the elf said coldly, stepping forward. The steward willed the eyepiece to lift and gave the newcomer the full benefit of his blazing gaze. The elf slowed, eyes narrowing a trifle, then came to a smooth halt, hand not—quite—touching the butts of a trio of wands sheathed at his hip.

Mardasper resisted the urge to smile tightly and asked carefully, "You venerate Holy Mystra, Lady of All Mysteries?" He used the diadem to truth-read, saving his own spells for any unpleasantness that might prove necessary.

The elf hesitated. "Betimes," he said at last, and that was truth. Mardasper suspected the newcomer meant that he'd gone on his knees to Mystra a time or two in conditions of great privacy, in hopes of gaining an edge over rival elf mages. No matter; here, it would suffice.

"All who enter here," the guardian said, raising the tip of the Lady Scepter just enough to make an elven eye flicker, "must obey me utterly and work no magic unbidden. Anyone who takes or damages even the

smallest thing from within these walls forfeits his life,
or at the least his freedom. You may rest within, and
take water from the fount, but no food or anything else
is provided—and you must surrender to me your name,
and all written magic and enchanted items you carry,
no matter how small or benign. They will be returned
upon your departure."

"I think not," the elf said scornfully. "I've no intention of ever becoming any man's slave, nor of yielding
items entrusted to me, long venerated in my family, into
the hands of anyone else—least of all a *human.* Do you
know who I am, steward?"

"One of the Fair Folk, almost certainly a mage and
probably of Cormanthan lineage, on the young side—
and greatly lacking in both prudence and diplomacy,"
Mardasper replied bleakly. "Is there more I should
know?" He caused the spell-gems on the diadem to
awaken and flicker, reinforcing them with the aroused
dazzle of the scepter. We may not all have blinking
staves, youngling, he thought, but . . .

Elven eyes flashed green with anger and that thin
mouth tightened like the jaws of a steel trap, but the
elf said merely, "If I cannot proceed freely—no."

Mardasper shrugged, lifting his arms from the
lectern to call the intruder's attention to the Lady
Scepter once more. He did not want a spell battle even
against a feeble foe, and he didn't need the ward-
warnings or the hovering staff to tell him this was no
feeble foe.

The elf shrugged elaborately, made his cloak swirl as
he ostentatiously turned to go, and let his gaze fall way
from the steward as if the man with the scepter were
a piece of crumbling statuary. In doing so, his eyes fell
across the open register—and suddenly blazed as
brightly as Mardasper's own accursed eye.

The elf whirled around again, surging forward like
a striking snake—and Mardasper practically thrust the
Scepter into his nose, snapping, "Have a *care,* sir!"

"This man!" the elf spat, stabbing a daggerlike finger onto the last name entered in the book. "*Is he still here?*"

Mardasper looked into that incandescent gaze from inches away, trying to keep the fear out of his own eyes and knowing he was failing. He swallowed once then said—his voice surprisingly calm in his own ears—"No. He visited only briefly, this morn, departing not long ago. Headed west, I believe."

The elf snarled like an angry panther and whirled away again, heading for the door. The staff followed him, trailing black spell flames, two large green gems in its head coming alight to look uncannily like eyes.

"Would you like to leave a message for this Elminster, if he should stop at the tower again?" Mardasper asked in the grandest, most doom-laden voice he could manage, as the elf practically tore the door open. "Many do."

The elf turned in the doorway, and let the staff fly into his hand before he snapped, "Yes! Tell him Ilbryn Starym seeks him and would be pleased to find him prepared for our meeting." Then he stormed out, the door booming shut behind him. Its rolling thunders told the tale of the violence of its closing.

Mardasper stared at it until the wards told him the elf was gone. Then he ran a hand across his sweat-beaded brow and almost collapsed across the lectern in relief.

The Lady Scepter flashed once, and he almost dropped it. That had been a sign, for sure—but had it been one of reassurance? Or something else?

Mardasper shook the scepter slightly, hoping for something more, but, as he'd expected, nothing more happened. Ahh, tear in the Weave! Blast! By Mystra's Seven Secret Spells—!

He snarled incoherently for a moment, but resisted the urge to hurl the scepter. The last steward of Moonshorn Tower who'd done that had ended up as ashes paltry enough to fit in a man's palm. His, actually.

Mardasper went back into his office under a heavy weight of gloom. Had he done the right thing? What did Mystra think of him? Should he have tried to stop the elf? Should he have allowed this Elminster fellow in at all? Of course the man couldn't have been *the* Elminster, the One Who Walks, could he? No, that one must be ancient by now, and only Mystra's—

Mardasper swallowed. He was going to fret over this all night and for days to come. He knew he was.

He set down the diadem and the scepter with exaggerated care, then sat back in his chair, sighed, and stared at the dark walls for a time. The priests of Mystra had been quite specific: a day in which strong drink of any sort passed his lips did not count in the marking of his service here.

Indeed. Quite deliberately he pulled out the three thick volumes at one end of the nearest bookshelf, reached into the darkness beyond, and came out with a large, dusty bottle. To the Abyss and beyond with the priests of Mystra and their niggling rules, too!

"Mystra," he asked aloud, as he uncorked the bottle, "how badly did I do?"

In his fingertips, the cork shone like a bright star for the briefest of instants—and shot back into the bottle so violently that his fingers and thumb were left bleeding and numb. Mardasper stared at them for a moment, then carefully put the bottle away again.

"So was that good . . . or bad?" he asked the gloom in bewilderment. "Oh, *where* are the priests when I need them?"

* * * * *

"Whoah!" Tabarast cried. "*Woaaaaah—*" His cry ended in a thump as his behind met the road hard, hurling dust in all directions. The mule came to a stop a pace farther on, gave him a reproachful look, and then stood waiting with a mournful air.

Beldrune sniggered as he overtook his winded colleague, urging it on with a small, feather-plumed whip, his splendid boots outthrust like tusks on either side of his mule. "You seem quite fond of fertile Faerûn beneath us this day, friend Baerast!" he observed jovially—an instant before his mule came to an abrupt stop beside the one Tabarast had lately been riding.

Overbalanced, Beldrune toppled helplessly over his mount's head with a startled yell, somersaulting onto the road with an impressive crash that made Tabarast wince, then sputter with repressed mirth as the two mules exchanged glances, seemed to come to some sort of agreement, and with one accord stepped forward, trampling the groaning Beldrune under hoof.

His groans turned to yells of rage and pain, and he flailed wildly with his arms until he was free of unwashed mule bodies and mud-caked mule hooves. "A rescue!" he cried. "For the love of Mystra, a rescue!"

"Get up," Tabarast said grimly, pulling at his hair. "This Chosen must be half the way to wherever he's going by now, and we can't even stay in the saddles of two smallish mules, by the Wand! Get *up,* Droon!"

"*Arrrgh!*" Beldrune yelled. "Let go of my hair!"

Tabarast did as he was bidden—and Beldrune's head fell back onto the road with a thump that sounded like a smaller echo of the one Tabarast had made earlier. The younger mage launched into a long and incoherent curse, but Tabarast ignored him, limping ahead to catch the bridles of their mules before the beasts got over the next rise in the road, and clean away.

"I've brought back your mule," he said to the still-snarling body on its back in the road. "I suggest we walk beside them for a time . . . we both seem to be a little out of practice at riding."

"If you mean we've been falling off all too often," Beldrune snarled, "then we are out of practice—but we won't get back in practice unless we mount up and ride!"

Suiting the action to the words, he hauled himself into the saddle of Tabarast's mule, hoping the change of mount would improve his ride a trifle.

The mule swiveled one eye to take in Tabarast standing beside it and someone else loudly occupying its back and didn't budge.

Beldrune yelled at it and hauled on the reins as if he was dragging in a monstrous fish. The mule's head was jerked up and back, but it started trying to twist the reins out of Beldrune's grasp, or draw them into its mouth by repeated chomping, rather than move even a single step forward.

Beldrune drew back his heels, wishing he was wearing spurs, and kicked the beast's flanks as hard as he could. Nothing happened, so he kicked again.

The mule shot forward, leaping up into the air and twisting as it did so.

Beldrune went over backward with what might have been a despairing sob, landed hard on one shoulder, and rolled helplessly back down the road. His splendid doublet was rapidly becoming a dung-stained rag as he tumbled along an impressive length of road before negotiating contact—a solid, leaf-shaking collision, to be precise—with one of a pair of duskwood trees by the roadside.

Tabarast snatched at the reins of the growling mule—until now, he hadn't known mules *could* growl—made sure he still had hold of the other mule's bridle, and looked back down the road. "Finished playing at bold knights on horseback?" he snapped. "We're on an important mission, remember?"

An upside-down Beldrune, who'd been staring at his booted feet a good way up the tree, above him, looked back at his colleague groggily for a moment, then slowly unfolded himself back into the road. When he was upright again, he raked showers of dust from his hair with one hand—wincing at the pains in his back this activity caused—and snarled, "With all the shouting you're doing, it's a safe bet that Elminster isn't within forty farms of here!"

The tree seemed to flicker for a moment, but neither of the two esteemed mages noticed.

Six

AT THE RIVEN STONE

Let stones be riven and the world be changed,
When next two such as these meet,
With howling chaos in the sky
And deception a gliding serpent round their feet.

Author unknown
from the ballad **Many Meetings**

composed sometime before The Year of the Twelverule

Sunlight stabbed down, and Elminster smiled. He was still in lands he'd never seen before, but more than one farmer along this rising road had assured him he was heading toward the Riven Stone.

Out of habit El glanced back to see if anyone was following him, then up at the sky; taking bird-shape had been a favorite tactic of elf mages who didn't look with friendly eyes on the first human who'd walked into their cozy midst, and changed Cormanthyr forever. Right now, however, both places seemed empty of foes—or any living creature, for that matter.

Briefly El wondered how far along the road those

two bumbling mages had gotten to yestereve on their recalcitrant mules. He chuckled. The way Mystra's whims ran, no doubt he'd find out soon enough.

The sky was blue and clear, and a brisk wind blew just this side of chilly; a grand day for walking, and the last prince of Athalantar was enjoying it. Rolling farm fields with rubblestone walls spread out on either side of the road; here and there, boulders too big to be moved thrust up out of the tillage like tomb markers or the snouts of gigantic, petrified monsters of the underearth. . . .

He was obviously remembering too many bards' ballads, and too few hours of plowing and haying. The air had that wet, earthy smell of fresh-plowed land, and if a certain Athalantan had to walk Toril alone, days like these at least made one feel alive and not a doddering survivor staggering toward a waiting grave.

The laughter of swift rushing water came to Elminster's ears from off to the left, and over the brow of the next rise its source came into view. A stream rushed past, cutting away across the fields in a small, deep-cut gorge. Ahead, it ran beside the road for a time, in its fall from what had to be a mill.

Ah, good. According to the last farmer, this must be Anthather's Mill. A tall fieldstone building, towering over a fork in the road. A fork, of course, which was bereft of any signs.

The stream rushed out of the pool below the mill dam, a creaking wheel turning endlessly in its wake. Men smudged white with flour were loading a cart by the roadside, adding bulging sacks to an already impressive pile. The horses were going to have a hard pull. One of the men saw El and murmured something. All of the men looked up, took their measure of the stranger, and looked back to their work, none of them halting in the hefting, tossing and heaving for a moment.

El spread his hands to show that he meant to draw no weapon, stopping beside the nearest man. "Well met," he said. "I seek the Riven Stone, and know not my road from here."

The man gave him an odd look, pointed up the left-hand road, and said, " 'Tis easy enough to find, aye—straight along that, a good stride, until you're standing in the middle of it. But yon's just a stone, mind; there's nothing there."

El shrugged and smiled. "I go following a vow, of sorts," he said. "Have my thanks."

The miller nodded, waved, and looked down for the next sack. Somewhat reassured, Elminster strode on.

It took some hours of walking, but the Riven Stone was clear enough. Tall and as black as pitch, it rose out of scrub woods in a huge, helmlike cone—cloven neatly in half, with the road running through the gap. There were no farms nearby, and El suspected the Stone enjoyed the usual "haunted" or otherwise fell reputation such landmarks always attracted—if they weren't deemed holy by one faith or another.

No sigils, altars, or signs of habitation met his view as he came around the last bend and saw just how large the stone was. The cleft must have been six man-heights deep or more, and the way through it was long and dim. The inside surfaces of the stone were wet with seeping groundwater, and the faintest of mists drifted underfoot there in the gap.

There, where someone was standing awaiting him. Mystra provides.

Elminster walked steadily on into the gap, a pleasant smile on his face despite the stirrings in him that his freedom to wander would end here—and darker forebodings.

Those misgivings were not lessened by what met his eyes. The figure ahead was human and very female. Alone and cloakless, dark-gowned, tall and sleek of figure; in a word, dangerous.

Had Elminster been standing in a certain dark hall in Tresset's Ringyl as a scepter fell to dust, rather than panting on a hilltop over the remains of a stag-headed shadow, he'd have seen this beautiful, dark-eyed sorceress before. As it was, he was looking into a pair of proud, cold dark eyes—did they hold a hint of mischief? Or was that suppressed mirth . . . or triumph?—for the first time.

Her legs, in black boots, were almost impossibly long. Her glossy black hair fell in an unbound flood that was longer. Her skin was like ivory, her features fine; just the pleasant side of angular. She carried herself with serene fearlessness, one long-fingered hand playing almost idly with a wand. Aye, trouble. The sort of sorceress folk cowered away from.

"Well met," she said, making of those words both a challenge and a husky promise, as her eyes raked him leisurely from muddy boots to untidy hair. "Do you work"—her tongue darted into view for an instant between parted lips—"magic?"

Elminster kept his gaze steady on those dark eyes as he bowed. Mindful of Azuth's directive, he replied, "A little."

"Good," the dark lady replied, making the word almost a caress. She moved the wand in her hand ever so slightly to catch his eyes, smiled, and said, "I'm looking for an apprentice. A *faithful* apprentice."

El didn't fill the silence she left after those words, so she spoke again, just a trifle more briskly. "I am Dasumia, and you are—?"

"Elminster is my name, Lady. Just Elminster." Now for the polite dismissal. "I believe my days as an apprentice are over. I serve—"

Silver fire suddenly surged inside him, its flare bringing back an image of the cracked stone ceiling of the best bedchamber in Fox Tower, and words of silver fire writing themselves across the ceiling, vivid in the darkness: "Serve the one called Dasumia." El swallowed.

"—ye, if ye'll have me," he concluded his sentence, aware of amused dark eyes staring deep into his soul.

"Yet I must tell ye: I serve Holy Mystra first and foremost."

The dark-eyed sorceress smiled almost lazily. "Yes, well—we all do," she said coyly, "don't we?"

"I'm sorry, Lady Dasumia," Elminster said gravely, "but ye must understand . . . I serve Her more closely than most. I am the One Who Walks."

Dasumia burst into silvery gales of laughter, throwing her head back and crowing her mirth until it echoed back off the stony walls flanking the two mages. "I'm sure you are," she said when she could speak again, gliding forward to pat Elminster's hand. "Do you know how many young mages seeking a reputation come to me claiming to be the One Who Walks? Well, I'll tell you—a dozen this last month, fully two score the month before that, snows and all, and one before you so far *this* month."

"Ah," Elminster replied, drawing himself up, "but they none of them were as handsome as me, were they?"

She burst out laughing again and impulsively hugged him. "A dream-vision told me to look for my apprentice here—but I never thought I'd find one who could make me laugh."

"Then ye'll have me?" El asked, giving no sign that he'd sensed her hug delivering many probing magics. More than one warm stirring in his innards told him Mystra's silver fire was hard at work countering hostile attempts to control and influence—and to leave behind at least three means of slaying him instantly by her uttering trigger words. Ah, but it was a wonderful thing to be a wizard. Almost as marvelous as being a Chosen.

Dasumia gave him a smile that held rather more triumph than welcome. "Body and soul I'll have you," she murmured. "Body and soul." She whirled away from him and looked back over her shoulder to purr provocatively, "Which shall we sample first, hmmm?"

* * * * *

"Now, *really*, Droon! I ask you: would we have had such widespread mastery of magic, such legions of capable or nearly capable mages, from sea unto sea and to the frozen wastes and uttermost east, if Myth Drannor still stood proud? Or would we have had closed, elite ranks of those who dwelt or had free admittance to the City of Song— and the rest of us left to fight for what scraps the glittering few deigned to toss to us, or that we could plunder from old tombs—and the liches lurking in them?" Tabarast turned in his saddle to make a point, almost fell out of it despite the tangle of sashes and belts he'd lashed himself on with, and thought it prudent to face forward again, merely gesturing airily with one hand. His mule sighed and kept on plodding.

"Come, come! We speak not of gems, Baerast," Beldrune replied, "nor yet cabbages—but magic! The Art! A ferrago of ideas, a feast of enchantments, an endless flood of new approaches and—"

"Free-flowing nonsense spoken by young mages," the older mage retorted. "Surely even you, young Droon, have seen enough years to know that generosity—truly open giving, not to an apprentice one can keep beholden or even spell-thralled—is a quality rarer and less cultivated in the ranks of wizards than in any other assembly of size or import in Faerûn today, save perhaps an orc horde. Pray weary my ears with rather less morology, if it troubles you not overmuch to do so."

Beldrune spread despairing hands. "Is any view that differs from your own but worthless idiocy?" he asked. "Or can it be—panoptic wind trumpet that you are—that some small shred of possibility remains that some truths the gods may not as yet have revealed unto wise old Tabarast, shrewd old Tabarast, *unthinking* old Tab—"

"Why is it that the young always resort so swiftly to personal offenses?" wise old Tabarast asked the world at large, loudly. "Name-calling and ridicule greet arguments that speak to a point, not foremost a person to attack or decry. Such a rude, unsettling approach makes a mountain of every monticule, a pernicious tempest of every chance exchange of remarks, and blackens the names of all who dare to hold recusant views. I disapprove strongly of it, Droon, I do. Such scrannel threats and blusterings are no worthy substitute for well-argued views—and all too often hold up a shield for jejune, even retrorse sciamachy, bereft of sense and waving bright purfle and clever verbiage where meaning has flown!"

"Uh, ah, ahem, yes," Beldrune said weakly. When Tabarast was riled, two words in ten was fair going. "We were speaking of the influence of fabled Myth Drannor on the practice of the Art across all Faerûn, I believe."

"We were," Tabarast confirmed almost severely, urging his mule over the summit of a monticle with a flourish of his tiny riding whip. The fact that it had broken in some past mishap, and now dangled uselessly from a point only inches above the handle, seemed to have utterly escaped his notice.

Beldrune waited for the torrent of grand but largely junkettaceous utterances that invariably accompanied any of Tabarast's observations of simple fact, but for once it did not come.

He raised his eyebrows in wonderment and said nothing as he followed his colleague over the hill. Hipsy—and plenty of it. 'Twas past time for hipsy. He slapped at the grand cloak rolled and belted at his hip, found the reassuring solid smoothness of his flask beneath it, and drew it forth. Tabarast had made this blend, and it was a mite watery for Beldrune's taste, but he didn't want to have to sit through *that* argument again. Next time, it'd be his turn, and there'd be more of the rare and heady concoction he'd heard called "brandy," and less water and wine.

Hmmm. Always assuming they both lived to see a next time. Adventure had seemed a grand thing a day ago—but he'd been thinking more of an adventure without mules. He'd be a hipshot, broken man if they had to ride many more days. Even with all the belts and sashes and lashings—which of course gave the demon-brained beasts a means of *dragging* mages who'd had the misfortune to fall out of their saddles helplessly along in the dirt until they could haul themselves hand-over-hand to the bridles, receiving regular kicks in the process—he'd fallen off more than twenty times thus far today.

Tabarast had managed an even more impressive Faerûn-kissing total, he reflected with a smirk, watching the old wizard bucketing down a steep descent with both legs sticking out like wobbling wings on either side of his patient mount. In another moment, he'd be—

Something that was dark and full of stars rushed past Beldrune like a vengeful wind, dealing his left leg a numbing blow and almost hurling him from his own saddle. He kept aboard the snorting, bucking mule only by digging his hands into its mane like claws and kicking out in a desperate, seesaw fight for balance.

Ahead of him, down the hill, he could see what was bearing down on poor, unwitting Tabarast: a slim, dark-cloaked elven rider bent low in the saddle of a ghostly horse, with a lightning-spitting staff floating along at his shoulder. Beldrune could see right through the silently churning hooves of the conjured mount as the elf swept down on Tabarast, swerved at the last instant to avoid a hard and direct collision, and stormed past, hurling mage and mule together over on their sides.

Beldrune hurried to his colleague's aid as swiftly as he dared, but Tabarast was working some magic or other that hoisted himself and the bewildered, feebly kicking mule upright again, and shouting, "Hircine lout! Lop-eared, fatuous, *rude* offspring of parents who should've known better! Ill-mannered tyrant of the road! *Careless* spellcaster! I shall impart some wisdom to your thumb-sized brain—see if I don't! It almost need not be said that I'll school you in humility—and safe riding—first!"

Ilbryn Starym heard some of those choice words, but didn't even bother to lift his sneer into a smile. *Humans.* Pale, blustering shadows of the one he was hunting. He must be getting close now.

Elminster Aumar—ugly hook nose, insolence *always* riding in the blue-gray eyes, hair as black and lank as that of a wet bear. That familiar, hungry tang rose into Ilbryn's mouth. Blood. He could almost taste the blood of this Elminster, who must die to wash clean the stain his filthy human hands had put on the bright honor of the Starym. As he topped a rise, Ilbryn stood up in the stirrups that weren't there and shouted to the world, "This Elminster must *die!*"

His shout rang back to him from the hilltops, but otherwise the world declined to answer.

*   *   *   *   *

Dusk almost always came down like a gentle curtain to close a glorious sunset at Moonshorn. Mardasper liked to be up on the crumbling battlements to see those sunsets, murmuring what words he could remember of lovelorn ballads and the chanted lays of the passing of heroes. It was the only time of the day—barring unpleasant visitors—when he let his emotions out, and dreamed of what he'd do out in Faerûn when his duty here was done.

Mardasper the Mighty he might become, stout-bearded, wise, and respected by lesser mages, rings of power glittering on his fingers as he crafted staves and tamed dragons and gave orders to kings that they dared not disobey.

Or he might rescue a princess or the daughter of a wealthy, haughty noble and ride away with her, using his magic to stay young and dashing but never taking up the robe and staff of a mage, keeping his powers as secret as possible as he carved out a little barony for himself, somewhere green.

Pleasant thoughts, soul-restoring and necessarily private . . . Wherefore Mardasper Oblyndrin was apt to grow very angry when something or someone interrupted his time alone, up on the battlements, to watch another day die into the west. He was angry now.

The wards warned him. The wards always warned him. Raw power, not held in check or under governance, always made them shriek as if in pain. Snarling at the happenstance, Mardasper was thundering down the long, narrow back stair before the intruder could have reached the doorstep. Precipitous it might be, but the back stair led directly to the third door in the entry hall; when the front door was hurled open, to bang against the wall and shudder at the impact, Mardasper was in place behind his lectern, white to his pinched lips and quivering in anger.

He stared out into the gathering night, but no one was there.

"Reveal," he said coldly, uttering aloud what he could have caused the wards to do silently, seeking to impress—or cause fear in—whoever was out there, playing pranks. It took magic of great power to force open the Tower door, with its intertwined glyphs, layers of active enchantments, and the runes set into its frame and graven on its hinges.

Too much power, he would have thought, to burn in any prank.

The wards showed him nothing lurking within their reach. Hmmph; perhaps that nose-in-the-air elf had left a timed magic behind and miscast on the timing. He couldn't think of anything fast enough to smite open a door and leave the reach of the wards so swiftly—and magic mighty enough to breach the door from afar would leave traces behind in the wards. So would a teleport or other translocation. The door's own magics should prevent a spell cast on it from surviving to take effect at any later time . . . so who—or what—had forced the door open?

Mardasper called on the power of the wards to close and seal the mighty door. After it had boomed shut, he stared at it thoughtfully without touching it for a long time, then murmured words he'd never used before, had never thought he'd have to use—the words that would force the awakened ward to expel any magic-wielding sentient in contact with it. The wards blazed white behind his eyes, finding nothing. If spellcasting beings were lurking nearby, they were either well out in the night-shrouded forest—

—or here, in the Tower, inside the wards already.

Mardasper looked at the door and swallowed, his throat suddenly dry. If there was an intruder in Moonshorn, he'd just sealed himself in with it.

Gods above. Well, perhaps it was time to earn his title as Guardian of the Tower. There was a lot of useful—and misunderstood, fragmentary, or forgotten— magic herein; potential realm-shattering weapons in the right unscrupulous hands. "Mystra be with me," he whispered, opened the door that led into the main stair, and started to climb.

*   *   *   *   *

The mist chimed only occasionally, and very softly, as it drifted across the parchment-strewn table like an eel ghosting its way among the rocks of an ocean reef. Occasionally it would pounce on a gem or a twisted fil-igree item placed as a paperweight by Tabarast and Beldrune, and a cold turquoise light would flare briefly. When the power drunk was very strong, the mist would swirl up in triumphant, flamelike bursts of white, winking motes of light that would dance above the table in triumph for a moment before dimming and dwindling into a drifting, serpentine mist once more.

From knickknack to gewgaw it darted, flaring as it drank, and growing ever larger. It was in mid-swirl when the door of the room suddenly opened, and the Guardian of the Tower peered in. Something in here had flashed, spilling a tongue of white light through the keyhole. . . .

Mardasper paused on the threshold and sent a seeking spell rolling out across the room. The mist faded and sank down behind the table, becoming nigh-invisible—and when the spell streamed through it, it allowed itself to be scattered rather than to resist and be found.

The spell washed into every corner of the room, then receded. In its wake, the wind sighed softly back together, not chiming even once.

Mardasper glared into the room, the flame from his blazing eye seeking what his spell could not see. There *must* be someone or something here; translocations wouldn't work inside Moonshorn.

His accursed eye saw it immediately: a breeze that was no breeze, but a living, drifting, incorporeal thing. In furious haste Mardasper lashed at it with a shatterstar spell—a magic designed to rend and burn ghostly and gaseous things.

The expected flames flared up, and the agonized scream with it. But the Guardian of the Tower was unprepared for what followed.

Instead of collapsing into sighing oblivion, the blazing, exploding mist drew together suddenly, rising with terrifying speed into the shape of a human head and shoulders—a head that was only eyes and long hair, trailing down onto a bust.

Mardasper took a pace back; who was this ghost-woman?

Fingers that were more smoke than flesh moved in intricate gestures, trailing the flames of the guardian's spell, and Mardasper frantically tried to think what spell he should use—this ghost that should not be able to withstand his shatterstar was casting magic!

An instant later, the ghostly outline of the sorceress grew a jaw and began to laugh—a high, shrill mirth that was almost lost in the sharp hiss of acid raining down on the guardian . . . and the shrieking death that followed.

Mardasper's melting, smoking bones tumbled to the floor amid a torrent of acid that made the floor erupt in smoke.

Over it all rose a cold, mirthless, triumphant laugh. Some might have judged that wild laughter to be almost a scream, but it had been a long time since the whirlwind had laughed aloud. It was a little out of practice.

Seven

DEADLY SPELLS FORBEAR THEE

Evil is no extravagance to those who serve themselves first.

Thaelrythyn of Thay
from **The Red Book of a Thayvian Mage**
published circa The Year of the Saddle

It was a cool day in late spring—the third greening of Toril to come and go since two mages had met in the Riven Stone—and the sky was ablaze in red, pink, and gold as the sun, in a leisurely manner, prepared to set. A tower rose like an indigo needle against that sky of flame, and out of the west something small and dark came flying to bank in a wide loop around that tower.

Heads looked up at it: a flying carpet, with two humans seated upon it, their figures dark against the fiery sky wherever the rays of the setting sun hadn't turned them the hue of beaten copper.

"Beautiful, is it not?" Dasumia purred, turning from surveying the tower. A green glint that El had long ago learned presaged danger was dancing in her eyes. She slid forward onto her elbows, cradling her chin in her hands, and regarded the tower with an almost satisfied air.

"Lady, it is," Elminster said carefully.

A teasing eye rolled up to stare into his own orbs. Ye gods, trouble indeed; Mystra defend.

His Lady Master pointed at the tower and said, "A wizard named Holivanter dwells there. A merry fellow; he taught the beasts he summoned to build it all sorts of comical songs and chants. He keeps talking frogs, and even gave a few of them wings with which to fly."

The carpet banked smoothly around the tower on its second orbit of the spire. The tower rose like a fairy-tale needle from neat, green walled gardens. Ruby-hued lamps glimmered in several of its windows, but it seemed otherwise tranquil, almost deserted.

"The house of Holivanter . . . pretty, isn't it?"

"Indeed, Lady," El agreed and meant it.

"Slay him," Dasumia snapped.

El blinked at her. She nodded, and pointed down at the slim tower with an imperious hand.

El frowned. "Lady, I—"

Little flames seemed to flicker in Dasumia's eyes as she locked her gaze with his. One elegant eyebrow lifted.

"A friend of yours?"

"I know him not," El replied truthfully. There was no way he could send a warning, or a defense, or healing; the man was doomed. Why betray himself in futility?

Dasumia shrugged, drew forth a dark, smooth rod from a sheath on her hip, and extended it with languid grace. Something caused the air to curdle in a line, racing down, down . . .

. . . And the upper half of Holivanter's tower burst apart with a roar, spraying the sky with wreckage. Smaller purple, amber, and blue-green blasts followed as various scorched magics within the tower exploded in their turns. El stared at the conflagration as its echoes rolled back from nearby hills, and debris hurtled at them. Blackened fingers spun past the carpet, trailing flame. Holivanter was dead.

Dasumia rolled back onto one hip and propped herself up with one arm, the other toying with the rod. "So tell me," she told the sky, in silken-soft tones that made Elminster stiffen warily, "just why you disobeyed me. Does killing mages come hard to you?"

Fear stirred cold fingers within him. "It seems . . . unnecessary," El replied, choosing his words very carefully. "Does not Mystra say the use of magic should be encouraged, not jealously guarded or hampered?"

Ah, Mystra. Her word had led him here, to serve this beguiling evil. He'd almost forgotten what it felt like to be a Chosen of Mystra, but in his dreams, El often knelt and prayed, or repeated her decrees and advice, fearing it would entirely slip away from him if he did not. Sometimes he feared that the Lady Dasumia was stealing his memories with creeping magic or walling them away behind mists of forgetfulness, to make him entirely her creature. Whatever the cause, it was getting harder, as the months passed, to remember anything of his life before the Riven Stone. . . .

Dasumia laughed lightly. "Ah, I see. The priests of the Lady of Magic say such things, yes, to keep us from slaying thieves who steal scrolls . . . or disobedient apprentices. Yet I pay them little attention. Every mage who can rival me lessens my power. Why should I help such potential foes rise to challenge me? What gain I from that?"

She leaned forward to tap Elminster's knee with the rod. He tried not to look at the little green lights winking into life around it and wandering up and down its length almost lazily. "I've seen you on your knees to Mystra, of nights," she told him. "You pray and plead with her, yes, but tell me: how much does she talk to you?"

"Never, these days," El admitted, his voice as low and as small as the despair he felt. All he had to cling to were his small treacheries, and if she ever discovered those , . .

Dasumia smiled triumphantly. "There you are—alone, left to fend for yourself. If there is a Mystra who takes any interest in mortal mages, she watches while the strong help themselves, over the bodies of the weak. Never forget that, Elminster."

Her voice became more brisk. "I trust your labors haven't faltered in my absence," she commented, sitting up—and raising the rod to point at his face like a ready sword. "How many whole skeletons are ready?"

"Thirty-six," Elminster replied. She lifted that eyebrow again, obviously impressed, and leaned forward to peer into his eyes, dragging his gaze to meet hers by the sheer power of her presence. El tried not to wince or lean away. In some ways, the Lady Dasumia was as, as—well, *awesome* at close quarters and as irresistibly forceful in her presence—as Holy Lady Mystra Herself. How, a small voice in the back of his mind asked, could that possibly be?

"You *have* been hard at work," she said softly. "I'd thought you'd spend some time trying to get into my books and a little more poking around my tower before you got out the shovels. You please me."

El inclined his head, trying to keep satisfaction—and relief—from his face and voice. She must not have discovered his rescue work, then.

With his spells, her most obedient apprentice had healed a servant and whisked him to a land distant, laden with supplies and white with fear. She'd taken the man to her bed but tired of him as the Year of Mistmaidens began, and one morning she had turned him into a giant worm and left him impaled on one of the rusting spits behind the stables to die in slow, twisting agony. El had left the transformed body of a man who'd died of a fever in the servant's place. Restless and reckless meddling, perhaps. Doom-seeking lunacy; that, too. Yet he had to do such things, somehow, working small kindnesses to make up for her large, bold evils.

It hadn't been his first small treachery against her cruelty . . . but there was always the chance that it would be his last. "My honesty has always outstripped my ambition," he said gravely.

Her mockery returned. "A pretty speech, indeed," she said. "I can almost believe you follow Mystra's dictates to the letter."

She stretched like a large cat and used the rod over one shoulder to scratch her back, putting it within easy reach of Elminster. "You must have far more patience than I do," she admitted, her eyes very dark and steady upon him. "I could never serve such an arbitrary goddess."

"Is it permitted to ask whom ye do serve, Lady Master?" El asked, extending his hands in a mute offering to accept the enchanted rod.

She poked at her back once more, smiled, and put the rod into his hands. Two of the rings she wore blinked as she did so.

Dasumia smiled. "A little higher . . . ah, yessss." Her smile broadened as El carefully used the rod to scratch the indicated spot, but she kept her eyes fixed on his hands, and the rings that had winked a moment ago now flickered with a constant flame of readiness.

"It's no secret," she said casually. "I serve the Lord Bane. His gift to me was the dark fire that slays intruders and keeps more cautious mages at bay. Did you know there's some fool of an elf who tests my wards with a new spell every tenday? He's been at it for three seasons now, as regular as the calendar; almost as long as you've been with me." She smiled again. "Perhaps he wants your position. Should I order you to duel him?"

El spreads his hands and said, "If it's your wish, Lady. I'd as soon not slay anyone unnecessarily."

Dasumia stared at him in thoughtful silence for quite a long time as the carpet rushed on away from the smoking stump of the tower and the dying day, and finally murmuring, "And deprive me of the entertainment elven futility brings me? No fear."

She rose up on her knees in a single smooth motion, plucked the rod out of El's hand, resheathed it, and in the same continuous movement reached out with both hands to take hold of his shoulders. Her slender fingertips rested lightly upon him, yet Elminster suddenly felt that if he tried to move out of their grasp, he'd find them to be claws of unyielding iron. In three years, this was the closest contact between them.

He held still as his Lady Master brought her face close to his, their noses almost touching, and said, "Don't move or speak." Her breath was like hot mist on Elminster's cheeks and chin, and her eyes, very dark and very large, seemed to be staring right into the back of his head and seeing every last secret he kept there.

She leaned a little way forward, just for a moment, and their lips met. An imperious tongue parted his own lips— and something that burned and yet was icy raced into his mouth, roaring down his throat and coiling up his nose.

Agony—burning, shuddering, get-away-from-it agony! El sneezed, again and again, clawing at fabric in a desperate attempt to keep from falling, knowing his whole body was shuddering. He was convulsing and sprawling on the carpet, sobbing when he could find breath enough . . . and he was as helpless as a child.

Yellow mists cavorted and flowed before his eyes; the darkening sky overhead kept leaping and turning, and he was thrashing against claws that held him with painful, immovable force.

For what seemed an eternity he coughed and struggled against the yellow haze, drenched with sweat, until utter exhaustion left him able to spasm no more, and he could only lie moaning as the lessening surges of pain ebbed and clawed their ways through him.

He was Elminster. He was as weak as a dried, rolled-up leaf blown in the wind. He was—lying on his back on the flying carpet, and the only thing that had kept him from falling off it in his throes was the iron grip of the sorceress he served, the Lady Dasumia.

Her hands loosened on him, now. One left his bruised
bicep—in which it had been sunk inches deep, like an
anchor of iron throughout his thrashings—to trail
across his brow, thrusting oceans of sweat away.

She bent over him in the gathering gloom of falling
night, as the breezes of the lofty sky slid over them
both, and said softly, "You have tasted the dark fire. Be
warned; if ever you betray me, it shall surely slay you.
As long as you worship Mystra more than you revere
me, Bane's breath shall be agony to you. Three apprentices, down the years, have kissed me unbidden; none
lived to boast of it."

Elminster stared up at her, unable to speak, agony
still ruling him. She looked into his eyes, her own orbs
two dark fires, and smiled slowly. "Your loyalty, however, outstrips theirs. You shall duel my worst foe for me
and best him—when you are ready. You'll have to learn
to kill first, though, swiftly and without reckoning the
cost. He'll not give you much time for reflection."

At last El found the strength to speak. His voice was
thick-tongued and halting, but it was speech nonethe-
less. "Lady, who is this foe?"

"A wizard Chosen by Mystra as her personal servant,"
the Lady Dasumia replied, looking away toward the last
traces of the setting sun. Beneath them, the carpet started to descend. "He left my side to do so and though he
could not follow the narrow path the Lady of Magic set
for him and is now called the Rebel Chosen, he's not
returned to me. Hah! Mystra must be unable to concede
that anyone could turn from blind worship of her."

Her eyes were burning as she turned back to meet
Elminster's gaze, and added in tones once more light and
casual, "Nadrathen is his name. You shall slay him for me."

The last prince of Athalantar looked at the night
sky rushing past and shivered once.

*   *   *   *   *

The rustling and croaking of night had begun in earnest in the thick stand of hiexel and thornwood and duskwood nearest the castle. As the flying carpet descended toward the tallest of the black towers, a pair of eyes blinked amid the fissured bark of a lightning-scarred duskwood and slowly sharpened into a coldly angry elven face. Roused anger glittered in Ilbryn Starym's eyes as he said softly, "Your wards may still my ears, proud Lady, but my spells work well enough when you are out over the wide world. Don't count over-much on your apprentice. His life is mine."

He glowered at the tallest towers of the lady's castle long after the carpet was gone from view, until his glare slid suddenly into a calmer look; a frown of thought-fulness rather than fury. "I wonder if anything in that mage's tower survived?" he asked the night. "It's worth the journey to see. . . ."

Dark-hued radiance flashed and curled like smoke, and the duskwood glared no more.

*   *   *   *   *

Dasumia's castle rose up into the sky above them in dark, forbidding ramparts. Tabarast watched the fly-ing carpet disappear into its many-turreted heart and grunted. "Well, that was exciting," he said. "Another day of splendid and energetic furtherance of the Art, I must say."

Beldrune looked up from the tankard of magically warmed soup he was cradling and spoke in tones of some asperity. "My memory may be failing me from time to time, esteemed Baerast, but did we, or did we not, agree to moan no more about wasted time and forgone opportunities? Our mission is, and remains, clear. Callow idiot this One Who Walks may be, but he—and what he chooses to do—are the most important developments in the Art in all Toril just now. I think we can afford to obey the dictates of a goddess—*the* goddess—and miss a few years of peering at fading, dusty writings in hopes of finding a new way of conjuring up floating lantern lights."

Tabarast merely grunted in wordless acknowledgment. A few lights blinked into life high in the turrets of Dasumia's castle, and the night noises resumed around them. They kept silent for a long time, crouched on little stools at the end of the hedgerow that marked the edge of the nearest tilled field to the Castle of the Lady, until Beldrune murmured, "Mardasper must have given us up for dead by now."

Tabarast shrugged and said, "He guards Moonshorn Tower, not we."

"Hmmph. Did he ever tell you about his fiery eye?"

"Aye. Something about a curse . . . he lost a spell duel to someone, and his service as guardian was payment to the priests of the Mysteries, to break the magic and restore him. Another poor mage-wits, driven into the service of the Lady who governs us all."

Beldrune lifted his head. "Do I hear the faith of Tabarast of the Three Sung Curses retunding? The divine graces of Holy Mystra losing their hold after all these years?"

"Of course not," Tabrast snapped. "Would I be sitting here the night through in all this cold damp if they were?" He thumbed the lid of his tankard open, took a long pull, and looked back at the castle towers in time to see one of the glimmering lights go out.

They sat and waited until their tankards were empty, but nothing else happened. The castle, it seemed, was asleep. Tabarast finally turned his gaze from it with a sigh. "We're all pawns of the Lady who minds the Weave, though—aren't we? It just comes down to whether you delude yourself into thinking you're free or not."

"Well, I *am* free," Beldrune snapped, his lips tightening. "By all means let these funny ideas prance through your head, Tabarast, and govern your days if you want them to, but kindly leave me out of the 'foolish puppet' drawer in your mind. You'll live longer if you grant that other mages might have scrambled out of it, too."

Tabarast turned to fix the younger mage with a wise and keen old glare. "*Which* other mages?"

"Oh, just the ones you meet," Beldrune grunted. "All of them."

*   *   *   *   *

Far from the turrets Tabarast and Beldrune were watching, and farther still from the shattered, smoking stump that had been the tower of Holivanter, another wizard's tower stood against the night sky.

This one was a modest roughstone affair studded with many small, loosely shuttered windows, sun boxes of herbs hanging from their sills. It stood alone in the wilderlands, bereft of village or muddy lane, and deer grazed contentedly around its very door—until a mist rising silently out of the grass settled upon them, and they sank down into oblivion, leaving only bones behind.

When there were no eyes left to see it, a chill, chiming whirlwind stole to the base of the tower and began to rise.

Floating up past climbing roses and ivy in eerie silence, it gathered itself in the air like a coiling snake—and lunged through a chink in a shutter halfway up the tower, pouring itself into the sleeping darkness beyond.

Dark chamber within opened into dark chamber, and the misty wind whirled, moaned as it gathered its might in that second room, a place of books and scroll-littered tables and dust—and became an upright, gliding thing of claws and jaws that slid out into the spiral stair at the heart of the tower, and up.

At the top of the tower, candlelight through an ill-fitting door danced reflections down the staircase, and an old and rough voice was speaking, alone, oblivious to the danger creeping closer, as clawed mists came gliding.

At the heart of a chalked symbol set with many candles, an old man in much-patched robes was on his knees, facing the chalk image of a pointing human hand. A blue radiance outlined the hand, and both it and the chalkwork were his doing, for he had dwelt long alone.

"For years I've served you, and the Great Lady, too," the wizard prayed. "I know how to smash things with spells and to raise them, too. Yet I know little of the world outside my walls and need your guidance now, O Azuth. Hear me, High One, and tell me, I pray: to whom should I pass on my magic?"

His last word seemed to echo, as if across a great gulf or chasm, and the blue conjured radiance suddenly shone almost blindingly bright.

Then it went out entirely as a wind rose out of the very floor, flowing from the chalked hand. The candles flared wildly, spat flames, and went out under its rushing onslaught, and out of the darkness that followed their deaths came a voice, deep and dry: "Guard yourself, faithful Yintras, for danger is very close to you now. I shall gather your Art unto me in the time of your passing . . . worry not."

With a crackle of leaking energy and a strange singing of the air, something blown on that wind flowed around the old wizard, winding around his trembling limbs to cloak him in warmth and vigor. With an ease and agility he hadn't felt in years, the old man sprang to his feet, raised his hands, and watched tiny lightnings crackle from one arm to the other with pleased wonder in his eyes, amid the gathering glimmer of unshed tears in his eyes. "Lord," he said roughly, "I am unworthy of such aid as this. I—"

Behind him, the door of the spell chamber split from

top to bottom, shrieking its protest as more than a dozen claws literally tore it apart, tossing down the splinters to reveal an open, empty door frame.

Something that glowed with a pale, wavering ghostliness stood at the head of the stair—something large, menacing, and yet uncertain. A thing of claws and ever-shifting jaws and tentacles and cruelly barbed mandibles. A thing of menace and death, now advancing leisurely into the spell chamber at an almost gloating, slow pace.

Yintras Bedelmrin watched death come for him, floating over wards that would have seared limbs at a touch, and swallowed, trembling.

Lightning leaped within him, as if in reminder, and suddenly Yintras threw back his head, drew in a deep breath and spoke as loudly and as imperiously as he could. "I am armored by Azuth himself, and need fear no entity. Begone, whatever you are. Go from here, forever!"

The old wizard took a step toward the thing of claws, lightning still leaping from arm to arm. Ghostly radiance rose up in a menacing wall of claws and reaching tentacles—but even as it did so, it was flickering, trembling, and darkening. Holes were opening in its overreaching substance, holes that grew with it.

With horrifying speed it expanded to loom almost to the ceiling, towering over the old man in the many-patched robes. Yintras stood watching it, not knowing what to do and so doing nothing.

A fatal creed for an adventurer, and no better for wizards. He quailed, inwardly, knowing death could come in moments, horrified that he might embrace it when he could have escaped it—just by doing the right thing, or *some*thing.

Claws snatched at him in a horrible mass lunge that left him entirely unaware that a tentacle that had grown savage barbs and long-fanged jaws was snaking around through the darkness to stab at him from behind and below.

Lightning cracked, raged white-hot in the air of the

spell chamber and was gone again, leaving—when his streaming eyes could see again—a feebly flickering gray mist cringing and writhing in the air by the door.

Yintras drew in a deep breath and did one of the bravest and most foolish things in his life thus far. He took a step toward the mist, chuckled, then took another step, raising his arms despite the lack of lightning or any feeling of surging or lurking power.

The mist gathered itself as if to do battle with him, rising and thickening into a small but solid mass, like a ready-raised shield trailing away into formlessness. The old wizard took another step, and the strange mist seemed to tremble.

He stretched forth a hand as if to grasp it. In a sudden wash of frigid air and a chiming of tiny, bell-like sounds, the mist broke into a swirling stream and was gone out the door in a flash, leaving only a mournful snarl in its wake.

Yintras watched it go and stared at the emptiness where it had been for a long anxious time. When at last he believed that it was truly gone, he went to his knees again to speak his thanks. All that came out were sobs, in a quickening rush that he found himself powerless to stop.

He crept forward in the darkness on knees and fingertips, trying to at least shape Azuth's name. Then he froze in surprise and awe. Where his tears had fallen, candle after candle was springing to life by itself, in a silently growing string of dancing warmth.

"Azuth," he managed to whisper at last. "My thanks!"

All of the candles went out in unison, then flared into life again. Yintras knelt in their midst, touched by glory and grateful for it. Sadness laced the edges of his bright delight too, and beneath all, he felt empty, utterly drained. He touched the smudged chalk that had once been the outline of a pointing hand and started to cry like a child.

Eight

THE SUNDERED THRONE

A throne is a prize that petty and cruel folk most often fight over. Yet, on bright mornings, 'tis but a chair.
Ralderick Hallowshaw, Jester
from **To Rule A Realm, From Turret To Midden**
published circa The Year of the Bloodbird

A shadow fell across the pages Elminster was frowning over. He did not have to look up to know who it was, even before a tress of glossy raven-black hair trailed across fading sketches and notations.

"Apprentice," Dasumia said beside his ear, in melodious, gentle tones that made El stiffen in alarm, "fetch the Orbrum, Prospaer on Nameless Horrors, and the Tome of Three Locks from my side table in the Blue Chamber, and bring them now to me in the Balcony Hall. Do off any items you may wear or carry that possess even the slightest dweomer, upon peril of your life."

"Aye, Lady Master," El murmured, glancing up to meet her eyes. She looked unusually stern, but there was no hint of anger or mischief about her eyes as she strode to a door that was seldom opened, stepped through it, and pulled it firmly closed behind her.

The solid click of its lock coincided with Elminster realizing he had to ask her what to do about the guardian of the Blue Chamber. Her spell-lock he could probably break—a test?—but the guardian would have to be slain if he was to do something so time-consuming as to cross the room, pick up three books, and attempt to carry them out again . . . or *it* would be the one doing the slaying.

If he slew it, she'd once told him, small malignant sentiences would be released from mirrors and orbs and tome-bindings all over the castle. They might rage for months before they were all recaptured and spellbound once more to obedience. Months of lost time she'd repay him for with the same duration of torment . . . and Elminster had tasted the Lady Dasumia's torments before.

Her favorite punishment seemed to be forcing him to fetch things on hands and knees that she'd thoroughly broken, so every movement was wobbling, grating agony, but sometimes—more often in recent days, as the Year of Mistmaidens abandoned spring for full summer—she preferred strapping El into a girdle of everhealing then stabbing him in succession with a slim sword tipped with poison, and a blade fashioned of jungle thorns as long as his forearm, dipped in flesh-eating acid. She seemed to enjoy the sounds of screaming.

These reflections took El only the few seconds needed to stride across the room and open the door Dasumia had passed through. Beyond it was the Long Gallery, a passage studded with alternating paintings and oval windows. It was an enclosed flying bridge the height of twenty men above a cobblestone courtyard, that linked the two tallest towers of the castle. Ever since two once-apprentices of the Lady had thought it a perfect venue for a duel and had slain each other amid conjured flames that threatened both attached towers, the Lady had caused the Gallery to be magic-dead: its very air quenched and quelled all spells, so Dasumia could do nothing but walk its considerable length; he'd have ample time to call out to her before she—

He snatched open the door, opened his mouth to speak—and stared in silence at a dark, lifeless, and very empty gallery.

Even if she'd been as swift as the fastest Calishite message-runners, and thrown dignity to the winds for a panting sprint the moment the door had closed, she'd have been no farther from him than mid-passage. There'd just not been time enough for anything else. Perhaps she'd banished the dead magic effect and not bothered to inform him. Perhaps—

He frowned and conjured light, directing it to appear at the midpoint of the passage. The casting was both simple and perfectly accomplished . . . but no light blossomed into being. The gallery was still death to magic.

Yet—no Lady Dasumia. Elminster turned away from that door looking very thoughtful.

*   *   *   *   *

El used the heavy, many-layered wards that the Lady had set upon the Blue Chamber to spin a modified maze spell that drew the guardian—a small, enthusiastic flying maelstrom of three barbed stingtails, raking claws, and a nasty disposition—into "otherwhere" for a long handful of moments. He was out and down the hall, with the door safely closed and the books under his arm, before it won its furiously hissing freedom.

Twice cobwebs brushed his face on his brisk jaunt along the Long Gallery, telling him the Lady Master hadn't passed this way recently—certainly not mere minutes ago.

The doors of the Balcony Hall stood open, star-studded smoke swirling gently out; the Lady had spun a spell-shield to protect her castle. This was to be a test, then, or a duel in earnest. He held the books in a stack out before him as he entered, and murmured, "I am come, Lady Master."

The books floated up out of his grasp toward the balcony, and from its height Dasumia said softly, "Close the doors and bar them, Apprentice."

El glanced up as he turned back to the doors. She was wearing a mask, and her hair was stirring about her shoulders as if winds were blowing through it. Spell-globes floated above and behind her; El saw much of her jewelry hanging in one, and the books were heading for another. Real magic was to be unleashed here.

He settled the bar and secured its chains without haste, giving her the time she needed to be absolutely ready. When facing the spells of a sorceress who can destroy you at will, it's best to give her little cause for irritation.

When he turned back into the room, the last glowspell had dimmed to a row of glimmering lights around the balcony rail; he could no longer see the sorceress who stood somewhere above him.

"It is time, and past time, Elminster, for me to assay this. Defend yourself as you're able—and strike back to slay, not gently."

Sudden light burst forth from on high: white, searing light that boiled forth at him from the face, bodice, and cupped hands of his Lady Master. Did she know of his treacheries?

Time enough to learn such things later . . . if he lived to enjoy a "later." El spun a hand vortex to catch it and sent it back at her, diving away when its fury proved too powerful for his defense, and broke his vortex apart in a snarling explosion that awakened short-lived fires here and there about the floor of the Hall. El spellsnatched one of them and threw it up at her, in hopes of spoiling another casting. It flickered as it plunged wide, but its brief radiance showed him

Dasumia standing as rigid as a post, with silver bands of magic whipping about her—bands that became flailing chains as they rattled free of her and hurtled down upon him.

He danced across the Hall, to win himself the few moments they'd need to chase after him, then put his hands together in a spellburst that shattered them. He'd placed and angled himself so as to spit the unused fire of his spell up at the balcony, wondering how long his dozen or so defensive or versatile spells could serve him against the gathered might of her magic.

This time, some of it reached her; he heard her gasp, and saw her throw her head back, hair swirling, in the blazing moment when her spell-shield failed under the searing, clawing assault of his strike.

Then he glimpsed the flash of her teeth as she smiled, and felt the first cold whisper of fear. Now would come agony, if she could burst through his defenses to bring him down. And sooner or later—probably sooner—she would bring him down.

Purple lightning spat out of dark nothingness in a dozen places along the balcony rail, and lanced down into the Hall, ricocheting here, there, and everywhere. El spun a swift armoring spell but felt burning agony above one elbow, and in the opposing thigh—and crashed bruisingly to the stone floor, biting his tongue as he grunted back a scream. His body bounced and writhed helplessly as lightning surged through it; he fought to breathe now, not to weave spells or craft tactics. Yet perhaps the tatters of his failing, fading armoring could be used to hurl her lightning back—for she'd spent no time to raise another spell-shield for herself.

El crawled and rolled, blindly and agonizingly, seeking to be out of the searing surge of the lightning, to where he could gasp for breath and make his limbs obey.

A rising whistling sound just above his head told El his armoring had survived—and could turn lightning aside quite effectively. He willed it down to above his head, to break the lightning that was holding him in thrall, then moved it to one side, rolling to stay in its shadow.

Lightning clawed at his foot for a moment; then he was free once more. Murmuring a paltry incantation to make his armoring larger and longer lasting, El rose into a crouch to peer at the last few lightnings crawling about the Hall. It was the work of a few moments to deflect these so until they could all be cupped in his armoring and hurled back up at the balcony, raking it for the briefest of instants before they boiled away under the onslaught of the Lady Dasumia's next spell.

This one was a wall of green dust he'd seen before; short-lived and unstable, but turning all living things it touched briefly to stone. El cast a wall of force as fast as he knew how, bringing it into being curved like a cupped hand to scoop dust aside and spill it back up onto the balcony.

As his "hand" moved one way, he trotted in another direction, hurling magic missiles at where his Lady Master must be crouching, to keep her from moving away from the area wherein her dust would be delivered back to her.

A moment later, the glowing green cloud spilled across the balcony, and it was too late for Dasumia to flee. El had the satisfaction of seeing her stiffen and grow still.

An instant thereafter, he was shouting in startled pain as sharp, slicing blades materialized out of the air on all sides. He threw himself to the floor and rolled, shielding his face and throat with tight-curled arms as he willed his forcewall back down out of the balcony like a swooping falcon to batter aside blades and shield him.

Shrieking from overhead told him his tactic had worked; he gasped out one of his two dispel magic incantations to clear the air of flying, razor-sharp metal, then gaped in fresh surprise, as the disappearance of the blades caused a shimmering serpent of force to fade into view in midair and snap down, lashing at his forcewall until it shattered and failed.

As he dodged away from the magical whip, El stole a glance at Dasumia up on the balcony, still leaning stonily out with one hand raised. She hadn't moved an inch. These spells hitting him now must be linked, so that breaking or trammeling one awakens the next!

Was she unaware of the hall around her, in her petrified state? Or could she still exact some measure of control over her magics?

El vaulted a lash of the whip that struck the floor so close by that it left his arm and shoulder tingling and sprinted for the balcony stairs. The whip followed, coiling like a gigantic snake.

He took the broad steps three at a time, sprinting for all he was worth, and was able to dive behind Dasumia's stony feet before the whip could find him. It crashed down beside his face, the force of its strike swirling up remnants of green dust. El found himself growing numb . . . and struggling not to move slowly, as he entwined one arm around his Lady Master's legs and tried to climb her, whilst the whip raged in the air around him but did not strike . . . and Elminster found he could not move at all.

The whip fell away into motes of fading light, and there was a moment of peaceful darkness in Balcony Hall.

"If my knees get chilled in future, I'll know who to summon," a familiar voice said from close above El's head, and he collapsed to Dasumia's ankles and the balcony floor, as his limbs were abruptly freed from thrall. She stepped away from him, turned with hands on hips, and looked down.

Their eyes met. Dasumia's held satisfaction and approval. "You're a sword ready enough to go into battle," she told him. "Go now, and sleep. When you're quite ready, you shall duel in earnest, elsewhere."

"Lady Master," Elminster asked, as he clambered to his feet, "is it permitted to ask whom I shall duel?"

Dasumia smiled and traced the line of his throat with one slender finger. "You," she said merrily, "are going to challenge Nadrathen, the Rebel Chosen, for me."

*   *   *   *   *

The Blood Unicorn flapped above the gates of Nethrar and the arched gate of the palace at its heart, telling every Galadornan that the King yet lived. As this bright summer day wore on, not a few eyes looked up at those standards again and again, seeking to learn if the ownership of the Unicorn Throne had changed.

For a season and more the aging, childless King Baerimgrim had lingered in the shadow of the tomb, kept alive after being savaged by the claws of the green dragon Arlavaunta only by his great strength and the Art of Court Mage Ilgrist. The once-mighty warrior was a thin and failing husk now, unable to sire children even with magical aid, and preoccupied by ever-present pain.

In the time of Baerimgrim's ailing, Galadorna had suffered under the skirmishes and mischief—crop-burning, and worse—of its five barons, all risen in ambition to be king after Baerimgrim. All had blood ties to the throne; all saw Galadorna as rightfully theirs . . . and Galadornans hated and feared all of them.

Inside the House of the Unicorn this day the tension was a thing thick and heavy enough to be cut with a knife—and there was no shortage of knives held ready in its dim, tapestry-hung halls. The King was no longer expected to see nightfall and had been carried to his throne and tied in place there by servants, sitting with grim determination on his face and his crown slipping aslant upon his brow. The wizard Ilgrist stood guard over him like a tall, ever-present shadow, his own somber black robes overlaid by the linked crimson-unicorns mantle of his office, and suffered no hands

but his own to straighten the crown or approach closely. There was good reason for his vigilance.

All five barons, like vultures circling to be in at a
dying, were prowling the palace this day. Ilgrist had
asked the eldest and most law-abiding among them, the
huge and bearded warrior whom men called the Bear,
to bring his seven best armsmen to bolster the throne
guard, and Baron Belundrar had done so. He stood
scowling around at the three doors of the throne room
right now, hairy hands laced through the hilts of the
many daggers at his belt. He was watching his men as
they stared stonily, nose to nose, at the far more numer-
ous troops of Baron Hothal, who like their master had
come to court this day in full armor, fairly bristling with
cross-scabbarded blades. At the heart of where they
stood thickest lurked their master in his own full
armor; some Galadornans said he never took it off save
to don new, larger pieces.

Other armsmen were here too, though out of their
armor—and looking as wary and uncomfortable over it
as so many unshelled crabs, among all the battle-ready
warriors. Some of them wore the purple tunics of Baron
Maethor, the suave and ever-smiling master of a thousand intrigues and even more Galadornan bedchambers. "Purple poisoners," some folk of the realm called
them, and not without cause. Other servants—some of
whom looked suspiciously like battle-worn hireswords
from other lands, not Galdornans at all—wore the scarlet of Baron Feldrin, the restless trickster who grew
gold coins at the end of his fingertips every time he
stretched out his hands to take things, it seemed . . .
and his hands were outstretched often.

Last among this fellowship of ready death strolled
the haughty magelings and quickblades of the baron
some folk at court deemed the most dangerous threat
to the freedoms enjoyed by all Galadornans: Tholone,
the scarred would-be mage and accomplished swords-
man, who styled himself "Lord" rather than Baron, and

had largely ignored the decrees and writ of the Unicorn Throne for almost a decade. Some said Arlavaunta had been called forth from her lair to attack the king by his spells—because Baerimgrim had been riding with many armed knights at his back to demand Tholone's renewed loyalty, and long-withheld taxes, when the dragon's attack had come.

"A flock of vultures," the king muttered, watching the liveried lackeys drifting into the throne room. "None of them people I'd choose to have standing by, watching me die."

Court Mage Ilgrist smiled thinly and replied, "Your Majesty has the right of it, to be sure." He made a small hand sign to one of the throne guards who held the balconies this day, to make stone cold sure no baronial crossbowmen just happened to idly mount the back stairs to gain a better view of things. The officer nodded and sent three guards down those stairs, one bearing a horn and the other two walking with slow, measured tread, the banner of the Blood Unicorn borne stretched out in splendor between them. It showed the leaping crimson "horned horse" forever silhouetted against a full moon, on a glittering cloth-of-gold field. When the banner had been laid flat at the king's feet, the guard with the horn blew a single high, ringing note, to signify open court was now in session—and the king would entertain public deputations and entreaties from all folk, no matter how high or low.

There were a few commoners in the hall this day—folk who always watched the king, or who'd not have missed today's expected danger and excitement no matter what doom might confront them—but none of them dared push forward through the throngs of baronial men. The throne faced a half-ring of armsmen who were glaring hard-eyed in every direction whilst fondling the hilts of half-drawn daggers all the while; if he'd had the strength, King Baerimgrim would have risen and walked about mockingly introducing them all to each other.

As it was, he just sat and waited to see who of the five circling vultures was boldest. War would come no matter what was decided here today . . . but he could do Galadorna one last service and leave its throne as strongly held as possible, to keep the bloodshed, if the gods smiled, paltry.

The Bear would stand with him, if need be. No prize, but the best of a bad lot. He believed in laws and doing the right thing . . . but how much of that was rooted in his firm belief that as senior Baron among the five, and head of the oldest and largest noble house, the right thing meant Belundrar on the throne?

It was hard to say which was the most dangerous threat: Tholone's loose-leashed magelings, Maethor's spies and poisons, or Hothal's brute blades-enough-to-reap-all. And what sort of surprise blade had Feldrin's gold been used to hire . . . or was he supporting one of the others? Or were the Lords of Laothkund or other covetous foreign powers dealing with him?

Ah, it began. Striding out from among the tensely waiting warriors toward Baerimgrim came a young, black-bearded man in the green and silver of Hothal—one of the few who'd not come to court this day full-armored for battle.

The envoy bowed low before the throne, and said, "Most gracious Majesty, all Galadorna grieves at your condition. My Lord Hothal knows deep sorrow at the fate of royal Baerimgrim but grieves also for the future of fair Galadorna if the Unicorn Throne falls empty, to be fought over at this time—or worse, offers sitting room to one whose malice or blundering ignorance will lead the realm into ruin."

"You make your concerns clear enough, sir," the king said then, his dry tones awakening chuckles all over the room. "Bring you also solutions, I trust?"

The reddening envoy responded sharply, "Majesty, I do. I speak on behalf of Hothal, Baron of Galadorna, who begs leave to take the crown at this time, peaceably"—his voice rose to ride over sounds of derision and dispute from many in the chamber—"and with fair regard for the rights and desires of others. My lord requests this honor not idly; he has been most diligent on Galadorna's behalf and has bade me reveal thus: in return for promises that bright-visaged peace and fair-handed justice shall continue to flourish in the realm, he enjoys the full support of the most puissant lord Feldrin, Baron of Galadorna, which that noble personage shall himself confirm."

All eyes turned to Feldrin, who smiled in his customarily sly, sidelong way, his eyes meeting no one's gaze—and nodded, slowly and deliberately.

"Moreover," the envoy continued, "My lord hath spoken with the enemies of Galadorna, with an eye to keeping them from our borders and out of our purses, that the land remain free and prosperous, with no shadow of war-fear upon our thresholds. In return for most favored prices on silver and iron from our deep forest mines, the Lords of Laothkund have agreed to a treaty of mutual peace and border respect."

Cries of anger, oaths, and gasps of exaggerated horror made such a din in the chamber that the envoy paused for some time before adding, "My Lord Hothal submits that as he leads a force that can best keep the realm safe and prosperous, the crown should pass to him, and—for the good of Galadorna—his rule be proclaimed as legitimate by yourself, Grave Majesty."

There was another uproar, quelled in an instant by the deep rumble of Baron Belundrar as he lurched forward to stand beside the throne. With obvious reluctance in his tone and anger in his eyes, he said, "I share the anger of many here that any Galadornan would deal in secret with the wolves of Laothkund. Yet—"

He paused to sweep the room with his glare, his green eyes fierce under his bushy black brows and his battered nose jutting like a drawn blade, before he resumed, "Yet I will support this bid for the crown, scheming though it may seem, so long as the rule of law and right be upheld. Galadorna must be ruled by the strongest—and must not become a land of knifings and monthly intrigues or executions."

As the Bear stepped back to better survey all of the doors once more, a murmur of agreement arose at his words—but again the talk stilled in a moment as another baron stepped forth and purred, "A moment, brave Belundrar! You speak as if you see no acceptable alternative to this admitted scheming, to guard the safety of fair Galadorna in the years ahead. Well, then, listen to me, and I'll provide an offer unstained by dealing with enemies in secret."

Lord Tholone ignored Belundrar's instinctive snarl and continued, turning in a slow circle with his hand out, to survey all in the room. "You've heard very real and loyal concerns for the safety of our beloved realm. I share that love for Galadorna and worry for the security of us all. Unlike others, however, I've busied myself not with dark back-passage deals, but with assembling the finest company of mages this side of the sea!"

There was snorts and spitting as many warriors expressed their disgust at any reliance on wizards—and the presence of hired outlander mages here.

A cold-eyed Tholone raised his purring voice a notch and continued firmly, "Only my mages can guarantee the peace and prosperity we all seek. To those who mistrust magic, I ask this: if you truly want peace, do you hire and consort with battle-hungry warriors? Galadorna scarcely needs such bloody folk as its lords."

He left a little silence then for murmurs of agreement but heard instead, in that roomful of fearful courtiers and simmering warriors, only stony silence and quickly added, "I command magic enough to make Galadorna not only safe but great—and to deal with any traitors in this chamber who plan to put other interests before the security and rebuilding of the Realm of the Blood Unicorn."

"Bah! We'll have no twisted sorcerers ruling the realm!" someone shouted from the press of armored men around Baron Hothal, and several voices echoed, "Twisted sorcerers!" in tones of anger. The king and the Court Mage Ilgrist, who was standing by the royal shoulder, exchanged glances of rueful amusement.

The tumult, which had reached the point of daggers glinting here and there as they were drawn, fell abruptly still and silent once more.

The most handsome of the barons of Galadorna had stepped forth, the smile that charmed Galadornan ladies all too often flashing forth like a deft and graceful sword. Baron Maethor might well have been a crown prince, so richly was he dressed, so perfect his flowing mane of brown hair, and so smoothly confident his manner. "It grieves me, men of Galadorna," he said, "to see such anger and open lawlessness in this chamber. This blustering of those who walk around with ready swords, and the merciless will to use them, is the very thing that must be stopped if the Galadorna we all love is to be saved from sinking into . . . a land not worth saving or dwelling in; just another warlord's den."

He turned to look around the room, ruffled cloak swirling grandly, every eye upon him, and added, "Therefore, my duty to the realm stands clear. I must and shall support Lord Tholone—"

There was a gasp of surprise, and even Tholone's jaw dropped. Maethor and Tholone were considered the two strongest barons by many, and everyone in the realm knew they were far from friends.

"—the one man among us who can make a difference. I must go to bed this night knowing I have done my best for Galadorna . . . and I can only do that if Lord Tholone willingly gives the most trustworthy of us all, good Baron Belundrar, the post of seneschal of Nethrar, in sole charge of all justice throughout the realm."

There was an approving murmur; Belundrar blinked at Maethor. The pretty boy baron wasn't called "the

Silver-Tongued Poisoner of Galadorna" for nothing. What was he up to?

Maethor gave everyone a last smile and glided quickly back within his protective ring of handsome aides in silks and leathers, with not-so-hidden daggers ready in their lace-wristed hands.

A stir of excited talk arose at this surprising—and to many, bright in promise—offer. A stir that rose sharply, only to fall away into tense silence once more, as the last baron slipped through his supporters to scuttle close to the throne, causing guards to stiffen and turn until Ilgrist waved them back.

Feldrin's big brown eyes roved around the chamber. His hands fluttered as nervously and as restlessly as always, as their thin, weak-looking owner bent near the ear of the king. Feldrin's fine but ill-fitting clothes were drenched with sweat, and his short black hair, usually straight-plastered to his skull, looked like a bird had been raking it for nesting material. He was almost dancing with fearful excitement as he whispered in the royal ear. On the other side of the throne, Ilgrist bent close to listen too, evoking one nervous glance from Feldrin—but only one.

"Most Just and Able Majesty," Feldrin breathed, along with a strong scent of parsley, "I too, in my not-so-bold way, love Galadorna and would at all costs see her escape the bloody ruin of war between us barons—moreover, I have good information that at least three ambitious lordlings of Laothkund will ride here with the best mercenaries they can muster if we do take up arms 'gainst each other, to carve away all of Galadorna that they can hold. These three have a pact; their men shall never turn on each other whilst any of us live."

"And so?" the king growled, sounding very much like Belundrar in his dislike of threats and whispered schemes. Feldrin wrung his hands nervously, his brown eyes very large as they darted this way and that, peering to see who might be close enough to hear. He lowered his voice still further and leaned close; Ilgrist pointedly raised one fist and let the ring on its middle finger gleam and glow for all to see. If Feldrin drew dagger on the king, it would be the last thing he ever did.

"I, too, will support Lord Tholone, if you, sire, can agree to my conditions—which you will appreciate must needs be kept secret. These are two: that Hothal be executed here and now—for he will never accept Tholone where you sit now, and will harry us all for years, spilling the best blood of the realm—"

"Including that of one Feldrin?" the king muttered, a smile almost creeping onto his face.

"I—I—well, yes, I do suppose, ahem-*hem,* and that brings us to the second hazard: the greater danger to Galadorna is the smiling snake yonder, Maethor. I need your royal promise that 'an accident' shall very soon befall him. He has been a tireless and always untrustworthy spinner of intrigues, master of lies and shadows and poison; the land has no need of him, no matter who holds the throne." Feldrin was almost panting now, streaming with sweat, out of fear at his own daring.

"And one Feldrin most assuredly has no need of such a pretty rival at scheming," Ilgrist murmured, so quietly that perhaps only the king heard.

King Baerimgrim thrust out a hand suddenly and caught hold of Feldrin's chin. He pulled, dragging the baron around to face him, and murmured, "I agree to these two conditions, so long as you stand steadfast and no one else dies by your hand, direction, or maneuverings. For your own good, I place one condition upon you, clever Feldrin: when you straighten up from here, look worried—not pleased."

The king thrust the whispering baron away, and raised a voice that held a quaver of enfeeblement, yet also the snap of command: "Lord Tholone! Attend us here, for the love of Galadorna!"

There was a momentary excited stir—in some corners of the throne room, almost a shout—then breathless silence.

Out of the heart of that waiting, watching stillness Lord Tholone came striding, face a pleasant mask, eyes wary. There was a faint singing in the air around him; his mages had been busy. No doubt daggers would prove futile fangs if thrown his way now or in the near hereafter.

If—given the number of wizards and warriors ready for battle and on edge with excitement—there would be a hereafter for anyone in this room.

The silence was utter as Tholone came to a stop before the Unicorn Throne, separated from the king only by the crimson and gold expanse of the Blood Unicorn banner.

"Kneel," Baerimgrim said hoarsely, "on the Unicorn."

There was a collective gasp of indrawn breath; such a bidding could mean only one thing. The king reached to his own head, and slowly—very slowly—did off the crown.

His hands did not tremble in the least as he raised it over Tholone's bent head—a head that had grown a triumphant, almost maniacal smile—and said, "Let all true Galadornans gathered here bear witness this day, that of my own free will, I name as my rightful heir thi—"

The crack of lightning that burst from the crown at that moment deafened men and hurled them back hard against the paneled walls. Baerimgrim and the Unicorn Throne were split in twain in a blackened, writhing instant, the crown ringing off the riven ceiling. As the blazing limbs of what had been the king slumped down amid the sagging wreckage of the throne, the golden unicorn's head that surmounted it sobbed aloud.

The court mage looked astonished for the first time, and snatched out a wand as he looked sharply at the painted wooden head . . . but whatever enchantment had made it speak had fled, and the head was cracking and collapsing into falling splinters.

Ilgrist glanced swiftly around the room. Feldrin was lying lifeless on the floor, his arms two scorched stumps and his face burned away, and Tholone was on his back, clawing feebly at gilding from the smoldering banner that had melted onto his face.

The court mage fired over them, calling forth the fury of the wand in his hand, and a veritable cloud of magic missiles sang and snarled their blue-white death around the room. Not a few of Tholone's magelings crumpled or slid down the wall, wisps of smoke issuing from their eyes and gaping mouths—then the air was full of curses and swords flashing in the hands of running men.

Fire leaped up in a circle around Ilgrist then, and the wand in his hand spat forth a last trio of magical bolts—they struck at mages who still stood, and one fell—before it crumbled.

The court mage let its ashes trickle from his hand as he looked calmly around the ring of angry armed men and said, "No, Galadorna is too important for me to allow such a mistake. Baerimgrim was a good king and my friend, but . . . one mistake is all that fells most kings. I trust the rest of you, gentlesirs, w—"

With a roar that shook the room, Belundrar the Bear launched himself through the flames, heedless of the pain, and leaped at Ilgrist.

The wizard coolly took a single step back, raising one hand. The knife in the baron's grasp, sweeping side-long at Ilgrist's throat, struck something that broke it, amid sparks, and sent the Bear's arm springing back involuntarily, to hurl the hilt into the balconies. The fire that blossomed in the wizard's hand caught the Bear full in the face, and his roar became a gurgling for the brief instant before his blackened, flaming body crashed face first into the floor.

Ilgrist lifted a fastidious foot to let it slide, blazing, past. "Are there any more heroes here today?" he asked mildly. "I've plenty more death in these hands."

As if that had been a signal, the air filled with hurled daggers and swords, spinning at the court mage from roaring men on all sides—only to ring off an invisible barrier, every last one of them, and fall away.

Ilgrist looked down at the body of Belundrar, which had broken his circle of fire and was busily being burnt in two by its flames, and murmured "Blasted to smoking ruin. A true patriot—and see how much he accomplished, in the end? Come, gentlesirs! Let us have your submission. I shall be the new king of—"

"Never!" Baron Hothal thundered. "I'll die before I'll allow su—"

Ilgrist's mouth crooked. "But of course," he said.

He made a tiny gesture with two of his fingers, and the air was suddenly full of the twang and hum of crossbows firing, from the throne guard up in the balconies, their faces white and blank, their movements mechanical.

Warriors groaned, clutched vainly at quarrels sprouting in their faces or throats, and fell. Hitherto-concealed crossbows spat an answer from many baronial armsmen around the chamber—and the helmless Hothal, his head transfixed by many bolts, staggered, then toppled onto his side.

Baron Maethor would have tasted as many flying deaths had he not possessed an unseen barrier of his own that kept both hurled daggers and crossbow bolts from him. Many of his unarmored men fell, but others surged forward to drive daggers into the faces of Hothal's armored guardsmen or raced up balcony stairs to carve out a bloody revenge on Galadorna's throne guard.

The chamber erupted in a flurry of hacking, stabbing steel, the thunder of armored men running, and screams—all too many screams. There was fresh commotion at two of the throne room doors, as royal soldiers with halberds in their hands elbowed ways into the room—then a bright flash and roar that shook the chamber even more than the lightning had and left dazzled men blinking.

Into the ringing echoes of the blast he'd caused, transforming a score of Baron Hothal's best knights into so many bloody scraps of armor embedded in riven paneling, the court mage shouted, "All of you—hold! *Hold,* I say!"

Commoners, throne guards, and the men of Maethor who were left, with their master in their midst, all turned to look at the wizard. The ring of fire around Ilgrist was gone, and the mage was pointing across the chamber, at—

The burned and broken body of Lord Tholone, now struggling jerkily to sit upright, its legs still much-twisted ruin. It turned sightless, despairing eyes to the watching men and worked jaws that had already drooled much blood for some time before trembling lips said the horribly flat and rattling words, "Pay homage to King Ilgrist of Galadorna, as I do."

Bonelessly the body slumped—an instant before it burst apart in a blast that spattered many of the surviving warriors. One of them snarled, "Magecraft said those words, not Tholone!"

"Oh?" Ilgrist asked softly, as the twisted, blackened crown of Galadorna flew smoothly out of the wreckage into his hand. "And if so, what will you do?"

He straightened the crown with a sudden show of strength, and unseen spell-hands lifted the mantle of court mage from his shoulders. It fell unheeded to the floor as he stepped forward, settled the battered crown upon his brow, and said loudly, "So let all Galadornans kneel before their new king. I shall rule over Galadorna as Nadrathen, a name I've known rather longer than 'Ilgrist.' Bow down!"

The shocked silence was broken by the rustlings and scrapings of several armsmen going clumsily to their knees. One or two of Maethor's men knelt; one was promptly knifed from behind by one of his fellows and fell on his face with a gurgling cry.

King Nadrathen regarded the knot of richly garbed men with a gentle smile and said to their midst, "Well, Maethor? Shall Galadorna lose all of its barons this day?"

There was a rustling from behind him. Nadrathen turned and stepped back in the same motion, protective magics plucking his feet from the floor, to drift gently down a good pace back—and stare in open-mouthed surprise.

The mantle of the Court Mage of Galadorna, let fall by Nadrathen scant moments ago, was rising from the floor again, to hang upright as though a rather tall man was wearing it.

As the wondering court watched, a body faded into view within the mantle—a hawk-nosed, raven-haired human wearing nondescript robes and a faint smile. "Nadrathen?" he asked. "Called the Rebel Chosen?"

"King Nadrathen of Galadorna, as it happens," came the cool reply. "And who might you be? The shade of a court mage past?"

"I am called Elminster—and by the Hand of Azuth and the Mercy of Mystra, I challenge thee to spell duel, here and now, in a circle of my rais—"

"Oh, by all the fallen *gods*," Nadrathen sighed, and black flames suddenly exploded out of his hands with a roar, racing in a thick cylinder, like a battering ram, at the newcomer.

"Die, and trouble my coronation no more," the new king of Galadorna told the sudden inferno of black flames that erupted where his spell had struck. All over the chamber murmuring armsmen were crouching low behind pillars and railings or slipping out doorways, and away.

Black flames howled up to the ceiling—and were gone, snarling up to some lofty otherwhere. The man in the mantle of court mage stood unchanged, save that one eyebrow was now raised in derision. "Ye have some aversion to rules of combat or defensive circles? Or were ye in some haste to remodel this part of thy castle?"

Nadrathen cursed—and stone blocks were suddenly raining down all around them, plunging down from empty air to shake the chamber with their thunderous landings. Stone shards sprayed in all directions as the floor shattered; more armsmen fled, shouting in fear.

No stones struck either Nadrathen or Elminster; it was the turn of the Rebel Chosen to lift his brows in surprise.

"You come well shielded," he granted grudgingly. "Ulmimber—or whatever your name is—do you know what I am?"

"An archmage of accomplished might," Elminster said softly, "named by Holy Mystra herself as one of her Chosen—and now turned to evil."

"I did not turn to evil, fool wizard. I am what I have always been; Mystra has known me for what I am from the first." The king of Galadorna regarded his challenger bleakly, and added, "You know what the outcome of our duel must be?"

El swallowed, started to nod, and then suddenly grinned. "Ye're going to talk me to death?"

Nadrathen snarled, "Enough! You had your chance, idiot, and now—"

The air above them was suddenly darker and full of a host of ghostly, faceless floating figures, cowled and robed, trailing away to nothingness as they swooped, thrusting cold and spectral blades at the hawk-nosed mage.

As those blades transfixed Elminster, they slid in without gore or resistance . . . and became dwindling smoke and sparks, taking their wielders with them.

Nadrathen gaped in astonishment. His words, when he could find them, came in a gasp. "You must be a Ch—"

Behind the self-styled king of Galadorna, unseen by either dueling mage, a long-fingered female hand had slid into view, protruding from the still-solid, upright back of the riven Unicorn Throne with blue motes of risen magic dancing around it. Those long, flexing fingers now leveled a deliberate finger at the back of the unwitting Rebel Chosen.

Nadrathen's eyes widened, bulging for one incredulous moment before all his glistening bones burst together out the front of his body. Behind them as they bounced, a bloody, shapeless mass of flesh slumped to the floor, spattering El's boots and the throne with gore.

El sprang back, gagging, but the bones and the horrible puddle that had been Nadrathen were already afire, blazing from within. Blue-white, wasted magic swirled above flames of bright silver as men cried out in disgust and fear all over the chamber. El watched a thread of silver rise straight up from those flames to pierce the ceiling and burn onward.

He never saw the sunlight stab down into the throne room from high above; he was staggering back to fall heavily on his knees by then, as magic that was not his own shocked into him, surging throughout his spasming, weeping body.

Baron Maethor swallowed. He dared not approach the man-high conflagration that had been "King" Nadrathen, but this challenger-mage was on his knees blindly vomiting silver flames onto the smoking floor. Galadorna could be free of over-ambitious mages yet.

"Hand me your blade," he murmured to an aide without looking, extending his hand for it. Just one throw would be enough, if—

A tall, slender feminine figure stepped from behind that conflagration, bare thighs above high black boots flashing through slashes in midnight-black robes. "I think I shall rule Galadorna," Dasumia said sweetly, blue motes still swirling about one of her hands. "Ascending my throne in this Year of Mistmaidens— this very hour, in fact. And you shall be my seneschal, Elminster of Galadorna. Rise, Court Mage, and bring me the fealty of yon surviving lords and barons—or an internal organ from each; whichever they prefer."

Nine

GLAD DAYS IN GALADORNA

*The wise ruler leaves time among audiences and prom-
enades for receptions of daggers—usually in the royal
back.*

Ralderick Hallowshaw, Jester
from **To Rule A Realm, From Turret To Midden**
published circa The Year of the Bloodbird

Dark fire snarled and spat, and the slender elf in
dark robes staggered back, groaning. Ilbryn Starym's
three hundredth or so encounter with the wards of dark
fire around the Castle of the Lady had not gone well.
Her power was still too great, even in her absence . . .
and where by the Trees Everlasting was she, anyway?

He sighed, glared up at the dark, slender towers so
high above him in the twilit sky, and—

Was sent almost sprawling by a hard and sudden
impact. He whirled to do battle with whatever fell guardian
had charged him and found himself staring at the receding boots of one of the two buffoon-mages who were also
encamped outside the walls of Dasumia's fortress.

Beldrune's excited shout floated back to the furious elf. "Baerast! Hearken!"

Tabarast looked up from a fire that just wouldn't light, shaking his scorched fingertips, and asked somewhat testily, "What is it now?"

"I was scrying Nethrar," Beldrune of the Bent Finger panted, "as the dream bid me, and there's news! The Lady Dasumia has just taken the throne and named the Chosen One as her seneschal. Elminster is Court Mage of Galadorna now!"

Ilbryn stared at the trotting mage's back for a moment, then broke into a fluid dash that swiftly brought him abreast of Beldrune. He reached up, caught hold of one bobbing shoulder in its fashionable slashed and pleated claret-hued silk, and snapped, "*What?*"

Spun around to face blazing elven eyes by fingers that felt like talons of steel, Beldrune groaned, "Let go, longears! You've fingers like wolf jaws!"

Ilbryn shook him. "What did you say?"

Tabarast fumbled in a belt pouch, dropped a shower of small, sparkling items, and held one up between finger and thumb, muttering something.

A lance of shining nothingness coalesced out of the air and thrust forward, unerring and as swift as leaping lightning. It took Ilbryn right in his ribs, shattering his shielding spell in a cascade of small and wayward cracklings and snatching him off his feet.

He hit the phandar tree with brutal force; ribs snapped like dry kindling crushed in a forester's fist. Ilbryn sobbed and choked and writhed, fighting for breath, but the spell held him pinned to the trunk. If it had been a real lance, he'd have been cut in two . . . but that knowledge afforded him scant consolation. Through red mists of pain he glared almost pleadingly at the two human mages.

Tabarast regarded the trapped elf mage almost sorrowfully and shook his head. "The problem with young elves is they've got all the arrogance of the older ones, with nothing to back it up," he observed. "Now, Beldrune, speak up for the hasty youngling here. What did you say?"

*   *   *   *   *

Curthas and Halglond stood very straight and still, their pikes just so, for they knew their master's turret window overlooked this section of battlements . . . and that he liked to look out often on moonlit nights and see tranquillity, not the gleam and flash of guards fidgeting at their posts.

They stood guard over one end of the arched bridge that linked the loftiest rooms of the Master's Tower with the encircling battlements. It was light enough duty. No thief or angry armsman for three realms distant would dare to come calling uninvited on Klandaerlas Glymril, Master of Wyverns. The dragonkin he held in spell-thrall were seldom unleashed; when they did come boiling out of their tower on swift wings, they were apt to be hungry, fearless, and savage of temper.

One guard risked a quick glance along the moonlit wall. The stout tower that imprisoned the wyverns stood, as usual, dark and silent. Like the rest of Glymril Gard, it had been raised by the Master's spells from the tumbled stones of an ancient keep, here on the end of a ridge that overlooked six towns and the meeting of two rivers.

It was moonlit and gloriously warm this night, even up on the ever-breezy battlements of Glymril Gard, and it was easy to drift into a reverie of other moonlit nights, without armor or guard duties, and—

Curthas stiffened and turned his head. Bells? What could be chiming up here on the battlements at this time of night?

He could see at a glance that the walls were deserted. Halglond was already peering down the walls and into the yards below, in case someone was climbing the walls or coming up the guard stairs. No. Perhaps someone's escaped falcon, still with its jesses, had perched nearby . . . but where?

The sound was faint, small—yet very close, not on the ground far below or in one of the towers. What by all the storm-loving gods could it *be?*

Now it seemed to be right under Halglond's nose, swirling. He could see a faint, ragged line of mist coiling and snaking in the air. He swept through it with his halberd, and small glowing motes of light gathered for a moment along its curved blade before winking out—like sparks without a fire.

The chiming wind curled away, moving along the battlements. He exchanged glances with Curthas, and they both trotted warily after it, watching it grow larger and brighter. From behind them came the faint squeal that heralded the shutters of the Master's turret window opening. Perhaps it was one of his spells . . . or not, but they'd best chase it down even so. This could well be a test of their diligence.

It led them to the Prow Tower at the end of the ridge, where rocks fell away in almost cliffs beneath the castle walls, and there it seemed to quicken its dancing and circling. Curthas and Halglond closed with it cautiously, separating to come at it from different directions, with halberds to the fore and crouching low to avoid being swept over the battlements into a fall, no matter how fierce the wind became.

The chiming rose to a loud and regular sound, almost annoying to the ears, and the mist that made it spiraled up into a vaguely human form taller than either of them. Both guards stabbed at it with their pikes, and suddenly it collapsed, falling to become a milky layer of radiance awash around their boots.

Curthas and Halglond traded looks again. Nothing met their probing pike thrusts, and the chiming was silent. They shrugged, took a last look around the curved tower battlements, and turned to head back to their posts, If the Master wanted to tell them what it had been, he would; if he kept silent about it, 'twould be best if they did, too, and—

Halglond pointed, and they both stared. Halfway back along the way they'd come, the mist was dancing along the battlements. It had a definite shape, now— and the shape was female, barefoot and in flowing skirts, with long hair flying free in her wake as she ran, a faint chiming in her wake. The guards could just see through her.

In unspoken accord they broke into a run. If she turned across the bridge they were supposed to be guarding . . .

She ran right past it, heading toward the binding-racks and bloodstains of Bloodtop Tower, where—when the Master had prisoners he no longer needed—the wyverns were sometimes allowed to feed. That was a good way off, and the ghostly lady seemed in no hurry; the pounding guards gained on her swiftly.

A dark-robed figure was coming across the bridge—the Master! Halglond hissed a curse, and Curthas felt like joining in, but the mage ignored them, turning to join the chase along the battlements well ahead of his two guards. He carried a wand in one hand.

The guards saw her turn, hair swirling in the moon-light, amid the binding-racks, and silently beckon the Master of Wyverns, as coyly as any lover in a minstrel's ballad. As he approached her, she danced away to the edge of the battlements. The hard-running guards saw him follow warily, wand raised and ready. Glymril looked back at them once, as if deciding whether or not to wait until they reached the Tower, and Curthas clearly saw amazement on his face.

Not of their master's making, then, and unexpected to boot. They did not slow in their now-panting sprint— but even so, Curthas knew the strange foreboding that precedes by instants the sure knowledge that one is going to be—just—too late.

The woman became a snakelike, formless thing, and the shocked guards heard a long, raw howl from Klandaerlas Glymril as something bright whirled around him in a swift spiral, climbing toward the moon.

An instant later the Master of Wyverns became a roaring column of flame that split the night with its sudden fury. Curthas clutched at Halglond's arm, and they came to a ragged, panting halt together, all too close to where the battlements joined Bloodtop Tower. There was a booming *thump,* and something exploded out of the pyre, trailing flames down into the inner courtyards: the wand.

The guards exchanged fearful looks, licked dry lips, and started to back away in fear. They had managed two strides before the stones beneath their feet rippled like waves on a beach and started to slump and fall.

They fell into oblivion with the gathering roar of Glymril Gard collapsing ringing in their ears.

As the moon saw that great fortress crash back down into the tumbled ruin it had been before Glymril's spells had rebuilt it, a bright and triumphant mist danced over the rising dust and fading screams, its chimes mixed with cold, echoing laughter.

*   *   *   *   *

The court mage looked at the guard captain's grim face and sighed. "Who was it this time?"

"Anlavas Jhoavryn, Lord Elminster: a merchant from somewhere south across the sea. Brass work, sundries; nothing important, but a lot of it. Many coins here over many seasons. His throat was cut."

Elminster sighed. "Maethor or one of the new barons?"

"L-lord, I know not, and hardly dare s—"

"Your *hunches*, loyal Rhoagalow."

The guard captain glanced nervously from side to side; El smiled crookedly and leaned over to put his ear right to the man's lips. "Limmator," the officer breathed hoarsely; El nodded and stepped back. No particular surprise if Rhoagalow was right; Limmator was the only baron—or lordling—in Galadorna busier in dark corners with bribe, threat, and ready knife than Maethor of the Many Whispers.

"Go and dine now," he told the exhausted guard officer. "We'll talk later."

Rhoagalow and his three armsmen hurried out; El took care not to sigh until the antechamber was quite empty.

He murmured something and moved two fingers a trifle. There was a faint thump behind one wall, as the spy there abruptly went to sleep. El gave the section of wall a mirthless smile and used the secret door he wanted to keep secret a little longer, taking the lightless passage beyond to one of the disused and dusty hidden rooms in the House of the Unicorn. A little time alone to think is a rare treasure some folk never seize for themselves . . . and others, the truly deprived in life, cannot.

Three barons had died so far this year, one of them with a dagger in his throat not two steps from entering the throne chamber, and six—no, seven—lesser lords. Galadorna had become a nest of vipers, striking at each other with their fangs bared whenever the whim took them, and the court mage was not a happy man. He had no friends; anyone he befriended soon ended up staring sightlessly at a ceiling of a morning. There were whisperings behind every door in the palace and never any true smiles when those doors opened. El was even getting used to the sight of dark ribbons of blood wandering out from behind closed doors; perhaps he should issue a decree commanding all doors in Nethrar be taken down and burned.

Hah to that. He was becoming what he knew they called him behind his back: "the Flapping Mouth That Spews Decrees." The barons and lordlings constantly tried to undercut royal authority, or even steal openly from the court, and his Lady Master was no help at all, using her spells too seldom to engender any fear that might in turn breed obedience.

There came a faint scratching sound from off to his left. Elminster pulled on the right knob and a panel slid open. Two young guardsmen peered into the dimness. "You sent for us, Lord Elminster?"

"Ye found the scrolls, Delver, and—?"

"Burned, and the ashes in the moat, lord, as you ordered, mixed with the dust you gave me. I used all of it."

Elminster nodded and reached out a hand to touch a forehead. "Forget all, loyal warrior," he said, "and so escape the doom we all fear."

The guard he'd touched shivered, eyes blank, then turned and hurried back into the darkness, unlacing his breeches as he went. He'd been heading for his quarters when the sudden, urgent need to use a garderobe had come upon him, and led him into the disused wing of the palace.

"Ingrath?" the court mage asked calmly.

"I found the Q—ah, *her* work in the Redshield Chamber and mixed in the white powder until I could see it no more. Then I said the words and got out."

El nodded and reached out his hand. "Ye and Delver are earning such handsome rewards. . . ." he murmured.

The guardsman chuckled. "Not the need to go to the jakes, please, lord. Let it be wandering trying to recall my youthful dalliances down here, eh?"

El smiled. "As ye wish," he said, as his fingers touched flesh. Ingrath's eyes flickered, and the forgetful warrior stepped around the still and silent mage, walked in a thoughtful circle around the room, found the panel, and trotted away again, his part in slowing Dasumia's evil forgotten once more.

Which might just keep him alive another month or two.

'Twould be safer if the two weren't friends and knew nothing of each other—but it had happened that the best warriors El could trust, after subtle but thorough mind-scrying, were fast friends. That should be no surprise, he supposed.

El paced the gloomy room, his mood dark enough to match it. Mystra's command to serve had been clear, but "serve in his own way" had always been Elminster's failing; if it was a flaw that was to doom him now, then let it be so. Some things a man must cling to, to remain a man.

Or a woman cleave to, to be herself . . . and there was certainly one lady in Galadorna doing just as she pleased. Queen Dasumia always seemed to be laughing at him these days and certainly cared nothing for the duties of being queen; she was seldom to be found on the throne or even in the royal castle, leaving El to issue decrees in her stead. Galadorna could sink into war and thievery without her noticing . . . and daily, as more slavers and unscrupulous merchants rushed in, knowing they'd be left more or less unrestricted in their dealings, the Lords of Laothkund were casting covetous eyes on the increasingly wealthy kingdom. One thing lawlessness among merchants does bring is full tax coffers.

El sighed again. The important thing was to make sure that with all this gold, lawlessness did not spread to the crown. Sweet Mystra forfend. Whatever would it be like to live in a land ruled by merchants?

*　*　*　*　*

Everyone ignored the splintering and crashing sounds of a table collapsing under two cursing men slugging each other and the shivering and tinkling sounds of breaking glass that followed as various nearby drinkers hurled bottles at the combatants, seeking to alter the odds of wagers just placed. Someone screamed from another room—a death cry that ended in a horrible, wet gurgle, and was answered by drunken applause. It was late, after all, and this was the Goblet of Shadows.

Nethrar had known wilder taverns in its time, but the days of golem dancers who ate their fees to enrich Ilgrist were gone, and the dens they'd done more than dance in were gone with them. The Goblet, however, was very much here—and those too afraid to brave its pleasures alone could always hire a trio of surly-looking warriors to guard them and make them—at least in their own eyes—seem a veteran member of a band of adventurers on dangerous business bent.

And there were the ladies. One such, a vision in blue silk and mock armor whose loops of chain and curves of leather did more to display than conceal, had just perched on the edge of a table not far from where Beldrune and Tabarast were nursing glasses of ruby-hued but raw heartsfire and grumbling, "Well aged? Six days, belike!" to each other.

Over their glasses, Beldrune and Tabarast watched the saucy beauty in the silks bending low over two young men at the table she'd chosen, giving them a view of the sort that older, more sober men have fallen headlong into before now. The two wizards cleared their throats in unison.

" 'Tis getting a might hot in here," Tabarast observed weakly, tugging at his collar.

"Over that side of the table, too?" Beldrune grunted, his eyes locked on the lady in blue. He flicked a finger, and through the din of chatter and laughter, singing and breaking glass, the two mages could suddenly hear a voice purring, as if it was speaking right in their ears: "Delver? Ingrath? Those names are . . . exciting. The names of daring men . . . of heroes. You *are* daring heroes, aren't you?"

The two young warriors chuckled and said something more or less in unison, and the saucy beauty in blue whispered, "How daring are you both feeling this night? And . . . how heroic?"

The two men laughed again, rather warily, and the beauty murmured, "Heroic enough to do a service for your queen? A—*personal* service?"

They saw her reach into her bodice and draw forth a long, heavy chain of linked gold coins that caught and held their hungry eyes as she flashed the unicorn-adorned Royal Ring of Galadorna.

Two sets of eyes widened, and looked slowly and more soberly up from the coins and the curves to the face above—where they found an impish grin followed by a tongue just darting into view between parted lips.

"Come," she said, "if you dare . . . to a place where we can . . . have more fun."

The watching wizards saw the two men hesitate and exchange glances. Then one of them said something, lifting his eyebrows in an exaggerated manner, and they both laughed rather nervously, drained their tankards, and rose. The queen looped her chain of coins around the wrist of one of them and towed him playfully off across the dim and crowded maze of tables, beaded curtains, and archways that formed the backbone of the Goblet.

Blue silk and supple leather swayed very close past the innocently tilted noses of Beldrune and Tabarast. When the second warrior had stalked past—hungry eyes, hairy arms and all—the two mages with one accord drained their heartsfires, turned to each other and turned red at the same time, tugged at their collars again, and cleared their throats once more.

Tabarast rumbled, "Ah—I think it's time to see the bottom of more than one tankard . . . don't you?"

"My thoughts exactly," Beldrune agreed. "After a keg or three of beer, now, mind you. . . ."

*   *   *   *   *

Deep in the dimness behind a pillar in the Goblet of Shadows, an elf whose face might have been cut from cold marble watched Queen Dasumia of Galadorna tow her two prizes out of the tumult. When they'd rounded a corner, out of sight, Ilbryn Starym turned his head to sneer down at the two blushing old wizards, who didn't see him. Then he glided off through the Goblet toward the exit he knew the queen would use, taking care to keep well back and well hidden.

*   *   *   *   *

Rhoagalow had brought word of another murder and a knifing whose victim might live. Elminster had handed him a hand keg of Burdym's Best from the royal cellar and told him to go somewhere safe and out of uniform to drink it.

Now the Court Mage of Galadorna was striding wearily bedward, looking forward to some solid hours of staring up into the darkness and getting some real thinking work done on the governance of a feud-festering little kingdom. Perhaps there'd be another assassination attempt in the wee hours. *That* would be jolly.

El's mood had a sword edge to it just now; an ache was already raging in his head from dealing with sharp-tongued merchants all day. Moreover, he couldn't seem to put an idea out of his mind—a rumor abroad in Nethrar courtesy of the two old bumbling mages from Moonshorn Tower, who seemed to have followed him here, that "Dasumia" was the name of the dread sorceress called the Lady of Shadows; could she and the queen somehow be related?

Hmmm. El sighed again, for perhaps the seven hundredth time this day, and out of habit glanced along the side corridor his passage had brought him to.

Then he came to a dead halt and peered long and hard. Someone very familiar was crossing the corridor farther down, using a passage parallel to his own. It was the queen, clad in blue silks and leather and chains like a tavern dancer—and she was leading two young men, warriors by their harness, whose hands and lips were hard at work upon her person as she led them along . . . out of view, and into a part of the House of the Unicorn Elminster had never yet visited. Cold fear stirred deep in his vitals as he recognized those two ardent men as his sometime tools against her, Delver and Ingrath.

His headache started to pound in earnest as he caught up his robes and sprinted as quietly but as swiftly as he could down the corridor toward the place where he'd seen Dasumia disappear. It was better not to use a concealment spell now, in case his Lady Master had a trailing spelltell active.

The queen was making no effort at stealth. The high, tinkling laugh she used as false flattery rang out as El reached the corner he thought was the right one and began hopping from pillar to pillar.

There followed the sounds of a slap, Delver's voice telling a jest he couldn't catch the words of, and more laughter. El abandoned stealth for haste as he saw the passage they'd used end at an archway. He was just in time to see the amorous trio leave the far end of that empty, echoing room through another arch.

One dark and disused chamber proved to lead into another, through a succession of open archways, and El took care to keep out of sight of anyone glancing back, and freeze whenever the sounds ahead ceased. He'd worked his way back to being a single chamber behind when some trick of eddying air currents made the voices of those he was following startlingly loud.

"Where by all the gods of battle are you *taking* us, woman?"

"Uh, *Your Majesty,* he meant to say. . . . This does look suspiciously like a way down to the dungeons."

Dasumia laughed again, a deep, hearty sound of pleasure this time. "Keep that hand right where it is, bold warrior . . . and no, don't-be-gentle-sirs, we're heading nowhere near the dungeons. You have a royal promise on that!"

El crept to the next archway like a hunting cat and peered around its edge—in time to hear the rattle of a beaded curtain, unseen around a corner, parting. Light flared out from beyond it; El took a chance, danced across the room to that corner, and took another chance: across the open, lit way they'd taken was another curtain. He could hide behind it and see into the lit area, if he just darted across the open way at the right moment not to be seen.

Now? He darted, halted, and tried to bring his breathing back to soundlessness, all in a handful of instants. He used the next handful, and the next, to stare at where the queen had taken her catches.

The brightly lit area beyond the curtains was only an antechamber; an archway in its far wall opened into a place lit by a red, evil-looking radiance. Flanking that arch were two fully armored guardians, with their visors down and curving sabers raised in their gauntlets—warriors without feet, whose ankle stumps were gliding along inches above the stone floor without ever touching it. Helmed horrors, men called them; magically animated armor that could slay as surely as living armsmen.

El watched them start menacingly forward, only to halt at a gesture from the queen. Dasumia strode between them without stopping, towing her living warriors, and El stole along boldly in their wake, watching those raised sabers narrowly. Before he reached the helmed horrors, they wheeled around and floated along after the trio, sheathing their swords soundlessly. El brought up the rear, moving very cautiously now.

The chamber beyond was very large and very dark, its only light coming from a glowing ruby-hued tapestry at the far end, a tapestry that displayed a black device larger than many cottages El had seen: the Black Hand of Bane.

The aisle that ran down the center of the temple was lined with braziers. As Dasumia strode between each pair of them, they burst spontaneously into flame. Delver and Ingrath were obviously having second thoughts about their royal night of passion; El could clearly hear them gulping as they slowed and had to be dragged along by Dasumia.

There were pews on either side of the aisle, some of them occupied by slumped skeletons in robes, others by mummified or still-rotting corpses. El ducked into an empty row, crouching low to the floor; he knew what must be coming.

"No!" Ingrath cried suddenly, twisting free of the queen's grasp and whirling around to flee. He moaned despairingly, an instant before Delver tore free of the chain of coins, began his own sprint—and screamed.

The two helmed horrors had been floating right behind them, gauntleted hands out and ready to close on their throats. Those steely fingers beckoned to them now, as the empty helms leaned horribly closer.

Moaning in despair, the two guardsmen turned back to face the queen. Dasumia was lying on the altar, propped up on one elbow and wearing rather less than she'd entered the temple with. Laughingly she beckoned them.

Reluctantly, the two warriors stumbled forward.

Ten

TO TASTE DARK FIRE

The best thing an archmage can do with his spells? Use them to destroy another archmage, of course—and himself in the doing. We'll plant something useful in the ashes.

Radishes, perhaps.

Albryngundar of the Singing Sword
from **Thoughts On A Better Faerûn**
published circa The Year of the Lion

Unseen drums boomed and rolled, beginning an inexorable, unhurried beat that shook the temple. El watched narrowly as a large hand of Bane—a trifle taller than a man and seemingly carved of some black stone—rose into view behind the altar block. A halo of wispy red flames rose and fell around its fingers, and by their flickering light, as Dasumia leaped lightly back down from the altar, Elminster saw two long, metal-barbed black whips lying crossed upon the altar where she'd been lying.

The drumbeats quickened very slightly. Seeking a better view, El drew up the hood of his robes to hide his

face in its cowl and slowly rose into a seated position
on his pew, becoming just another slumped form among
the many corpses. His decaying neighbors were no
doubt onetime victims of rituals here. Delver and
Ingrath—and one Elminster, too, for that matter—
might well soon join them, if the Court Mage of Galadorna didn't act with precise timing and do just the
right things in the moments just ahead.

The two warriors stood facing Dasumia, and they
were trembling with fear. She took their hands and
spoke to them. The words were lost to El in the sound
of the drums, but she was obviously reassuring them.
From time to time she embraced or kissed them, ignoring—as they could not—the hulking helmed horrors
floating just behind their shoulders.

The queen turned, took up the whips, and handed one
to each man. Leaning back against the altar, she snapped
a command to them and held up her hands toward the
dark, unseen ceiling in a gesture of summoning.

With great reluctance they swung the whips in her
direction—with no force, so the barbed lengths simply
brushed against her and bounced off harmlessly. Elminster heard Dasumia's angry order this time: "Strike!
Strike or die!"

She held up her hands in a summoning once more, and
the whips lashed out at her in earnest this time. Her body
jerked under the blows, and a wisp of blue silk fell away.
She hissed encouragement to Ingrath and Delver, who
struck harder, their whips cracking. A lash wrapped
around her, baring one of her breasts.

At their next blows, the first weals marked Dasumia, and she groaned at them to strike harder still. The
guardsmen obeyed tentatively at first. Then with spirit
as she shouted at them to strike ever harder, staring
up at them as she had more than once overwhelmed
Elminster with her will.

Delver and Ingrath reeled, then bent to their task,
putting all their fear of dying here and resentment at

her entrapping them behind each blow. Blood-drenched blue silk and smooth flesh beneath rapidly vanished under a rain of blows from whips that glistened dark with blood.

Abruptly Dasumia threw back her head and howled at them to stop. Delver, weeping hysterically, failed to do so—and the helmed horror behind him snaked out a gauntlet and caught his arm in a grip that halted his frantic flailing in mid-swing.

She looked more like a beast skinned for the roasting spit than a naked woman, now, but as Dasumia drew her arms down and put her hands on her hips to explain the next part of the ritual, she might have been imperiously gowned and giving orders to kneeling courtiers. She showed no trace of pain despite the blood coursing down her limbs, moving easily and with her usual wanton sway of the hips as she ordered Ingrath onto the altar, to lie on his back.

Anger was rising in Elminster. Anger and revulsion. He had to do something. He had to make this stop.

El tried to recall what he'd once heard a drunken worshiper of Bane say about this sort of ritual. Sacrifices being cut to death by priests flailing with sharp swords, was it? Or a floating Hand of Bane crushing sacrifices in its grip . . . aye, that was it.

Dasumia had mounted the guardsman on the altar and was crying out, "Strike! Strike!" to Delver, who was moving reluctantly forward with his whip to obey her, when El knew he could watch no longer.

The whip cracked down, trailing blood at each swing, and El found himself tingling with rage and with risen power—power throbbing at his very fingertips.

He was a Chosen of Mystra, however hazily he recalled what that had meant. "Mystra," he murmured, "guide me."

However evil his Lady Master had turned out to be, he could not watch her blood raining down any longer while he did nothing, and two good men drew closer and closer to their deaths. That black hand behind the altar would slowly rise, then reach out to crush them—as it was moving now!

Horrified, Elminster reached out with his will, using the one spell he could unleash without speaking or moving. Hopefully he could remain an anonymous corpse for a few moments more. He moved not against the hand—that would come next—but to disable the foes who were sure to come diving down on him the moment he was discovered. He could feel the webwork of linkages, now, coursing out from the altar. With infinite care he detached one linkage from a helmed horror, shifting it to a section of ceiling beyond the floating thing rather than severing it outright. If he could get one step further before being discovered. . . .

Dasumia stiffened and sat up, ignoring the continuing bite of the lash. She glared around the temple, seeking the intruder. El shrugged and broke the bindings of the second helmed horror with savage abruptness.

Dark and terrible eyes bored into him. Then, slowly, Dasumia's lips twisted into a smile. She sat back on the altar, reclining again on one elbow with an air of amusement, and watched him.

Silently, their limbs jerking, Delver and Ingrath began to shuffle toward Elminster. Obviously in thrall, they thrust the bloody whips they carried back over their shoulders, ready for the first lashing strike. The barbs that had so mutilated Dasumia glistened red with her blood as the guardsmen lurched nearer . . . and nearer. . . .

El's shearing spell was still active, and he was loathe to spend another magic when the duel of his life was waiting, sneering at him up on the altar. Yet what good would it do to break her thrall upon the warriors, when with another spell—no doubt to her a trifling magic— she could restore it?

Delver and Ingrath stumbled stiffly nearer, their faces locked and impassive, their eyes horrified and rolling, pleading with him for aid or mercy or release. . . .

El snapped the linkages that controlled them with brutal force. Ignoring their suddenly spasming bodies and uncontrolled spitting and ululating, he rode the shock of the magical backlash into their minds, feeling the same pain they did. It was he who cried out in agony—but they toppled bonelessly to the floor, senseless.

It had worked. El discovered he'd bitten his lip. He shot a glance at the altar, but Dasumia hadn't moved. She was still reclining at her ease, soundlessly laughing—and the blood and whip cuts were fading from her skin, melting away as if they'd never been.

El drew in a deep breath and glanced behind him to be sure there were no other helmed horrors, arriving Bane worshipers, or any other menace that might strike from behind. He found nothing. He thought he saw a movement among the corpses along the darkest row of pews, right at the back, but he could not be sure and could see nothing moving when he stared hard at that place. He dared not turn his back on Dasumia any longer.

Wheeling around, he found her still lying at ease on the altar, whole and healed now, her body quite bare. She laughed aloud, and El gritted his teeth against the rage now boiling up in his throat and with iron control worked his next magic with precision. Lady Master or no, he was going to bring that huge, hovering black hand of stone crashing down on the altar. He was—

The Hand resisted him utterly. Dasumia's laughter rose into real mirth as he snarled and strained to move it. He could feel the linkage, he could insinuate his will into its flows, to grasp at the magic—and it ignored him, remaining as rigid as an iron bar despite his best efforts to budge it. He was—he could . . . he could not.

As the Queen of Galadorna hooted at him, El abandoned the spell with a snarl and worked another magic, hiding his gestures from her, down below the back of the pew in front of him.

When he was ready, a seeming eternity later, he stood up and hurled his magic through her cruel laughter—

not at the deadly, beautiful woman on the altar, or at the altar itself, a stone block that positively throbbed with ebbing and flowing magic he could not hope to overmaster. The floor beneath one end of it, however. . . .

Flagstones heaved, buckled, and shattered into shards, their cracks louder than those the whip had made. The floor rippled like a wave of stone, sending slivers of stone clattering against the back wall of the temple, and suddenly subsided, opening a huge pit. There must be cellars down there his magic could shove the earth and stone into, to clear a space so swiftly.

Dasumia sprang calmly off the altar to land on her feet, facing him. She smiled approvingly, saluted him, then turned to watch as the altar block shivered, teetered, and tipped over, sliding into the chasm with a thunderous crash.

"Shattered . . . how destructive of you," Dasumia observed merrily. "Care to destroy anything else?"

In grim, wordless answer Elminster snatched a stall-plate from the end of his pew and broke it across his knee, cracking the hand of Bane. Dying enchantments spat black sparks. He cast its wooden shards onto the floor and reached for the next plate.

Dasumia laughed. "So, has it come to a duel between us two at last, brave Elminster? Are you ready to dare me at last?"

"No," Elminster almost whispered. "Have ye forgotten what I told ye, when first we met at the Riven Stone? I serve Mystra first . . . and *then* Dasumia . . . then Galadorna. Tell me: who does Dasumia serve first?"

Dasumia laughed again. "Choices have prices," she said almost merrily. "Prepare to pay yours."

Her hands rose in a simple gesture, and almost immediately Elminster felt a tightness in his throat, a choking feeling that grew steadily worse. His legs and hips seemed to shift under him, his clothes began to feel tight . . . then more than tight.

El struggled to rise, and saw that his fingers were becoming stubby, bloated things, like mismatched, mottled sausages. So was the rest of him. Clothing began to split and disintegrate then, with tearing sounds like whip strikes.

The shredded remnants of the mantle of Court Mage of Galadorna fell away in tatters as El wallowed about, trying to rise on legs that kept changing in length and thickness. Dasumia was howling with laughter as he fell over to one side or another, growing steadily larger until he was pressed tight against the pew in front of his own in a grip that grew steadily more viselike. He was as fat as two cart barrels now, and still growing. He tried to spin the gestures of another spell with fingers that dangled and wobbled and were as long as his forearm—a forearm that was now as broad as his chest had been, before it, too, had started growing. . . .

Then his own spell took hold, and the tightness was suddenly gone as the pews in front of him, behind him, and under him all tore free of the floor, trailing dust as they rose—and tumbling him onto the floor, a grotesque mass of sliding, many-folded flesh that lay on its back, panting. El heaved and struggled, gasping for breath, and managed to get over onto one side, facing his foe.

The moment he could see her, three pews flashed through the air at her under his grim bidding, like gigantic lances. Dasumia ducked, rolled, then back flipped, turned as she landed, and in the same motion flexed her magnificent legs and sprang. All three pews missed, crashing into the floating black hand with a splintering fury that shook the room. One of the fingers broke off the hand, leaking magical radiances as it went.

Dasumia hissed something fast and harsh—and almost instantly El found himself rising into the air. Up and up he rose, uncontrollably, trying to see what was where around the temple as he went. Was she going to lift him and drop him, or—?

El caught sight of something lying in the aisle and got an idea. He worked the spell he needed in furious haste, knowing that a bruising impact with the cob-webbed stone ceiling was coming up fast.

He finished the spell just in time to throw one arm up in front of his face and turn his nose aside before slamming hard into the ceiling—sending startled bats screeching away in a wild flapping of wings—and find-ing that her magic was still pressing on him, pinning him against the dank stone.

He scrabbled with his arms and elbows, trying to roll over so he could see Dasumia—and not dark, dirty stone an inch from his eyelashes. He needed to be able to see, to work the spell he'd cast.

Grunting and gasping, he managed to roll his pon-derous bulk over in time to see a tightly smiling Dasumia magically raise one of the shattered pews he'd hurled at her into the air—and send it right back at him.

Larger and larger it loomed as El scrambled along the ceiling trying to get out of its way, using his great bulk to catch and kick at vault ribs that would have been ten feet or more out of his reach if he'd been his proper size . . . El tried to concentrate on his own spell, down below, and ignore the oncoming pew.

He never saw the slim, dark-robed figure that stood up in the back pew to take calm, careful aim at him, fix his position in mind, then begin to cast its own deadly spell.

As El moved, the pew curved in the air to follow, Dasumia's smile broadening with anticipatory glee at the coming impact. The end that would strike Elmin-ster was a splayed mass of jagged wooden splinters, most of them as long as a man was tall.

Dasumia took three swift steps sideways to get a better look at the situation—and that was all El need-ed. He rolled over a roof vault, wheezing like some great aerial whale, and in its lee called on his spell. Two whips rose from the aisle like eager, awakened snakes, to pounce on the Queen of Galadorna.

As the pew struck the ceiling with a crash that sent him bouncing off the ceiling tiles amid showers of dust, El had a brief glimpse of Dasumia's startled face as bloodied black leather whipped around one wrist and jerked down, throwing her onto her back. She struck her head on the floor and cried out in pain—and that was all the time the two whips needed. The wrist that had dragged her down was bound fast to her ankle, the other whip did the same on her other side, and one whip slapped its handle across her eyes, blinding her with tears, while the other thrust its handle into her open mouth, effectively gagging her.

Most of the pew broke away and showered the temple below with shards of wood as the gigantic missile cartwheeled away from the roof vault. Ilbryn Starym didn't even have time to flee as the rest of the pew plunged into the pew right in front of where he was sitting, sending riven wood in all directions and hurling him helplessly into the air, tumbling head over heels in the midst of his own conjured ball of magical flames to strike the back wall of the temple with a crash. He slid slowly and brokenly down that wall, his screams fading.

Abruptly El found himself plummeting to the ground. He grinned savagely; this must mean Dasumia was either falling unconscious or abandoning her spell in favor of something desperate. He sent the whips an urgent command to thrust their captive aloft, so he could give her the same sort of fall if she overcame him, or his own landing was too . . . hard.

Gods! El knew bones had shattered, even before he rolled over like some sort of agonized elephant and tried to scramble to his feet. Scrambling didn't work, but he did get upright by throwing his great bulk to one side, then trying to climb it with his clumsy legs. He got himself turned around in time to see his whips suddenly swinging empty, their captive gone from their entangling midst.

A moment later, a cold, cold pain slid into his side and out again, and he knew where she'd gone. He didn't bother to try to turn and face her, just to see a sword dripping with his own blood and to give her a better target to stab at, but concentrated on ignoring the pain and calling up another spell. The blade slid into him once more, but El knew his great bulk kept him safe from her slitting his throat—she couldn't reach it without so much climbing that he'd be able to simply topple over onto her to win this fight forever. He threw himself backward and heard her startled curse and the clangor of a dropped sword bouncing on stone. Now he did start to turn, heaving himself around. If the blade was close enough, he could throw himself on it and bury it.

He met Dasumia's startled eyes—and she brought one hand to her mouth, glanced down at the sword lying so close to him—and vanished, just moments before El completed his spell.

It was a blood magic incantation. El threw back his head and shrieked at the pain. As the magic healed his wounds, it felt like fire raging through his gigantic body— fire that flared, raged, then swiftly faded as the healing neared completion. It could also teleport him to wherever his freshly shed blood might be—on the floor beneath him, on the sword mere feet away . . . and on the hands of the queen, wherever she might be!

The spell flashed, the temple around him twisted, and he was suddenly behind the altar, where a crouching Dasumia was looking up at him in startled surprise. He reached out to clutch at her should she try to flee, and threw himself off-balance so as to fall on her. Dasumia back flipped again, her heels grazing the floating Black Hand of Bane—and El crashed down inches away from her frantically rolling form. He grabbed at her, but couldn't reach, and was still huffing and wallowing and trying to pivot his great bulk around so that his bloated and deformed arm could reach her when she fetched up against the back wall of the temple and cast another spell, favoring him with a catlike smile of triumph.

Something flashed. El turned his head in time to see one of the floating helmed horrors flow and twist, breaking apart into a whirling sphere of jagged metal shards—shards that came out of their dance in a stream that leaped right at him.

El threw one ponderous arm up in front of his eyes and throat, and with the other grabbed blindly, felt Dasumia's struggling form, closed his grasp mercilessly, and hauled her like a rag doll back up in front of him as a shield.

As searing shards cut into him in three places or more, El heard Dasumia gasp, a sound that was cut off sharply. When he lowered his shielding arm, he saw that she was biting her lip, blood trailing down her chin and eyes closed in her contorted face. Jagged shards had transfixed her in a dozen places, and she was shuddering. The blue-white motes of magic leaking from her might be contingencies . . . or might be something else. As he watched, a shard drooped, dangled, then broke off and fell, visibly smaller. Another seemed to be melting into her, and another—gods!

The sudden pain made Elminster drop his foe. Her ravaged body fell onto his great bulk—and the real pain began. A burning . . . smoke was rising from where she lay sprawled on his mounded flesh, and she was slowly sinking.

Acid! She'd turned her blood to acid, and it was eating away at him and at the shards. Well, the watching gods knew he'd spare flesh in plenty to lose, but he had to get clear of her. He snatched at her, threw her as hard as he could at the floating Hand of Bane, and had the satisfaction of seeing her strike it limply and stick for a moment before her own weight peeled her free, to fall from view behind the altar. Wisps of smoke curled up from the hand as a little left-behind acid ate at it, too.

El sat back grimly and sighed. Unconscious she might be, but he lacked the strength to crush her. Perhaps if he pushed her into the pit and shouldered those two loose pews into it on top of her . . .

Nay, he could not be so cruel. And so, when she awakened, Elminster Aumar would die. He was almost out of spells and still trapped in this grotesquely enlarged form, probably unable to fit through the passages that had brought him here. He could do little more to stop the evil Lady Master whom Mystra had sent him to serve. Her magic overmatched his, as his outstripped that of a novice. She would make a magnificent and able servant of Mystra, a better Chosen than he, if she were only biddable enough to obey anyone.

He shut his eyes against the banner of Bane and called up a mental image of the blue-white star of Mystra. "Lady of Mysteries," he said aloud, his voice echoing in the now-silent temple, "one who has been thy servant cries to ye in his need. I have failed thee, and failed in my service to the one called Dasumia, but see in her strength that could well serve thee in my place. Succor this Dasumia, I pray, and—"

Sudden, searing cold shocked him into an inarticulate cry. He could feel himself trembling uncontrollably as magic stronger than he'd ever felt before surged through him. Numbly he waited for whatever killing strike Dasumia would deal him, but it did not come. Instead, a warmth gently grew within the ice, and he felt himself relaxing, even as a strange crawling sensation swept over him. He was healed, he was growing smaller and lighter and himself again, and a face that he could barely see through flooding tears was bending over him.

Then he heard a voice speaking to him tenderly, a voice that belonged to the Queen of Galadorna but no longer held the cold cruelty of Dasumia. "So you pass the test, Elminster Aumar, and remain the first and dearest of my Chosen—even if your brains are too addled to recognize when a ritual of Bane is being perverted, bringing pleasure to his altar instead of pain, and shedding the blood of someone willing." A fond and musical laugh followed, then the words, "I am proud, this night."

Gentle arms enfolded him, and Elminster cried out in wonder as he felt himself lifted up, in a soaring flight that should have smashed them both into the ceiling but did not, reaching high and clear into the stars instead.

*   *   *   *   *

The roof of the House of the Unicorn burst apart, towers toppling, as a column of silver fire roared up into the night. As men on the battlements screamed and cursed, something chill and chiming that had been coiled hungrily around a spire close by their heads fled in a misty parabola, to drift away low over the streets of Nethrar, cowering in the night.

*   *   *   *   *

Silver fire danced on dark water, throwing feeble reflections onto purple-bordered tapestries of deepest black. High on those tapestries, in purple thread, were worked their sole adornments: cruel, somehow feminine smiles.

The inky waters of the scrying font rippled, and the scene of silver fire soaring up out of a castle was gone.

Someone close above the water said excitedly, "You saw? I know how we can use this."

"Tell me!" a cold voice snapped, sharp with excitement, then in lower tones, in another direction, said more calmly, "Cancel the Evenflame service. We'll be busy—and undisturbed, mark you, Sister Night—until further notice."

*   *   *   *   *

And so it was that Galadorna lost its queen and its
court mage in the same night, less than a tenday before
the armies of Laothkund rolled down from the tree-girt
hills to set Nethrar ablaze, and shatter the Unicorn Kingdom forever.

BOOK TWO

SUNRISE ON A DARK ROAD

Eleven

MOONRISE, FROSTFIRE,
AND DOOM

Adventurers are best used to slay monsters. Sooner or later, they become your worst monsters, and you have to hire new ones to do the obvious thing.
Ralderick Hallowshaw, Jester
from **To Rule A Realm, From Turret To Midden**
published circa The Year of the Bloodbird

"Seems peaceful enough, don't it?" the warrior rumbled, looking around from the height of his saddle at the forest of hiexel, blueleaf, and gnarled old phandar trees that flanked both sides of the road. Birds called in the distant depths of its shade gloom, and small furry things scuttled here and there among the dead leaves that carpeted its mossy stumps and mushroom-studded dead falls. Golden shafts of sunlight stabbed down into the forest here and there, lighting little clearings where shrubs fought each other for the light, and the moss-draped creepers were fewer.

"Don't say such foolhead things, Arvas," one of his companions growled. "They sound all too much like the sort of cues ambushing brigands like to follow. That sentence of yours sounds like something that should end with an arrow taking you in the throat—or the chunk of road your charger's standing on rising up to be revealed as the head of some awakened titan or other."

"I'll take the 'or other,' you merry-faced killjoy," Arvas grunted. "I just meant I don't see claw-sharpening marks on trees, bloodstains . . . that sort of thing—which should make you even more cheerful."

"You can be sure the High Duke didn't hire us to block the Starmantle road while we argue about things I'd rather other ears didn't hear about," a deeper voice said sharply. "Arvas, Faldast—stow it!"

"Paeregur," Arvas said in weary tones, "have you looked up and down this road recently? Do you see anyone—*anyone*—but us? Block the road from what, may I ask? Since the deaths began, travel seems to have just about stopped along here. Possibly about the same time you got this funny idea into your head that you're somehow entitled to give the rest of us orders! Was it that new armor, the heavy helm pressing hard on your brains? Or was it the new thrusting codpiece with the—"

"Arvas, *enough!*" said someone else, in exasperation. "Gods, it's like having a babbling drunk riding with us."

"Rolian," his halfling comrade said, from somewhere below the level of the humans' belts, "it is having a babbling drunk riding with us!"

There was a general roar of laughter—even echoed, albeit sarcastically, by Arvas himself—and the Frostfire Banner urged their mounts into a trot. They all wanted to find a good defensible place to camp before dark, or have time to get back to Starmantle if no such site offered itself, and it wouldn't be all that many hours, now, before the shadows grew long and the sun bright and low.

High Duke Horostos styled himself lord over the rich farmlands west of Starmantle, along a forested cliff of a coast that offered few harbors (and no good ones). As realms went, it was a quiet and safe land, plagued by the usual owlbears and stirges from time to time, the odd band of brigands, thieving peddlers; small problems that a few armsmen and foresters with good bows could handle.

Lately, it seemed, at about the time the worst winter snows ended and folk considered the useful part of the Year of the Awakening Wyrm to have begun, the High Duchy of Langalos had somehow acquired a big problem.

Something that left no tracks, but killed at will—passing merchants, woodcutters, farmers, livestock, and alert war bands of the Duke's best armsmen alike. Even a high-ranking priest of Tempus, traveling with a large mounted and well-armed bodyguard, had gone missing somewhere along the wooded road west of Starmantle, and was thought to have fallen afoul of the mysterious slayer. Could this be the "Awakening Wyrm" of the prophecies?

Perhaps, but hired griffon-riders flying over the area had found no sign of large caves, scorched or broken trees or any other marks of large beasts . . . or any sign of brigands or their encampments, for that matter. Nor had the few foresters who still dared to venture anywhere near the trees seen anything—and one by one, these were disappearing too. Their reports told of a land that seemed barren of any beast so large as a fox or hare; the game trails were grown over with ferns.

So the High Duke had reluctantly opened his coffers while he still had subjects to tax and refill them and had hired the classic solution: a band of adventurers—in this case, hireswords who'd been thrown out of service to wealthy Tethyrians for a variety of reasons, and gathered as the Frostfire Banner to seek their fortunes in more easterly lands, where their past indiscretions would be less well known.

The money offered by Horostos was both good and needed. The Banner were ten in all, and numbered among their ranks a pair apiece of mages and warrior-priests, yet they went warily. This was unfamiliar country to them—but death knows all lands, intimately and often.

So it was that cocked but unloaded crossbows hung across several saddles, though it was bad for the strings, and no one rode carelessly. The forest stayed lovely—and deserted.

"No stags," Arvas grunted once, and his companions, nodding their replies, realized how silent they'd fallen. Waiting for the blow to fall.

A goodly way west of Starmantle the road looped around and beneath an exposed spur of rock, an outcropping that pointed out to sea and upward like the prow of some great buried ship. Once the sun sank low and the Banner knew they had to turn around, they settled on the rocky prow as their camp.

"Yon's as good a place as the gods provide, short of bare hilltops. One to watch along the road and down the cliffs, and two to face the forest along the neck of it, here, tie up our horses below and be-damned to anyone trying to use the road by night, and we're set," Rolian grunted.

Paeregur gave a wordless grunt as his only answer. The tone of that grunt sounded unconvinced. The silence of fear hung heavy over the camp that night, and evenfeast was eaten in hushed tones.

"We're as close to death as we've ever been," the halfling muttered as they rolled themselves in their cloaks, laid weapons to hand, and watched the stars come out over the water.

"Will you belt up about dying?" Rolian hissed. "No one can come at us unseen, we've set a heavy watch, the dippers and the shields are ready for a fast wakening . . . what more can we do?"

"Ride out of here and go back to Tethyr," Avras said quietly—yet the camp had grown so still that most of them heard him. Several heads turned, wearing scowls . . . but no one said a word in reply.

Overhead, as deep night came down, the stars began to come out in earnest.

* * * * *

"What's that?" Rolian breathed, beside Paeregur's ear. "D'you hear it?"

"Of course I hear it," the warrior replied quietly, rising silently to his feet and turning slowly, his drawn blade glinting in the light of the new-risen moon. He could hear it best to the west, somewhere very close by, a thin, aimless chiming sound. A bridle? A bell on a minstrel's instrument, or on the harness of a wayward horse? Or—the little fey ones, come calling?

After a moment he took a few cautious crouching steps across the rock spur, picking his way between the still forms of his sleeping fellows. A thin thread of mist was drifting in the lee of the rock spur—strange, that, with the moon rising—but there was nothing to be seen. Not even seabirds, or an owl. In fact, that was why this was so eerie—the woods were still. No scuffling, no night cries or the shrieks of small animals being caught by larger prowlers . . . nothing. Paeregur shook his head in puzzlement, and turned slowly to go back. There it was again, that faint chiming.

He turned back to the west again and became a listening statue. After a time the chiming was gone. The tall warrior shrugged, glanced down at the horses below the prow—and froze.

Where were the horses? He took two quick strides to the other side of the prow, in case they'd all shifted to the east of the overhang—their lead-reins were long enough—but, no. They were gone. "Rolian," he growled, beckoning sharply, and ran along the prow to its very tip, where the still, cowled form of Avras sat facing out to sea, his sword across his knees. Hah! Some watch guard he'd turned out to be!

"Avras!" he hissed, clapping a heavy hand on the warrior's shoulder, "where are the horses? If you've been drinking again, so help me I'm g—"

The shoulder under his hand crumpled like a thing of dry leaves and kindling, and the faceless husk of Avras pivoted toward him for a moment before collapsing into ash. The man's skull tumbled out to bounce off Paeregur's boot before falling out and down to the road below with a dull clatter.

Paeregur almost fell off the spur recoiling in horror. Then he scrambled back along it to the first of his sleeping companions, and turned the blankets back with the point of his blade. A skull grinned up at him.

"Gods," he sobbed, slashing with his sword tip at the next cloak. His blade caught on the garment and dragged it half off; bones spilled out in a confusion of ash and collapse. Paeregur knew real gut-wrenching terror for the first time in his life. He wanted to run, anywhere, away from here.

Rolian was taking a damned long time to arrive.

Paeregur glanced along the spur to where Rolian had been sitting beside him, facing the forest—had been whispering to him, only a few breaths ago. Where had—?

The chiming, coming again—only this time, from among the wall of dark trees they'd been facing—sounded almost mocking. A little mist was curling around their trunks, and Rolian—

Rolian was standing in those trees with his sword in the crook of his arm and the laces of his codpiece in his hands, in the eternal wide-legged pose of men relieving themselves in the woods, facing away into the darkness. Paeregur started to relax, then fresh fear coiled in the pit of his stomach. Rolian was standing very still. Too still.

"Frostfire *awake!*" Paeregur roared, with all the volume he could muster; the very rocks rang back his shout, and an echo came back faintly from the depths of the forest. He was running as he bellowed, back along the spine of the spur toward Rolian . . . already knowing what he'd find.

He came to a stop behind that still form and tried to peer past it. Fangs? Eyes? Waiting blades? Nothing; the moonlight was enough to show him nothing but trees. He stretched out his sword gently. "Rolian?"

The warrior gave a long, formless sigh as he toppled forward into the trees. He broke into three pieces before he hit the ground, his blade bouncing away among dead leaves . . . and left Paeregur staring at a pair of empty boots and a tangle of slumped clothing. Ye bloody grave-sucking gods!

The tall warrior took two quick steps back from that place and spun around. Was he the only one left alive? Had any—but no. He almost shouted with relief: the mage Lhaerand was on his feet, face pinched with sleepy disapproval, as was the giant among them, slow-witted but loyal Phostral, his full plate armor make him a gleaming mountain in the moonlight. Two. Two of them all.

"Something has killed all the others," Paeregur told them tightly. "Something that can slay in a moment, and silently."

"Oh?" Lhaerand snarled. "Then what's that?"

It was the chiming again, only loud and insistent now, as if standing in triumph over them. Suddenly the mist was back, sliding past their feet and bringing its own chill with it as it drifted along the spur. Paeregur's eyes narrowed.

"Lhaerand," he said suddenly, "can you hurl fire?"

"Yes, of course," the mage snapped. "At who? I—"

"*At that!*" Paeregur shouted, fear making his voice almost a scream. "*Now!*"

And as if it could hear his words, the mist thickened into bright smoke, and struck, snakelike, at Phostral. The giant warrior had raised his blade and moved to challenge it even before Paeregur's cry; his companions could only see his back, and hear a faint sighing—was that a sizzle, at the heart of it? A gurgle?—in the instant before his blade fell from his hand. The gauntlet went with it, and nothing was left behind: the vambrace ended in a stump. Then, slowly, Phostral turned to face his companions.

His helm was empty, his head entirely burnt away, but something was filling it or at least holding it where it should be, above the armored wall of the warrior's chest. The thing that had been Phostral staggered toward them, moving slowly and tentatively. The mage stepped back and started to stammer out a spell.

Instantly the gigantic armored form turned toward him and toppled, crashing down on its face—or where its face had been—as a white whirlwind boiled up out of it, chiming. Paeregur shouted in fear, waving his sword and knowing it would avail him nothing—but Lhaerand shrieked and sprinted the length of the spur, with the mist-thing in cold and chiming pursuit.

The mage never tried to turn and fight. He ran as fast as he could and leaped, high and far, out over the road to somewhere above the cliffs beyond—where he howled all the way down to a wet and splintering end.

So that was a despairing death. Paeregur swallowed. What better would a heroic one be?

And how would any minstrel know, once he was bones and ash?

The whirlwind came back along the spur slowly, chiming almost coyly—as if it was toying with him.

The tall warrior set his jaw and raised his sword. When he judged the mist was near enough, he slashed at it and danced to one side, then planted himself to drive a vicious backhand back through its chiming whiteness.

Unsurprisingly, his blade met nothing, though its edge seemed to acquire a line of sparks. Even as he noticed them, in his frantic trot along the spur, they winked out.

He circled, tripping on someone's helm and almost falling, to lash out with his blade again. Once more he clove nothing, gasped his way aside from looming mist, and slashed through it again with the same utter lack of effect. The mist swirled, leaping over his head, and he dodged aside to avoid having it fall on him. It continued its sinuous rush, curving around his vainly thrusting blade to dart in along his sword arm.

At the last instant, it turned into him rather than grazing past—and blazing agony exploded through him. Paeregur was dazedly aware that he was screaming and staggering away vainly slapping at empty air with his arm.

His only arm.

Nothing remained on the other side but a twisted mass of seared flesh and leather, all melted together. There was no blood . . . but there was no arm left at all. His sword arm. Paeregur looked wildly about as the ribbon of mist floated almost mockingly past, and saw his sword lying atop a huddled mess that had once been a priest of Tymora. Much good Lady Luck had brought them all, to be sure. He ran unsteadily, not used to one side of him being a lot lighter than the other, over to his blade and scooped it up.

He was still straightening when the burning pain came again and he fell heavily onto his tailbone on the rock, watching an empty boot spin away. It had taken his leg.

He struggled to rise, to move at all, his remaining boot heel kicking vainly against the uneven stone, and waved his blade defiantly. The mist closed in and he made of himself a desperate whirlwind, spinning around and around with his blade constantly slashing the air. He rang it off the stone around him twice, once hard enough to chip the edge, and cared not. He was going to die here . . . what good is a pristine blade to a dead man?

The mist came at him again in an almost gloating dive, its chiming rising around him as he twisted and slashed desperately. When the burning came again, it was in his intact thigh and he was rolling helplessly over, flailing at nothing with his useless sword. One limb at a time—it *was* toying with him.

Was he going to be reduced to a helpless torso, unable to do anything but stare as it slew him very slowly?

A few panting breaths later, as he stared up at the uncaring stars through swimming eyes, he knew the answer was going to be—yes.

He wondered just how long the mist would make him suffer, then decided he was past caring. Almost his last thought was a rueful realization that all who die slowly enough to know what is happening must come to a place beyond caring.

He was . . . he was Paeregur Amaethur Donlas, and he had come to his cold end here on a rock in the wilderlands of the accursed High Duchy of Langalos in the early summer of the year seven hundred and sixtyseven (as Dalereckoning ran) with no one to mourn or mark his passing, and his dead comrades all around him.

Well, have my thanks, all you vigilant gods.

Paeregur's last thought was that he really should remember the name of that star . . . and that one, too. . . .

*   *   *   *   *

The Crypt of the Moondark family was overgrown with brambles, creepers, and contorted, curving trees deformed by warding enchantments that were still strong after centuries. The Moondark house, a happy mingling of elf and human blood, had been known for its fell sorcery, but no Moondarks had walked Faerûn for something like one hundred and sixteen winters . . . and Westgate was quite content about that. No more powerful spells that might challenge a king or discomfit self-styled nobles, and no more need to be polite to half-bloods who were graceful, handsome, learned, bright, all too merry—and all too insistent on fairness and honesty in ruling. There was even a sign, much more recent than the spell-locked gates: "Behold the ending of all who insist too much."

Elminster smiled grimly at that little moral notice. It was the first thing to crumble into dust at the touch of his most powerful spell. The long-untested wards beyond were the next thing. Dawn was almost upon Westgate, and he wanted to be safely inside the tomb-house before folk took to the streets.

The guards at the corner were still yawning and dozing against the outer wall of the crypt as Elminster slipped inside. On his short walk along the statue-flanked path to the doors of the pillared tomb house, El's magic burnt away an astonishing number of magical triggers and traps. An odd thing for one in the service of Mystra to practice . . . but then Mystra dealt in a healthy array of "odd things." What he was here to do was one of his most important tasks as a Chosen, one he spent a lot of time at these days. One that seemed to awaken an almost girlish glee in the Lady of Mysteries.

Elminster Aumar would do anything to see her smiling so.

The door wards, falling beam trap, and weave-of-jutting-blades traps were all to be expected, were anticipated, and were dealt with in but a few seconds. The fact that folk from time to time had to enter a family tomb for legitimate purposes—burials, not thefts—meant that such defenses had to be of a lesser order. In a matter of a few calm breaths Elminster was inside the dark chamber, with the door shut and spell-sealed behind him, and a radiance of his own making awakening everywhere along the low, cobwebbed ceiling.

Moondarks lay crumbling on all sides of him in stacked stone coffers that must have numbered nearly a hundred. The oldest ones were the largest, carved with ornate scenes along the sides, their lids effigies of the deceased; the more recent ones were plain stone boxes, some lacking even names. Thankfully none were stirring in undeath; he was running late as it was and never liked to hurry the fun part.

The bright and wealthy Moondarks had even been considerate enough to leave a funeral slab in the center of the crypt—a high table on which the coffin of the most recently dead could lie during a last service of remembrance, before it was muscled onto one of the stacks of the dead that lined the walls, to be left undisturbed forever. Or at least until a clever Chosen of Mystra happened along.

Elminster hummed a tune of lost Myth Drannor as he laid out his cloak on the empty slab—a large but nondescript lined leather cloak that wasn't much of any color anymore and sported more than the usual assortment of patches. The inside of the cloak bore several large, crude pockets, though they seemed flat and empty as El patted them affectionately then turned away to wander around the chamber peering at dark corners, particular caskets, and even the underside of the funeral slab.

When he returned from his stroll, he slid his fingers into an upper pocket and drew forth a lacing-wrapped flask full of an amber liquid. Holding it up, he murmured, "Mystra, to thee, as always. A pale shadow of the fire of thy touch." A long, gasping pull later, El stoppered the flask, sighed contentedly, and put it away again—in a pocket that still looked empty.

He dug in the next empty pocket with both hands and drew forth a wand in a shabby, almost crumbling wyvernskin case. He'd spent two careful spells and a lot of running around trailing the case along the rough stone blocks of an old castle wall getting the case to look this elderly. He was even prouder of the wand, discolored by decades of handling that he'd accomplished in a few minutes with goose grease, sand, and soot. Now, Eaergladden Moondark had died destitute, begging his

kin for a few coppers with which to buy a roasting-fowl
. . . but who save one Elminster was still alive to
remember that? So accomplished a mage as Eaergladden could quite well have had a wand, and of course a
spellbook—El reached back into the empty pocket and
pulled forth a worn and bulky tome with huge, much-
battered brass corners—that he hadn't sold in his last
year of life, after all. Not to mention the usual dagger
enchanted so as not to rust or go dull, and to glow upon
command; these enchantments were made to last, say,
three centuries by a hire-cast elven longlook spell, from
one of the poorer Myth Drannan apprentices. Aye, so.

El calmly lifted the lid of Eaergladden's casket, murmured, "Well met, Master Mage of the Moondarks,"
and gently laid the wand, dagger, and spellbook in the
proper places around the mummified skeleton that had
been Eaergladden. Then he closed the casket and went
back to the cloak for a few scrolls—on carefully aged
parchment—and a battered little book of magical observations, copied runes, and half-finished spells that
should lead even a half-wit to the creation of a spell
that would temporarily imbue the non-magically gifted
with the ability to carry and cast a spell placed in them
by a mage.

This work took up much of his time in the service of
Mystra, these days; at her bidding, Elminster traveled
Faerûn visiting ruins and the tombs of dead mages,
planting "old" scrolls, spellbooks, minor enchanted
items, and even the occasional staff for later folk to
find—and all such leavings were in truth items he'd
just finished crafting, and made to look old. Almost
always, part of the treasures he left for others includ-
ed notes that should lead anyone with a gift for magic
to experiment and successfully create a "new" spell.

Mystra cared not overmuch who found these magics,
or how they used them—so long as ever more magic
was in use and ever more folk could wield it, rather
than a few archwizards lording it over the spell-poor or

magically barren, as had happened in the days of lost
Netheril. El loved this sort of work and always had to
fight a tendency to linger in the ruins and crypts, mis-
chievously letting his lights and spell-effects be seen
by others, to lure exploring adventurers toward his
leavings.

"About as subtle as an orc horde," Mystra had once
termed these tactics, pouting prettily, and El knew she
was right. Wherefore today he firmly took up his cloak,
worked the powerful spell Azuth had given him that
obliterated all traces or magical echoes of his visit, and
left in the form of a shadow. The thoughtful shadow
restored a few of the wards and traps in his wake before
he slipped back out onto the street, inches distant from
the back of a guard whose attention was on a gold coin
that seemed to have fallen from the sky moments
before. Unnoticed, the shadow turned solid and strolled
away.

The cloaked, hawk-nosed figure had been gone from
sight around a corner for exactly the time it took to
draw in a single good, deep breath when a dark horse
came trotting through the steady stream of walking
folk and clopped to a halt in front of the guard.

That worthy looked up, raising an eyebrow in both
query and challenge, to see a young, maroon-robed elf
in a rich cloak peering down at the coin in the guard's
weathered palm.

The guard closed his fingers around it hastily and
said, "Aye? What d'you want, outlander?"

"Myth Drannan, was it not?" the elf asked softly.
"Found hereabouts?"

The guard flushed. "Paid to me fair and square, more
like," he rumbled.

The elf nodded, his gaze now lingering long and considering on the overgrown crypt the guard was standing duty in front of. The Moondarks . . . that bastard
house of dabbling mages. And all of them who'd found
their way home to die now shared a stone tomb-house,

such as humans favor. In good repair, by the looks of it, with its wards still up. It was closed up much too securely for inquisitive birds or scurrying squirrels to pluck up a gold coin and carry it outside the walls. His eyes narrowed, and his face grew as sharp as honed flint, causing the guard to warily raise his weapon and shrink back behind it.

Ilbryn Starym dropped the man a mirthless and absentminded smile and rode on toward the Stars and Sword.

Wizards who came to Westgate always stayed at the Sword, in hopes of being there when Alshinree wandered in and did her trance-dance. Alshinree was getting old and a bit gaunt, now; her dances weren't the affairs they'd once been, with the house crowded with hungrily staring men. Her dance, too, was usually just so much playacting and drunken mumbling . . . but sometimes, a little more often than once in a month, it happened. An entranced Alshinree uttered words of spells not known since Netheril fell, advice that might have come from the Lady of Mysteries herself, and detailed instructions as to the whereabouts, traps, and even contents of certain archmages' tombs, ruined schools of wizardry, sorcerous caches, and even long-forgotten abandoned temples to Mystra.

Bad things happened to mages who so much as spoke to Alshinree outside the Sword or who tried to coerce or pester her within its walls, so they contented themselves with booking rooms at the inn so often that some of them could be considered to have been living there. Even if a certain human mage—one Elminster, formerly Court Mage of Galadorna, before the fall of that realm—had not taken a room at the Sword, it held the best gathering of folk in Westgate who might just have seen him hereabouts or heard something of his deeds and current doings.

The hard looks thrown his way by every guard and many merchants he'd passed suddenly hit home; Ilbryn

blinked, looked all around, and found that he was gal-
loping his startled mount down the street, its hooves
slipping and sliding on the cobbles. He reined in and
settled the horse into a careful walk thereafter. The
bright, sparkling spell-animated sign of the Stars and
Sword loomed ahead, and the champion of Starym
honor steered his mount through the bustling folk to—
he hoped—some answers, or even the man he sought.

As he gathered the reins together in one hand to free
the other for the bellpull that would summon hostelers
to see to his horse, Ilbryn discovered that something he
carried in a belt-pouch had found its way into his hand,
and was now clenched there: a scrap of red cloth that
had been part of the mantle of office of the Court Mage
of Galadorna. Elminster's mantle.

The elf looked down at it, and although his hand
remained rock steady, his handsome face slowly slipped
into a stony, brooding mask. His eyes held such glittering menace that both hostelers recoiled and had to be
coaxed back.

As he swung himself down from the saddle and
reached for the handle of the Sword's finely carved front
door, Ilbryn Starym smiled softly.

And as one of the hostelers put it, "That were worse
than 'is glaring!"

Still smiling, Ilbryn put one hand—the one flickering with the risen radiance of a ready, deadly spell—
behind his back, and with the other opened the door
and went in.

The hostelers lingered, half-expecting to hear a ter-
rific crash, or smoke, or even bodies hurled out through
the windows . . . but their hoped-for entertainment
never came.

Twelve

THE EMPTY THRONE

It must bother most wizards a lot that for all their spells, they can't seize immortality. Many try to become gods, but few succeed. For this, let us all be very thankful.
Sambrin Ulgrythyn, Lord Sage of Sammaresh
from **The View From Stormwind Hill**
published circa The Year of the Gate

Far to the east of Westgate, even as a smiling elf slipped into an inn expecting trouble, a mist drifted through an old, deep forest.

It was a mist that sparkled and chimed as it went, moving purposefully through the trees. Sometimes it rose up into an almost humanoid, striding form, bulking tall, thick and strong; at other times it moved like an ever-leaping, undulating snake. No birds called in the shade around it, and nothing rustled in the dead leaves underfoot. Only its own whirling breezes stirred the creepers and tatters of hanging moss it wound its way through; silence ruled the forest it traversed.

This was no wonder; earlier chiming hungers had left not a creature alive in that part of the forest to witness its haste. The chiming mist had left the graveyard of the Frostfire Banner far behind, moving for miles along the deserted road to a place where most eyes would have missed the sapling-studded, overgrown remnants of a lane turning off into the woods.

The mist drifted along the dips and turns of that road, passing like eager smoke across crumbling stone bridges that took the road across rivulets, to the deep green place where the road ended . . . and the ruins began.

The lines of gigantic old trees flanking the overgrown road gave way to a litter of creeper-shrouded, sagging wagons and coaches. Beyond lay thickets, at their hearts overgrown mounds that had once been stables and cottages. Beyond the thickets rose shadow-tops so tall that their gloom choked away thickets and lay in endless shadow over the rotting ruin of a drawbridge across a deep, muddy cleft that had once been a moat . . . and the stone pillars or teeth within the moat, that had once been the stout buttresses of mostly fallen walls. Walls that had once frowned down on Faerûn from a great height, formed a massive keep.

The long-fallen fortress was more forest and tumbled stone, now, than a building. The mist moved purposefully through the tangle of leaning trees and creepers that grew in its inner spaces, as if it knew what chambers could be found where. As it went, the walls became taller. Here and there ceilings or roofing had survived, though all of the archways gaped open and doorless, and there were no signs that anyone—or anything—dwelt within.

The mist came to a gently chiming halt in a chamber that had once been large and grand indeed. Gaps in its walls showed the forest just outside, but there was still a ceiling, and even furniture. A rotting-canopied bed larger than many stable stalls, stood with ornate gilded bedposts and cloth of gold glinting among the green mildew-fur of its bedding. Close by stood a lounge, canted over where one leg had broken, and beyond that several stools were enthusiastically growing mushrooms. A little way farther on, across the cracked marble floor, a peeling, man-high oval mirror stood beside a sagging row of wardrobes. Water was dripping down onto what had once been a grand table in another part of the room—and beyond it, in the darkest, best-roofed rear of the chamber, stood a ring-shaped parapet. Within the knee-high circular wall was only deeper darkness . . . and when the mist began to move, it headed straight for this well.

As it approached, sudden flashes of light occurred in the air above the parapet.

The mist hesitated, rose a little higher, and ventured closer to the well.

The radiance reached for it, brightening, and was echoed by similar glows that crawled snakelike along the stone walls and the surrounding floor, outlining hitherto-invisible runes and symbols.

The mist danced for a moment among these flame-like tongues of silent light—then swooped, in a plunge that took it right down into the well. Elaborate traceries of magic flashed and flared into visibility for a moment as the mist arrowed past, seeming to lash and claw at it, but when it had disappeared down the well, these fading remnants of guardian spells lapsed into quiescence once more.

The shaft was a good distance across and fell straight down, a long and lightless way. It ended in a floor of uneven, natural stone—one end of a vast and dark natural cavern.

The mist moved into this velvet void with the confidence of someone who moves through utter darkness to a familiar spot. It chimed softly as its own faint radiance revealed something in the emptiness ahead: a tall, empty stone seat, facing it as it approached.

The mist stopped before it reached the man-sized throne, and hovered above a semicircle of large, complex runes that were graven into the floor in front of the throne. If the throne had been the center seat of a barge, facing ahead, the runes formed the rounded prow of the barge.

The mist seemed to linger for a time in thought, then the breeze of its movements suddenly quickened into a brisk whirlwind, spiraling around and around as it sparkled and chimed. As it swept up to violent speed, dust rose and whirled with it, pebbles rolled at its bidding, and the whirlwind rose into a horned, shifting column.

Arms it grew, and absorbed again, then humps or moving lumps that might have been heads or might have been other things, before it flashed once, then grew very dim.

No whirlwind or snake of mist now glowed in the darkness. Where the mist had been stood the translucent, ghostly shape of a tall, thin woman in a plain robe, her feet and arms bare, her hair a knee-length, unruly tangle, her eyes rather wild. She threw up her arms in triumph or glee, and mad laughter broke out of her, harsh and high and shrill, echoing back from dark and unseen stony crevices.

* * * * *

"You dare to doubt visions sent by our Lady Who Sings In Darkness?" the voice from behind the veil asked in dry tones. "That sounds perilously close to heresy—or even unbelief—to me."

"N-no, Dread Sister," a second female voice replied, a trifle too hastily. "My wits fail me—a personal flaw, no act of unbelief or discourtesy to the Nightsinger— and I cannot see why this shrine must be established in the depths of a wood, where none dwell and none will know of its existence or location."

"It is needful," the veiled voice replied. "Lie down upon the slab. You shall not be chained; your faith shall be demonstrated by your remaining in place upon it while the owlbear feeds. Offer yourself to it without resistance, and be free of fear. My spells shall keep you alive, whatever it devours of you—and no matter how painful it seems, no matter what wounds you sustain, you shall be restored wholly when the rite is done. I have survived such a ritual, in my day, and so have a select few here. To do this is a mark of true honor; the blood of someone so loyal is the best consecration we can offer the Dread Mistress Of All."

"Yes, Dread Sister," the underpriestess whispered, and the trembling of her body could be heard in her voice. "W-will I . . . will my mind be untouched by watching something eat me?" Her voice rose into what was almost a shrill shriek of horror at the thought.

"Well, Dread Sister," the veiled voice purred calmly, "that is up to you. The slab awaits. Dearest of those I've guided, make me proud this day, not ashamed. I shall be watching you—and so shall one who is far, far greater than any of us shall ever be."

* * * * *

"By Mystra's smile, that feels good!" Beldrune said wonderingly, as he stretched and wiggled his fingers experimentally. "I *do* feel younger; all the aches are gone." He swung himself up to a sitting position, rubbing at his face around his eyes, and from between his fingers fixed Tabarast with a level look.

"Truth time, trusted colleague of the arcane," he said firmly. "Wizards of a certain standing don't just 'find' new spells on hitherto-blank back pages of their spellbooks. Where did it really come from?"

Tabarast of the Three Sung Curses looked back over the tops of his thumb-smudged spectacles rather severely. "You grow not old gracefully, most highly regarded Droon. I detect a growing and decidedly unattractive tendency in yourself, to open disbelief in the testimony of your wiser elders. Crush this flaw, my boy, while yet you retain some friendly relations with folk who can serve as your wiser elders—for 'tis sure that, given your advancing age and wisdom, these are few, and shall be fewer henceforth."

The older wizard took a few thoughtful paces away, scratching the bridge of his nose. "I did indeed just find it, on a page that has always been blank, that I have looked to fill with a spell puissant enough to be worthy of the writing these last three decades. I know not how it came to be there, but I believe—I can only believe— that the sacred Hand of the Lady is involved somehow. Spare me the hearing, the spittle and drawn breath, of your usual lecture on Mystra's utter and everlasting refusal to give magic to mortals."

Beldrune blinked. Tabarast waited, carefully not smiling.

"Very well," the younger mage said after a pause that seemed longer than it truly was, "but you leave me, now, with very little to say. Some silences, I fear, are going to stretch."

Then Tabarast did smile—an instant before asking in innocent tones, "Is that a promise?"

Fortunately, a rejuvenated Beldrune of the Bent Finger proved to be every bit as bad a shot with hurled pillows as the old one had been.

*   *   *   *   *

Though not a living creature could be seen in the deep shade of the duskwoods, here where their trunks stood so close together that they might have been gigantic blades of grass, the lone human could feel that someone was watching him. Someone very near. Swallowing, he decided to take a chance.

"Is this the place men call 'Tangletrees'?" he asked the air calmly, sitting down on the huge and moss-covered curve of a fallen tree trunk, and setting his smooth-worn staff aside.

"It is," came a grave reply, in a voice so light and melodious that it could only have been elven.

Umbregard, once of Galadorna, resisted his instinctive desire to turn toward where the voice seemed to have come from, to see who might be there. Instead, he smiled and held out his hands, empty palms upward. "I come in peace, without fire or any ill will or desire to despoil. I come seeking only answers."

A deep, liquid chuckle came to his ears, then the words, "So do we all, man—and the most fortunate of us find a few of them. Be my guest for a time, in safety and at ease. Rise and go around the two entwined trees to your right, down into the hollow. Its water, I suspect, will be the purest yet to pass your lips."

"My thanks," Umbregard replied, and meant it.

The hollow was cold and as dark as a cave; here the leaves met close overhead, and no sun at all touched the earth. Faintly glowing fungi gave off just enough light to see a stone at the edge of the little pool, and a crystal goblet waiting on it. "For my use?" the human mage asked.

"Of course," the calm voice replied, coming from everywhere and nowhere. "Do you fear enslaving enchantments, or elven trickery?"

"No," Umbregard replied. "Rather, I do not want to give offense by seizing things overboldly."

He took up the goblet—it was cool to the touch, and somehow softer in his fingers than it should have been—dipped it into the pool, and drank. As the ripples chased each other across the water, he thought he saw in them a sad, dark-eyed elf face regarding him for a moment . . . but if it had ever truly been there, it was gone in the next instant.

The water was good, and seemed at once both invigorating and soothing. The man let it slide down his throat, closed his eyes, and gave himself over to silent enjoyment.

Somewhere a bird called and was answered. It was all very peaceful . . . he sat up with a start, fearing for one awful moment that he had slept under an elven spell, and carefully set the goblet back on the stone where he'd found it.

"My thanks," he said again. "The water was every bit as you said it would be. Know that I am Umbregard, once of Galadorna, and have fled far since that realm fell. I work magic, though I can boast no great power, and I have prayed to Mystra—the goddess of magic humans venerate—often in my travels."

"And what have you prayed to her for?" the elven voice asked in tones of pleasant interest, sounding very close. Again Umbregard quelled the urge to turn and look at its source.

"Guidance in what good and fitting things magic can be used for, to build a life for one who is not interested in using spells as blades to threaten or thrust into others," he replied. "Galadorna, before its fall, had become a nest of spell-hurling vipers, each striving to bring rivals down and not caring what waste and ruin they wrought in the doing. I will not be like that."

"Well said," the elf said, and Umbregard heard the goblet being dipped then lifted up out of the pool. "Yet it is a long and hard wandering through the shadowed wood for one of your kind, to here. What brought you hence?"

"Mystra showed me the way, and this duskwood grove," Umbregard replied. "I knew not who I'd meet here, but I suspected it would be an elf, once of Myth Drannor . . . for such a one would know what it was to choose a path after the fall of your home and all you held dear."

He could clearly hear a wince in the elven voice as it replied, "You certainly have the gift of speaking plainly, Umbregard."

"I mean no offense," the human mage replied, turning quickly and offering his hand.

A moon elf male in a dark blue open-front shirt and high booted tight leather breeches was sitting perhaps another handspan away, the goblet raised in his hand. He seemed weaponless, though two small objects—black, teardrop-shaped gemstones that twinkled like two dark stars—floated in the air above his left shoulder.

He smiled into Umbregard's wonderstruck eyes and said, "I know. I am also known, among my folk, for my uncommon bluntness. I am called, in your tongue, Starsunder; a star fell from the sky at the moment of my birth, though I doubt whatever it heralded had anything at all to do with me."

The human mage gasped, shrank back, and said, "That's one of the . . ."

The elf's eyebrows lifted. "Yes?" he asked. "Or blurt you out a secret you must now try to keep?"

Umbregard blushed. "Ah, no . . . no," he said. "That's one of the sayings of the priests of Mystra. 'Seek you one for whom the stars fall, for he speaks truth.' "

Starsunder blinked. "Oh, dear. My role, it seems, is laid out for me," the elf said with a smile, drained the goblet, and set it down on the stone just as carefully as Umbregard had done. In soft silence, it promptly vanished.

"What truths have you come to hear?" the elf asked, and in that moment Umbregard came to understand that the lacing of laughter in an elf's voice is not always mockery.

He hesitated for a moment, then said, "Some in Galadorna whispered that the man Elminster, who was our last court mage, also lived in Myth Drannor long ago, and worked dark magic there. I know this is a human I ask about, and that I presume overmuch—why should you freely yield secrets to me, at all?—but I must know. If humans can live long years as elves do, how . . . and why? At what tasks should they spend all this time?"

Starsunder held up a hand. "The flood begins," he joked. "Hold at these for now, lest your remembrance of answers I give be lost in the rushing stream of your next query, and the one to follow, and so on." He smiled and leaned back against a tree root.

"To your first: yes, the same man named Elminster dwelt in Myth Drannor from before the laying of its mythal to some time after, learning and working much magic. Those who hated the idea of a human thrusting his way in among us elves—for he was the first, or among the first—and many folk who came to Myth Drannor, once it was open to all, and envied him his power, might have termed some of his castings 'dark,' but I cannot in truth judge them so, or his reasons for working this or that enchantment."

Umbregard opened his mouth to speak, but Starsunder chuckled and threw up a hand to still him. "Not yet, please; bald and important truths shouldn't be rushed."

Umbregard flushed, then smiled and sat back, gesturing to the elf to continue.

There was a twinkle in Starsunder's eyes as he spoke again. "Humans who master magic enough—or rather, *think* they've 'mastered' magic enough—try many ways to outlive their usual span of years. Most of these, from lichdom to elixirs, are flawed in that they twist the essential nature of persons using them. They become new—and many would judge, I among them, 'lesser'—beings in the process. If you ask me how you could live longer, I would say the only unstained way to do so . . . though it will change you as surely as the lesser ways . . . is the one Elminster has taken . . . or perhaps been led into. I know not if he ardently sought it and worked toward it, drifted into it, or was forced or pushed into it. He serves Mystra as a special servant, doing her bidding in exchange for longevity, special status, and powers to boot. I believe he is called a 'Chosen' of the goddess."

"How did he get to be chosen for this service?" Umbregard asked slowly. "Do you know?"

"I know not," Starsunder replied, "but I do know how he has continued it for what to humans is a very long time: love."

"Love? Mystra loves him?"

"And he loves her." There was disbelief or incredulity in the confusion written plainly on the human mage's face, so Starsunder added gently, "Yes, beyond fondness and friendship and the raging desires of the flesh; true, deep, and lasting love. It is hard to believe this until you've truly felt it, Umbregard, but listen to me. There is a power in love greater than most things that can touch humans . . . or elves, or orcs for that matter. A power for good and for ill. Like all things of such power, love is very dangerous."

"Dangerous?"

Starsunder smiled faintly and said, "Love is a flame that sets fire to things. It is a greater danger to mages than any miscast spell can ever hope to be."

He leaned forward to lay a hand on Umbregard's arm, and said almost fiercely, as they stared into each other's eyes, "Magic gone awry can merely kill a mage; love can remake him, and drive him to remake the world. Our Coronal's great love drove him to seek a way for Cormanthyr that remade it . . . and, most of my folk would say, in the end destroyed it. I was yet young one warm night, out swimming for a lark, with no magic of my own to be felt—something that probably kept me alive then—when the Great Lady of the Starym, Ildilyntra who had loved the Coronal and been loved by him, slew herself to try to bring about his death, driven by her love for our land, just as he was—and both of them seared in their striving by their denied yet thriving love for each other."

The moon elf sighed and shook his head. "You cannot feel the sadness that stirs in me when I hear them again in my head, arguing together—and you are the first human after Elminster to know of that night. Mind and mark, Umbregard: to speak of this secret to others of my kind may mean your swift death."

"I shall heed," Umbregard whispered. "Say on."

The elf smiled wryly and continued, "There's little more to say. Mystra chose this Elminster to serve her, and he has done well, where others have not. The gods make us all different, and more of us fail than succeed. Elminster has failed often—but his love has not, and he has remained at his task. Bravery, I think your bards term it."

"Bravery? How can one armored and aided by a god fear anything? Without fear to wrestle with and reconquer, again and again, where is bravery?" Umbregard asked, excitement making him bold.

Something like fondness danced in Starsunder's eyes as he replied, "There are many gods; divine favor marks a mortal for greater danger than his 'ordinary' fellow and is very seldom a sure defense against the perils of this world—or any other. Only fools trust in the gods so much that they set aside fear entirely, and dismiss or do not see the dangers. I have seen bravery among your kind often; it seems something humans are good at, though more often I see in them recklessness or foolish disregard for danger that others who see less well might term bravery."

"So what is bravery?" Umbregard asked. "Standing in the path of danger?"

"Yes. Staying at one's post or task, as diligent as ever, knowing that at any time the sword waiting overhead may fall, or seeing fast-approaching doom and not abandoning all to flee."

"Please know that I mean no disrespect, but I *must* know: if such is bravery, how is it," Umbregard whispered, fear in his own eyes at his own daring, "that Myth Drannor—Cormanthyr—fell, and you still live?"

Starsunder's answering smile held sadness. "A race and a realm need obedient fools to survive, even more than they need brave—and soon dead—heroes." He stood up, and made a movement with his hand that might have been a wave of farewell. "You can see which I must be. If ever you meet this Elminster of yours face to face, ask him which of the two he is—and bring back his answer to me. I must Know All; it is my failing." Like a graceful panther, he padded up out of the hollow into the duskwood grove above.

"Wait!" the human mage protested, rising and stumbling up into the trees in the elf's wake. "I've so much more to ask—must you go?"

"Only to prepare a place for a human to snore and a meal for us both," Starsunder replied. "You're welcome to stay and ask all the questions you can think of for as long as you want to tarry here. I've few friends left here among the living and this side of the Sundering Seas."

Umbregard found himself trembling. "I would be honored to be considered your friend," he said carefully and found himself trembling, "but I must ask this: how can you trust me so? We've but spoken for a few moments of your time, no more; how can you measure me? I could be a slayer of elves, a hunter of elven treasure—an elfbane. I give you my word I am no such thing . . . but I fear human promises to elves have all too often rung empty down the years."

Starsunder smiled. "This grove is sacred to two gods of my kind: Sehanine and Rillifane," he said. "They have judged you. Behold."

The eyes of the human wizard followed the elf's pointing hand to the moss-covered fallen tree and the wooden staff leaning there. Umbregard knew its familiar, well-worn length as well as he knew the hand that held it. That staff had accompanied him for thousands of miles, walking Faerûn, and was both old and fire-hardened, its ends bound shod with copper to keep them from splitting. Yet for all that, while he'd sat talking in the hollow, it had thrown forth green shoots in plenty up and down its length—and every shoot ended in a small, beautiful white flower, glowing in the shade.

*   *   *   *   *

In a colder darkness, a ghostly woman stopped laughing and let her hands fall. The echoes of her cold mirth rolled around the cavern for some time, while she looked around at its dark vastness almost as if seeing it for the first time, her eyes slowly becoming sharp and fierce and fiery.

They were two glittering flames when she moved at last, striding with catlike, confident grace to a particular rune. She touched the symbol firmly with one foot, watched it fill with a bright blue-white glow, then stood with arms folded, watching, as wisps of smoke rose from the radiance to form a cloud like a man-sized spark—a cloud that suddenly coalesced into something else. A legless, floating image of a youngish-looking man, eager and intense of manner, faced the empty throne, hanging in midair above the rune that had spawned it.

As the image began to speak, the ghostly woman strode around the runes to the throne, leaned on one arm of that seat, and watched the image's speech.

It wore robes of rich crimson trimmed with black, and golden rings gleamed on its fingers—their hue matched by the blazing gold of the man's eyes. He had tousled brown hair and the untidy beginnings of a beard, and his voice fairly leaped with eager confidence.

"I am Karsus, as you are Karsus. If you behold this, disaster has befallen me, the first Karsus—and you, the second, must carry on to glory."

The image seemed to pace forward but actually remained above the rune. It waved one hand restlessly and continued, "I know not what you recall of my—our—life; some say my mind is less than clear, these days. Know that many mages of our people have achieved great power; mightiest of these, the archwizards of Netheril, rule their own domains. Mine, like many, is a floating city; I named it for us. I am the most powerful of all the archwizards, the Arcanist Supreme. They call me Karsus the Great."

The image waved a dismissive hand, blazing eyes still fixed on the throne. The ghostly woman was murmuring along with the words she'd obviously heard many times before. Something that might have been a faint sneer played about her lips.

"Of course," the image went on, "given your awakening, none of that may mean anything. I may not have been slain by a rival or suffered a purely personal doom—Karsus the city and the glory of Netheril itself may have fallen in a great war or cataclysm; we have made many foes, the greatest of them ourselves. We war among ourselves, we Netherese, and some of us war within ourselves. My wits are not always wholly my own. You may well share this affliction; watch for it, and guard against it."

The image of Karsus smiled; arching a sardonic eyebrow, the ghostly woman smiled back. Karsus spoke on. "Perhaps you'll have no need of these recording spells of mine, but I've prepared one for each speculum you see on the floor in this place; a series of spellcasting lessons, lest you face the perils of this world lacking certain enchantments I've found crucial. Our work must continue; only through power absolute can I—we—find perfection ... and Karsus exists, has always existed, to achieve perfection and transform all Toril."

The watching woman laughed at that, a short and unpleasant bark. "Mad indeed, Karsus! Destiny: reshape all Toril, Oh, you were certainly competent to do *that.*"

"Your first need may now be for physical healing, and I have anticipated the recurrence of this need in time to come, in a life where you may lack loyal servant mages or anyone you can trust. Know, then, that touching the speculum that evoked this image of me, while speaking the word '*Dalabrindar,*' will heal all hurts. This power can be called upon as often as desired for so long as this rune remains unbroken, and can so serve anyone who speaks thus. The word is the name of the wizard who died so that this spell might live; truly, he has served us well, and—"

"Wasted words, Karsus!" the ghostly woman sneered. "Your clone was a headless mummy decorating this throne when I first saw it! Who slew it here, I wonder? Mystra? Azuth? Some rival? Or did the great and supreme sleeping Karsus fall to a passing adventurer-mage of puny spells, who thought he was beheading a lich?"

". . . many another spell will serve where these do not, but I have here preserved demonstrations of my casting of enchantments of lasting usefulness and . . ."

The ghostly woman turned away from the words she'd heard so many times before, nodding in satisfaction. "They'll do. They'll do indeed. I have here a lure no mage can resist." She strode across the rune again, and the image vanished in mid-word, the radiance winking out of the graven stone to let darkness rush back into the cavern.

"Now, how to let living mages know of it, without causing them to crowd in here by the elbowing thousands?" ghostly lips asked the utter darkness.

The darkness did not answer back.

A frowning ghost strode to the bottom of the shaft and began to blur, unraveling in a spiraling wind of her own making, until once more a whirlwind of flickering lights danced in the darkness, spiraling slowly up the shaft. "And how to keep my mage-catches here for more than one night?"

At the top of the shaft, the chiming whorl of lights hovered over the well ring, and a soft, echoing voice issued from it. "I must weave mighty spells, to be sure. The runes must respond only to me—and then only one a month, no matter what means are tried. That should cause a young mage to linger here long enough."

With sudden vigor the mist darted to one of the rents in the walls and plunged through it, snaking through the trees trailing wild laughter and the exultant shout, "Long enough for a good feed."

Thirteen

KINDNESS SCORCHES STONE

Cruelty is a known scourge, too seldom clever—for which we should all thank the gods. Kindness is the stronger blade, though more often scorned. Most folk never learn that.

Ralderick Hallowshaw, Jester
from **To Rule A Realm, From Turret To Midden**
published circa The Year of the Bloodbird

The tall, thin stranger who'd given them a cheerful smile as he'd gone into the Maid was back out again in far less than the time it took to drain a tankard.

The two old men on the bench squinted up at him a mite suspiciously. Folk seldom turned their way—which is why it was their favorite bench. It sat in the full shadow of the increasingly ramshackle porch of the Fair Maid of Ripplestones. A cold corner, but at least it wasn't in the full dazzle of the morning sun.

The stranger was, though, his face outlined in gold as he tossed his nondescript cloak back to lay bare dark and dusty robes and breeches that bore no badge or adornment, as—wonders of the Realms!—Alnyskavver came bustling out with the best folding table, and a chair . . . and food!

The tavern master shuttled back and forth, puffing, as the two old men watched a meal the likes of which they'd not seen in many a year accumulate under their very noses: a tureen of the hot soup that'd been making two old bellies rumble all morn, a block of the sharpest redruck cheese—and *three* grouse pies!

Baerdagh and Caladaster scratched at various itches and glared sourly at the hawk-nosed stranger, wondering why by all the angry gods he'd had to choose *their* bench as the place to set his mornfeast on. Everything they'd dreamed of being able to afford for months now was steaming away under their noses. Just who by the armpit of Tempus did he think he was, anyway?

The two old men exchanged looks as their all-too-empty bellies rumbled, then with one accord stared the stranger up and down. No weapon . . . not much wealth, either, by the looks of him, though his travel-scuffed boots were very fine. An outlaw who'd had them off someone he knifed? Aye, that would fit with all the money thrown out on a huge meal like this, coming down out of the wilderlands a-starving and with stolen coins in plenty.

Now Alnyskavver was back with the haunch of venison they'd smelled cooking all yestereve, all laid out cold amid pickled onions and sliced tongue and suchlike, on the platter used when the High Duke came by . . . it was too much to bear! Arrogant young bastard.

Shaking his head, Baerdagh spat pointedly into the dust by the stranger's boots and started to shift himself along the bench, to get out and away before this young glutton tucked into such a feast as this under their very noses and drove him and his empty vitals wild.

Caladaster was in the way, though, and slower to move, so the two old men were still shifting their behinds along the bench when the tavern master came back again with a keg of beer and tankards.

Three tankards.

The stranger sat down and grinned at Baerdagh as the old man looked up with the first glimmers of amazement dawning on his face.

"Well met, goodsirs," he said politely. "Please forgive my boldness, but I'm hungry, I hate to eat alone, and I need to talk to someone who knows a fair bit about the old days of Ripplestones. Ye look to have the wits and years enough . . . what say we make a deal? We three share this—and eat freely, no stinting, ye keeping whatever we don't eat now—and ye give me, as best ye know, answers to a few questions about a lady who used to live hereabouts."

"Who are you?" Baerdagh asked bluntly, at about the same time as Caladaster said under his breath, "I don't like this. Meals don't just fall out of the sky. He must have paid Alnyskavver to get even a quarter of this out here on a table, but what's to say we won't have to pay summat, too?"

"Our thin purses," Baerdagh told his friend. "Alnyskavver knows just how poor we are. So does everyone else." He nodded his head toward the tavern windows. Caladaster looked, already knowing what he'd see. Near everyone in the place was crowded up against the dirty glass, watching as the hawk-nosed stranger poured two full tankards and slid them across the table, emptying eating forks and trencher knives out of the last tankard and sliding them across too.

Caladaster scratched his nose nervously, raked a hand down one of his untidy white-and-gray mutton-chop whiskers—a sure sign of hurried, worried thought—and turned back to the stranger. "My friend asked who you are, an' I want to know too. I also want to know whatever little trick you've readied for us. I can leave your food an' just walk away, you know."

At that moment, his stomach chose to protest very loudly.

The stranger ran a hand through unruly black hair and leaned forward. "My name is Elminster, and I'm doing some work for my Lady Master; work that involves my finding and visiting old ruins and the tombs of wizards. I've been given money to spend as I need to, in plenty—see? I'll leave these coins on the table . . . now, if I happen to vanish in a puff of smoke before ye pick up that tankard, there's enough here for ye to pay Alnyskavver yourselves."

Baerdagh looked down at the coins as if they were a handful of little sprites dancing under his nose, then back up at the stranger. "All right, that tale I'll grant," he said slowly, "but why us?"

Elminster poured his own tankard full, set it down, and asked, "Have ye any idea what weary work it is, spending days wandering around a town of increasingly suspicious folk, peeking over fences and looking for headstones and ruins? By the first nightfall, farmers always want to thrust hayforks through me. By the second, they're trying to do it in droves!"

Both old men barked short and snorting laughs at that.

"So I thought I'd save a lot of time and suspicion," the stranger added, "if I just shared a meal with some men I liked the look of, with years enough under their belts to know the old tales, and where so-and-so lies buried, and—"

"You're after Sharindala, aren't you?" Caladaster asked slowly, his eyes narrowing.

El nodded cheerfully. "I am," he said, "and before ye try to find the right words to ask me, know this: I will take nothing from her tomb, I'm not interested in opening her casket, performing any magic on her while I'm there, or digging up or burning down anything, and I'd be happy to have ye or someone else from Ripplestones along to watch what I do. I need to be able to look around thoroughly—in good bright daylight—and that's all."

"How do we know you're telling the truth?"

"Come with me," Elminster said, doling out platters and cutting into one of the pies. "See for thyselves."

Baerdagh almost moaned at the smell that came out of the opened pie with the rush of steam—but he'd no need to; his stomach took care of the utterance for him. His hands went out before he could stop himself. The stranger grinned and thrust the platter bearing the slice of pie into his hands.

"I'd rather not go about disturbing dead sorceresses," Caladaster replied, "an' I'm a bit old for clambering around on broken stones wondering when the roof's going to fall down on my head, but you can't miss Scorchstone Hall; you came—"

He broke off as Baerdagh kicked him under the table, but Elminster just grinned again and said, "Say on, please; I'm not going to whisk away the meal the moment I hear this!"

Caladaster ladled himself a bowl of soup with hands that he hoped weren't shaking with eagerness, and said thickly, "Friend Elminster, I want to warn you about her wards. That's why no one plundered the place long since, an' why you didn't see it. Trees and thorn bushes an' all have grown around it in a wall just outside the shimmering . . . but I recall, before they grew, seeing squirrels and foxes and even birds a-wing fall down dead when they so much as brushed Sharindala's wards. You came right past it on your way in, just after the bridge, where the road takes that big bend; it's bending around Scorchstone." He took a big bite of cheese, closed his eyes in momentary bliss, and added, "It burned after she died, mind; *she* didn't call it Scorchstone."

Baerdagh leaned close across the table to breathe beer conspiratorially all over Elminster and whisper roughly, "They say she walks there still, you know—a skeleton in the tatters of a fine gown, still able to slay with her spells."

El nodded. "Well, I'll try not to disturb her. What was she like in life, d'ye know?"

Baerdagh jerked his head in Caladaster's direction. The older man was blowing on his soup to cool it; he looked up, stroked his chin, and said, "Well, I was nobbut a lad then, do you see, and . . ."

One by one, overcome with curiosity, the folk of Ripplestones were drifting out of the Maid or down the street to listen—and, no doubt, to enthusiastically add their own warnings. Elminster grinned, sipped at his tankard, and waved at the two old men to continue. They were plowing through the food at an impressive rate; Baerdagh had already let out his belt once, and it lacked several hours to highsun, yet.

* * * * *

In the end, the two old men were content to let their good friend Elminster go alone up to Scorchstone Hall, though Caladaster gravely asked the hawk-nosed mage to stop by their neighboring cottages on his way out, if'n he needed a bed for the night, or just to let them know he'd fared safely. El as gravely promised he would, guessing he'd find deafening snores behind barred doors if he returned before the next morning. He helped the old men carry home the food their groaning-full bellies wouldn't let them eat and bought them each another keg of beer to wash it down with. They looked at him from time to time as if he was a god come calling in disguise but clasped his hand heartily enough in almost tearful thanks and wheezed their way indoors.

El smiled and went on his way, waving cheerfully to the scattering of Ripplestones children who came trailing after him—and the mothers who rushed to drag

them back. He turned and walked straight into the
thick-standing trees that hid Scorchstone Hall from
view. The last watchers from afar, who'd wandered
down from the Maid with their tankards in their hands,
spat into the road thoughtfully, agreed that Ripplestones had seen the last of another madman, and
turned away to drift back to the tavern or about their
business.

The shimmering was as Caladaster had described
it—but sighed into nothingness at the first passage
spell El attempted. He became a shadow once more, in
case more formidable traps awaited, and drifted quietly into the overgrown gardens of what had once been a
fine mansion.

It had burned, but only a little. What must have been
a tower at the eastern front corner was now only a
blackened ring of stones among brambles, attached to
the house beyond by a rock pile of its fallen walls—but
the gabled house beyond seemed intact.

El found a place where a shutter sagged, and drifted into the gloom through a window that had never, it
seemed, known glass. The dark mansion beyond had
its share of leaks, mold, and rodent leavings, but it
looked for all the world as if someone cleaned it regu-
larly. The shadowy Chosen found no traps and soon
reverted to solid form to poke and peer and open. He
found sculptures, paintings smudged where someone
had recently scrubbed mold away, and bookshelves full
of travel journals, scholarly histories of kingdoms and
prominent families, and even romantic novels. Nowhere
in the house that he could see, however, was there any
trace of magic. If this Sharindala had been a mage, all
of her books and inks and spell-substances must have
been destroyed in the fire that brought down her tower
. . . and presumably the lady had perished therein, too.

El shrugged. Well, a searcher in days to come
wouldn't know that if he did his work properly. A forgotten scroll on a shelf here, a wand in a wooden box

hidden behind this tallchest, and a sheaf of incomplete spell notes thrust into that book *there*. Now to put a few more scrolls in the closets he'd seen up in the bedrooms, and his work here was done. Magic enough to set a mageling on the road to mastery, if shrewdly used, and—

He opened a closet door and something moved.

Cowered, actually, as handfire blazed between Elminster's fingers. Brown and gray bones shifted and shuffled into the deepest corner of the closet, holding a wobbling wand pointed at him. El saw glittering eyes, a wisp of cloth that might once have been part of a gown, and a snarl of long brown hair that was falling out of the shriveled remnant of a scalp as the skeleton brushed against the walls. He stepped back, holding up a hand in a "stop" gesture, hoping she'd not trigger that trembling wand.

"Lady Sharindala?" he asked calmly. "I am Elminster Aumar, once of Myth Drannor, and I mean no harm nor disrespect. Please come out and be at ease. I did not know ye still dwelt here. I'll pay ye proper respects, then withdraw from thy house and leave ye in peace."

He retreated to the door, put on his cloak and summoned up defenses in case the undead sorceress did use the wand, and waited, watching the open closet door.

After a long time, that dark-eyed skull peered out— and hastily withdrew. El leaned against the door frame and waited.

After a few moments more, the skeleton hesitantly shuffled out of the closet, looking in all directions for adventurers who might be waiting to pounce. She held the wand upward, not leveled upon him, and came to a stop halfway down the room, gazing at him in silence.

El offered her the chair beside him with a gesture. She didn't move, so he picked up the chair and carried it to her.

The wand came up, but he ignored it—even when magic missiles spat forth and streaked at him, trailing blue fire.

His spell defenses absorbed them harmlessly; El felt only gentle jolts as they struck. Pretending they'd never existed at all—or the second volley, that tore into his face from barely an arm's length away—the last prince of Athalantar set down the chair and gestured to the walking remains of Sharindala, then to the chair, offering it to her. Then he bowed and went back to the doorway.

After a long, silent moment, the skeleton went to the chair and sat down, crossing its legs at the ankles and leaning back on one arm of the chair out of long habit.

Elminster bowed again. "I apologize for my intrusion into thy home. I serve the goddess Mystra and am here on her bidding to leave magic for later searchers to find. I shall restore thy wards and trouble ye no more. Is there anything I can do for ye?"

After a long while, the skeleton shook its head, almost wearily.

"Would ye find lasting rest?" El asked gently. The wand shot up to menace him. He held up a staying hand and asked, "Do ye still work magic?"

The hair-shedding skull nodded, then shrugged, holding up the wand.

El nodded. "I've not searched for any magic ye may have hidden. I've only added, not taken away." A thought occurred to him, then, and he asked, "Would ye like to know new spells?"

The skeleton stiffened, made as if to rise, then nodded so emphatically that hair fell out in handfuls.

El reached into his cloak and drew forth a spellbook. Muttering a word over it, he strode back across the room, ignoring the hesitantly lifted wand—which spat nothing more at him—and gently placed the tome in her lap, holding it as her free hand came across to clasp it.

Her other hand dropped the wand and reached up impulsively to clasp his arm. Rather than pulling free, El reached out slowly to place his own hand over the dry, bony digits on his forearm and stroked them.

Sharindala trembled all over, and for a long time blue-gray eyes and dark points of light in the sockets of a fleshless skull stared into each other.

El withdrew his stroking hand and said, "Lady, I must go. I must place more magic elsewhere—but if I survive to return to Ripplestones in time to come, I'll stop and visit ye properly."

He received a slow but definite nod in answer.

"Lady, can ye speak?" El asked. The skeleton stiffened, then the hand on his arm became a fist that smashed down on the arm of the chair in frustration.

El bent over and tapped the book. "There's a spell in here, near the back, that can change that for ye. It requires no verbal component, obviously—but I want ye to remember something. When ye have some unbroken time to devote to things and have mastered that spell, I want ye to hold this tome and say aloud the words, 'Mystra, please.' Will ye remember?"

The skull nodded once more. El took hold of bony fingertips and brought them to his lips. "Then, Lady, fare thee well for now. I go, but shall return in time. Be happy."

He straightened, gave her a salute, and strode out of the room. The skeleton managed a wave at its last glimpse of his smiling face, then its hand fell to the book, cradling it as if it would never let go.

For a long time the skeleton that had been Sharindala sat in the chair, staring at the door and shuddering. The only sound in the room was a dry clicking as fleshless jaws worked. She was trying to weep.

* * * * *

"But there's *more!*" Beldrune hissed, creeping forward with his fingers held out like claws before him.

Spellbound, the circle of pupils watched him with nary a titter at the appearance of an old and overweight wizard trying to tiptoe like an actor overplaying the part of a skulking thief. "This mighty mage has walked *these* very streets! Here—just outside, down yon alley, not three nights past—I saw him *myself!*"

"Think of it," Tabarast took up the telling excitedly, never knowing that the mage they were speaking of was at that moment kissing the fingertips of a skeleton. "We've walked with him, we studied magic at his very elbow in fabled Moonshorn Tower—and soon, just perhaps, you too may have this opportunity! To talk with the supreme sorcerer of the age—a man touched by a god!"

"Nay," Beldrune leered suggestively, "a man touched by a *goddess!*"

"Think of it!" Tabarast put in hastily, flashing a warning glare at young Droon. Don't the young ever think of anything *else?* "The great Elminster has lived for centuries! Some believe him to be a Chosen One, personally favored by the goddess Mystra—that's what my colleague was *trying* to say—and records are clear: he is a man who dwelt in fabled Myth Drannor when elven magic flowed like water, was respected enough to be accepted into a noble elf family there, advise their ruler, the Coronal—and even survive the darkness of its destruction at the hands of a shrieking army of foul fiends! Hard to believe? Ask the folk of Galadorna about Elminster's survival in the face of the fell magic of an archpriestess of Bane, while defying her in her very temple! This was before Galadorna's fall, when he was the court mage of that realm."

"Aye, all this is true," Beldrune agreed, taking up the tale. "And don't forget: he's been seen here—fearlessly strolling out of the tomb of the mage Taraskus in broad daylight!"

There were gasps at this last piece of news and many involuntary glances toward the windows.

A ghostly shape that had been floating outside one of those windows, listening intently, prudently fell away and dissolved into mists.

"I've lived for centuries, too," it murmured, chiming as it gathered speed to go elsewhere. "Perhaps this Elminster will make a fitting mate . . . if he's alive and human, and not some cleverly cloaked lich or crawling netherplanar spirit." Unaware that excited pupils were crowding the windows to glimpse her as a supposed magical manifestation of the very mage she was musing about, the sorceress drifted away, murmuring, "Elminster . . . 'tis time to go hunting Elminsters."

Fourteen

THE ELMINSTER HUNT

The deadliest sport among the Zhentarim is vying for supremacy within its dark ranks . . . and in particular, the doom of the too young and nakedly ambitious: to be sent Elminster hunting. I'll wager that this has always been a perilous pastime. Some are wise enough, as I was, to use it as a chance to "die" our ways out of the Brotherhood. It was interesting—if a trifle depressing—to hear, while in disguise, what folk said of me, once they thought me safely dead. One day I'll return and haunt them all.

Destrar Gulhallow
from **Posthumous Musings of
a Zhentarim Mageling**
published circa The Year of the Morningstar

The darkness never left Ilbryn Starym. It never would, not since the day when the last hunting lodge of the Starym had been torn apart in spells and flame, their proud halls in Myth Drannor already fallen, and the Starym had been shattered forever.

If any of his kin still lived, he'd never found trace of them. Once proud and mighty, the family that had led and defined Cormanthyr for an age was now reduced to one young and crippled cousin. If the Seldarine smiled, with his magic he might be able to sire children to carry on the family name . . . but only if the Seldarine smiled.

Again, it had been the Accursed One, that grinning human Elminster, his spells splashing around the temple as he fought the queen of Galadorna. A thousand times Ilbryn had relived those searing instants of tumbling down the temple, broken and aflame. To work magic that would restore his leg and smooth his skin to be what it had once been would ruin spells he'd never mastered; the spells that had cost him so much, to keep his ravaged innards working. Years of agony—if he lived that long—lay ahead. Agony of the body to match the agony in his heart.

"Have my thanks, human," he snarled to the empty air. The horse promptly jostled him, sending stabbing pains through his twisted side, as it clopped across a worn and uneven bridge. Ahead, through the pain, he saw a signboard. On his sixth day out of Westgate, riding alone on a hard road, it was a welcome sight; it told him he was getting somewhere . . . even if he didn't know quite where that *some*where was.

"Ripplestones," he read it aloud. "Another soaring human fortress of culture. How inspiring."

He drew his bitter sarcasm around himself like a dark cloak and urged his horse into a trot, sitting up in his saddle so as to look impressive when human eyes began their startled looks at him; an elf riding alone, all in black and wearing the swords and daggers of an adventurer, with—whenever he let the spell lapse—one side of his face a twisted, mottled mass of burn scar.

The weaponry was all for show, of course, to make his spells a surprise. Ilbryn dropped one hand to a smooth sword pommel and caressed it, keeping his face hard and grim, as the road rounded a thick stand of trees and Ripplestones spread out before him.

He was always wandering, always seeking Elminster. To hunt and slay Elminster Aumar was the burning goal that ruled his life—though there'd never be a House Starym to return to with triumphant news of avenging the family unless Ilbryn rebuilt it himself. He was close on Elminster's trail now; he could taste it.

He put out of his mind how many times he'd been this close before and at the end of the day had closed his fingers on nothing.

Ah, a tavern; The Fair Maid of Ripplestones. Probably the only tavern in this dusty farm town. Ilbryn stopped his horse, threw its reins over its head to enact the spell that would hold it like a statue until he spoke the right word, and began the bitter struggle to dismount without falling on his face.

As it was, his artificial leg clanked like a bouncing cartload of swords when he landed, and he clung to a saddle strap for long seconds before he could clear his face of the pain and straighten up.

The two old men on the bench just sat and watched him calmly, as if strange travelers rode up to the Fair Maid every day. Ilbryn spoke gently to them, but grasped the hilts of a blade and a throwing dagger as a sort of silent promise of trouble to come . . . if they wanted trouble.

"May this day find you in fortune," he said formally. "I hope you can help me. I'm seeking a friend of mine, to deliver an urgent message. I must catch him! Have you seen a human wizard who goes by the name of Elminster? He's tall, and thin, with dark hair and a hawk's nose . . . and he steps into every wizard's tomb he passes."

The two old men on the bench stared at him, frowning, but said not a word. A third man, standing in the tavern door, gave the two on the bench an even odder look than he'd given Ilbryn and said to the elf, "Oh, *him!* Aye, he went in Scorchstone right enough, and soon

came out again, too. Headed east, he did, into the Dead
Place."

"The Dead Place?"

"Aye; them as goes in comes not out. There's nary a
squirrel or chipmunk 'tween Oggle's Stream and Rairdrun Hill, just this side of Starmantle. We go by boat,
now, if'n we have to. No one takes the road, nor goes
through the woods, neither. A tenday an' some back,
some fancy adventuring band—an' not the first one,
neither—hired by the High Duke hisself went in . . . and
came not out again. Nor will they, or my name's not
Jalobal—which, a-heh, 'tis. Mark you, they'll not be
seen again, no. I hear there's another band of fools yet,
jus' set out from Starmantle . . ."

The elf had already turned and begun the struggle
up into his saddle again. With a grunt and a heave that
brought a snarl of pain from between clenched teeth,
he regained his seat on the high-backed saddle and took
up his reins to head on east.

"Here!" Jalobal called. "Aren't you be stayin', then?"

Ilbryn twisted his lips into a grim smile. "I'll never
catch him if I stop and rest wherever he's just moved
on from."

"But yon's the Dead Place, like I told thee."

With two swift tugs, the elf undid the two silver
catches on his hip that Baerdagh had thought were
ornamental and peeled aside his breeches. Inside was
no smooth skin, but a ridged mass of scars that looked
like old tree bark, a sickly yellow where it wasn't
already gray. The twisted burn-scarring extended from
his knee to his armpit—and above the knee were the
struts and lashings that held on a leg of metal and wood
that the elf had not been born with.

"I'll probably feel at home there," the elf told the
three gaping men thinly. "As you can see, I'm half dead
already." Without another word or look in their direction, he pulled the catches closed and spurred his
mount away.

In shocked silence, the three men watched the dust rise, and beyond it, the bobbing elf on his horse dwindle from view along the overgrown road toward Oggle's Stream.

"Didj'ye see? Did d'ye see?" Jalobal asked the two silent men on the bench excitedly. They stared at him like two stones. He blinked at them then bustled back into the Maid to spread word about his daring confrontation with the scorched elf rider.

Baerdagh turned his head to look at Caladaster. "Did he say 'catch him up' or just 'catch him'?"

"He said 'catch him,' " Caladaster replied flatly. "I noticed that in particular."

Baerdagh shook his head. "I'd not like to walk in a mage's boots, for all their power. Crazed, the lot of them. Have you noticed?"

"Aye, I have," Caladaster replied, his voice deep and grim. "It passes, though, if you stop soon enough." And as if that had been a farewell, he got up from the bench and strode away toward his cottage.

Something flashed as he went, and the old man's hand was suddenly full of a stout, gem-studded staff that Baerdagh had never seen before.

Baerdagh closed his gaping mouth and rubbed his eyes to be sure he'd seen rightly. Aye, there it was, to be sure. He stared at Caladaster's back as his old comrade strode down the road home, but his friend never looked back.

*   *   *   *   *

Despite the gray sky and cool breezes outside, many a student had cast glances out the windows during this day's lesson. So many, in fact, that at one point Tabarast had been moved to comment severely, "I doubt very much that the great Elminster is going to perch like a pigeon on our windowsill just to hear what to him are the rudiments of magic. Those of you who desire to grasp a tenth of his greatness are advised to face front and pay attention to our admittedly less exciting teachings. All mages—even divine Azuth, the Lord of Spells, who outstrips Elminster as he outstrips any of you, began in this way; learning mage-lore as words dropping from the lips of older, wiser wizards."

The glances back diminished noticeably after that, but Beldrune was still sighing in exasperation by the time Tabarast threw up his hands and snapped, "As the ability to focus one's concentration, that cornerstone of magecraft, seems today to utterly elude all too many of you, we'll conclude the class at this point, and begin—with fresh insight and interest, I trust—on the morrow. You are dismissed; homeward go, *without* playing spell pranks this time, Master Maglast."

"Yes sir," one handsome youth replied rather sullenly, amid the general tumult of scraping chairs, billowing cloaks, and hurrying bodies. Muttering, Tabarast turned to the hearth, to rake the coals out into a glittering bed and put another log on the fire. Beldrune glanced up at the smoke hanging and curling under the rafters—when things warmed up, that chimney would profit from a spell or two to blast it clean and hollow it out a trifle wider—then clasped his hands behind him and watched the class leave, just to make sure no demonstration daggers or spell notes accidentally fell into the sleeves, scrips, boots, or shirt fronts of students' clothing. As usual, Maglast was one of the last to depart. Beldrune met his gaze with a firm and knowing smile that sent the flushing youth hastily doorward, and only then became aware that a man who'd sat quietly in the back of the class with the air of someone whose thoughts are elsewhere—despite the gold piece he'd paid to be sitting there—was coming slowly forward. A first timer; perhaps he had some questions.

Beldrune asked politely, "Yes? And how may we help you, sir?"

The man had unkempt pale brown hair and washed-out brown eyes in a pleasantly forgettable face. His clothing was that of a down-at-heels merchant; dirty tunic and bulging-pocketed overtunic over patched and well-worn breeches and good but worn boots.

"I must find a man," he said in a very quiet voice, stepping calmly past Beldrune to where Tabarast was bending over the hearth, "and I'm willing to pay hand-somely to be guided to him."

Beldrune stared at the man's back for a moment. "I think you misunderstand our talents, sir. We're not . . ." His voice trailed off as he saw what was being drawn in the hearth ashes.

The nondescript man had plucked up a kindling stick from beside the fire and was drawing a harp between the horns of a crescent moon, surrounded by four stars.

The man turned his head to make sure that both of the elderly mages had seen his design, then hastily raked ashes across it until his design was obliterated.

Beldrune and Tabarast exchanged looks, eyebrows raised and excitement tugging at the corners of their jaws. Tabarast leaned forward until his forehead almost touched Beldrune's and murmured, "A Harper. Elminster had a hand in founding them, you know."

"I do know, you dolt—*I'm* the one keeps his ears open for news, remember?" Beldrune replied a trifle testily, and turned to the Harper. "So who do you want us to find for you, anyway?"

"A wizard by the name of Elminster. Yes, our founder; *that* Elminster."

The pupils, had any returned to spy on the hearth with the same attention they'd paid to the windows, would at that moment have witnessed their two elder-ly, severe tutors squealing like excited children, hop-ping and shuffling in front of the fire as they clapped their hands in eagerness, then gabbling acceptances without any reference to fees or payments to the down-at-heels merchant, who was calmly returning the stick to where he'd found it in the center of the happy tumult.

Beldrune and Tabarast ran right into each other in their first eager rushes toward cupboards, laughed and clawed each other out of the way with equal enthusiasm, then rushed around snatching up whatever they thought might come in remotely useful on an Elminster hunt.

The worn-looking Harper leaned back against the wall with a smile growing on his face as the heap of "essentials" rapidly grew toward the rafters.

* * * * *

"What befell, Bresmer?" The High Duke's voice didn't hold much hope or eagerness; he wasn't expecting good news.

His seneschal gave him none. "Gone, sir, as near as we can tell. One dead horse, seen floating by fishermen. They took Ghaerlin out to see it; he was a horse tamer before he took service with you, lord. He said its eyes were staring and its hooves and legs all bloodied; he thinks it galloped right down the cliff, riderless, fleeing in fear. The boat guard report that the Banner didn't light the signal beacon or raise their pennant . . . I think they're all dead, lord."

Horostos nodded, hardly seeing the wineglass he was rolling between his fingers. "Have we found anyone else willing to take us on? Any word from Marskyn?"

Bresmer shook his head. "He thinks everyone in Westgate has heard all about the slayings—and so does Eltravar in Reth."

"Raise what we're offering," the High Duke said slowly. "Double the blood price."

"I've already done that, lord," the seneschal murmured. "Eltravar did that on his own, and I thought it prudent to confirm his offers with your ducal seal. Marskyn has being using the new offer for a tenday now . . . it's the doubled fee all of these mercenaries are refusing."

The High Duke grunted. "Well, we're seeing the measure of their spirit, at least, to know who not to hire when we've need in future."

"Or their prudence, lord," Bresmer said carefully. "Or their prudence."

Horostos looked up sharply, met his seneschal's eyes, then let his gaze fall again without saying anything. He brought his wineglass down to the table so hard it shattered into shards between his fingers, and snapped, "Well, we've got to do *something!* We don't even know what it is, and it'll be having whole villages next! I—"

"It already has, lord," Bresmer murmured. "Ayken's Stump, sometime last tenday."

"The woodcutters?" Horostos threw back his head and sighed at the ceiling. "I won't have a land to rule if this goes on much longer," he told it sadly. "The Slayer will be gnawing at the gates of this castle, with nothing left outside but the bones of the dead."

The ceiling, fully as wise as its long years, deigned not to answer.

Horostos brought his gaze back down to meet the eyes of his expressionless, carefully quiet seneschal, and asked, "Is there any hope? Anyone we can call on, before you and I up shields and ride out those gates together?"

"I did have a visit from one outlander, lord," Bresmer told the richly braided rug at his feet. "He said to tell you that the Harpers had taken an interest in this matter, lord, and they would report to you before the end of the season—if you could be found. I took that as a hint to tarry here until at least then, lord."

"Gods *blast* it, Bresmer! Sit like a babe trembling in a corner while my people look to me and say, 'There goes a coward, not a ruler'? Sit doing nothing while these mysterious wandering harpists murmur to me what's befalling in my land, and to stay out of it? Sit watching money flow out of the vault and men die still clutching it, while crops rot in the fields with no farmers left alive to tend them, or harvest them so we won't starve come winter? *What would you have me do?*"

"It's not my place to demand anything of you, lord," the seneschal said quietly. "You weep for your people and your land, and that is more than most rulers ever think to do. If you choose to ride out against the Slayer come morning, I'll ride with you . . . but I hope you'll give shelter to those who want to flee the forest, lord, and bide here, until a Harper comes riding in our gates to at least tell us what is destroying our land before we go up against it."

The High Duke stared at the shards of the wineglass in his lap and the blood running down his fingers, and sighed. "My thanks, Bresmer, for speaking sense to me. I'll tarry and be called a coward . . . and pray to Malar to call off this Slayer and spare my people." He rose, brushing glass aside impatiently, and acquired the ghost of a grin as he asked, "Any more advice, seneschal?"

"Aye, one thing more," Bresmer murmured. "Be careful where you do your hunting, lord."

*   *   *   *   *

A chill, chiming mist dived between two curving, moss-covered phandars, and slid snakelike through a rent in a crumbling wall. It made of itself a brief whirlwind in the chamber beyond, and became the shifting, semisolid outline of a woman once more.

She glanced around the ruined chamber, sighed, and threw herself down on the shabby lounge to

think, tugging at hair that was little more than
smoke as she reclined on one elbow and considered
future victories.

"He must not see me," she mused aloud, "until he
comes here and finds the runes himself. I must seem . . .
linked to them, an attractive captive he must free, and
solve some mystery about; not just how I came to be here,
but who I am."

A slow smile grew across her face.

"Yes. Yes, I like that."

She whirled around and up into the air in a blurred
whirlwind, to float gently down and stand facing the
full-length, peeling mirror. Tall enough, yes . . . She
turned this way and that, subtly altering her appearance to look more exotic and attractive—waist in, hips
out, a little tilt to the nose, eyes larger . . .

"Yes," she told the glass at last, satisfaction in her
voice. "A little better than Saeraede Lyonora was in life
. . . and yet—no less deadly."

She drifted toward one of the row of wardrobes,
made long, slender legs solid enough to walk; it had
been a long time since she'd strutted across a dance
floor, to say nothing of flouncing or mincing.

The wardrobe squealed as it opened, a damp door
dropping away from the frame. Saeraede frowned and
went to the next wardrobe where she'd put garments
seized recently from wagons—and victims—on the road
. . . when there had still been wagons.

Her smile became catlike at that thought, as she
made her hands just solid enough to hold cloth, wincing at the empty feeling it caused within her. To become
solid drained her so much.

As swiftly as she dared, she raked through the
gowns, selecting three that most caught her eye, and
draped them over the lounge. Rising up through the
first, she became momentarily solid all over—and
gasped at the cold emptiness that coiled within her.
"Mustn't do this . . . for long," she gasped aloud, her

breath hissing out to cloud the mirror. "Dare not use . . . too much, but these *must* fit. . . ."

The blue ruffles of the first gown were flattened and wrinkled from their visit to the wardrobe; the black one, with its daring slits all over, looked better but would tear and fall apart most easily. The last gown was red, and far more modest, but she liked the quality it shouted, with the gem-highlighted crawling dragons on its hips.

Her strength was failing fast. Gods, she needed to drain lives soon, or . . . With almost feverish speed she shifted her shape to fill out the three gowns most attractively, fixed their varying requirements in her mind, and thankfully collapsed into a whirlwind again, dumping the red gown to the ground in a puddle.

As mist she drifted over it, solidifying just her fingertips to carry it back to the wardrobe and hang it carefully away.

As she returned for the other two garments, an observer would have noticed that her twinkling lights had grown dim, and her mist was tattered and smaller than it had been.

By the time the wardrobe door closed behind the last gown, Saeraede had noticed that she was a little dimmer now. She sighed but couldn't resist coalescing back to womanly form for one last, critical look at herself in the mirror.

"You'll have to do, I suppose . . . and another thing, Saeraede," she chided herself. "Stop talking to yourself. You're lonely, yes, but not completely melt-witted."

"Try over there," a hoarse male voice said then, in what was probably intended to be a whisper. It was coming from the forest beyond the ruin, through one of the gaps in the walls. "I'm sure I saw a woman yonder, in a red gown. . . ."

The ghostly woman froze, head held high, then smiled wolfishly and collapsed into winking lights and mist once more.

"How thoughtful," she murmured to the mirror, her voice faint and yet echoing. "Just when I need them most."

Her laughter arose, as a merry tinkling. "I never thought I'd be around to see it, but adventurers are becoming almost . . . predictable."

She plunged out through a hole in the wall like a hungry eel. Seconds later, a hoarse scream rang out. It was still echoing back off the crumbling walls when there was another.

Fifteen

A DARK FLAME RISING

And a dark flame shall rise, and scatter all before it, igniting red war, wild magic, and slaughter. Just another quiet interlude before the fresh perils of next month . . .
Caldrahan Mhelymbryn, Sage of Matters Holy
from **A Tashlutan Traveler's Day-Thoughts**
published in The Year of Moonfall

Dread Brother Darlakhan.

It had a ring to it. It would go well with the branding and the whip scars that crisscrossed his forearms. He'd worked hard with a paste of blood and urine and black temple face paint to turn those scars into dark, permanent, raised ridges. His eagerness to take branding in the temple rituals had not gone unnoticed.

The wind off the Shaar was hot and dry this night, and he'd been looking forward to a quiet evening of prostrate prayer on the cold stone of the cellar floor—but the adeptress he'd paid to flog him first had come to him with a harshly whispered mission instead: by Dread Sister Klalaera's command, he was to immediately bear this platter of food and wine to the innermost chambers of the House of Holy Night.

"I'm excited for you, Dread Brother," she'd whispered in his ear, before she'd given him the customary slap across the face. Kneeling, he'd clawed at her ankles with even more than the usual enthusiasm, his heart pounding with his own excitement.

He'd *thought* the cruel Overmistress of the Acolytes had been eyeing him rather closely for the last tenday or so; was this his chance at last?

When he was alone, he hastened to fix the mantle of shards around him, tucking it up firmly between his thighs so as to make it draw blood before his first step, instead of walking with infinite care to avoid its wounds, as most did. Then he took up the platter, held it high, and made a silent prayer to the all-seeing goddess.

Oh, holy Shar, forgive my presumption, but I would serve you as the dark night wind, the barbed black blade, your scourge and trusted hand, not merely as a temple puppet at Klalaera's whims.

"Shar," he breathed aloud, in case anyone was spying from behind panels and thought he'd been quailing or daydreaming instead of praying. He raised and lowered the platter in salute and set off briskly through the dimly torchlit halls of the temple. The smooth, black marble was cold under his bare feet, and his limbs tingled where threads of blood trickled down.

He walked straight and tall, never looking back at the naked novices crawling along in his wake, licking up his blood where it fell, and gave no sign he'd heard grunts and sobs and muffled screams behind the doors he passed, as the ambitious clergy of the House made their own pain sacrifices to Holy Shar.

He heard the rumble of the lone drum long before he reached the Inner Portal, and his excitement grew to an almost unbearable singing within him. A High Ritual, unannounced and unexpected, and he was to be part of it.

Dread Brother Darlakhan. Oh, yes. A measure of

power at last. He was on his way to greatness.

Darlakhan rounded the last pillar and strode to the archway where the two priestesses crossed their razor-sharp black blades before him, then drew them back across his chest with the most delicate of strokes as he held the platter high out of the way. They turned toward him this night, and Darlakhan stopped, trembling, to receive their ultimate accolade: they let him watch as they shook his blood from the points of their swords into cupped palms, and brought it to their mouths.

He whispered, "As Shar wills," to them, making of his tone a thanks, then strode on down the last passage to the Inner Portal, the drumbeat growing louder before him.

He was surprised to find the Portal itself unguarded. A black curtain adorned with the Dark Disk hung in the customarily empty Portal Arch. Darlakhan slowed for a moment, wondering what to do, then decided he must follow the procedure all acolytes were trained in, as if nothing was occurring out of the ordinary.

He paused at the Portal, swept his elbows out to make the shards slash at him one last time—and to keep them out of the way as he knelt—and went to his knees, extending the platter at the full stretch of his arms and touching his forehead to the cold marble of the threshold.

Swift hands snatched the platter away, and others beheaded him with a single keen stroke.

A long, sleek arm snatched up the blood-gargling head by its hair. An oiled body stretched and thrust Darlakhan's head into a brazier, ignoring the flames that raced back down oiled flesh. "The last," that someone murmured, pain making the voice tight.

"Then know peace, Dread Sister," someone else said, touching her with the black Quenching Rod that drank all fire. The drum rolled one last time and fell silent, a long-nailed hand made a gesture, and black flames roared up out of a dozen braziers with a collective crackle and snarl.

Each brazier in the circle held a blackening, severed head. Each tongue of dark flame rose up in a twisting, flowing column to feed a dark sphere overhead.

The Sacred Chamber of Shar, the most holy room in the House of Holy Night, was crowded indeed. All of the cruel and powerful upper priestesses of Shar were gathered here in their black and purple, beneath the sphere of roiling shadows. All of them streamed blood from open wounds, all of their eyes were bright with excitement, and all of their attention was now fixed on the sphere that loomed so large above their heads, as tall as six men.

Something swam into view briefly, within the sphere: a human arm, slender and feminine, white skinned and clawing vainly at nothing. Then an elbow was seen, and suddenly, the head and shoulders of a feebly struggling human female swam into view. All that could be seen of her was bare, and she was thrashing about in the fire, seemingly blind. Despair was written large across her face, the eyes dark, staring pools, the mouth open in an endless, soundless scream.

There was a murmur of puzzlement and surprise from among the gathered priestesses—and the tallest among them, resplendent in her horned black headdress and her mantle of deepest purple, stepped forward and brought the long lash in her hand down with brutal force across the bare back of a man kneeling under the sphere. Sweat flew in all directions; he was drenched and gleaming.

"Explain, Dread Brother High," the Darklady of the House commanded, her voice sharp. "We were promised by you—and, in a sending, by the Flame of Darkness herself—that your striving would bring us great power and great opportunity. Even if this wench is some great queen of Faerûn, I see no power nor opportunity here save the grubby achievement of seizing a land and its coffers. Explain both well and speedily—and live."

The senior priest of the House looked at the struggling figure in the sphere as he let his hands fall to his sides, then slumped back to the marble floor, exhausted. Through his gasps, the priestesses saw the bright flash of his smile.

"It is a success, your Darkness," he said when he could find breath enough. "This is an avatar of the goddess Mystra, though of much less power than most she sends forth. We cannot harm it without unleashing magics too wild for all of us together to hope to control, but while we keep it trapped thus, we can tap the Weave whenever it strives to, gaining magic to power spells studied—and cast—as wizards do. This avatar must have been tainted by its flirtation with Bane . . . there is a lasting weakness here, I believe."

"Time enough for such musings later," said Darklady Avroana firmly. Her voice was still cold and biting, but the eagerness on her face and the tapping of her whip against her own thigh rather than across the face of High Brother Narlkond betrayed her excitement and approval. "Tell me of these spells. We sit and study as mages do, and fill our minds—and what then?"

"No power floods into those memorized patterns until our captive here seeks to touch the Weave," replied the senior priest, rolling over to face her on his knees, "which happens every few hours or so. It seems unable not to strive to, for that is its essential nature, and—"

"How long can we keep this up?" Avroana snapped, gesturing up at the sphere with her whip.

"So long as we have enthusiastic believers in the Dark Mother to furnish us with their heads."

"More have been called hither," said the Darklady, her lips shaping—for a very brief instant—a smile that was as cold as the glacial ice that seals shut a northern tomb. "They've been told we mount a holy crusade."

"Your Darkness," High Brother Narlkond replied, with a soft smile of his own, "we do."

*   *   *   *   *

"This is what in human speech would be called the Lookout Tree," said the moon elf, sitting down on a huge leaf—which promptly curled and flexed around him to form a couch that cupped him like a giant, gentle hand.

Umbregard stared around at the view between the great arched branches that split apart where they stood to soar still farther up into the thin, cold air. "By the gods," he said slowly, "those are clouds! We're looking down on the *clouds!*"

"Only the lowest sort of clouds," Starsunder said with a smile. "Oh, didn't you know? Yes, different shapes of clouds hang at different levels, just as fish in a lake seek levels in the water that suit them."

"Fish—?" the human mage asked, then grinned and said, "Never mind; we stray swiftly from my original questioning."

Starsunder grinned back. "Now do you see how it was that humans studied in Myth Drannor for centuries," he said, "and some of them still learned only a handful of the spells they came seeking? The best of them didn't even mind."

Umbregard shook his head. "Oh, to have been there," he whispered longingly, sitting down rather gingerly on another leaf. It promptly tumbled him into its center—he had time for only the briefest of startled murmurs—and folded itself around him, to leave him upright, enthroned in warm comfort.

"Well, ahem," he offered in pleased surprise, while Starsunder chuckled. "Nice, very nice." He looked at Starsunder's chair, still clearly alive and attached to the gigantic shadowtop tree they'd climbed so laboriously to the top of, up a spiral stair that had seemed endless. "I suppose there's no chance of getting a chair like this anywhere else but in the Elven Court?"

"None," Starsunder said with a wide smile, "at all. Sorry."

Umbregard snorted. "You don't sound sorry at all. Why did we have to sweat our weary ways up here, step after thousandth step; what's wrong with using spells to fly?"

"The tree needed to get to know you," his elf host explained. "Otherwise, when you sat down just now, it'd quite likely have hurled you off into yonder clouds like a catapult . . . and I'd have had no human wizards to chat with this evening."

Umbregard shuddered at the vision of being help-lessly thrust out, out into the oh-so-empty air, before starting that terrible, long plunge . . .

"*Aghh!*" he shrieked, waving his hands to sweep away his mental vision. "Gods! Away, away! Let's get back to our converse! When we were eating—ohh, that treejelly! How d—no. Later, I'll ask that later. *Now* I want to know why you said, when we were eating, that Elminster stands in such danger just now—and stands also so close to being an even greater danger to us all . . . why?"

Starsunder looked out over miles of greenery toward the distant line of mountains for a moment before he said, "Any human mage who lives as many years as this Elminster outstrips most human foes of his own mak-ing; they die while he lives on. His very longevity and power make him a natural target for those of all races who would seize him, or his powers from him, or his supposed riches and enchanted items. Such perils con-front all mages who've enjoyed any success."

Umbregard nodded, and his elf host continued.

"It's reasonable to suppose that a wizard of greater success attracts greater attention, and so greater foes, yes?"

Umbregard nodded again, sitting forward eagerly. "You're going to tell me about some great mysterious foes that Elminster's now facing?"

Starsunder smiled. "Such as the Phaerimm, the Malaugrym, and perhaps even the Sharn? No."

Umbregard frowned. "The Phaerr—?"

Starsunder chuckled. "If I tell you about them, they won't be mysterious any longer, will they? Moreover, you'll live the rest of your days in fear, and no one will believe you when you spread word of them. Each time you speak of them will increase the likelihood that one of their number will feel sufficient need to silence you— and so bring to a brutal and early end the life of Umbregard. No, forget them. It's good practice for mages, forgetting and letting go of things that interest them. Some of them never learn how, and die long before their time."

Umbregard frowned, opened his mouth to say something, and shut it again. Then it popped open once more, and he said almost angrily, "Well then, if we're to speak of no foes, what special danger does Elminster face?"

A small, tightly curled leaf at Starsunder's elbow opened then to reveal two glass bowls full of what looked like water. He passed one of the bowls over to Umbregard and they drank together.

It was water, and the coolest, clearest that Umbregard had yet tasted. As it slid down to every corner of his being, he felt suddenly fully awake and vigorous. He turned his head to exclaim about how he felt, looked into Starsunder's eyes, and saw sadness there. He hesitated in speaking just long enough for the moon elf to say deliberately, "Himself."

"Himself?" By the gods, had he been reduced to an echo? And was this his sixth evening here with Starsunder . . . or his seventh?

Yes. He was like a small child invited into the converse of adults, seeing a longer, graver view of Faerûn around him for the first time. With a sudden effort, Umbregard held his tongue and leaned forward to listen.

Starsunder rewarded him with a slight smile and added, "With all the friends, lovers, foes, and even realms of his youth gone, Elminster will feel increasingly alone—and as is the way of humans, lonely. He will cling to all he has left—his power and accomplishments of magecraft—and begin to chafe at the bargain that has robbed him of his youth, and of all the things he might have done, but did not . . . in short, he will become restless in the service of Mystra."

"No! You said so yourself: love—"

"It is the way of humans," Starsunder continued calmly, "and of us all, at differing times in our lives . . . but now it is I who digress. In short, Elminster will for the first time as a mature mage of power—as opposed to an ardent, easily-distracted youth—be ready to notice temptations."

"Temptations?"

"Chances to use his power as he sees fit, without the bidding of, or restrictions decreed by others. The desire to do just as he pleases, ignoring consequences for good or ill, smashing all who stand against him. To do whatever he's idly thought of doing, pursuing every whim."

"And so?"

"And so, while he's about it, every living creature on or under fair Toril must cower and hide—for what fate will Umbregard enjoy, if it strikes a passing Elminster that a handful of Umbregard tripes will make a good toy, or meal, for the next few minutes?"

The elf let his words hang in silence for a time, waiting for Umbregard to speak.

Soon enough the human wizard was unable to resist doing so. "Are you saying," he asked softly, "that we—I—or someone . . . must set out to destroy Elminster now, to save all Toril?"

Starsunder shook his head almost wearily. "Why is it that humans love that word so much? 'Destroy!' " He set his water bowl back into the leaf and asked with a smile, "If you succeeded, Umbregard the Mighty, tell me: who then would protect Toril from *you?*"

*   *   *   *   *

If I was a lurking Slayer, I would want a lair . . .

"Sweet Mystra," Elminster murmured, smiling despite himself, "whatever you do, stop me from *ever* trying to be a bard." He took another step along the crumbling wall of the ruin, the slight scrape of his boot on damp dead leaves seeming very loud in the eerie quiet of the empty forest.

Somehow he knew this crumbling keep had to be linked to whatever was killing folk and forest creatures hereabouts. He'd felt it clear out along the coast road, calling him here . . . calling him . . .

He stopped and glared up at the mossy stones. Could a spell be at work on him, drawing him here?

He'd have felt any simple charm or suggestion . . . wouldn't he?

Abruptly El wheeled around and started back across the sagging bridge, heading away from the ruins at a steady pace. He looked back once, just to be sure nothing was speeding toward his back, but all seemed as quiet as before. He still felt as if he was being watched, though.

He studied the toothlike remnants of walls for a long time, but nothing moved and nothing seemed to change. With a shrug, El turned around again and headed back down the road.

He hadn't gone far when he saw it—out of the corner of his eye, expected but yet not what he'd expected—a woman watching him from between two duskwood trees. He spun toward the trees, but there was no one there. He turned slowly on his heel, all around, but he saw no watching human, or anyone flitting from tree to tree or crouching in any hollow. He'd have heard the dead leaves rustling at any such movement, anyway.

With a little smile, El turned back to the road and an unhurried trudge along it back to the coast road. He suspected he'd not have to wait long before seeing that face peering at him again—for that was what it had been; no gowned figure, but a head and a neck. She could even be a floating ghost.

If she was the Slayer, that could well explain the lack of tracks to follow or creatures for the High Duke's men to corner. The manner of slaying even argu—

There she was again, peering at him from a tree ahead. This time El didn't rush forward but turned slowly to look in all directions . . . and as he'd expected, that face peered at him from a tree behind him, back toward the ruins, just long enough for their eyes to meet.

He smiled slowly and walked back to that second tree. He was only a few paces from it when a ghostly face turned to regard him from high in a tree a good distance closer to the ruins. Elminster gave her a cheery wave this time and allowed himself to be led back to the ruins. The sooner he got to the bottom of this, the sooner he could be away from here before dark, and on about the main task Mystra had set him.

He went the other way around the walls this time, just to cover new ground, and found himself looking, through gaps in the crumbling stonework, into a vast chamber that seemed to have furniture in it. He moved carefully nearer through the tangle of stunted shrubs and fallen stone, peering.

"There!" a voice snarled—human, rough, and not far away. As Elminster ducked low and spun around, he heard the familiar hum of approaching arrows. The life those arrows sought was his.

* * * * *

Ilbryn Starym reined in at the sentry's startled yell and held up an empty hand. "I come in peace," he began, "alone—"

By then javelins were whizzing his way and men
with hastily-drawn swords in their hands and fear and
astonishment warring on their faces were leaping
through the trees on all sides. "Elves!" one of them
roared. "I *told* you 'twas elves, all along—"

The elf sighed, threw off his cloak with the word that
made the world dark, and backed his snorting mount to
one side. Its sudden jerk told him one of the javelins had
found a mark even before it reared up, spilling him out
of his saddle, and came crashing down heavily on its
side—inches away from Ilbryn. The elf rolled away as
hard as he'd ever done anything in his life. A stray hoof
numbed his good hip and had probably laid it open, too.

Bloody humans! Can't even ride along woodland
trails without getting jumped by idiot adventurers
arrogant enough to pitch their encampments *right*
across the trail itself.

Ilbryn found his feet, stumbled awkwardly away
until he ran into a tree, and propped himself against it.
The humans were blundering around in the little corner of nightfall he'd made, hacking at each other—of
course, the fools!—shouting in alarm, and generally
despoiling their camp and the woods immediately
around them. If these were the Slayers, they were more
than inept . . . no, these must be one of the bands of
hireswords—hah! They thought he was the Slayer!

Right, then . . .

Cloaked in darkness only he could see through,
Ilbryn watched the fray rage for a time as he caught
his breath and peered around, seeking mages or
priests who might have the wits and power to end his
spell. Once he unleashed another, his darkness would
fall like a dropped cloak—so he wanted that spell to be
a good one.

Two of this benighted band of adventurers were
dead already at the hands of their fellows, and as Ilbryn
watched, a third met a screaming end spitted on two
javelins. The stronger of his slayers ran him back

against a tree and left him pinned to it and vomiting his lifeblood away. The elf shook his head in disgust and kept looking . . . there!

That man by the tent, bent over the scrolls. Ilbryn readied his spell, then plucked up a stone from beside his tree, measured the throw with narrowed eyes—and threw. The stone bonged off the pot and spilled it into the fire.

The man with the scrolls whipped his head around to see what had befallen, and two other adventurers came loping back through the trees, employing that most favorite of human words, "What?" in the midst of many oaths.

A goodly group. Now, before they all ran off again! Ilbryn steadied himself against the tree, cast the spell as quietly as he could but with unhurried care, and was rewarded, an instant before its end, with the human mage hissing, "Hoy, all—*be still!* Listen!"

The seven-odd adventurers obediently stopped their shouting and rushing about, and they stood like statues as the darkness fell away—and waist-high whirling shards of steel melted out of the empty air and cut them all in half. A few of them even saw the elf standing against a tree sneering at them.

The crouching mage was beheaded, his blood exploding all over the scrolls as he slumped forward into the dirt. Seeing that, Ilbryn didn't bother to survey the slain any longer; he was listening hard now for the sounds of the living. At least two, and possibly as many as four, were still lurking close by.

One of them ran right past him, shrieking in horror as he sprinted into the bloody camp. Sweet trembling trees, were all humans this *stupid?*

Evidently they were; two others joined the first, weeping and yelling. Ilbryn sighed. It wouldn't be long before even fools such as these noticed a motionless elf standing against a tree. Almost regretfully he sent forth the spellburst that slew them.

Its echoes were still ringing off the trees around when he heard the slight scrape of a boot that made him spin around—to stare at a lone, horror-struck human warrior three paces away, coming toward him with sword raised.

"*You're* the Slayer?" the man asked, face and knuckles white with fear.

"No," Ilbryn told him, backing away around the tree.

The man hesitated, then resumed his cautious advance. "Why did you kill my sword brothers?" he snarled, snatching out a dagger to give himself two ready fangs.

Ilbryn took another step back, keeping the tree between them, and shrugged. "You made a mistake," he told the human, as they started to slowly circle the tree, watching each other's eyes. "I was riding along the trail, at peace and intending no harm to you—and you attacked me, more than a dozen to one. Brigands? Adventurers? I'd no time to parley or see who you were. All I could do was defend myself. A little thought before swinging swords could have saved so much spilled blood." He smiled mockingly. "You should be more careful when you go out in the woods. It's dangerous out here."

That evoked the rage he'd hoped it would; humans were so predictable. With a wordless roar the warrior charged, hacking furiously. Ilbryn let the tree take most of the blows, waited until the blade got caught, then darted forward to snatch the man's dagger hand aside with one of his own hands—and press the other to the man's face, delivering the spell that would take his life.

Flesh smoked and melted; gurgling, the man went to his knees. By the despairing moan he made thereafter, he knew he was dying, even before he started clawing at his own flowing flesh, trying to get air.

"Not that I was unhappy to slay you all," Ilbryn told him lightly, "seeing as how you cost me a perfectly good horse." He stepped back and shot a look all around, in case other surviving adventurers—or the Slayer, whoever that might be—was approaching. No such peril seemed at hand.

The warrior made a last choking noise, then seemed to relax. "After all," Ilbryn told him, "This is the Dead Place, I'm told."

The elf turned away to walk through the camp and see if there was anything he might put to his own use. A few paces along he stopped, looked around again for foes, and bent rather stiffly and plucked up a good, slender blade from among the trodden leaves.

"Just in case," Ilbryn told the torn body of its dead, staring owner, whose fingers would forever be stretched out now toward the blade he'd let fall, the blade that now was no longer there. As the elf reached out with his own sword to cut free the scabbard from amongst the gory, tangled harness, he added almost merrily, "You never know when you'll need a good blade, after all."

Sixteen

IF MAGIC SHOULD FAIL

*If magic should fail, Faerûn shall be changed forever—
and not a few folk would welcome those changes. For one
thing, the very land itself might tilt under the hurrying
weight of the oppressed and aggrieved, chasing down
now-powerless mages to settle old scores. I wonder what
a river of wizards' blood would look like?*

Tammarast Tengloves, Bard of Elupar
from **The Strings of a Shattered Lyre**
published in The Year of the Behir

"Begone! Mighty events shake all Faerûn, and the
holy ones within cannot come out to speak to you now!
For the love of Mystra, begone!"

The guard's voice was deep and powerful; it rolled
out over the gathered crowd like a storm-driven wave
crashing across the sands of a beach . . . but when it
died away, the people were still there. Fear made their
voices high and their faces white, but they clung to the
front steps of the House of the Ladystar as if for their
very lives and would not be moved.

The guard made a last grand "get hence" gesture and stepped back off the balcony. "I'm sorry, Bright Master," he murmured. "They feel something is very wrong. It'd take the hounding spells of Mystra herself to shift them now."

"Do you dare to blaspheme *here,* in the holy place itself?" the high priest hissed, eyes blazing with fury. He drew back his hand as if to strike the guard—who stood a head taller than he, despite his own great height—then let it fall back to his side, looking dazed. "Lost," he said, lips trembling. "All is lost. . . ."

The guard enfolded the Lord of the House in a comforting embrace, as one holds a sobbing child, and said, "This shall pass, lord. Wait for nightfall; many shall leave then. Wait, know peace, and watch for some sign."

"You have some guidance for this counsel?" the high priest asked, almost desperately. He could not keep a quaver from his voice.

The guard patted his shoulders and stepped away with the grave reply, "Nay, lord—but look you; what else can we do?"

The Lord of the House managed a chuckle that was perilously close to a sob, and said, "My thanks, loyal Lhaerom." He drew in a deep breath, threw back his head as if donning his dignity like a mantle, and asked, "What do warriors do when they must wait and watch inside their walls, dawdling until a great blow falls on them?"

Lhaerom chuckled in return. "Many things, lord, most of which I leave to your wits to conjure up. There is one thing of comfort we undertake, which I suspect me your question seeks: we make soup. Pots and pots of it, as good and rich as we can manage. We let all partake, or at least smell if they cannot sup."

The high priest stared at him for a moment, then raised his hands in a "why not?" gesture and commanded the silently watching underpriests, "Get hence! To the kitchens, and make soup! Go!"

"You'll find, lord," the hulking guard added, "that—"

"Lhaerom," one of his fellow guards snapped, "fresh trouble." Without another word the guard turned away from the Lord of the House and ducked back out onto the balcony. The priest took two steps after him—only to find a guard barring his way. "no, lord," he said, face carefully expressionless. " 'Twouldn't be wise. Some of them are throwing stones."

Outside, the bright sun fell on the closed bronze doors of the House of the Ladystar. Many fists fell thereon, too, and the guards and gatepriest had long since stopped answering knocks and cries for aid. They paced anxiously back and forth inside the gate, casting anxious glances at the bolts and bars, wondering if they'd hold. All of the spikes that could be found in the temple cellars had long since been driven between the stones to wedge the doors against being forced inward. The bright marks on those spikes told how often this morning the doors had already been sorely tested. The priest licked dry lips and asked, for perhaps the fortieth time, "And if this all gives way? What—"

The guard nearest him waved violently for him to fall silent. The priest frowned and opened his mouth to snap an angry response, then his eyes followed the guard's pointing hand to the doors and his jaw dropped almost to chest.

A man's hand was protruding *through* the bronze, magic crackling around his wrist where it passed through the thick metal. It was gesturing, forming the hand signs used between clergy of Mystra when enacting silent rituals.

The priest watched a few of them, then hissed, "Stay here!" and went pounding up the steps to a door that led into the barbican. He had to get onto that balcony. . . .

The hands of the tall man in the black cloak were trembling as he drew them back from the doors. He knew he'd been seen and knew the mood of the crowd pressing in behind him. "It's no use," he said loudly. "I can't get in."

"You're one of 'em, though, aren't ye?" a voice snarled, close by his ear.

"Aye, I saw him—used a spell, he did!" put in another, high with fear and anger—or rather, the angry need to lash out.

The man in the black cloak made no reply, but looked up at the balcony in desperate hope.

It was rewarded. Two burly guards came into view with long pikes in their hands—pikes fully able to reach down, into, and through anyone standing near the gate—and asked gruffly, more or less in unison, "Yes? You have lawful business in this holy house?"

"I do," the man in the black cloak told them, ignoring the angry mutterings that rose in a wave after his words. "Why are the gates closed?"

"Great doings on high demanding contemplation on the part of all ordained servants of Mystra," the guard thundered.

"Oh? Is there an orgy going on in there, or just a pig-wallowing feast?" someone called from the thick of the crowd, and there were roars of agreement and derision. "Aye, let us in! We want some too!"

"Begone!" the guards bellowed, straightening to face the entire crowd.

"Does Mystra live?" someone cried.

"Aye!" Others took up the call. "Does the goddess of magic yet breathe?"

The guard looked scornful. "Of *course* she does," he snarled. "Now go away!"

"Prove it!" someone yelled. "Cast a spell!"

The guard hefted his pike. "I don't cast spells, Roldo," he said menacingly. "Do you?"

"Get one of the priests—get 'em all!" Roldo called.

"Aye," someone else agreed. "And see if one of them—just *one* of them—can cast a spell!"

The roar of agreement that followed his words shook the very temple walls, but through it the man in the black cloak heard one of the guards mutter, "Aye, and make it a good big fireball, right about *there*."

The other agreed, not smiling.

"Look," the man in the black cloak said to them, "I *must* speak to Kadeln. Kadeln Parosper. Tell him it's Tenthar."

The nearest guard leaned over. "No, *you* look," he said coldly. "I'm not opening these gates for anybody . . . short of holy Mystra herself. So if you can come back holding hands with her, and the two of you asking very nicely to come in, all right, but otherwise . . ."

A third figure was on the balcony, peering around the guard's shoulder. It wore the cloak and helm of a guard, but no gauntlets, and the helm—which was far too big for it—kept slipping forward over its face.

An impatient hand shoved the helm back up out of the way, and the white, worried face of Kadeln, Tome-priest of the Temple, stared down at his friend. "Tenthar," he hissed, "you shouldn't have come here. These people are wild with fear."

"You know," the man in the black cloak remarked almost casually, "standing down here with them, I'd begun to notice that." Then his control broke and he almost clawed his way up the wall to the balcony, ignoring a warning pike thrust. The dirty blade stopped inches from his nose and hung there warningly. Tenthar paid it not a blind bit of attention.

"Kadeln," Tenthar was snarling, "*what's going on?* Every last damned magic I work goes wild, and when I study—nothing. I can't *get* any new spells!"

"It's the same here," the white-faced priest whispered. "They're saying Mystra must have died, and—"

One of the guards hauled Kadeln away from the edge of the balcony, and the other jabbed viciously with his pike; Tenthar flung himself desperately back out of its reach and tumbled down the bronze doors to the ground.

The crowd melted away a few paces as if by magic, and he found himself lying in a little cleared space with the pike once more hanging a handspan above his throat. "Who are you?" the guard behind it demanded. "Answer, or die. I have new orders."

Tenthar sat up and thrust the pike head away with one contemptuous hand. When he scrambled to his feet, however, he took care to be a good two paces beyond its reach.

"Tenthar Taerhamoos is my name," he said sternly, opening his cloak to reveal rich robes, and a gem-studded medallion blazing on his chest. "Archmage of the Phoenix Tower. I'll be back."

And with that grim promise the archmage whirled around and pushed his way almost proudly through the crowd. All around him were murmurs of "It's *true!* Mystra's dead? Magic all undone?" and the like.

A stone spun out of somewhere and struck Tenthar on the shoulder. He did not stop or try to turn but struggled onward through bodies disinclined to let him pass. "An archmage?" someone cried. "With no spells?" another asked, close at hand. Another stone struck Tenthar, on the head this time, and he staggered.

There was a roar of mingled awe and exultant hunger all around him, and someone shrieked, "Get him!'

"Get him!" a thunderous chorus echoed. Tenthar went to his knees, looked up to see boots and sticks and hands coming at him from all sides, clutched his precious medallion to guard against the spell going wild, and said the words he'd hoped not to have to say.

Lightning crackled out in all directions, and Tenthar tried not to look at the dying folk dancing to its hungry surges around him. Chain lightning is a terrible thing even when unaugmented; with the medallion involved, well . . .

He sighed and stood up as the last of the screams died away, watching the bobbing heads of those who'd lived to flee grow smaller as they ran across the fields. He'd best be running, too, before some bloodthirsty idiot rallied them or the folk here who were only stunned and twitching recovered enough to seek revenge.

The smell of cooked flesh was strong; bodies were heaped on all sides. Tenthar gagged, then broke into a trot. He never even saw the pike hurled at him from the balcony; it fell well short and struck, quivering, in the dirt.

A blackened body rose from among the dead and tugged it free. "The thing I hate most about these little games," it remarked to the empty air, "is the *cost*. How many lives will be snuffed out before it's over, this time?"

Another blackened thing rose, shrugged, touched the pike, and said sadly, "There's always a price . . . all our power, and we can't change that."

There were two shimmerings in the air—and the two blackened bodies were gone. The pike winked out of sight an instant later.

"Are there archmages under every stone out yonder? Or just what bloody dancing gods were *those?*" the guard who'd thrown the pike barked, more fear than anger in his tones.

"Mystra and Azuth," the priest beside him whispered. The guards turned to look at Kadeln—and gasped in amazement. The missing pike had just appeared in the priest's shuddering hands. He stared at them, eyes full of wonder, and moaned, "Mystra and Azuth, they were. Standing right there, with the symbols they've granted us to know them by glowing above their heads—right *there!*"

He tried to point out into the litter of bodies, but decided to faint instead. He did it very well, eyes rolling up and body folding down. One of the guards caught him out of force of habit, and the other snatched hold of the pike.

If gods were going to come calling, he didn't want to be standing there unarmed.

* * * * *

"Mystra is dead!" the Darklady declared exultantly. "Her priests find their spells to be but flickering things, and mages study and find no power behind their words. Magic is now ours alone to command—ours to control!"

The purple flames that raged in the brazier before her cast strange lights on her face as she raised eyes that were very large and dark to gaze at them all. Around the flames sat her eager audience: the six priests of the Dark Lady who'd agreed to work as wizards, harnessing for their spells the power of what had already become known in the temple as the Secret in the Sphere. With them she could make the House of Holy Night the mightiest temple of Shar in all Faerûn—and the faith of the Nightbringer the most powerful in all Toril. It might not even take long.

"Most loyal Dreadspells," the high priestess told them, "you have a great opportunity to win the favor of Shar, and power for yourselves. Go forth into Faerûn and seek out the most capable mages and the largest holds of magic. Slay at will, and seize all you can. Bring back tomes, rare things, and anything that bears the tiniest glow of magic. You *must* slay any of those servants of Mystra called the Chosen if you meet with them. We here shall work most diligently with our spells to try to find them for you."

"Your Darkness?" one of the wizards asked hesitantly.

"Yes, Dread Brother Elryn?" Darklady Avroana's voice was silken; a clear warning to all that anyone who dared to interrupt her had better have a *very* good reason for doing so—or she'd soon give them one.

"My work involves farscrying our agents in Westgate," Elryn said quickly, "and rumor now abroad in that city speaks of many recent sightings of a Chosen in the vicinity of Starmantle . . . something about going into a 'Dead Place' . . ."

"I, too, have heard such tidings," the Darklady agreed eagerly. "My thanks for giving us a location, Elryn. All of you shall go there immediately—and there begin your holy task. Thrust your hands into the flames—oh, and *most* loyal Dreadspells, bear in mind that we can see and hear you always."

Six faces paled—and six hands were reluctantly extended into the flames. Darklady Avroana laughed delightedly at their fear and let them burn for a few moments ere she said the words that teleported them all elsewhere.

*   *   *   *   *

It was very peaceful in the woods around the shrine—and, since the killings had begun and fear had driven folks away, very quiet.

Most days Uldus Blackram was alone on his knees before the stone block, halfheartedly lashing himself a few times—gently, so as not to make much noise—and whispering prayers to the Nightsinger.

The shrine had been founded so nicely, consecrated with blood and a wild ritual that still made Uldus blush to remember it. Now there were no black-robed ladies to dance and whirl barefoot around the horned block and no one to lead him in the half-remembered prayers . . . so he did a lot of just thanking Shar for keeping him alive on his stealthy visits to the woods. He hoped she'd forgive him for not coming at night anymore.

"May your darkness keep me safe from the Slayer," Uldus breathed, his lips almost touching the dark stone. "May you guide me to power and exultation over mine enemies, and make of me a strong sword to cut where you need things cut, and slash where it is your will to slash. Oh, most holy Mistress of the Night, hear my prayer, the beseeching of your most loyal servant,

Uldus Blackram. Shar, hear my prayer. Shar, answer my prayer. Shar, heed m—"

"Done, Uldus," said a voice from above him, crisply.

Uldus Blackram managed to strike his head on the altar, somersault over backward to get a good four paces away, and get to his feet all in one blurred flurry of movement.

When he froze, half turned to flee and panting hard, he was looking back at six bald-headed men in black and purple robes, standing in a semicircle around the altar facing him, with faint amusement on their faces.

"Lords of the Lady?" Uldus gasped. "Have my prayers been answered at last?"

"Uldus," the oldest of them said pleasantly, stepping forward, "they have. At last. Moreover, a fitting reward has been chosen for you. You're going to guide us into the Dead Place!"

"P-praise Shar!" Uldus replied, rolling his eyes wildly upward as he toppled to the turf in a dead faint.

"Revive him," Elryn commanded, not bothering to keep the contempt from his face or voice. "To think that such as this worship the Most Holy Lady of Loss."

"Well," one of the other wizards commented, bending over the fallen Uldus, "we all have to start somewhere."

* * * * *

The glowing spellsphere orbited the throne at an almost lazy pace. Saeraede gave it only casual attention, absorbed as she was in sending images of her peering self out into the trees to lure this bold Elminster back to her castle.

Aye, let us gently tease this fittingly powerful and somewhat attractive mage hence.

Yet the news was clear enough, from all the mages she covertly farscried. Word of the death of Mystra was

spreading like wildfire, spells were going wild all over
Faerûn, mages were shutting themselves up in towers
before grudge-holding commoners could get to them—
or tarrying too long, and getting caught on the ends of
pitchforks in a dozen realms, and on and on.

It was time to move at last and make Saeraede
Lyonora once more a name to be feared!

Abruptly something tore through one of her images.
Saeraede sat up with a frown, and peered, trying to find
out what it had been. The spellsphere abruptly lost its
scene of city spires and flapping griffon wings beneath
armored riders and acquired the dappled gloom of the
forest above her. A forest that held a crouching Elminster, several of her floating faces, and—

Arrows snarled through her conjured visage and the
dead leaves beyond, to thud into the forest loam and send
Elminster scrambling around the other side of a tree.

Arrows?

"Damned adventurers!" she roared, her cry ringing
back to her off the cavern roof, and sprang up from the
throne. The spellsphere winked out as it fell, the radiance around the stone seat faded—but she was already
whirling up the shaft, her eyes spitting flames of mage-
fire. Were a bunch of blundering sword swingers going
to shatter her long-nursed plans *now?*

*   *   *   *   *

The fittingly powerful and somewhat attractive
Elminster boldly dodged another arrow, hurling himself
on his face in wet moss and dead leaves as another dark
shaft whined past his ear like an angry hornet and
fetched up in the trunk of a nearby hiexel with a very
solid thunk.

El scrambled up, drawing breath for a curse, and
flung himself right back down on his face again. A

second shaft hummed past low overhead, joining the first.

The hiexel didn't look to be enjoying these visitations too much, but Elminster hadn't time to survey its sadness—or do anything else but charge to his feet, leap over a fallen tree, and whirl around behind its rotting trunk. He bobbed up into view right away, betting that the two archers wouldn't have had time to put fresh arrows to their strings just yet. He had to see them.

Ah! There! He loosed a stream of magic missiles at one, then ducked down again, hearing the approaching thud of booted feet running hard in his direction.

It was time to get gone and be blessed quick about it!

He sprinted away, downhill and dodging from side to side, hearing crashing in his wake that heralded the coming of someone large, heavy, armored, and sword-waving. He didn't stop to exchange pleasantries, but whirled around a tree to let the grizzled armsman have some magic missiles full in the face. The man's head jerked back, wisps of smoke burst from his mouth and eyes, and he ran on blindly for another dozen paces before stumbling and crashing to the ground, dead or senseless.

"Dead or senseless." Hmm; 'twould do as a motto for some adventuring bands, to be sure, but . . .

It was time to circle around and take care of that second archer, or he'd be fleeing through the forest feeling phantom arrows between his shoulder blades for the rest of the day . . . or until they brought him down.

El trotted a goodly way off to the right and started to work his way back toward the ruin, keeping as low and as quiet as possible. It didn't matter if he spent hours worming his way closer, so long as he wasn't seen too soon. He had to get close enough to—

A grim-looking man in leathers, with a bow ready-strung in his hand, stepped into view around a gnarled phandar not twelve paces away. He couldn't help but see a certain hawk-nosed mage the moment he lifted his eyes from the arrow he'd just dropped. El lifted his hand to shoot forth his last magic missiles spell.

A moment later the archer exploded into whirling bones and fire. El had a brief glimpse of two dark eyes—if they were eyes—in a confused whirlwind of mist. Then whatever it was had gone, and scorched bones were thudding down onto the moss.

The Slayer?

It had to be. The talk had been all of something that burned its victims when it killed; this was it. "Well met," Elminster murmured to the empty woods, and went cautiously forward. He knew he'd already find nothing but ashes and bones of the rest of the adventurers, but just in case . . .

Sprawled garments, weapons, and bones were everywhere he looked, as he drew near the overgrown keep. The ruins seemed deserted again. A tense silence hung over them, almost as if something was waiting and watching for his approach. El stole back to the gaps in the wall he'd looked into before. That big chamber, where he'd seen the wardrobes and . . . a mirror? That would bear another look, to be sure.

He peered very cautiously into that vast room again and met those dark eyes once more, the mist they were at the heart of swirling around a wardrobe as its doors banged open. Then the mist flared into blinding brilliance and he couldn't see what was taken out of the wardrobe. Whatever it was, the whirlwind spun around and around it, almost as if deliberately hiding it from his view in its bright and chiming tatters, as it sped away across the room. El almost clambered in the gap after it to see better, but paused prudently when the glowing mist did.

It lingered in the farthest, darkest corner of the room for a moment, hovering above what looked like a well, then plunged down into that ring-shaped opening and out of sight.

"Ye want me to follow, do ye?" Elminster murmured, looking at the well. He glanced around the room, taking in the peeling mirror, the row of wardrobes—the open one holding an array of feminine apparel—the lounge, and the rest . . . then walked straight to the well.

"Very well," he said with a sigh. "Another reckless leap into danger. That does seem to be what this job most entails."

And he clambered over the edge of the well, dug his hands into the first of a row of handholds in the stone and tapped with the toes of his boots for another, found it, and started down. He might need his hellbent flying spell for getting back out again.

*   *   *   *   *

She laid out the three gowns on the stone at the bottom of the shaft as gently as a nurse stroking a sick child, and as gently set loose stones from the rubble over them. The exacting effort cost her much energy, but she worked swiftly, heedless of the cost, and darted away before her quarry got to the top of the shaft to look down.

A moment later she was sinking into one of the runes that sustained her, hiding her misty self entirely. She had been hungry too long, and the incessant chiming was even getting on *her* nerves.

Brandagaeris had been a mighty hero, tall and bronzed and strong; she had fed on him for three seasons, and he had come to love her and offer himself willingly . . . but in the end she had drained him and gone hungry again. That was her doom; once her own body had fallen to dust, what remained was a magic that needed to feed on the living—or dwell within, and necessarily burn out the innards of a young, strong, vital body. Brandagaeris had been one such, the sorcerer

Sardon another . . . but somehow mages, clever as they were, lacked something she craved. Perhaps they had too little vitality.

She hoped this Elminster wouldn't be another such disappointment. Perhaps she could win his love, or at least his submission, and not have to fight him long to taste what power a Chosen held.

"Come to me," she whispered hungrily, her words no more than the faintest of sighings above the deep-graven rune. "Come to me, man-meal."

Seventeen

A FINE DAY FOR TRAVEL

Travel broadens the mind and flattens the purse, they say. I've found it does rather more than that. It shatters the minds of the inflexible, and depletes the ranks of the surplus population. Perhaps rulers should decree that we all become nomads.

Then, of course, we could choose to stay only within the reach of those rulers we favor—and I can't conceive of the chaos and overburdened troops and officials that would be found in any realm in which folk could choose their rulers. Thankfully, I can't believe that any people would ever be crazed enough to do that. Not in this world, anyway.

Yarynous Whaelidon
from **Dissensions of a Chessentan**
published in The Year of the Spur

"You're doing just fine, brave Uldus," Dreadspell Elryn said soothingly, prodding their trembling guide with the man's own sword. Brave Uldus arched away from the blade, but the noose around his neck—held tight and short-leashed in the fist of Dreadspell Femter—kept him from entirely missing its sharp reminder. Dreadspell Hrelgrath was walking along close by, too, his dagger held ready near the ribs of their unwilling guide.

"Shar is very pleased with you," Elryn told the man, as they went on along the almost invisible game trail, deeper into the Dead Place. "Now just show us this ruin . . . oh, and Uldus, reassure me again: it is the *only* ruin or building or cave or construct you know about, anywhere in these woods, is it not?"

Choking around his noose, Uldus assured him that it was, oh, yes, Dread Lord, indeed it was, may the Nightbringer strike me down now if I lie, and all the watching gods bear witness—

Femter didn't wait for Elryn's sign this time before jerking the noose tight enough to cut Uldus off in mid-babble. The guide silently clawed at his throat, stumbling, until Femter relented enough to let him breathe again.

"Iyrindyl?" Elryn asked, without turning his head.

"I'm watching, Dread Lord," the youngest Dreadspell replied eagerly. "The first sign of walls or the like, I'll cry hold."

"It's not walls I'm seeing," the deep drawl of Dreadspell Daluth put in, a few strides later, "but an elf—alone, and walking with a drawn sword in his hand, yonder."

The Sharran priests stopped, unnecessarily clapping their hands over the mouth of their guide, and glared through the trees. A lone elf looked back at them, disgust written plain on his face.

A moment later, Elryn snarled, "Attack!" and the Sharrans surged forward, Elryn and Daluth standing still to hurl spells. They saw the elf sigh, take off his cloak and hurl it high over a tree branch, then turn to face them, crouching slightly. "Damned human adventurers!" he cried. "Haven't I killed enough of you *yet?*"

*   *   *   *   *

Ilbryn Starym watched the wizards run toward him—*charging* wizards? Truly, Faerûn was plunging deeper into madness with every passing day—took up the blade that was battle-booty from the last band of fools, and said a word over it. When he threw it like a dart at the onrushing men, it glowed, split into three, and leaped away like three falcons diving at separate targets.

At the same moment, a tree just behind the line of running wizards turned bright blue and tore itself up out of the earth with a deafening groan, hurling earth and stones in all directions. Someone cursed, sounding very surprised.

An instant later, a sheet of white lightning broke briefly over the running mages, and a man who seemed to have a noose around his neck convulsed, clawed at the air for a few moments and shrieked, "My *reward!*" and fell to earth in a twisted heap. The wizards ran on without pause, and Ilbryn sighed and prepared to blast them to nothingness. His three blades should have done *some*thing.

One of the running mages grunted, spun around, and went down with something glowing in his shoulder. Ilbryn smiled. One.

There was a flash, someone cried out in surprise and pain, and the three remaining wizards burst through the still-shimmering radiance and came on, one of them shaking fingers that trailed smoke. Ilbryn lost his smile. Some sort of barrier spell, and it had taken both of his other blades.

He raised his hands and waited. Sure enough, now that they were close enough to him that the army of Ilbryn and the army of half a dozen mages could count each other's teeth, the panting wizards were coming to a halt and preparing to hurl spells at him.

Ilbryn cloaked himself in a defensive sphere, leaving only a keyhole open for his next spell. If his measure of these dolts was correct, he'd not have overmuch to fear in this battle . . . even with the wizard who'd taken his blade slowly crawling to his feet and the two who hadn't come running strolling slowly closer in the distance.

Abruptly the air in front of Ilbryn's sphere was filled with blue flowers, swirling about as they drifted to earth. An elf mouth crooked into a smile. By the startled oaths coming to his ears, *that* hadn't been supposed to happen. Perhaps he was caught up in some school of wizardry's battle test of the inept apprentices. He waited politely to see what else would come his way.

A moment later, he blinked with new respect. The earth was parting with a horrible ripping sound, between the boots of one of the mages—and racing toward Ilbryn, zigzagging only slightly as it came. Trees, boulders, and all were hurled aside in the chasm's swift advance, and Ilbryn readied his lone flight spell, just in case. He'd have to time this just right, collapsing the sphere and bounding aloft more or less in one smooth sequence.

The chasm swerved and snarled on past, trailing the awed yells of a wizard who seemed astonished he'd cast it. Ilbryn's eyes narrowed. What sort of madmen were these?

Well, he'd wasted more than enough time and magic on them already. He hurled a quick spell of his own out of the keyhole, and stood watching as the trunk of the shadowtop he'd shattered, a goodly distance above the wizards, spun about almost lazily, then came crashing down.

Wizards shouted and hurled themselves in all directions, but when the dancing, flailing branches receded to a shivering, one man lay broken like a discarded doll under a trunk ten times his girth.

Ilbryn risked another spell through the keyhole. Why not a volley of magic missiles? These idiots seemed almost like bewildered actors *playing* at being mages, not foes to fear at all.

He hoped, a moment later, that he hadn't just given the gods some sort of awful cue.

*　*　*　*　*

"If Mystra is dead, what's helping *his* spells?" Dread-spell Hrelgrath snarled, puffing his way back to where Elryn stood watching, cold-eyed.

"Whatever god of magic elves pray to, dolt," Daluth answered—an instant before blue-white bolts of force came racing their way.

"Back!" Elryn snapped, "I don't think these can miss, but *back*, anyway! This is costing us too much!"

Elryn's prediction proved to be right; none of the bolts missed. The Dreadspells grunted and staggered their ways back through the trees, hoping the elf wouldn't bother to follow them.

"Femter?" Elryn snapped.

A head snapped up. "I'll be all right, the next time the power surges into us," Femter replied grimly. "Some sort of magical blade. Can't use my arm, though."

"Our guide—dead?"

"Very," Femter said shortly, and there were a few dark chuckles.

"Iyrindyl?"

"Down. Forever. Half a tree fell on him."

Elryn drew in a deep breath and let it out in a ragged sigh, very conscious of the unseen eyes of Darklady Avroana upon him. "Right—consider that fiasco our first battle-practice. There'll be no more charging into any fray. From now on, we creep through these woods like shadows. When we find the ruin, we wait for the Weave to feed us once more, then—and only then, even if it takes all night—we advance. Out in these woods, only the Chosen really matters to us, and I'm not going to be caught off-guard again."

*   *   *   *   *

"*That's* a good plan," Ilbryn agreed sarcastically, as he let his clairaudience collapse, said farewell to the idiot wizards and their chatter, and cast the guidance spell that would take him to these ruins they'd been heading for. He bid it seek out man-touched stone, in any mass larger than four men—which should eliminate tombstones and the like—and in *this* general direction . . .

Almost immediately he felt the pull of the magic. Ilbryn followed it obediently, striding off through the woods along an invisible but unwavering line. Ah, but magic could be useful at times.

*   *   *   *   *

It had been cold and dark in Scorchstone Hall for many years. Too cold for the living.

A skeleton threw back the shutters of one window to let the sun in and went back to a table where a spellbook lay. Sitting down carefully in the stoutest chair left in the Hall, the skeleton took up the tome, clutched it to its ribcage with both bony arms enfolded around it, and called on the power of the spell it had cast earlier. The power that let it speak.

It said only two words, firmly enough that they echoed back from the dark corners of the room. "Mystra, please."

Blue-white fire burst forth from the book. The skeleton almost dropped the book in surprise, its bony fingertips clawing at its covers, as the flames that burned nothing washed over its bones, racing from the book to . . . her.

Sharindala shuddered as blue-white fire ran up and down her limbs, leaving something in its wake. She stared down at her glowing bones in wonder, then back at the book, feeling something rising in her throat.

* * * * *

Baerdagh stiffened at the sudden sound that came through the trees, and almost dropped his walking stick. He turned, to be absolutely sure that the faint weeping was coming from Scorchstone.

It was. In the very heart of that ruined mansion, a woman was sobbing—crying as if she'd never find breath to speak again. In dark, haunted Scorchstone, where the skeletal sorceress walked.

Baerdagh broke into a frantic shuffle, heading for the Maid—where strong drink, and plenty of it, would be waiting.

* * * * *

"Along here, it should be," Beldrune said, as they came around the bend and almost rode down an old man with a walking stick, who looked to have just taken up trotting, and was wheezing loudly to let the world know. "There! Up ahead, on the left—the Fair Maid of Ripplestones. We can get a good meal there, and decent beds a few doors on, and ask in both places about where Elminster's been hereabouts. I know he likes to look at old mages' towers."

"And their tombs, too," Tabarast put in. "It's been some years since I stopped here, but old Ralder, if he's still alive, used to roast a mean buck."

The down-at-heels Harper with the pale brown hair and eyes, riding between them, nodded pleasantly. "Sounds good," was all he said, as they slowed their horses at the ramshackle porch and rang the gong that would bring the stable boys.

An old man sitting on a bench deep in one corner of the porch looked at them sharply—especially at Tabarast—as they strode inside. After a moment, he got up and drifted into the Maid on their heels.

It seemed Caladaster was hungry enough for a second earlyevenfeast this day. By the time Baerdagh came puffing up to the front door of the Maid, Caladaster was sitting with the three horsemen who'd almost ridden him down as if they'd known each other for years.

"Aye, I know this Elminster, right enough," Caladaster was saying, "though a few days back I'd have answered you differently. He came walking up to this very tavern. Baerdagh—oh, hey! *This* is Baerdagh; come sit down with us, old dog—and I were warming yon bench, where you saw me just now, and he came striding up and bought us dinner—a huge feast it was, too!—in return for us telling him about Scorchstone Hall. Gods, but we ate like princes!"

"We can do no less," the youngest, poorest-looking of the three horsemen said then, saying his first quiet words since handing a stable boy some coins. "Eat hearty, both of you, and we'll trade information again."

"Oh, a-heh. Well enough . . . that's very kind of you, to be sure," Caladaster said heartily as he watched platters of steaming turtles and buttered snails brought to the table. Alnyskavver even winked at him as the tankards were set down beside them. Caladaster blinked. Gods, he was becoming a local lion!

"So where and what is Scorchstone Hall?" Beldrune asked almost jovially, plucking up a tankard and taking a long pull at it. Baerdagh didn't fail to notice the face the newcomer made at the taste of the brew or how quickly he set down the tankard again.

"A ruined mansion just back along the road a ways," he said quickly, determined to earn his share of the meal. "You passed it on your way in—the road bends around it, just this side of the bridge."

"It's warded," Caladaster said quietly. "You gentlesirs are mages, are you not?"

Three pairs of eyes lifted to him in brief silence until Tabarast sighed, took up a buttered snail that must have burned his fingers, and grunted, "It shows that badly, does it?"

Caladaster smiled. "I was a mage, years ago. Still am, I suppose. You have the look about you . . . eyes that see farther than the next hedge. Paunches and wrinkles, but yet fingers as nimble as a minstrel's. Not to mention the wardings on your saddlebags."

Beldrune chuckled, "All right, we're mages—two of us, at any rate."

"Not three?" Caladaster's brows rose.

The man with the pale brown eyes and the tousled hair smiled faintly and said, "Here and now, I harp."

"Ah," Caladaster said, carefully not glancing at the regulars in the Maid, who were bent almost out of their chairs straining not to miss a word of what passed between these travelers and the two old tankard-tossers. Wizards, now! And haunted Scorchstone! Mustn't miss this. . . .

A Harper and two wizards, hunting Elminster. Caladaster felt a little better, now, about telling them things. Hadn't Elminster had summat to do with starting the Harpers?

"Scorchstone Hall," Caladaster continued, in a voice so low that Baerdagh's sudden humming completely cloaked it from the ears of folk at other tables, "is the home of a local sorceress—a lady by the name of Sharindala. A good mage, and dead these many years. Of course, there are the usual tales of her being seen walking around past her windows, as a skeleton and all . . . but you'd have to be a damned good tree-climber to get to where you could just see a window of the Hall—let alone look through its closed shutters!"

He got smiles at that, and continued, "Whatever—Elminster asked us all about her, and we warned him about the wards, but it's my belief he went in there and did summat. We asked him to stop by our places—we live, Baerdagh an' I, in the two cottages hard by Scorchstone, 'twixt there and here—when he was done, so's we'd know he'd fared well—"

"And we wouldn't have to go in there looking for his body," Baerdagh growled and went back to his humming. Tabarast and the Harper exchanged amused glances.

Caladaster gave his old friend what some folks would call a dirty look and took up his tale again. "He did drop by to see us—looked right happy, too, though he had a little sadness about him, like folk get when they remember friends now gone, or see old ruins they remember as bright and bustling. He said he'd a 'task' to get on with, and had to head east. We warned him about the Slayer, o' course, but—"

"The Slayer?" the Harper asked quietly. Something about his words made the whole Maid fall silent, from door to rafters.

Alnyskavver, the tavern master, moved quickly forward. "It's not been seen here, lords," he said, "whatever it be. . . ."

"Aye, you're safe here," someone else grunted.

"Oh? Then why'd old Thaerlune pack up and move back to—"

"He *said* he was going to see his sister, her bein' sick an' all—"

Caladaster's open hand came down on the table with a crash. "*If* you don't mind," he said mildly into the little silence that followed and turned to the three travelers again.

"The Slayer is summat that has the High Duke, up in his castle Starmantle way, very worried. Summat is killing everything that lives in the forest, or travels the coast road past it, between Oggle's Stream—just beyond us here—and Rairdrun Hill. Cows, foxes, entire bands of hired adventurers, and several of 'em, too—everything. They've taken to calling it the Dead Place, this stretch of woods, but no one knows what's doing the killing. Some say the dead have been burned away to bones, others say other things, but no matter. We don't know what killer we're facing, so folk've been calling it the Slayer." He looked around the taproom. "Well enough? Said it all, didn't I?"

There were various grunts and grudging agreements, one or two hastily shushed dissenting opinions, and Caladaster smiled tightly and lowered his voice again. "Elminster walked straight into the Dead Place, he did, an' must be there now," he said. "I don't know right why he had to go there . . . but it's summat important, isn't it?"

There was a brief silence again. Then the Harper said, "I think so," at the same moment as Tabarast snapped, "*Everything* Elminster does is important."

"You're going after him?" Caladaster asked, in a voice that was barely above a whisper.

After a moment, the Harper nodded again.

"I'm going with you," Caladaster said, just as quietly. "That's a lot of woods, an' you'll need a guide. Moreover, I just might know where he was headed."

Beldrune stirred, "Well," he said gravely, "I don't know about that. You're a bit old to be going adventuring, and I'd not want to be—"

"Old? *Old?*" Caladaster asked, his jaw jutting. "What's *he*, then?" He pointed at Tabarast. "A blushing young lass?"

That old mage fixed Caladaster with a gaze that had made far mightier men quail, and snapped, " 'Just might know' where Elminster was heading to? What did he tell you—or are you guessing? *This* blushing young lass wants to know."

"There's a ruin in that forest," Caladaster said quietly, "in, off the road. You can tramp around in the trees all day waiting to get eaten by the Slayer while you search for it, or I can take you right to the ruin. If I'm wrong—well, at least you'll have one more old, overweight mage and his spells along for the jaunt."

"Overweight?" Tabarast snapped. "Who's overweight?"

"Ah," Beldrune said, clearing his throat and reaching for a dish of cheese stuffed mushrooms that Alnyskavver had just set down on the table, "that'd be me."

"I don't think it's a good idea to bring one more man along," Tabarast said sharply, "whom we may have to protect against the gods alone know what—"

"Ah," the Harper said quietly, laying a hand on Tabarast's arm, "but I think I'd very much like to have you along, Caladaster Daermree. If you can leave with us in the next few minutes, that is, and not need a night longer to prepare."

Caladaster pushed back his chair and got up. "I'm ready," he said simply. There was something like a smile deep in the Harper's eyes as he rose, set a stack of coins as tall as a tankard on the table—many eyes in the room bulged—and said, "Tavern master! Our horses— here's stabling for a tenday and for the feast. If we come not back to claim them by then, consider them yours. We'll walk from here. You set a good table."

Baerdagh was staring up at his old friend, his face pale. "C-Caladaster?" he asked. "Are you going yon, in truth—into the Dead Place?"

The old wizard looked at him. "Aye, but we can't take along an old warrior, so don't fear. Stay—we need you to eat all the rest of this for us!"

"I—I—" Baerdagh said, and his eyes fell to his tankard. "I wish I wasn't so old," he growled.

The Harper laid a hand on his shoulder. "It's never easy—but you've earned a rest. You were the Lion of Elversult, were you not?"

Baerdagh gaped up at the Harper as if he'd just grown three heads, and a crown on each one. "How did you know about that? *Caladaster* doesn't know about that!"

The Harper clapped his shoulder gently. "It's our business to remember heroes—forever. We're minstrels, remember?"

He strode to the door and said, "There's a very good ballad about you. . . ."

And then he was gone. Baerdagh half rose to follow, but Caladaster pushed him firmly back down. "You sit, and eat. If we don't come back, ask the next Harper through to sing it to you." He went to the door, then turned with a frown. "All those years," he said, scowling, "and you never told me you were the Lion! Just such a little thing it slipped your mind, huh?"

He went out the door. Tabarast and Beldrune followed. They just gave him shrugs and grins at the door, but Tabarast turned with his fingers on the handle and growled, "If it makes you feel better, you're not the only one who doesn't know what's going on!"

The door scraped shut, and Baerdagh stared at it blankly for a long while—long enough that everyone else had come back from the windows and watching the four men walk out of town, and sat down again. Alnyskavver lowered himself into the seat beside Baerdagh and asked hesitantly, "You were the Lion of Elversult?"

"A long time ago," Baerdagh said bitterly. "A long time ago."

"If you could go back to some moment, then," the tavern master asked a tankard in front of him softly, "what moment would it be?"

Baerdagh said slowly, "Well, there was a night in Suzail . . . We'd spent the early evening running through the castle, there, chasing young noble ladies who were trying to put their daggers into one another. Y'see, there was this dispute about—"

Turning to Alnyskavver to properly tell him the tale, Baerdagh suddenly realized how silent the room was. He lifted his eyes, and turned his head. All the folk of Ripplestones old enough to stand were crowded silently around him in a ring, waiting to hear.

Baerdagh turned very red and muttered, "Well, 'twas a long time ago. . . ."

"Is that when you got that medal?" Alnyskavver asked slyly, pointing at the chain that disappeared down Baerdagh's none-too-clean shirtfront.

"Well, no," the old warrior answered with a frown, "that was . . ."

He sat back, and blushed an even darker shade. "Oh, gods," he said.

The tavern master grinned and slid Baerdagh's tankard into the old warrior's hand. "You were in the castle in Suzail, chasing noble ladies up and down the corridors, and no doubt the Purple Dragons were chasing you, and—"

"Hah!" Baerdagh barked. "They were indeed—have you ever seen a man in full plate armor fall down a circular stair? Sounded like two blacksmiths, fighting in a forge! Why, we . . ."

One of the villagers clapped Alnyskavver's shoulder in silent thanks. The tavern master winked back as the old warrior's tale gathered speed.

* * * * *

"Not all that much more sun today," Caladaster grunted, "once we're in under the trees."

"Umm," Beldrune agreed. "Deep forest. Lots of rustlings, and weird hootings and such?"

Caladaster shook his head. "Not since the Slayer," he said. "Breezes through the leaves, is all—oh, and sometimes dead branches falling. Otherwise, 'tis silent as a tomb."

"Then we'll hear it coming all the easier," the Harper said calmly. "Lead on, Caladaster."

The old wizard nodded proudly as they strode on down the road together. They'd gone some miles and were almost at the place where the overgrown way to the ruins turned off the coast road, when a sudden thought struck him—as cold and as sudden as a bucket of lake water in the face.

He was very careful not to turn around, so that the Harper could see his face—this Harper who'd never given his own name. But from that moment on, he could feel the man's gaze on him—a cold lance tip touching the top of his spine, where his neck started.

The Harper had called him by his full name. Caladaster Daermree.

Caladaster *never* used his last name . . . and he hadn't told the Harper his last name; he never told anyone his last name. Baerdagh didn't know it—in fact, there was probably no one still alive who'd heard it.

So how was it that this Harper knew it?

Eighteen

NO SHORTAGE OF VICTIMS

*The one certainty in a coup, orc raid, or well-side gossip
session is that there'll be no shortage of victims.*
                    Ralderick Hallowshaw, Jester
    from **To Rule A Realm, From Turret To Midden**
          published circa The Year of the Bloodbird

It was dark and silent, once the scrape of his boots
had stilled. He was alone in the midst of cold, damp
stone, the dust of ages sharp in his nostrils—and a
feeling of tension as something watched him from the
darkness, and waiting.

Elminster let himself grow as still as the stone handholds he still clung to, faced the aware and lurking
darkness, and called up one of the powers Mystra had
granted him. It was one he'd used far too little, because
it required quiet concentration, and time . . . far more
time than most of the beings he shared Faerûn with
were ever willing to give him. Too often, these days, life
seemed a headlong hurry.

His awareness ranged out through the waiting,

listening darkness. Things both living and unliving he could not see, but magic, when El concentrated just . . . *so,* he could feel so keenly that he could make out surfaces on which dweomer clung, the tendrils of spell-bindings, and even the faint, fading traces of preservative magics that had failed.

All of those things lay before him. Faint magics swirled everywhere, none of them strong or precisely located, but outlining a large cavern or open space. A good way off, on the floor of this chamber or cavern—or down in a pit, he could not tell which—several closely clustered nodes of great, not-so-slumberous magical might throbbed and murmured ceaselessly. El blinked.

Trap or no trap, he had to see what waited here that could hold such magical might. He'd been led here; the swirling sentience that had done it was watching him or at least knew of his coming—so what was the point of stealth? El cast a stone-probing spell, seeking pits or seams ahead of him. Shrouded in its eerily faint blue glow, he stepped warily forward.

Great expanses of the floor were the natural rock of the cavern; as El proceeded, this gave way smoothly to a floor of huge stone slabs, smooth-polished and level; no mosses had stained them, but here and there, the fine white fur of salts leaching out of age-old rock trailed fingerlike across the stone.

A throne or seat of the same stone faced Elminster—empty of magic, surprisingly, though it was almost hidden from view behind the dazzle thrown off by the seven nodes of magic when he viewed it with his magesight. Thankfully, the seat was empty.

El sighed, threw back his head, and stepped forward. Seven nodes blinding in their magical might. Predictable or not, he could not ignore such power and remain Elminster. He smiled, shook his head ruefully—and took another step.

He might well die here, but he could not turn away.

*   *   *   *   *

The human was coming nearer. The Great Foe would soon be within reach—but also close to the runes that were too powerful to safely approach.

Too close.

He would probably get only one chance, so it would have to be a shattering blow that even a great god-touched mage could not hope to survive. After all these years, a few days or even months more would matter not at all. The slaying stroke did.

The strike that would reveal him and harm the Foe all at once had to be one that destroyed—or at least ruined his foe into something powerless but aware— aware of the pain he would then deal to it at leisure, and of who was harming it during that long, dark time . . . and why.

So wait a bit more, like a patient ghost in the shadows.

Two dark eyes that blazed like two inky flames of fury peered from the depths of one of the darkest clefts in the rear of the cavern and watched the wary wizard step forward to his doom.

Years consumed by the ache to avenge, the gnawing need that ruled him night and day . . . years that had all come down to this.

*   *   *   *   *

"Yes, Vaelam?" Dreadspell Elryn asked, his voice dangerously soft and silky. A long, tense creeping advance to a ruin where powerful foes were almost certainly waiting for them had not improved his temper— especially after one of his boots had found its first muddy, water-filled old burrow hole. That had occurred three paces before his other boot found the second. He'd lost count, since then, of how many creeper thorns had torn at him and raked across his hands and face . . . and all of it, of course, watched sneeringly from afar by the cruel upperpriestesses of the House, among them the Darklady herself.

Vaelam was practically dancing with excitement, his eyes large and round. The foreguard of the Sharran "wizards" was a thin, soft-spoken priest, both careful and thorough in his duties. He was more excited, now, than Elryn had ever seen him.

"Dark Brother," he hissed excitedly, "I've found something."

"No," Elryn murmured, frowning, "Really? You *do* surprise me."

"It's a stone," Vaelam continued, astonishingly not catching Elryn's thick sarcasm at all—or displaying uncommonly swift skill at hiding his recognition of it. "A stone with writing on it."

"Writing that says . . . ?"

"Well, ah, just one letter actually—but one as long as a man is tall. It's a 'K'!"

"No!" Femter gasped sarcastically. "Could it be?"

"Brother, it is," Vaelam confirmed. He seemed genuinely oblivious to their derision.

"Show us," Elryn ordered curtly, and raised his voice a trifle. "Brothers, move slowly, keep apart, and watch the trees around. I don't want us crowded together when someone strikes from hiding. If we arrange things so that one fireball might take care of all of us, a hostile mage might not be able to resist his opportunity, hmm?"

"Aye," Daluth murmured, at the same time as someone else—Elryn couldn't tell who—muttered, "Thinks of everything, our Elryn."

Dark thoughts or not, the "wizards" of Shar reached the stone slab Vaelam had found without incident. It lay between two mossy banks, almost entirely covered with years of rotting, fallen leaves, but the K could clearly be seen. The deep-graven letter sprawled across

a little more ground than one of the ornate temple
chairs would cover; the stone slab seemed both old and
huge.

Elryn leaned forward, not bothering to hide his own
swift-rising excitement. Magic. This had to have something to do with magic, strong magic . . . and magic was
what they were here for.

"Uncover it all," he ordered and stood back prudently to watch as this was done. The stone proved to be as
long across, or longer, than a man laid out straight on
his back, and twice that in the other direction, as well
as being—at the one point where the ground dipped,
along its edges—at least as thick as the length of a
short sword.

When they were done uncovering it, the Sharrans
stared at the massive slab . . . and it lay there patient-
ly looking back at them.

It knew who would blink first.

After the silence grew uncomfortably long and the
lesser priests started snatching sidelong glances at
their leader, Elryn sighed and said, "Daluth, work the
spell that wizards use to reveal magic. I can see no
trigger to this—but there must be one."

Daluth nodded and did so. Elryn was as shocked as
everyone else when he raised his head slowly and said,
"No magic at all. None upon yon slab or around it. Nothing but what few things we carry, within reach of my
spell."

"Impossible," Elryn snapped.

Daluth nodded. "I agree . . . but my spell cannot lie
to me, can it?"

As Elryn stood glaring at him, there was a common
gasp of relief—of held breaths let out—from the other
Sharrans, and they strode forward to stand on the slab
as if it had been calling to them.

Elryn whirled, a shout of warning rising to his lips—
a shout that died unuttered. The priests under his command strode across the slab, scraped their boot heels

on it, stomped and strolled, staring about at the trees
as if the slab was an enspelled lookout that gave them
some sort of special sight. No bolts of lightning burst
from the stone to slay them, and none of them shifted
shape, screamed, or acquired unusual expressions on
their faces.

Instead, one by one, they shrugged and fell silent,
blinking at each other and back at Elryn, until Hrelgrath said what they were all thinking: "But there must
be *some* magic here, some purpose for this—and it can't
be the lid of a tomb, or you'd need a dragon to lift it on
and off."

Daluth raised a brow. "And because we have no dealings with dragons, no one does? What if this is some
sort of storage box built by a dragon, for its own use?"

"In the midst of a forest? Right out in the open and
down low, not girt about with rock? Admitting my
unfamiliarity with wyrms, that still *feels* wrong to me,"
Femter replied. "No, this smacks of the work of men—
or dwarves working for men, or mayhap even giants
skilled at stonemasonry."

"So what or who doth the 'K' refer to?" Vaelam burst
out. "A king, or a realm?"

"Or a god?" Daluth echoed quietly, and something in
his voice brought all eyes upon him.

"Kossuth? In a forest?" Hrelgrath said in puzzled
tones.

"Nay, nay," Vaelam said excitedly. "What was the
name of that mage in the legend, who defied the gods
to steal all magic and become himself lord over all
magic? Klar . . . no, *Karsus*."

And as that name left the young Sharran's mouth,
he vanished, gone in the instant ere he could draw
breath. The slab where he had stood, so close between
Femter and Hrelgrath that they could easily have jostled elbows with him, was empty.

Those two brave and steadfast priests sprang and
sprinted away from the slab with almost comical haste,

as Daluth nodded grimly, his eyes fixed on the spot where Vaelam had stood, and Elryn said slowly, "Well, well . . ."

The four remaining priests stared at the slab in silence for a few tense moments before the most exalted Dreadspell said almost gently, "Daluth, stand upon the letter and utter the name Vaelam did."

Daluth cast a quick glance at Elryn, read in his face that this was a clear and firm order, and did as he was bid. Femter and Hrelgrath shifted uneasily as they watched their most capable comrade wink out of existence, and the appropriate one couldn't suppress a low groan of fear when Elryn said, "Now do likewise, Hrelgrath."

Hrelgrath was trembling so with fear that he could barely shape the name "Karsus," but he vanished as swiftly and utterly as his predecessors. Femter shrugged and strode onto the slab without waiting for an order, looking back for Elryn's nod of assent when he'd planted his boots squarely in the center of the giant letter. The nod was given, and another false wizard disappeared.

Now alone, Elryn looked around at the trees, saw nothing moving or watching, shrugged, and followed his fellow Sharrans onto the slab.

Even before their battle with the elf who'd slain Iyrindyl with such casual ease, he'd thought this entire scheme of holy Sharrans trying to be mages was wrong—dangerously wrong. Dreadspells, indeed. Still, if by some miracle what lay at the other end of this teleport was not one huge trap, it just might lead to enough magic to win them Darklady Avroana's holy approval—and survival long enough to enjoy it. He smiled slowly at that thought, said, "Karsus," with slow deliberation, and watched the world whirl away.

*   *   *   *   *

A red radiance lit up the darkness, gleaming back from a hundred curves of metal and countless gems. The light was coming from the floor—wherever they'd walked, the boot prints were a-glow.

It was too late to cry out a warning about awakening guardian spells or beings—Vaelam was already wading through knee-deep, shifting wonders to pluck at a gauntlet whose rows of sapphires were winking with their own internal light: the lambent glow of awakened magic, echoed in sinister chatoyance from a dozen places around the crypt. The low-ceilinged room was crammed with heaped treasures, most of them strange to the eye, and all of them, by the looks of it, harboring magic.

Elryn managed to keep from gasping aloud, but he was conscious of the quick glance Daluth threw him and knew his awe and wonder must be written plainly on his face.

The junior Dreadspells certainly hadn't wasted any time. Hrelgrath seemed to be waltzing with an armored figure as he tried to wrest a gorget from it, and a row of sheathed wands slapped and dangled against Femter's right thigh, depending from a gem-encrusted belt that enwrapped his waist as if it had been made for him. It had altered to fit him, of course. The eager-eyed priest was already reaching into another heap of armbands and anklets, seeking out something else that had caught his eye. Vaelam was drawing on the gauntlet, now, his eyes already on something else.

Only Daluth stood empty-handed, his hands raised to deliver a quenching spell should one of the reckless younger Dreadspells unleash something that could doom them all.

Elryn darted glances in all directions, saw nothing moving by itself and no doors or other ways out of the stone-walled room, and asked quietly, "Oh most diligent Dreadspells, has anyone spared a thought for how we'll be able to leave this place?"

"Karsus," Hrelgrath said clearly, the gorget clutched triumphantly in his hands.

Nothing happened, but Vaelam was already pointing into the farthest, dimmest corner of the chamber. "Another 'K' in a clear spot of floor yonder," he reported. "That'll be it."

"Aye, but to take us back out—or in deeper, to somewhere else unknown?" Daluth asked.

"Moreover, if I was intending to slay thieves who found their way hence uninvited, the way out is where I'd place guards of one sort or another," Elryn added, then—having not moved a pace from where he'd appeared—said, "Karsus" carefully. No whirling before his eyes occurred again, but he was unsurprised.

Slithering metallic sounds heralded Vaelam's continued digging—and as Elryn watched, he saw Femter slip something into his robes, his fingers working at a hitherto-hidden underarm pouch.

"Take nothing you cannot carry," the senior Dreadspell warned, "and be fully prepared to surrender unto the Darklady every last item of magic we bear out of this place, no matter how trifling. We are not unobserved, now and always."

Femter's head snapped up, and he blushed as he found Elryn's eyes upon him. He opened his mouth to say something, but Daluth forestalled him by asking the room at large, "Has anyone found something whose powers are obvious?"

He was answered by shaken heads and frowns.

Elryn used the toe of his boot to open a small black coffer, lifted his eyebrows to the ceiling when he saw the row of rings it contained, snapped it shut again, then blinked at what had lain next to it.

"Daluth," he asked quietly, inclining his head toward the heap of gleaming mysteries by his boot, "that circlet—hasn't that symbol been used to mean healing?"

Daluth pounced on the diadem. It was of plain but massy gold over some more durable metal, and it bore the device of a gleaming sun cupped in two stylized hands. "Yes," he said excitedly. He held it up to show the others and snapped, "Find more of these. Leave off looking at other things for now."

The lesser Dreadspells did as they were bid, digging and tossing aside treasures, and rising, from time to time, with cries of satisfaction. Daluth took the items they proffered—four circlets and a bracer—and Elryn snapped, "Enough. All of you, take only so much as what you can wear or carry, and leave swords and helms and suchlike behind. We dare not try to awaken anything here. Gird yourselves as if for battle; I don't want to see anyone staggering under an armload of loose items."

He reached down and plucked up a number of scepters from among a litter of metal-bound tomes, platters and smaller boxes. Then, as if in afterthought, he casually picked up the black coffer, its dozen rings riding safely hidden inside it.

A few moments of work with the long thongs that always rode in his belt pouch, and the scepters were riding ready at his hip, the coffer hidden down the front of his breeches. Elryn was ready. He said briskly, "Vaelam, the honor is yours, I believe. Take us from this place."

The youngest Dreadspell looked at the clear space at the back of the crypt, waiting in silence for him, swallowed, and said, "You said there might be guards. . . ."

Elryn nodded. "I have every confidence that you'll deal with them quite capably," he said flatly, and waited.

Reluctantly the youngest priest-turned-wizard picked his way through the crowded room, slowing as he approached the letter on the floor. Four pairs of eyes watched him go, their owners crouching down behind heaps of unidentified magic. Vaelam sent them all a look of mingled anger and despair, drew himself erect, and snapped, "Karsus."

As swiftly and as silently as he'd first left them, Vaelam disappeared.

As if that had been a signal, something moved in the heap nearest to Hrelgrath, rising amid a clatter of many small things sliding and tumbling as the Sharran stumbled back, moaning in wordless alarm.

"Do nothing," Elryn snapped. In frozen silence the four men watched a glowing sword rise into view, its naked and glittering blade aimed somewhere between Daluth and Elryn. It seemed a good five or six feet long, its ornate hilt a-wink with many lustrous gems, an ever-changing array of runes and letters flickering momentarily up and down the blue flanks of its blade.

"Hrelgrath," Elryn ordered, "follow Vaelam. Keep low, and do nothing in haste. Go now."

When the second sweating Dreadspell winked elsewhere, the sword in the air seemed to shiver for a moment, but otherwise moved not. Elryn watched it for a while, then said slowly, "Femter, follow the others."

Again the sword stayed where it was. When only Daluth and Elryn were left, the senior Dreadspell asked his most capable comrade, "In case some spell prevents us from ever returning here, is there anything in particular we should bear with us?"

Daluth shrugged. "It'd take years to examine all that's here—and even then, we'd only know a few powers of each thing. This is utterly . . . fantastic. There's more magic crowded in here around us than I think all who worship Holy Shar, in their thousands, can muster. If I have to take just one thing—let it be that stand of staves, yonder. Four staves, I think; almost one for each of us, and all of them sure to hold some sort of magic we can wield in a battle. If we can awaken them, we can at least play convincingly at being archmages . . . for a little time."

"Let's hope it's long enough, a little time," Elryn agreed, "when it comes. Two each?"

They gave the floating sword another long look, slipped carefully past it, and Daluth took the two staves under one arm and pulled out a wand he'd found earlier in the other. The healing circlets bulged in his scrip.

Elryn looked down at Daluth's ready wand, smiled tightly, and quoted the saying, "We dare not trust anyone save Holy Shar herself." As he spoke, he raised the wand already in his own hand into view so that Daluth could see it.

"I mean this for perils I may find beyond the teleport," Daluth said carefully, "not for—closer dangers." His voice changed, sharpening in alarm. " 'Ware the sword!"

Elryn whirled around to find the sword hanging just as before. He was still turning as he heard Daluth add calmly, "Karsus."

The senior Dreadspell sprang wildly sideways, just in case Daluth had found the urge to trigger his wand irresistible and sprawled on a heap of enspelled clothing. Glowing mesh flickered under him as he slithered painfully down it, traveling over an array of sharp points; hastily Elryn clawed his way upright, snatched another look at the sword, and found it still motionless.

He looked around the room, down at the red footprints already beginning to fade to the hue of old blood, around at the thankfully motionless heaps of treasure, and cast his gaze once more down at the clothes he'd fallen on. Surely that was a stomacher, such as haughty ladies wore . . . he caught up one garment then another, feeling the tingling of powerful magic surging through his fingertips. They were all gowns, with cutouts in the meshes beneath ornate bodices.

Elryn of Shar looked at the shoulders of one, frowning in consideration . . . then shrugged and began to strip off his own clothes. He'd best hurry, if he was to be swift enough to keep the others out of mischief—or, knowing this lot, just from wandering off without him. Struggling in the growing dimness while trying to keep his eye on the sword floating nearby, Elryn was briefly glad they'd found no mirror that he'd have to look at himself in. He could imagine Avroana's mirth as she watched him battling the unfamiliar garment—and when at last he stood on the letter on the floor, and with one wary eye on that floating blade, uttered the name "Karsus," it was just this snarled side of a heartfelt curse.

*   *   *   *   *

The smoking stump of what must have been an old and large duskwood gave mute testimony to the effectiveness of something one of the younger Dreadspells had awakened. Elryn stared at it with dark anger rising in him, but before he could say anything, Femter was thrusting a ring at him excitedly.

"Dark Brother, look! This ring—against the best seeking Brother Daluth can cast—completely cloaks the dweomers of all magic in contact with its wearer! One could go into the presence of a king armed for a beholder war and strike with impunity."

"Such bold stratagems are usually more effective in ballads than in real life," Elryn replied severely, "to say nothing of prudence." He looked for Daluth and found him carefully taking forth one circlet after another from his scrip.

"Ah," the leader of the Dreadspells announced in satisfaction, "a wiser way to spend time. Let us all heal ourselves, then devote a short time to examining wands and staves before resuming our journey to the ruins."

Several more trees suffered in the moments that followed. The healing items all proved to be of more effectiveness than a single use. Two of the staves proved to have no more battle-worthy spells than the ability to spit forth the streaking bolts men called "magic missiles," but the others could unleash beams of ravening fire and explosive bursts of magic . . . and two of those seemed able to drain touched magic items and even the spells of their wielders upon command, to power their most destructive attacks.

"What shining luck!" Vaelam laughed, blasting a helpless shadowtop sapling to ashes.

"Luck? Holy Shar led us to this spot, Dark Brother," Elryn said severely, playing to the priestesses watching from afar. "Shar guides us always . . . you will do well never to forget that."

"Of course," Vaelam said hastily, then laughed heartily as the staff in his hands snarled again—and another tree vanished in roiling flames that fell away into streamers of smoke diving down to the leaf mold all around.

"Vaelam of Shar," Elryn said sharply, "stop that wasteful destruction at once. I'd rather not have this forest aflame around us or every druid and mage within a hundred miles appearing around us to give battle. Have you forgotten Iyrindyl's fate already?"

Vaelam grimaced, but he couldn't seem to stop fondling and hefting the staff, like a warrior who's just been handed a superb blade.

"My apologies, Dark Brother," he said, chastened, "I-I got caught up in its power." He licked his lips, firmly grounded the staff, and asked, as if seeking approval, "Do you know how tempting it is just to blast down everything that irritates or stands against you?"

"Yes, Vaelam, as a matter of fact, I do," Elryn replied, and wiggled the wand in his hand—the wand pointed at Vaelam's face—ever so slightly to draw the younger man's eyes. As Vaelam saw, and paled, the senior Dreadspell continued grimly, "It's just one of many such temptations."

Erlyn smiled tightly and thrust the wand back into his belt. "Aye," he added slowly, setting out at a steady pace in the direction of the ruins. "One of many."

He gestured curtly for the Dreadspells to follow. Reluctantly, they did so. Vaelam stopped to cast a longing look back at the stone slab, and the woods beyond it—and found himself looking right into the coldly smiling eyes and leveled staff of Daluth, who was watchfully bringing up the rear.

Vaelam managed a halfhearted smile, but Daluth's eyes grew no warmer. The youngest surviving Dreadspell swallowed, turned, and trudged off toward doom.

$$* \quad * \quad * \quad * \quad *$$

"Now, *this* curling of the leaf, on the other hand, tells you that this is a si—"

Starsunder paused in mid-word and straightened up suddenly, almost knocking his head against Umbregard's. The human mage stumbled hastily back out of the way as the elf threw out his hands.

Still standing dramatically stiff with his arms spread, the moon elf threw back his head and opened his mouth as if trying to taste the sky.

Silence fell. Umbregard watched his statuelike friend for what seemed like a very long time before he dared to ask, "Starsunder?"

"You expect someone else to jump into this body just because I stop moving?" came the mild reproof, as Starsunder turned his head, spun around, and took hold of Umbregard's arm all in one smooth motion. "Do you know of some body snatching, wizardly peril I'm unaware of?"

"W-where are we going?" Umbregard asked in lieu of a reply, as the slender moon elf practically dragged him around and between trees, dark green half cloak swirling.

"Where we're needed, and urgently," Starsunder said almost absently, urging the human he was towing into a trot.

"And where—" Umbregard was puffing now, even though they were descending a fern-covered slope rather than climbing, "—might *that* be?"

"In a forest almost as old as this one, across an arm of the sea," Starsunder replied, his voice as calm and his breathing as steady as if he'd been lounging at ease on a giant leaf rather than racing through the woods, leaping fallen trees and roots, and swinging around forest giants. "No place that humans remember a name for."

"Why?" Umbregard almost shouted, sprinting as fast as he ever had in all his life, with the slim elf still half a stride faster than he and threatening to drag his arm out of its socket.

"Trees are burning," Starsunder told him with a frown, "suddenly, as if struck by lightning or firestorm, where there's no storm in the sky to do such harm— and here we are!"

They plunged between two shadowtop trees that seemed perfectly matched, growing not three feet apart—and somewhere in the gloom between a blue haze plucked them and hurled them far away.

Umbregard's next step was in a different forest—one more dry and empty of calling birds and rustling animals. He gaped and tried to look behind him, but at that moment Starsunder let go of his arm and took hold of his chin. Staring into Umbregard's eyes from inches away, the moon elf murmured, "Make no unnecessary noise, and don't call out to anyone you see . . . even if they're old friends. Hmmm; especially if they're old friends."

"Why?" Umbregard asked, almost despairingly; why had he bothered to learn to speak any other word but "why"?

"You'll live longer," Starsunder said, laying two gentle fingers across the human mage's lips. "That's why."

*   *   *   *   *

The Phoenix Tower was dark and cool and lonely. With his fortress ringed by thick thorns, jagged rubble, and a break- neck chasm dug by his golems literally as they were falling apart, Tenthar felt secure from intrusion by all save the most persistent adventurers. If any such came calling, he'd just have to be very good at hiding . . . or dying.

The Archmage of the Phoenix Tower had long ago passed beyond loneliness into boredom—after all, how often can one read old and familiar spellbooks that one dare not try any castings out of? He was tired of trudging down to the cellars in the dark to gobble mushrooms like some sort of tomb beast. For that matter, he was tired of trudging everywhere rather than flying—and never leaving the Tower.

All he'd seen of Faerûn these last rides was the view his windows commanded. He lived from dawn to dusk, not daring to frivolously use any of the eight precious candle ends he'd found—he, Tenthar Taerhamoos, who was used to conjuring light as needed, almost without thinking. A light after dark might attract the attention of adventurers or hungry beasts that someone was in the shuttered tower. Not two days ago he'd slammed and bolted the shutters just in time. He'd spent most of the rest of the day crouched behind them, dry-mouthed in fear, listening to an angry peryton flap and slash with its horns at the old wood that he hoped would hold fast.

And if such foes got into the Tower, what could he do? He had no particular strength or skill at arms, and his spells failed him all the time, now—or at least, whenever he didn't bolster them with the precious power of his medallion, which was growing more feeble with each use.

He'd called on it too often in the early days of this spell-chaos, when he'd been frantic to find out what was

happening, and why. Now he was just sitting in the endless gloom waiting for magic to obey him once more—
or someone to force their way into the Phoenix Tower
and kill him.

Each morning Tenthar went down into the underpantry, cast a simple spell from his memory, and grimly watched it turn the stone walls purple or make them
start to melt or be goaded into a mad display of sprouting flowers—or whatever new idiocy struck Mystra's
whimsy that day. Each morning he hoped spells would
return to normal and he could begin life as the Archmage of the Phoenix Tower again.

Every day his visit to the underpantry disappointed
him.

Every day he grimly climbed back up into the cold
and lonely kitchens, boiled himself some beans and cut
a little more green mold off the huge wheel of cheese
under the marble hood before he climbed the stairs to
the big window, to study anew the spell he'd miscast.
Every day he grew a little more despairing.

It had almost gotten to the point where, given the
right goad, he'd use his medallion to fly away from this
place. He could find some distant realm where no one
would know his face, seek work there as a scribe, and
try to forget that he'd ever been an Archmage and summoned monsters from other worlds.

Aye, for the ghost of an excuse he'd—

Something shattered in the next room; it seemed a
dozen bells rang amid the musical clatter of glass. Tenthar was up and through the door in an instant, peering—ah!

The spelltale he'd laid upon the elven tree-gate in
the Tangletrees . . . someone had just used it to travel
south to the woods near Starmantle. That was it. He
was sick of hiding and doing nothing.

"The elves are on the move," Tenthar Taerhamoos
told the glass shards at his feet grandly. "I must be
there—at least I'll be able to learn as much about this

chaos of spells as they do." He cut himself a large wedge
of cheese with his dagger, wrapped it up in an old blan-
ket with his traveling spellbook, and thrust the bundle
into a battered old shoulder bag. Settling the blade back
in its sheath, Tenthar called up the flickering power of
his medallion, and cast a spell he'd had ready for a long
time.

"Farewell, old stones," he told his Tower, casting
what might be his last look around at it. "I'll return—
if I can."

A moment later, the floor where he'd stood was
empty. A moment after that, another spelltale shattered
in the room where no one was left to hear.

All too often, an archmage's life is like that.

*   *   *   *   *

Excitement burned within her, leaping to the back of
the throat she no longer had in a way it hadn't for years.
*Gently, Saeraede. Lose nothing now out of haste . . . you're
centuries past trembling like a maid, or should be.*

Like a wisp of dark smoke in the darkness, Saeraede flew up a thin crevice at the back of the cavern,
back to the main room above.

She'd prepared this spell long ago, and he'd disturbed none of her preparations. In a trice it was
done, gray smoke flowing out to settle like old stone
over the top of the shaft. Its veil would seem like a
raised stone floor to anyone on the surface, the well
mouth completely concealed—and her quarry would
be trapped beneath its web just as surely as if it was
solid stone.

Saeraede gave herself a bare breath of time to gloat
before plunging back down through the cold dark stone.
*Now to let myself be freed by my savior prince . . . and
bring him willingly to the slow slaughter.*

She plunged through the cavern like an arrow coming to earth; Elminster frowned and looked up, feeling some magical disturbance—but could sense nothing, and after a long, suspicious time of probing into the dusty darkness, he resumed his cautious advance. That was more than time enough for Saeraede to steal up into one of the runes through the cracked stone beneath, causing it to glow faintly.

Elminster stopped in front of it and stared at the unfamiliar curves and crossings. He didn't recognize any of these sigils. They looked both complex and old, and that of course suggested lost Netheril . . . or any of a score of its echoes, the fleeting realms that had followed its fall, with their self-styled sorcerer-kings; if any of the rotting old histories he'd read down the years had it right.

Only this one was glowing. El stared at it intently. "Sentience slumbreth here," he murmured, "but whose?"

Only silence answered him. The last prince of Athalantar acquired the ghost of a smile, sighed, and cast an unbinding.

The quiet echoes of his incantation were still rolling back to him from the walls all around when a ghostly head and shoulders erupted from the pale starry glow of the rune.

The eyes were dark and melting flecks in a head whose long and shapely neck yearned up from shoulders of striking beauty. Long hair flowed down over lush breasts, but it seemed his unbinding could free no more of this apparition from the grip of the now pulsing rune.

"Free me!" The voice was a tattered whisper, sighing from a lonely afar. "Oh, if the kindness and mercy of the gods mean anything to you, let me be *free!*"

"Who are ye?" El asked quietly, taking a pace back and kneeling to look more closely into the ghostly face, "and what are these runes?"

Ghostly lips seemed to tremble and gasp. When her voice soared out once more, it held the high, singing note of one who has triumphed over pain. "I am Saeraede . . . Saeraede Lyonora. I am bound here, so long I know not how many years have passed."

At the last few words, she seemed to grow dimmer and sank back into the rune as far as her shoulders.

"Who bound ye here?" Elminster asked, casting a quick look at the empty, watchful darkness all around. Aye, that was it; he could not shake the feeling that he was being watched . . . and not merely by the dark and spectral eyes floating near his feet.

"I was bound by the one who made these runes," the whispering shade told him. "Mine is the will and essence that empowers them, as the seasons pass."

"Why were ye bound?" El asked quietly, staring into eyes that seemed to hold tiny stars in their depths, as they melted pleadingly into his.

Her answer, when it came, was a sigh so soft that he barely heard it. Yet it came clearly: "Karsus was cruel."

The eyebrows of the last prince of Athalantar flew up. He knew that name. The Proudest Mage of All, who in his mad folly had dared to try to seize the power of godhood and suffered everlasting doom.

The name Karsus meant peril to any mage of sense. Elminster's eyes narrowed, and he stepped back and forthwith murmured a spell. Bound spirit, undead, wizardly shade or living woman, he would know truth when she spoke it—and falsehood. Of course, this Saeraede was likely to have been a sorceress of some accomplishment, perhaps an apprentice or rival of Karsus, for her to have been chosen for such a binding. She would know he'd just cast a truthtell.

Their eyes met in shared knowledge, and Elminster shrugged. She would answer as truthfully as she could, concealing only by her brevity. Like dueling swordsmen, they'd have to weigh each other's words and fence carefully. He cast a spell he should have used before entering the shaft, calling up a mantle of protection around himself, and stepped forward again.

Unseen beyond the faint shimmer of his mantle, fresh fury flared in eyes watching from the deep darkness at the back of the cavern.

"What will or must ye do, if freed?" El asked the head.

"Live again," she gasped. "Oh, man, free me!"

"What will freeing ye do to the runes?"

"Awaken them once each," the ghostly head moaned, "and they'll then be exhausted."

"What powers have the awakened runes?"

"They call up images of Karsus, who instructs all who view them in ways of magic. Karsus meant them for the education of his clone, hidden here."

"What became of it?" El asked sharply, hurrying to hear her answer as the truthtell ran out.

Dark, star-shot eyes stared steadfastly into his. "When awareness returned to me after my binding—a long time had passed, I think—I found it headless and wizened on the throne. I know not how it came to be that way."

His spell had failed before the second word had left those phantom lips, but somehow El believed her.

"Saeraede, how do I free ye?" he asked.

"If you have a spellquench or another unbinding, cast it upon me . . . not on the rune, but on me."

"And if I lack such magics?"

Those dark eyes flickered. "Stand over me, so that your mantle touches the rune, and I am within it. Then cast a magic missile, and let its target be the rune. In what follows, you should be unharmed—and I, freed. Be warned: 'twill cost you your mantle."

"Prepare thyself," Elminster told her, and stepped over her.

"Man, I have been waiting for an age, it seems; I am well prepared. Touch not the rune with your boots."

The last prince of Athalantar made sure his feet were clear of the glowing sigil, and made a careful casting. Blue-white radiance surged around him, roiling and tugging, the rune beneath him flared to blinding brilliance, and he heard Saeraede gasp.

Her breathing was ragged and swift as she surged up into the collapsing mantle beside him. As El stepped back, he saw wild delight in her face. All of the magic seemed to be rushing into her, and with each passing moment she grew more solid . . . more substantial. Her flickering, wraithlike form grew whole and acquired a dark gown. She was broad of shoulders, slim-waisted, and as tall or taller than he; her hair was an unbound, waist-length flow of velvet black, her brows startlingly dark tufts above eyes of leaping green. Her face was proud and lively—and very, very beautiful.

"Hail, savior mage," she said, eyes glowing with gratitude, as the last fires of magic fled into her. A single tongue of flame escaped from between her lips as she spoke. "Saeraede stands in your debt." She hesitated, reaching out one slender hand. "May I know your name?"

"Elminster, I am called," El told her, keeping a careful pace out of reach.

"Elminster," she breathed, eyes sparkling, "oh, have my *thanks!*"

She hugged herself, as if scarcely believing that she was whole and solid once more—and stepped forward off the rune. Her feet seemed to have grown spike-heeled, pointed black boots.

The moment she moved off it, the rune erupted. A column of white fire burst up from it, twice the height of a man, and smoke surged out in all directions from its snarling. Elminster took a pace back, eyes narrowing—and something unseen in the darkness of a deep crevice stirred and made as if to spring forth . . . but remained where it was, not all that far from the mage's unsuspecting back.

"Saeraede," El snapped, keeping his eyes on the unfolding magic, "what is this?"

"The magic of the rune," she replied, smiling at him. "Karsus prepared it to impress intruders. 'Tis harmless, a parade of illusions. Watch."

She turned to look at the column of flame, folding her arms, mild interest on her face. As she did so, the surging smoke seemed to freeze and thicken.

The archway of glowing runes solidified out of the smoke and air with startling swiftness. It occurred behind the fiery column, framing it, a wall that looked every bit as old and as solid as those of the cavern around—but hovered a few feet above the smooth stone floor. The runes around the arch matched those graven on the floor, save that all were afire, and even spitting lightning . . . the risen lightning of awakened magic, now crawling between them almost continuously.

Saeraede stood calmly watching, and El, struck by a sudden thought, glided to her elbow and indicated the empty throne. "Will ye sit, lady?"

Saeraede gave him a dazzling smile, raised a hand in wordless thanks—not quite touching him—and sat upon the throne. No change in it, or her, was apparent to El's intent eyes. Hmmm, well. Nothing learned there.

As Saeraede crossed her legs and leaned back in ease upon the stone seat, the column of flame grew a face—a youthful face ringed by tousled hair and the stubble of a beard aborning, its eyes two points of blazing gold. They were fixed on the throne, and when Elminster swung his left arm in a sudden, wild flourish, the eyes did not move to follow it.

The air in the cavern was suddenly alive with a singing tension. The proud mouth opened, and the voice that issued from it crashed and rolled like thunder through Elminster's mind as well as through the cavern. "*I am Karsus!* Behold me, and fear. I am The Lord of Lords, a God Among Men, Arcanist Supreme. All magic is my domain, and all who work it or trifle

with it without my blessing shall suffer. Begone, and
live. Tarry, and the first and least of my curses shall
begin its work upon you forthwith, gnawing memories from your brain until naught is left but a sighing
shadow."

Elminster looked sharply at Saeraede at those last
words, but she sat calmly watching as the hair on the
flaming head spat a halo of lightning out to the runes,
the echoes of its mighty voice still rolling around the
cavern as they faded, leaving it shaking and dust-
ridden. They burst into showers of sparks and fell, taking the illusion of the arch and its wall with them.

Still wearing its cruel smile, the face closed its eyes
and shrank back into the column of flame, fading as it
did so. In a few moments the flames fell back into the
rune, and it winked out, becoming mere dark and lifeless grooves in the stone floor.

"Did that curse afflict ye?" Elminster demanded,
striding around to where he could see Saeraede.

She lifted the edge of her beautiful mouth in a wry
smile. "Never . . . nor has it touched anyone, for 'tis all
a bluff. Believe me; I've seen it many times down the
years, whenever I grew overly lonely for the sight and
sound of another human. 'Tis an empty warning, no
more."

El nodded, almost trembling in his eagerness, and
asked, "How can one see the scenes held by the other
runes—and just what is in each?"

Saeraede pointed. "In this next rune lie two of the
most destructive spells devised by Karsus—magics
none else have attained since—as well as a defensive
shielding of surpassing strength and a healing magic;
he placed them thus in case his new self should have
urgent need to do battle."

Her pointing finger moved. "The rune beyond holds
another four magics, as powerful as the battle-spells but
of more mundane usage. One creates a floating 'worldlet'
to serve as a stronghold for the mage who uses magic to

modify it further; one can stop and hold the waters of a river while digging out a new course for its bed; one can shield an area permanently against specific spells or schools of spells with precision—so that one can allow a lightning bolt but deny chain lightning, say; and the last can coddle and keep from harm a living human while permanently altering one limb or organ—Karsus most often used that to move heart or brain to an unexpected place, or graft beast claws where hands had been or extra eyeballs from others . . . he also gave some men gills to work under the sea for him, as I recall."

Saeraede waved her hand at the curving row of runes. "The others hold lesser magics, four in each—and Karsus himself demonstrates all castings, noting drawbacks, details, and effective strategies."

She watched the hunger in Elminster's face and suppressed a smile. She had seen this so many times before . . . even Chosen, it seemed, were like eager children when offered new toys. She waited for the question she knew would come.

Elminster licked lips that were suddenly dry, before he could swallow and say quietly, "I asked how one can awaken these runes, lady, to view what waits within . . . and ye've not answered that. Is there some secret here, some hazard or caution?"

Saeraede gave him a warm and welcoming smile. "Nay, sir. As you're not Karsus and able to work the magics that respond only to his blood, there's but a matter of time—and your patience."

El raised a questioning eyebrow, and her smile broadened and slid into sadness.

"Only I can activate the runes," the woman on the throne added softly, "and I can call forth the power of only one in a month, by means of a nameless spell bound into me by Karsus. 'Tis a spell I know not how to cast, nor can I teach it to another. I can only call on it when the time is right—and I have no doubt 'tis the sole reason I still exist."

Elminster opened his mouth to say something, his eyes alight with eager fire, but Saeraede held up a hand to stay his speech, and added, "You asked of a hazard? There is one, and 'tis thus: long years must have passed since I was bound here, for my powers have faded indeed. I can awaken one rune, and no more. To open another will destroy me—and all of the magic stored here will drain away and be lost; it cannot persist without me."

"So there is no way to see the spells Karsus stored here—or at least, more than one foursome of them?"

"There is a way," Saeraede said softly, her eyes on his. "If you use that last spell I spoke of, not to give me gills or a tail, but to pass magical strength into me . . . the magic of another spell that heals, or imparts vitality, or places the vital, flowing power of Art in items, to recharge them. All of these should work."

Elminster frowned in thought. "And we must bide here a month, to see the rune that holds that spell?"

Saeraede spread her hands. "You freed me and woke the first rune. I am yet able to awaken a rune, now— and I owe you my very life. Would you like to see the rune I spoke of, which holds the spell that will let me live to unlock the others for you?"

"I would," El said eagerly, striding forward.

Saeraede rose from the throne and held up her hands in warning.

"Remember," she said gravely, "you'll see Karsus instructing himself how to cast those spells, and the rune will then be dead forever, its spells—spells neither you nor any living mage may now be able to cast—lost with it."

She took two slow steps away from Elminster, then turned back to face him, pointing down at the rune. "If you want to preserve its power and be able to view it again hereafter, there is a way . . . but it will call greatly on your trust."

Elminster's brows rose again, but he said merely, "Say on."

Saeraede spread empty hands in the age-old gesture traders use to show they are unarmed, and said gently, "You can channel energy into the rune through me. Touch me as I stand upon the rune, and will your spell to seek the rune as its target. The bindings set within me by Karsus will keep me from harm and deliver the fury of your magic into the rune. One powerful spell ought to do it . . . or two lesser ones."

The eyes of the last prince of Athalantar narrowed. "Mystra forfend," he murmured, raising a reluctant hand.

"Elminster," Saeraede said beseechingly, "I owe you my life. I mean you no harm. Take whatever precautions you see fit—a blindfold, bindings, a gag." She extended her arms to him, wrists crossed over each other in a gesture of submission. "You have nothing to fear from me."

Slowly, Elminster stepped forward and took her cold hand in his.

Nineteen

MORE BLOOD THAN THUNDER

The thunder of a king's tongue can always spill more blood than his own weight in gold before dawn the next morning.

Mintiper Moonsilver, Bard
from the ballad **Great Changes Aborning**
first performed circa The Year of the Sword and Stars

Saeraede's touch was cold—colder than icy rivers he'd plunged into, colder even than the bite of blue glacial ice that had once seared his naked skin.

Gods! Elminster struggled to catch his breath, too shocked even to moan. The face so close to his held no hint of triumph, only anxious concern. El stared into those beautiful eyes and roared out his pain in a wordless shout that echoed around the cavern.

It was answered a moment later by a greater roar, a rumbling that shook the cavern and split its gloom with a flash of light—a flash that made all of the runes briefly catch fire, and sent a slim, stealthy figure shrinking back hastily into its crevice, unregarded.

One of her best spells, shattered like a glass goblet hurled to stones—and it could not be any doing of this helpless, shuddering mage in her hands. Oh, dark luck rule: were there spells on a Chosen that called for aid by themselves?

Saeraede straightened, eyes blazing, and snarled, "Who—?"

The light that stabbed down the shaft this time was no flash of destruction but a golden column of more lasting sorcery. Four figures rode its magic smoothly down into the cavern of the throne, boots first.

Three of the men in that column of light were old and stout and amazed. Caladaster, Beldrune, and Tabarast were all staring in awe at their companion. The quiet Harper had just broken a spell that had shaken the very trees around in its passing, and swept away a thick stone floor in the doing with a casual wave of his hand. He'd taken a few steps forward, smiled reassuringly at them, and another gesture had swept them up into waiting radiance and borne them down the shaft together in its glowing heart.

"Elminster," the fourth man said crisply, as his boots touched the stone floor as lightly as a falling feather kisses the earth, "stand away from yon runes. Mystra forbids us to do what you are attempting."

A gasping Elminster had only just then recovered the power of speech. He turned with a stiff, awkward lurch, limbs trembling, and said sharply through lips that were thin and blue, "Mystra forbids us to do, never to look. Who are you?"

The man smiled slightly, and his eyes became two lances of magical fire, stabbing across the cavern at Saeraede. "Call me—Azuth," he replied.

*　*　*　*　*

"The spell failed again, l-lord," the man in robes said, his voice not quite steady.

The Lord Esbre Felmorel nodded curtly. "You have our leave to withdraw. Go not where we cannot summon you in haste, if need be."

"Lord, it shall be so," the wizard murmured. He did not—quite—break into a run as he left the chamber, but the eyes of both guards at the door flickered as he passed.

"Nasmaerae?"

Lady Felmorel lifted unhappy eyes to his and said, "This is none of my doing, lord. Prayers to Most Holy Azuth are as close as I come to the Art now. This I swear."

A large and hairy hand closed over hers. "Be at ease, lady. I cannot forget that hard lesson any more than you can; I know you forget not, and transgress not. I have seen your blood upon the tiles before the altar, and seen you at prayer. You humiliate yourself as only one who truly believes can."

A smile touched his lips for a moment, and stole away again. "You frighten the men more now than you ever did when you ruled this castle by your sorcery, you know. They say you talk with Azuth every night."

"Esbre," his lady whispered, holding her eyes steady upon his despite the blush that had turned her face, throat, and beyond crimson, "I do. And I am more frightened right now than ever I was when Azuth stripped my Art from me before you. All magic is awry, all over the Realms. It will be down to the sharpest sword and the cunning of the wolf once more, and not one of our hired mages will be able to aid us!"

"And what is so bad about trusting only in sharp swords and the strong arms and cunning of warriors?"

"Esbre," the Lady Nasmaerae whispered, bringing her lips up to brush his—but too slowly for him to miss seeing the bright glimmer of unshed tears welling up in her eyes, "How long can you stand against foe after foe without the spells of our mages to hew them down for you? How many sharp swords and how much cunning does an orc horde have?"

*   *   *   *   *

A chiming as of many bells rang out across the chamber. It nearly deafened Elminster, as the chill wind that carried it raced through him, searing him once more into frozen immobility. The ghostly mist that had been Saeraede was spiraling about him, coiling and twining—seemingly unharmed by the beams of fire Azuth had hurled, that roared through her into Elminster.

Ice, then fire—fire that lifted him off his feet in a whirlwind of battling mist and flames and set him down again staggering, too overwhelmed to do more than bleat in wordless pain.

"Here," Tabarast mumbled, through lips that were white and trembling with fear, "that's our Elminster you're smiting, sir—Your, er, Divineness, sir!"

"Break free of her," the Harper who was Azuth said quietly, his gaze no longer flaming—but now bent on the pain-narrowed eyes of Elminster, "or you are doomed."

"I'd say you're doomed anyway," a sneering voice said from above—and five staves spat in unison, hurling a rending rain of doom down the shaft.

*   *   *   *   *

The Overmistress of the Acolytes strode through the black curtain of hanging chains with every inch of the cruel authority that made her so feared among the underclergy. The cruel barbed lash rode upon her shoulder, ready to snap forward at the slightest act or omission that displeased her, and her face beneath the horned black mask wore a smile of cruel anticipation. Even the two guardian Priestesses of the Chamber shrank back from her; she ignored them as she strode on, the metal-shod heels of her thigh-high black boots clicking on the tiles, and shouldered through the three curtains of fabric into the innermost place of the Darklady's contemplation—the Pool of Shar.

A figure moved in the gloom beyond the pool: a figure in a familiar horned headdress and deep purple mantle. Dread Sister Klalaerla went to her knees immediately, holding forth her lash in both hands.

With leisurely tread the Darklady came around the inky waters and took it from her. The Overmistress immediately bowed forward to kiss the knife-blade toes of the Darklady's boots, holding her tongue against the cold, bloodstained metal until the lash came down across her own back.

It burned, despite the webwork of crossed lacings that were part of her own garb, but it was a mark of pride not to flinch or gasp; she held firm, waiting for the second blow that would mark her superior's displeasure, or the rain of cuts that meant Avroana's fury was aroused.

None came, and with a smooth motion that almost managed to conceal her relief, she straightened to a sitting position once more, for Avroana to put the lash to her lips. She kissed it, received it back, and relaxed. The ritual was satisfied.

"Your Darkness?" she asked, as was the custom.

"Klalaerla," the Darklady said, almost urgently—her familiarity made the Overmistress stiffen with excitement—"I need you to do something for me. Despite Narlkond's assurances, those five Dreadspells are going to fail us. You must be the striking hand that rewards them for their misdeeds. If they betray the House of

Holy Night, you must bring the justice of the House to them, whatever the danger to yourself. I demand it. The Flame of Darkness *herself* demands it. Dearest of my believers, will you do this for me?"

"Gladly," Klalaerla said, and meant it. To travel outside the House once more! To breathe the free winds of Faerûn, out in the open, and see lands spread out before her once more! Oh, Avroana! "Lady most kind," she said, her voice trembling, "what must I do?"

*   *   *   *   *

The noise smote their ears like a blow. Dust curled up, the ground shuddered and heaved beneath their boots, and here and there around the ruins slabs of stone whirled aloft, thrust into the air by geysers of rocketing vapor.

The five Dreadspells exchanged awed, delighted glances, the roaring of their unleashed magic swallowing their shouts of excited approval, and poured down death until Elryn slapped at their arms and waved the scepters in his hands—weapons he'd snatched from his belt after his staff sputtered out.

When he had their attention, the senior Dark Brother aimed the scepters at an angle toward the floor beside the shaft. If their fire burst through into the cavern below, it would burn an angled path reaching to where Elryn's spying spell had shown him the staggering Chosen, near a throne and a ring or half-ring of runes that could perhaps, just perhaps, be made to explode.

The destruction of a Chosen was, after all, their holy mission. As Femter, Vaelam, and Hrelgrath aimed their staves with undaunted enthusiasm, Elryn stepped back a pace or two and saw Daluth, on the far side of the group, doing the same. They exchanged mirthless smiles. If there was a backlash, someone had to survive to take word to the distant Darklady—or, if it raced along the linkage she used to spy on them all, to see what fate she suffered. Perhaps it would even be one that would let two false wizards go their separate ways in Faerûn, so heavily laden with enchanted items that they could barely stand.

A more prudent time for such moondreams would come later—when they weren't standing in a haunted ruin near sunset, at the heart of a killing forest emptied of life, with a known Chosen and a madman who thought he was a god and the ghost of a sorceress locked in battle somewhere close by under their feet, hurling spells around and over old and powerful spell runes cut into the stone floor for some old and very important purpose.

The thunder of destructive magic roared on unabated as the junior Dreadspells laughed and exulted in the sheer rush of power under their command. Walls toppled, smashing wardrobes flat, as the floors that supported them melted away and tumbled into an ever-lengthening chasm. Trees all around groaned and creaked as the ground shifted.

Daluth kept his own wands trained straight down, at the self-styled Azuth and his companions. He'd seen the casual waves of a hand that had wrought what it took most archmages long and complicated rituals to achieve. God or avatar or boldly bluffing archmage, whatever it was must be destroyed.

Elryn aimed his scepters to fire through the opened, dust-choked space in the wake of the three staves— which were now, one by one, shuddering to exhaustion, to be tossed aside in favor of Netherese scepters whose blasts were almost as potent. Chosen or not, no lone wizard could stand unscathed in the face of such destruction. Elryn snarled as a scepter crumbled to dust, and snatched forth another to replace it. No, there was no chance at all that a man could survive this. Why, then, was he so uneasy?

*   *   *   *   *

The end of the cavern vanished in tumbling stones and the flash and rock spray of spell-wrought explosions. Floor slabs bounced upward as a shock wave rolled through them, toppling the throne. More rocks broke away and fell from the ceiling, bouncing amid the roiling fury there; on his knees, a dazed Elminster watched through pain-blurred eyes as the collapse of the ceiling continued in a rough line heading toward him, chunks of stone larger than he was crashing down or being hurled aside in an endless roaring tide.

Someone or something aloft must be trying to slay him, or destroy the runes . . . not that he faced any dearth of foes nearer at hand.

Saeraede, who must have lied to him about everything except who put the runes here, was riding him like a mounted knight, her claws around his throat and searing his back with talons of icy iron. He knew before he tried that no amount of rolling or smashing himself into a wall could harm or dislodge her; how can one crush or scrape away a wisp of ghostly mist?

Move he must, though, or be buried or torn apart by the snarling, smoking bolts and beams of magic that were gnawing their way through earth and stone to reach him. El groaned and crawled a little way along heaving stones—until the runes of Karsus erupted into white-hot columns of flame, one by one. As they licked and seared the collapsing ceiling, magic played all around the cavern, purple lightning dancing and strange half-seen shapes and images forming and collapsing and forming again in an endless parade.

The last prince of Athalantar smashed his nose and shoulder into a floor-slab that was heaving upward to meet him, and rolled over with a gasp of pain and despair. As he clawed at the edges of the stone with bloody, feeble fingers, trying to drag himself upright again, the stone melted away into smoke and rending magic burst into him.

Ah, well, this is it . . . forgive me, Mystra.

But no agony followed, and nothing plucked at his flesh, to melt and sear and reave. . . .

Instead, he was rolled over as if by the empty air, and glowing nothingness enclosed him in ropes of radiance. Dimly, through his tears and the roiling motes of light, Elminster saw magic rushing toward him from all sides, being drawn to him, veering in its dancing to race in.

Wild laughter rose around him, high and sharp and exultant. Saeraede! She was wrapped around him, clinging in a web of glowing mists that grew thicker and brighter as she gorged herself on magic, a ghost of bright sorcery.

Sunlight was stabbing down into the riven cavern, now, but the dancing dust cloaked everything in gloom—everything but the rising giant built around Elminster's feebly writhing form. The rune-flames were twisting in midair to flow into Saeraede, and she was rising ever higher, a thing of crackling flame. El strained to look up at her—and two dark flecks among the magical fire became eyes that looked back at him in cold triumph . . . until a mouth swam out of the conflagration to join them and gave him a cruel smile.

"*You're mine now, fool*," she whispered, in a hoarse hiss of fire, "*for the little while you'll last. . . .*"

*   *   *   *   *

"Lord Thessamel Arunder, the Lord of Spells," the steward announced grandly, as the doors swung wide. A wizard strode slowly through them, a cold sneer upon his sharp features. He wore a high-collared robe of unadorned black that made his thin frame look like a tomb obelisk, and a shorter, more lushly built lady in a gown of forest green clung to his arm, her large brown eyes dancing with lively mischief.

"Goodsirs," he began without courtesies, "why come you here to me once more this day? How many times must you hear my refusal before the words sink through your skulls?"

"Well met, Lord Arunder," said the merchant Phelbellow, in dry tones. "The morning finds you well, I trust?"

Arunder gave him a withering glare. "Spare me your toadying, rag seller. I'll *not* sell this house, raised by mighty magic, nor any wagon length of my lands, no matter how sweetly you grovel, or how much gold you offer. What need have I for coins? What need have I for gowns, for that matter?"

"Aye, I'll grant that," one of the other merchants grunted. "Can't see him looking like much in a good gown. No knees for it."

"No hips, neither," someone else added.

There were several sputters of mirth from the merchants crowded at the doorway; the wizard regarded them all with cold scorn, and said softly, "I weary of these insults. If you are not gone from my halls by the time I finish the Ghost Chant, the talons of my guardian ghosts shall—"

"Lady Faeya," Hulder Phelbellow asked, "has he not seen the documents?"

"Of course, Goodsir Phelbellow," the lady in green said in musical tones. Favoring them all with a smile, she stepped from her lord and drew forth a strip of folded vellum, "and he's signed them, too."

She proffered them to Phelbellow, who unfolded them eagerly, the men behind him crowding around to see.

The Lord of Spells gaped at the paper and the merchants, then at Faeya. "W-what befalls here?" he gasped.

"A sensible necessity, my lord," she replied sweetly. "I'm so glad you saw the good sense in signing it. A most handsome offer—enough to allow you to retire from your castings entirely, if you desire."

"I signed nothing," Arunder gasped, white-faced.

"Oh, but you did, lord—and so ardently, too," she replied, eyes dancing. "Have you forgotten? You remarked at the time upon the hardness and flatness of my belly that made your penmanship such ease. You signed it with quite a flourish, as I recall."

Arunder stiffened. "But . . . that was—"

"Base trickery?" one of the merchants chuckled. "Ah, well done, Faeya!"

Someone else barked with laughter, and a third someone contributed a murmur of, "That's rich, that is."

"Apprentice," the Lord of Spells whispered savagely, "*what have you done?*"

The Lady Faeya drew three swift paces away from him, into the heart of the merchants, who melted aside to make way for her like mist before flame, and turned back to face him, placing her hands on her hips.

"Among other things, Thessamel," she told him softly, "I've slain two men this last tenday, who came to settle old scores since your spells failed you—and word spread of it."

"*Faeya!* Are you *mad?* Telling these—"

"They know, Thess, they know," his lady told him with cold scorn. "The whole town knows. Every mage has his hands full of wild spells, not just you. If you paid one whit of attention to Faerûn outside your window, you'd know that already."

The Lord of Spells had turned as pale as old bones and was gaping at her, mouth working like a fish gasping out of water. Everyone waited for him to find his voice again; it took quite a while.

"But . . . your spells still work, then?" he managed to ask, at last.

"Not a one," she said flatly. "I killed them with this."
She drew forth the tiny dagger from its sheath at her
hip, then threw back her left sleeve to lay bare a long,
angry-looking line of pine gum and wrapped linens.
"That's how I got *this*."

"Were these merchants also coming to—to—?" Arunder asked faintly, swaying back on his heels. His hands
were trembling like those of a sick old man.

"I went to them," Faeya told him in biting tones, "to
beg them to make again the offer you so *charmingly*
refused two months ago. They were good enough to
oblige, when they could well have set their dogs on me:
the apprentice of the man who turned three of them
into pigs for a night."

There were angry murmurs of remembrance and
agreement from among the merchants around her;
Arunder stepped back and raised a hand to cast a spell
out of sheer habit—before dropping it with a look of sick
despair.

His lady drew herself up and said more calmly, "So
now the deal's done. Your tower and all these lands,
from high noon today henceforth, belong to this cabal
of merchants, to use as they see fit."

"And-and what happens to me? Gods, woma—"

Faeya held up a hand, and the wizard's ineffectual
gibbering ended as if cut off by a knife. Someone chuckled at that.

"We, my lord, are free to live unmolested in the
South Spire, casting spells—so long as they harm or
work ill upon no one upon this holding—as much as we
desire . . . or are able to. You, Thess, receive two hundred thousand gold pieces—that's why all of these good
men are here—all the firewood we require, and a dozen
deer a year, prepared for the table."

Without a word, Hulder Phelbellow laid a sack upon
the side table. It landed with the heavy clink of coins.
Whaendel the butcher followed him, then, one by one,
all of the others, the sacks building up until they were

reaching up the wall, atop a table that creaked in protest.

Arunder's eyes bulged. "But . . . you can't have gold enough, none of you!"

His lady rejoined him in a graceful green shifting, and laid a comforting hand on his arm. "They have a backer, Thess. Now thank them politely. We've some packing to do—or you *will* be wearing my gowns."

"I-I—"

Her hitherto gentle hand thrust hard into his ribs.

"My lords," Arunder gulped, "I don't know how to thank you—"

"Thessamel," Phelbellow said genially, "you just did. Have our thanks, too—and fare thee well in the South Spire, eh?"

Arunder was still gulping as the merchants filed out, chuckling. The noises he was making turned to whimpers, however, when their withdrawal revealed the man who'd been sitting calmly behind them all the while, the faint glow of deadly magics playing along the naked broadsword that was laid across his knees. That blade was in the capable grasp of the large and hairy hands of the famous warrior Barundryn Harbright, whose smile, as he rose and looked straight into the wizard's eyes, was a wintry thing. "So we meet again, Arunder."

"You—!" the wizard's snarl was venomous.

"You're my tenant now, mage, so spare me the usual hissed curses and spittle. If you anger me enough, I'll take you under my arm down to the stream where the little ones play, and spank your behind until it's as red as a radish. I'm told that won't hamper your spellcasting one bit." One large, blunt-fingered hand waved casually through the air past Arunder's nose.

The wizard blinked in alarm. "What? Who—?"

"Told me so?" Harbright lifted his chin in a fond smile that was directed past Arunder's shoulder.

The Lord of Spells whirled around in time to see Faeya's catlike smile drifting out the door they'd come in by, together. The rest of her accompanied it, a vision in forest green.

Lord Thessamel Arunder moaned, swayed on his feet, and turned, on the verge of tears of rage, to run away from it all—only to come to an abrupt halt, with a squeak of real alarm, as he found himself about to run right into the edge of Harbright's glowing blade.

His eyes rose, slowly and unwillingly, from the steel that barred his way to the huge and hulking warrior who held it. There was something like pity in Barundryn Harbright's eyes as he rumbled, "Why are wizards, with all their wits, so slow to learn life's lessons?"

The blade swept down and away, seeking its sheath, and a large and steadying hand came down on the wizard's shaking shoulder. "Mages tend to live longer, Arunder," Harbright said gently, "if they manage to resist their most attractive temptations."

*   *   *   *   *

The Sharrans were beginning to sweat now, from the sheer strain of aiming and holding steady as the Art they wielded punched aside old stones and earth, to lay open a fortress and slay the beings below. Elryn watched Femter wince and shake the smoking fragments of a ring off one finger, as Hrelgrath tossed aside his third wand and Daluth slid one failing scepter back into his belt.

"Enough," Elryn bellowed, waving his hands. "Enough, Dreadspells of Shar!" Something had to be saved in case they met with other foes this day—or, gods above, there was someone still alive down there.

The priests-turned-wizards turned their heads in the sudden peace to blink at him, almost as if they'd forgotten who and where they were.

"We have a holy task, Dark Brothers," Elryn remind-ed them, letting them hear the regret in his voice, "and it is not melting away earth and stone in a forgotten ruin in the heart of a forest. Our quarry is the Chosen; how fares he?"

Three heads peered at roiling dust. All five looked down the shaft where they'd begun, where the dust was but a few flowing tongues. There was rubble down there, and—

One of the Sharrans cried out in disbelief.

The Harper who'd claimed to be Azuth was looking calmly back up at them, standing more or less where he'd been when their barrage began. The three old men, still blinking at him in awe, stood around him. He, they, and the floor around the bottom of the shaft seemed untouched.

"Finished?" he asked quietly, looking up at them with eyes of steady, storm-smoke gray.

Elryn felt cold fear catch at the back of his throat and slide slowly down into the pit of his stomach, but Femter snarled, "Shar take the man!" and snatched a wand from his belt.

Before Elryn or Daluth could stop him, Femter leaned over the well and snarled the word that sent a streak of flame down, down into the gloom below, straight at the upturned face of the gray-eyed man.

The Harper didn't move, but his mouth somehow stretched wider than a man's mouth should be able to—and the flames fell right into him. He shuddered for a moment as all of the fire plunged into his vitals. By the stumbling of the three old men around him, it seemed some sort of magic was keeping them at bay, moving them as he moved.

A moment later the fireball burst with a dull rum-bling. The Harper stood with an unconcerned expres-sion on his face as smoke whirled out of his ears.

He gave the watching Sharrans a reproving look and remarked, "Needs a little more pepper."

* * * * *

The Dreadspells were screaming and fleeing wildly even before Azuth lowered his head and looked again across the riven cavern at Elminster. "I mean what I say," he said gravely. "You must get free of her."

"I—can't," Elminster gasped, staring into the dark eyes of Saeraede, as she reared up over him in triumph like some sort of giant snake, twining around him in large and tightening coils.

"And you never will," she breathed triumphantly, her cold lips inches from his. He could feel the chilling frost of her breath on his face as she purred, "With the powers of a Chosen and all the might Karsus left here, I can defy even such as *him*."

She lifted her head to give Azuth a challenging glare as she clamped one giant hand of solid mist around El's throat. Other tentacles of mist rose around them both in a protective forest, undulating and lashing the tossed and shattered stone slabs.

The last prince of Athalantar struggled to breathe in her grasp, so throttled he couldn't speak or shout, as the ghostly sorceress leisurely turned the uppermost spire of her mists to a lush and very solid human torso, curvaceous and deadly.

Slim fingers grew fingernails like long talons, and when they were as long as Saeraede's hand, she reached almost lovingly for his mouth.

"We'll just have the tongue out, I think," she said aloud, "to forestall any nasty—ah, but wait a bit, Saeraede, you want him to tell you a few things before he's mute. . . . Hmmmm . . ."

Razor-sharp talons drifted just inches past Elminster's tightly constricted throat, to slice into the first flesh she found bared. Plowing deep gashes across the strangling mage's neck, she flicked his blood away in droplets that were caught in her whirling mists and held her bloody talons exultantly up to the sunlight.

"Ah, but I'm *alive* again," Saeraede hissed, "alive and whole! I breathe, I *feel!*" She brought that hand to her mouth, bit her own knuckles, and held the hand out toward the grimly watching avatar of Azuth to let him see the welling blood. "I bleed! I *live!*"

Then she screamed, swayed, and stared down, dark eyes widening in disbelief, at the gore-slick, smoking sword tip that had just burst through her breast from behind.

"Some people live far longer than they should," said Ilbryn Starym silkily from behind the hilt, as he stared gloating into the eyes of the mage still frozen in Saeraede's grasp. "Don't you agree, Elminster?"

*   *   *   *   *

A door was flung wide, to boom its broken song against a heavily paneled wall. It had been years since the tall, broad-shouldered woman who now stood in the doorway, her eyes snapping in alarm and anger, had worn the armor she hated so much—but as she stood glaring into the room, the half-drawn long sword at her hip gleaming, she looked every inch a warrior.

Sometimes Rauntlavon wished he was more handsome, strong, and about ten years older. He'd have given a lot for so magnificent a woman to smile at him.

Right now, she was doing anything *but* smiling. She was looking down at him as if she'd found a viper in her chamber pot—and his only consolation was that he wasn't the only mage rolling around on the floor under her dark displeasure; his master, the gruffly sardonic elf Iyriklaunavan, was gasping on the fine swanweave rug not a handspan away.

"Iyrik, by all the gods," the Ladylord Nuressa growled, "what befell *here?*"

"My farscrying spell went awry," the elf snarled back at her. "If it hadn't been for the lad, here, all those books'd be aflame now, and we'd be hurling water and running with buckets for our lives' worth!"

Rauntlavon's face flamed as the ladylord took a step forward and looked down at him with a rather kinder expression. "I-it was nothing, Great Lady," he stammered.

"Master Rauntlavon," she said gently, "an apprentice should never contradict his master-of-magecraft . . . nor belittle the judgment of any one of The Four Lords of the Castle."

Rauntlavon blushed as maroon as his robes and emitted the immortal words, "Yujus-yujus-er-ah-uhmmm, I, ah—"

"Yes, yes, boy, brilliantly explained as usual," Iyrik-launavan said dismissively, rolling to his elbows. "Now belt up and look around the room for me: is anything amiss? Anything broken? Smoldering? Aflame? Hop, now!"

Rauntlavon hopped, quite thankfully, but kept his attention more on what two of The Four Lords of the Castle were saying. They'd all been debonair and successful adventurers, less than a decade ago, and one never knew what wild and exciting things they might say.

Well, nothing about mating dragons *this* time.

"So tell me, Iyrik," the Ladylord was saying in her I-really-shouldn't-have-to-be-*this*-patient voice, "just *why* your farscrying spell blew up. Is it one of those magics you'd just be better off not trying? Or were you distracted by some nubile elf maid seen in your spying, perhaps?"

"Nessa," the elf growled—Rauntlavon had always admired the way he could look so agile and elegant and youthful, and yet be more gruff than any dwarf—as he rose and fixed her with one glaring that's-*quite*-enough eye, "this is serious. For us all, everywhere in Faerûn.

Stop playing the swaggering warrior bitch for just a moment and listen. For once."

Rauntlavon froze, his head sunk between his shoulders, wondering if folk really survived the full fury of Great Lady Nuressa a-storming—and just how swiftly and brutally she'd notice him and have him removed from the room.

Very and with iron calm, it seemed.

"Master Rauntlavon," she said calmly, "you may leave us now. Close the door on your way out."

"Apprentice Rauntlavon," his master said, just as calmly, "it is my will that you abide with us. Send Master Rauntlavon out, and close the door behind him, remaining here with us."

Rauntlavon swallowed, drew in a deep breath, and turned around to face them, hardly daring to raise his eyes. "I-I've found nothing amiss at this end of the chamber," he announced, his voice higher and rather more unsteady than he wished it would be. "Shall I examine the other half of it now . . . or later?"

"Now will be fine, Rauntlavon," the ladylord said in a voice of velvet menace. "Pray proceed."

The apprentice actually shivered ere he bowed and mumbled, "As my Great Lady wishes."

"It's a wonderful thing to make men and boys fear you, Nessa, but does it really make up for your years under the lash? The escaped slave gets even by enslaving others?" His master's voice was biting; Rauntlavon tried not to let his momentary hesitation show. The ladylord had been a slave? Kneeling naked under a slaver's lash, in the dust and the heat? Gods, but he'd never have—

"Do you think we can leave my past careers in my own bedchamber closet, Iyrik?" the ladylord said almost gently. Her next sentence, however, was almost a battlefield shout. "Or is there some pressing need to *tell all the world?*"

"I won't tell anyone, I won't—I swear I won't!" Rauntlavon babbled, going to his knees on the rug.

He heard the Great Lady sigh and felt ironlike fingers on his shoulder, hauling him back to his feet. Other fingers took hold of his chin and turned his head as sharply as a whip is flicked. The apprentice found himself staring into the Lady Nuressa's smoky eyes from a distance of perhaps the length of his longest finger.

"Rauntlan," she said, addressing him as he liked his handful of friends to—a short name he'd had no idea any of the lords even knew about, "you know that one of the most essential skills any wizard can have is to keep the right secrets, and keep them well. So I shall test you now, to see if you're good enough to remain in the castle as a mage-in-training . . . or a wizard in your own right, in time to come. Keep my secret, and stay. Let it out—and be yourself shut out of our lands, chased to our borders with the flat of my blade finding your backside as often as I can land it."

Rauntlavon heard his master start to say something, but the ladylord made some sort of gesture he couldn't see behind her back, and Iyriklaunavan fell silent again.

"Do you understand, Rauntlan?"

Her voice was as calm and as gentle as if she'd been discussing haying a field; Rauntlavon swallowed, nodded, squirmed under the hard points of her gaze, and managed to say, "Great Lady, I swear to keep your secret. I shall abide by your testing . . . and if ever I let it slip, I shall come to you myself to admit the doing, so the chase can begin at your convenience."

Her dark brows rose. "Well said, Master Apprentice. Agreed, then."

She took a quick step back from him and lifted her gown unhurriedly to display a tanned, muscular leg so long and shapely that he swallowed twice, unable to tear his eyes from it. Somewhere far, far away, his master chuckled, but Rauntlavon was lost in the slow but

continuing rise of fine fabric, up, up to her hip—he was
swallowing hard, now, and knew his face must be as
bright as a lamp—where his eyes locked on a purplish-
white brand. The cruel design was burned deep into her
flesh, just below the edge of the bone that made her hip
jut out. She traced a circle around it with one long finger and asked in a dry voice, "Seen enough, Rauntlan?"

He almost choked, trying to swallow and nod fervently at the same time, and somewhere in the midst
of his distress the gown went to her ankles again, her
hand clapped his shoulders like a club crashing down,
and her deep voice said in his ear, "So we have a secret
to share now, you and I. Something to remember." She
shoved him away gently and added, "I believe this end
of the room hasn't been fully inspected yet, Master
Apprentice."

Her voice was a brisk goad once more, but somehow
Rauntlavon found himself almost grinning as he strode
away to the end of the room and announced, "Inspection resumes, Great Lady—and sharing begins!"

His master laughed aloud, and after a moment
Rauntlavon heard a low, thrilling murmur that must
have been the ladylord chuckling.

She used the lash of her voice on Iyriklaunavan
next, breaking off in mid-chuckle to snap, "Enough time
wasted, mage. You frighten me up from my table with
a map half drawn and my soup growing cold, then go
all coy about why. What's so 'serious' that your apprentice must hear about it alongside me? Do you think you
can get around to telling me about this oh-so-serious
matter before, say, *nightfall?*"

"I meant it when I said this was serious, Nessa,"
Rauntlavon's master said quietly. "Put the edge of your
tongue away for a moment and listen. Please."

He paused then, and—wonders! Rauntlavon even
turned around to see, earning him an almost amused
glance from the Great Lady—the Ladylord Nuressa
gave him silence, waiting to hear him speak.

Iyriklaunavan blinked, seeming himself surprised, then said swiftly, "You know that magic—all magic not bolstered by draining a few sorts of enchanted items— is going wrong. Spells twisting to all sorts of results, untrustworthy and dangerous. Some mages are hiding in their towers, unable to defend themselves against anyone who might try to settle grudges. Magic has gone wild. If fewer folk knew about it, I'd say that this should be *our* secret—Rauntlavon's and mine own—for you to keep, or else. It will come as no surprise to you that many mages have been trying to find out why this darkness has befallen. I am one of them."

"And that's even less of a surprise," the Lady Nuressa said quietly. Rauntlavon's head snapped around to regard her somber face. He'd never heard her speak so gently before. She sounded almost . . . tender.

"I have no items to waste in bolstering my spells," Iyriklaunavan continued, "so the boy—Rauntlavon—has been my bulwark, using his spells to steady mine. Word has even come to us that some wizards—and even priests of the faiths of the Weave—believe divine Mystra and Azuth themselves have been corrupting magic deliberately, for some purpose mortals cannot even hazard."

"You worship our gods of magecraft?"

"Nessa," Iyriklaunavan said calmly, "I don't even *have* a bedchamber closet to keep *my* secrets in. I'm trying to hurry this, really I am; just listen."

Nuressa leaned back against one of the lamp-girt pillars that held up the ceiling of the spell chamber, and gestured for the elf mage to continue. She didn't even look irritated.

"Just now we were seeking but had not yet called up a place in our scrying, the enchantment being just complete," Iyriklaunavan continued, "when I felt one thing, and saw another. I think everyone in Faerûn who was attempting a scrying at the time felt what I did: the willful, reckless release of many wizards' staves at once, in one place, all directed at the same target."

"You mean mages everywhere feel it, whenever one wizard blasts another?" Nuressa's voice was incredulous. "No wonder you're all so difficult."

"No, we do not normally feel such things—nor have the violence of feeling anything strike us so hard that our own spells collapse into wildfire," Rauntlavon's master told her. "The reason we did this time was the target of this unleashing: the High One. I saw him, standing at the bottom of a shaft with three mortal mages, while magic seeking to destroy him rained down—and his attention was elsewhere."

"Azuth? Who was crazed enough to use magic to try to blast down a god of magic?" The ladylord looked surprised.

"That I did not see," Iyriklaunavan replied. "I did, however, see what Azuth was regarding. A ghostly sorceress, who was trying to slay a Chosen of Mystra."

"What's that?" the Great Lady asked. "Some sort of servant of the goddess?"

"Yes," the elf mage said grimly, "and he was someone you might remember. Cast your thoughts back to a day when we fled from a tomb—a tomb furnished with pillars that erupted in eyes. A mage was hanging above us there, asleep or trapped, and came out after we fled. He asked you what year it was."

"Oh, yesss," the ladylord murmured, her eyes far away, "and I told him."

"And thereby we earned the favor of the goddess Mystra," Iyriklaunavan told her, "who delivered this castle into our hands."

The Lady Nuressa frowned. "I thought Amandarn won title to these lands while dicing with some merchant lords—hazarding all our coins in the process," she said.

Rauntlavon stood very still, not wanting to be ejected again now. Surely this was an even more dangerous secret than—

"Amandarn lost all our coins, Nessa. Folossan nearly killed him for it—and they had to flee when he stole a few bits back to buy a meal that night and got caught at it. The two of them hid in a shrine to Mystra—rolled right in under the altar and hid under its fine cloth. There they slept, though both of them swear magic must have dragged them into slumber, for they'd had little to drink and were all excited from their flight and the danger. When they awoke, all of our coins were back in Amandarn's pouch—along with the title to the castle."

The Great Lady's brow arched and she asked, "And you believe this tale?"

"Nessa, I used spells to glean every last detail of it out of both their heads, after they told me. It happened."

"I see," the Great Lady said calmly. "Rauntlavon, be aware that this is another secret shared between us here—and only us here, or you'll have to flee four Lords of the Castle, not merely one."

"Yes, Great Lady," the apprentice said, then swallowed and faced them both. "There's something I should say, now. If something happens to Great Azuth—or Most Holy Mystra—and magic keeps crumbling, we all share a grave problem."

"And what is that, Rauntlavon?" The Lady Nuressa asked, in almost kindly tones, her fingers caressing the pommel of her long sword.

Rauntlavon's eyes dropped to those fingers—whose fabled strength was one of the rocks upon which his world stood—then back up to meet her smoky eyes.

"I think we must pray for Azuth or find some way to aid him. The castle was built with much magic," he told the two lords, the words coming out in a rush. "If its spells fail, it will fall—and us with it."

The Great Lady's expression did not change. Her eyes turned to meet those of the Lord Iyriklaunavan. "Is this true?"

The elf merely nodded. Nuressa stared at him for a moment, her face still calm, but Rauntlavon saw that her hand was now closed around the hilt of the long sword and gripping so tightly that the knuckles were white. Her eyes swung back to his.

"Well, Rauntlavon—have you any plan for preventing such doom?"

Rauntlavon spread empty hands, wishing wildly that he could be the hero, and see love for him awaken in her eyes . . . wishing he could give her more than his despair. "No, Nuressa," he was astonished to hear himself calmly whispering. "I'm only an apprentice. But I will die for you, if you ask me."

*   *   *   *   *

He drew his blade out of the swaying sorceress with savage glee, to thrust it into the Great Foe he'd pursued for so long, the grasping, stinking human who'd dared to stain bright Cormanthyr with his presence and doom the House of Starym; now helpless before him, able to move just his eyes—fittingly—to see whence his doom came.

"Know as you die, human worm," Ilbryn hissed, "that the Starym aven—"

And those were the last words he ever spoke, as all the magic that the ancient sorceress had drawn into herself rushed out again, in a fiery flood of raw magical energy that consumed the blade that had spilled it and the elf whose hand held that blade, all in one raging wave that crashed against the far wall of the cavern and ate through solid rock as if it was soft cheese, thrusting onward until it found daylight on a slope beyond, and the groan of toppling trees and falling stones began in earnest.

Saeraede wailed, flames streaming from her mouth, and fell away from Elminster, her mists receding into a standing cloud whose dark and despairing eyes pleaded with his for a few fleeting moments before it collapsed and dwindled away to whirling dust.

El was still staggering and coughing, his hands at his ravaged throat, when Azuth strode forward and unleashed a magic whose eerie green glow flooded the runes and the dust that had been Saeraede alike.

Like a gentle wave rolling up a beach, the god's spell spread out to the crevice Ilbryn had hidden in and every other last corner of the ravaged cavern. Then it flickered, turned a lustrous golden hue that made Beldrune gasp, and rose from the floor, leaving scoured emptiness behind.

Azuth strode through the rising magic without pause, caught hold of the reeling Elminster by the shoulders, and marched him one step farther. In mid-stride they vanished together—leaving three old mages gaping at a fallen throne in a shaft of sunlight in a pit in the forest that was suddenly silent and empty.

They took a few steps toward the place where so much death and sorcery had swirled—far enough to see that the runes were now an arc of seven pits of shivered stone—then stopped and looked at each other.

"They're gone an' all, eh?" Beldrune said suddenly. "That's it—all that fury and struggle and in the space of a few breaths . . . that's it. All done, and us left behind an' forgotten."

Tabarast of the Three Sung Curses raised elegantly white tufted eyebrows and asked, "You expected things to be different, this once?"

"We were worthy of a god's personal protection," Caladaster almost whispered. "He walked with us and shielded us when we were endangered—danger he did not share, or he'd never have been able to deal with that fireball as he did."

"That was something, wasn't it?" Beldrune chuckled. "Ah, I can see myself telling the younglings that . . . a little more pepper, indeed."

"I believe that's why he did it," Tabarast told him. "Yes, we were honored—and we're still alive, unlike that ghost sorceress and the elf . . . that's an achievement, right there."

They looked at each other again, and Beldrune scratched at his chin, cleared his throat and said, "Yes—ahem. Well. I think we can just walk out, there at the end where the fire burst out of the cavern, that way."

"I don't want to leave here just yet," Caladaster replied, kicking at the cracked edge of one of the pits where a rune had been. "I've never stood with folk of real power before, at a spot where important things happen . . . and I guess I never will again. While I'm here, I feel . . . alive."

"Huh," Beldrune grunted, "*she* said that, an' look what happened to her."

Tabarast stumped forward and put his arms around Caladaster in a rough embrace, muttering, "I know just how you feel. We've got to go before dark, mind, and I'll want a tankard by then."

"A lot of tankards," Beldrune agreed.

"But somewhere quiet to sit and think, just us three," Tabarast added, almost fiercely. "I don't want to be sitting telling all the drunken farmers how we walked with a god this night, and have them laugh at us."

"Agreed," Caladaster said calmly, and turned away.

Beldrune stared at his back. "Where are you going?"

The old wizard reached the rubble-strewn bottom of the shaft and peered down at the stones. "I stood just here," he murmured, "and the god was . . . there." Though his voice was steady, even gruff, his cheeks were suddenly wet with tears.

"He protected us," he whispered. "He held back more magic than I've ever seen hurled before, in all my life, magic that turned the very rocks to empty air . . . for us, that we might live."

"Gods have to do that, y'see," Beldrune told him. "Someone has to see what they do and live to tell others. What's the good of all that power, otherwise?"

Caladaster looked at him with scorn, anger rising in his eyes, and stepped back from Beldrune. "Do you *dare* to *laugh* at divine—"

"Yes," Beldrune told him simply. "What's the good of being human, elsewise?"

Caladaster stared at him, mouth hanging open, for what seemed like a very long time. Then the old wizard swallowed deliberately, shook his head, and chuckled feebly. "I never saw things that way before," he said, almost admiringly. "Do you laugh at gods often?"

"One or twice a tenday," Beldrune said solemnly. "Thrice on high holy days, if someone reminds us when they are."

"Stand back, holy mocker," Tabarast said suddenly, waving at him. Beldrune raised his eyebrows in a silent question, but his old friend just waved a shooing hand at him and strode forward, adding, "Move those great booted hooves of yours, I said!"

"All right," Beldrune said easily, doing so, "so long as you tell me why."

Tabarast knelt in the rubble and tugged at something; a corner of bright cloth amid the stones. "Gems and scarlet fineweave?" he asked Faerûn at large. "What have we here?"

His wrinkled old hands were already plucking stones aside and uncovering cloth with dexterous speed, as Beldrune went to one knee with a grunt and joined him at the task. Caladaster stood over them anxiously, afraid that, somehow, a ghostly sorceress would rise from these rags to menace them anew.

Beldrune grunted in appreciation as the red gown, with gem-adorned dragons crawling over both hips, was laid out in full—but he promptly plucked it up and handed it to Caladaster, growling as he waved at more cloth, beneath, "There's more!"

The daring black gown was greeted with an even louder grunt, but when the blue ruffles came into view and Tabarast stirred around in the stones beneath enough to be sure that these three garments were all they were likely to find, Beldrune's grunts turned into low whispers of curiosity. "Being as Azuth wasn't wearing them, that I saw, these must have come from *her*," he said.

Tabarast and Caladaster exchanged glances. "Being older and wiser than you," his old friend told him kindly, "we'd figured out that much already."

Beldrune stuck out his tongue in response to that and held up the blue gown for closer scrutiny.

"Do these hold power, do you think?" Tabarast asked, the black gown dangling from his fingers as Caladaster suppressed a smirk.

"Hmmph. Power or not, I'm not wearing this backless number," Beldrune replied, turning the blue ruffles around again to face him. "It goes down far enough to give the cool drafts more'n a bit of help, if you know what I mean. . . ."

Twenty

NEVER HAVE SO MANY
OWED SO MUCH

Never before in the history of this fair realm have so many owed so much to the coffers of the king. Never fear but that he'll come collecting in short order—and his price shall be the lives of his debtors, in some foreign war or other. He'll call it a Crusade or something equally grand . . . but those who die in Cormyr's colors will be just as dead as if he'd called it a Raid To Pillage, or a Head Collecting Patrol. It is the way of kings to collect in blood. Only archmages can seize such payments more swiftly and recklessly.

Albaertin of Marsember
from **A Small But Treasonous Chapbook**
published in The Year of the Serpent

"Doomtime," that deep voice boomed in Elminster's head. "Mind you make the right choices." Somehow, the Athalantan knew that Azuth was gone, and he *was* alone in the flood of blue sparks—the flood that he'd thought was Azuth—whirling him over and over and down . . . to a place of darkness, with a cold stone floor under his bare knees. He was naked, his gown and dagger and countless small items of magery gone somewhere in the whirling.

"Robbed by a god," he murmured and chuckled. His mirth left no echo behind, but what happened to it as it died away left him thinking he was somewhere underground . . . somewhere not all that large. His good feeling died soon after his chuckle; Elminster's innards felt—ravaged.

It was damp, and a chill was beginning to creep through him, but El did not rise from his knees. He felt weak and sick, and—when he tried to seek out magic or call up his spells—all of his powers as a Chosen and as a mage seemed to be gone.

He was just a man again, on his knees in a dark chamber somewhere. He knew that he should be despairing, but instead he felt at peace. He had seen far more years than most humans and done—so far as he could judge, at least by his own standards—fairly well. If it was time for death to come to him, so be it.

There were just the usual complaints: *was* it time for his death? What should he be doing? What was going on? Who was going to stop by and furnish him with answers to his every query—and when?

In all his life, there had only been one source for succor and guidance who wasn't certain to be long dead by now, or entombed and asleep he knew not where . . . and that one source was the goddess who made him her Chosen.

"Oh, Mystra, ye've been my lover, my mother, my soul guide, my savior, and my teacher," Elminster said aloud. "Please, hear me now."

He hadn't really intended to pray . . . or perhaps he had, all along, but just not admitted it to himself. "I've been honored to serve ye," he told the listening darkness. "Ye've given me a splendid life, for which—as is the way of men—I've not thanked thee enough. I am content to face now whatever fate ye deem fitting for me, yet—as is the way of wizards—I wish to tell thee some things first."

He chuckled, and held up a hand. "Save thy spells and fury," he said. " 'Tis only three things."

Elminster drew in a deep breath. "The first: thank ye for giving me the life ye have."

Was something moving in the gloom and shadows beyond where his eyes served him reliably?

He shrugged. What if something was? Alone, unclad, on his knees without magecraft to aid him; if something did approach him, this is how he'd have to greet it, and this was all he had to offer it.

"The second," El announced calmly. "Being thy Chosen is really what I want to spend out my days doing."

Those words echoed, where the darkness had muffled his words before. El frowned, then shrugged again and told the darkness earnestly, "The third, and most important to me to impart: Lady, I love thee."

As those words echoed, the darkness disgorged something that did move and reveal itself and loom all too clearly.

Something vast and monstrous and tentacled, slithered leisurely toward him.

* * * * *

"Was it a god?" Vaelam asked, white to the lips. Shrugs and panting were the first answers he got from his fellow Dreadspells, as they lay gasping in the hollow. Scraped and scratched by tree limbs in their run and thoroughly winded, they were only now shedding the heavy cloak of terror.

"God or no god," Femter muttered, "anyone who can withstand all we hurled down on his head—and *swallow* fireballs, for Shar's sake!—is someone I don't want to stand and face in battle."

"For Shar's sake, indeed, Dread Brother," someone said almost pleasantly from the far side of the hollow, where the ferns grew tall and they hadn't been yet. Five heads snapped around, eyes widening in alarm—

—and five jaws dropped, the throats beneath them swallowed noisily, and the eyes above them acquired a look of trapped fear.

The masked and cloaked lady floating in the air just above their reach, reclining at her ease on nothing, was all too familiar. "For there is a Black Flame in the Darkness," the cruel Overmistress of the Acolytes purred, in formal greeting.

"And it warms us, and its holy name is Shar," the five priests murmured in a reluctant, despairing chorus.

"You are far from the House of Holy Night, Dread Brothers, and unused to the ways of wizards—all too apt to stray, and in sore need of guidance," Dread Sister Klalaera observed, her voice a gentle honey of menace. "Wherefore our most caring and thoughtful Darklady Avroana has sent the House of Holy Night . . . to you."

"Hail, Dread Sister," Dreadspell Elryn said then, managing to keep his voice noncommittal. "What news?"

"News of the Darklady's deep displeasure at your leadership, most bold Elryn," the Overmistress said almost jovially, her eyes two spark-adorned flints. "And of her will: that you cease wandering Faerûn at your pleasure and return to the place from whence you so lately fled. Immense power lies there—and Shar means for us to have it. I know you'd not want to fail Most Holy Shar . . . or disappoint Darklady Avroana. So turn about and return thence, to serve Shar as capably as I know you can. I shall accompany you, to impart the Darklady's unfolding will as you return to the mission you were sent here for. Now rise, all of you!"

"Return?" Femter snarled, his hand darting to one of the wands still at his belt. "To duel with a god? Are you *mad,* Klalaera?"

The other Dreadspells watched silently, neither rising nor snarling defiance, as something unseen flashed between the Overmistress, at her ease with her head propped on her hand, and Femter Deldrannus, the wand still on its way out of his belt and not yet turned outward to menace anyone.

The priest shrieked and clutched at his head with both hands, hurling the wand away and staggering forward, his limbs trembling.

They watched him spasm and convulse and babble for what seemed like a very long time before Klalaera raised one languid hand and closed it in a casual gesture—and Femter collapsed in mid-word, falling in a sprawled and boneless heap like a dangle-puppet whose string had been cut.

"I can do the same to any of you—and all of you, at once," the Overmistress drawled. "Now rise, and return. You fear death at the hands of this 'god' you babble of—well, I can deliver you sure and certain death to set against one that may happen . . . or may not. Would any of you care to kneel and die here and now—in agony, and in the disfavor of Shar? Or will you show the Flame of Darkness just a little of the obedience she expects from those who profess to worship her?"

As Dread Sister Klalaera uttered these biting words, she descended smoothly to the ground, drawing from her belt the infamous barbed lash with which she disciplined the acolytes in her charge. The Dreadspells turned their faces reluctantly back toward the ruins they'd left so precipitously and began to trudge up out of the hollow—to the serenade of her whip crashing down on the defenseless back of the motionless Femter.

At the lip of the hollow, they turned in unspoken accord to look back—in time to see Femter, head lolling and eyes glazed, rise to his feet in the grip of fell magic and stagger after them, his back mere ribbons of flesh among an insect-buzzing welter of gore, his boots leaving bloody prints at every step. Klalaera shook drops of his dark blood from her saturated lash and gave them a soft smile. "Keep going," she said silkily. "I'll be right behind you."

*   *   *   *   *

Despite the floating menace of the Overmistress behind them, the five Dreadspells slowed cautiously as they climbed the last wooded ridge before the ruins. Blundering ahead blindly could mean swift doom . . . and a delay could well bring them to a shaft now empty of dangerous mages, leaving the ruins free for scavenging.

"Careful," Elryn murmured, the moment he heard the creak of leather that marked Dread Sister Klalaera bending forward to bring her lash down hard on someone's shoulders . . . probably his. "There's no need for anyone to strike alone in the fray, if we work together, and—"

"Avoid making pretty little speeches," Klalaera snapped. "Elryn, shut your mouth and lead the way! There's nothing between us and the ruins save a couple of stumps, a lot of waste lumber, your own fears, and—"

"Us," a musical voice murmured; an elven voice. Its owner rose up from the other side of the ridge, a scabbardless sword made of wood held in both his hands. "A walk in the woods these days holds so many dangers," Starsunder added. "My friend here, for instance."

The human mage Umbregard rose up from behind the ridge on cue and favored the Sharrans with a brief smile. He held a wand ready in either hand.

The Overmistress snapped, "Slay them!"

"Oh, well," Starsunder sighed theatrically, "if you *insist.*" Magic roared out of him then in a roaring tide that swept aside wand-bolts, simple conjurations, and the lives of struggling Hrelgrath and dumbfounded Vaelam alike.

Femter screamed and fled blindly back into the trees—until Klalaera's unseen magic jerked him to a halt as if a noose had settled about his neck, and spun him around, thrashing and moaning, for the slow stagger back into the fray.

Beams of light were stabbing forth and wrestling in the roiling air as Elryn and a snarling Daluth sought to strike down the elf mage, and Umbregard used his own wands to disrupt and strike aside their attacks.

Daluth shouted in pain as an errant beam laid bare the bone of his shoulder, flesh, sinews, and clothing all boiling away in an instant. He staggered back a pace or two, at about the same time as Umbregard went over backward in a grunt and a shower of sparks, leaving the elf standing alone against the Sharrans.

The Overmistress of the Acolytes found her coldest, cruel smile and put it on. It widened slowly as Starsunder's shielding spell darkened, flickered, and began to shrink under the bolts and bursts streaming from the wands of the Dreadspells.

"I don't know who you are, elf," Klalaera remarked, almost pleasantly, "or why you chose to get in our way—but it's quite likely to be a fatal decision. I can slay you right now with a spell, but I'd rather have some answers. What is this place? What magic lies here that makes it worth you losing your life over?"

"The only thing that amazes me more about humans than their habit of splitting up fair Faerûn into separate 'places,' one seemingly having no connection to the next," Starsunder replied, as casually as if he'd been idly conversing with an old friend over a glass of moonwine, "is their need to gloat, threaten, and bluster in battle. If you *can* slay me, do so, and spare my ears. Otherwise—"

He sprang into the air as he spoke, leaving Sharran wand-blasts to ravage elfless stumps and ferns, and collapsed his shield into a net of deadly force that clawed at the Overmistress.

She writhed in the air, sobbing and snarling, until her desperate mental goading dragged the wild-eyed Femter over to stand beneath her. Then she collapsed her own defenses—and Starsunder's attack, still gnawing at them—down into the helpless Dreadspell, in a deadly flood that left him a tottering, blinded mass of blood and exposed bone.

The joints of Femter Deldrannus failed, and he sought his last, eternal embrace with the earth, ignored by all. He hadn't even been given time to scream.

A gasping Overmistress tumbled away through the air as her flight spell began to collapse.

Elryn roared in wordless victory as his wand-bursts found Starsunder at last, spinning the elf around in a swarm of biting bolts. Umbregard was struggling to rise, his face sick with pain as he watched his friend beset.

Daluth leveled his own wand at the human mage at point-blank range, across the smoking bodies of fallen fellow Dreadspells, and smiled a slow and soft smile at the horrified human.

Then he spun around and smashed Dread Sister Klalaera out of the air with all the might the wand in his hand could muster.

It crumbled away, leaving him holding nothing, as the lash all of the House of Holy Night hated and feared so much blazed from end to end and spun high into the trees, hurled by a spasming body in black leather that was crumpling into smoking ruin.

Crumpling—then snarling into a standing stance once more, surrounded by crackling black flames, the face that had been Klalaera's working and rippling beneath dead, staring eyes as her lips thundered, "Daluth, you shall die for that!"

The voice was thick and roaring, but the two surviving Dreadspells recognized it, Elryn's head snapping around from the task of rending the convulsing, darkening body of the elf mage.

"You are cast out of the favor of Shar—die friendless, false priest!" Darklady Avroana thundered, through the lips that were not hers.

The bolt of black flame that the body of the Overmistress vomited forth then swept away the errant wizard-priest, an old and mighty tree beyond him, and a stump that dwarfed them both, shaking the forest all around and hurling Elryn to the ground.

The last Dreadspell was still struggling to his feet as Klalaera's dangling body, still streaming black flames, floated forward. "Now let us be rid of meddling mages, elf and human both, and—"

The sphere of purple flame that came out of nowhere to hit what was left of the Overmistress tore her apart, spattering the trees around with tatters of black leather.

"Ah, fool, that's one thing none of us will ever be rid of," a new voice told the dwindling, collapsing sphere of black flames that hung where Klalaera had been.

Elryn gaped up at a human who stood holding a smoking, crumbling amulet in his hand, a black cloak swirling around him. "Faerûn will always have its meddling mages," the newcomer told the dying knot of flames in tones of grim satisfaction. "Myself, for instance."

Elryn put all of his might into a lunge at this new foe, swinging his belt mace viciously and jumping into the air to put all his weight behind the strike.

His target, however, wasn't there to meet the blurred rush of metal. The newcomer slid a knife into the priest's throat with almost delicate ease as he stepped around behind the last Dreadspell, and said politely, "Tenthar Taerhamoos, Archmage of the Phoenix Tower, at your service—eternally, it appears."

Choking over something ice cold in his throat that would not go away as the pleasant world of trees and dappled shade darkened around him, Elryn found he lacked the means to reply.

*   *   *   *   *

Purple flames exploded over the Altar of Shar with a sudden flourish, scorching the bowl of black wine there. The chosen acolyte held the glowing knife that was to be slaked in it aloft and kept fervently to his chanted prayer, not knowing that bursts of purple fire weren't part of this most holy ritual.

So intent was he on the flowing words of the incantation that he never saw the Darklady of the House stagger and fall past him across the altar, her limbs streaming purple fire. Wine hissed and sputtered under her as she thrashed, faceup and staring at the black, purple-rimmed circle that adorned the vaulted ceiling high above. Avroana was still arching her body and trying to find breath enough to scream as the prayer reached its last triumphal words . . . and the knife swept down.

With both hands the acolyte guided the consecrated blade, the runes on its dark flanks pulsing and glowing, down, down to the heart of the bowl, the very center of—Darklady Avroana's breast.

Their eyes met as the steel slid in, to the very hilt. Avroana had time to see triumphant glee dawning in the acolyte's eyes amid the wild horror of realizing his mistake before everything grew dim forever.

*   *   *   *   *

Gasping, Starsunder managed to raise himself on one arm, his face creased with pain. Large, weeping blisters covered all of his left flank—save where melted flesh glistened in dangling droplets and ropes of scorched sinew. Umbregard half staggered and half ran to his side, trying not to look at the Archmage of the Phoenix Tower, his foe of many years.

Fear of what Tenthar might do, standing so close at hand behind him, was written clearly on Umbregard's face as he knelt by Starsunder and carefully cast the most powerful healing spell he knew on the stricken elf. He was no priest, but even a fool could see that an unaided Starsunder hadn't long to live.

The elf mage shuddered in Umbregard's arms, seemed to sag a trifle, then breathed more easily, his eyes half closed. His side still looked the same, but the organs only partially hidden beneath the horrible seared wounds were no longer wrinkled or smoking. Still . . .

A long hand reached past Umbregard, its fingers glowing with healing radiance, and touched Starsunder's flank. The glow flared, the elf shuddered, and the last fragments of something that had hung on a chain around the archmage's neck fell away into drifting dust. Tenthar rose hastily and stepped back, his hand going to his belt.

Umbregard looked up at the wand that hand had closed around, and hesitantly asked its owner, "Is there going to be violence between us?"

Tenthar shook his head. "When all Faerûn hangs in the balance," he replied, "personal angers must be set aside. I think I've grown up enough to set them aside for good." He extended his hand. "And you?"

*   *   *   *   *

Elminster knelt on the cold stone as the slithering, tentacled bulk drew nearer . . . and nearer. With almost indolent ease a long, mottled blue-brown tentacle reached out for him, leathery strength curling around his throat. Icy flames of fear surged up his back, and El trembled as the tentacle tightened almost lovingly.

"Mystra," he whispered into the darkness, "I—"

A memory of holding a goddess in his arms as they flew through the air came to him unbidden, then, and he drew on the pride it awakened within him, forcing down his fear. "If I am to die under these tentacles, so be it. I've had a good life, and far more of it than most."

As his fear melted, so did the slithering monster, melting into nothingness. It hung like clinging smoke around him for a moment before sudden light washed over him. He turned his head to its source—and stared.

What his eyes had told him was probably a bare stone wall, though the cloak of gloom made it hard to see properly, was now a huge open archway. Beyond was a vast chamber awash in glowing golden coins, precious statuary, and gems—literally barrels full of glistening jewels.

Elminster looked at all its dazzle and just shrugged. His shoulders had barely fallen before the treasure chamber went dark, all of its riches melting away . . . whereupon a trumpet sang out loudly behind him.

El whirled around to see another vast, grand, and warmly lit chamber. This one held no treasure, but instead a crowd of people . . . royalty, by their glittering garb, crowns, and proud faces. Human kings and scaled, lizardlike emperors jostled with merfolk who were gasping in the air, all crowding forward to lay their crowns and scepters at his feet, murmuring endless variations on, "I submit me and all my lands, Great Elminster."

Princesses were removing their gem-studded gowns, now, and offering both gowns and themselves to him, prostrating themselves to clutch at his ankles. He felt their featherlike fingers upon him, stared into many worshiping, awed, and longing eyes, then shut his own firmly for a moment to gather the will he needed.

When he opened them, an eternity later, it was to say loudly and firmly: "My apologies, and I mean no offense by my refusal, but—no. I cannot accept ye, or any of this."

When he opened his eyes, everything was melting away amid growing dimness, and off to his right another light was growing, this one the dappled dance of true sunlight. Immeira of Buckralam's Starn was gliding forward across a bright room toward him, her arms outstretched and that eager smile on her face, offering herself to him. As she drew near, shaping his name soundlessly on her lips, she pulled open the bodice of her dark blue gown—and Elminster swallowed hard as the memories rose up in a sudden, warm surge.

* * * * *

The sun fell through the windows of Fox Tower and laid dappled fingers across the parchments Immeira was frowning over. Gods, how did anyone make sense of such as this? She sighed and slumped back in her chair—then, in a sort of dream, found herself rising to glide across the room, toward its darkest corner. Halfway there her fingers began to pluck at her catches and lacing, to tear open the front of her gown, as if offering herself to—empty air.

Immeira frowned. "Why—?" she murmured, then abruptly shivered, whirled around, and did up her gown again with shaking fingers.

Her busy fingers clenched into fists when she was done, and she peered in all directions around the deserted room, her face growing pale. "Wanlorn," she whispered. "Elminster? Do you need me?"

Silence was her answer. She was talking to an empty room, driven by her own fancies. Irritated, she strode back to her chair . . . and came to a halt in mid-stride, as a sudden feeling of being watched washed over her. It was followed by a surge of great peace and warmth.

Immeira found herself smiling at nothing, as contented as she'd ever felt. She beamed at the empty room around her and sat back down with a sigh. Dappled sun danced across her parchments, and she smiled at a memory of a slender, hawk-nosed man saving the Starn while she watched. Immeira sighed again, tossed her head to send her hair out of her eyes, and returned to the task of trying to decide who in the Starn should plant what, so that all might have food enough to last comfortably through the winter.

                    *   *   *   *   *

Her warm, yearning eagerness and hope, her delight . . . Elminster reached for Immeira, a broad smile growing on his own face—a smile that froze as the thought struck him: was this spirited young woman to be some sort of reward for him, to mark his retirement from Mystra's service?

He snatched back his hands from the approaching woman and told the darkness fiercely, "No. Long ago I made my choice . . . to walk the long road, the darker way, and know the sweep of danger and adventure and doom. I cannot turn back from it now, for even as I need Mystra, Mystra needs me."

At his words, Immeira and the sun-dappled room behind her melted away into falling motes of dwindling light that plunged down far below him in the great dark void he hung within, until his eyes could see them no more.

Abruptly fresh sunlight washed in from his right. Elminster turned toward it, and found himself gazing into a long chamber lined with rows of bookshelves that reached up to touch its high ceiling. Sunlit dust-motes hung thick in the air, and through their luster Elminster could see that the shelves were crammed with spell tomes, with not an inch of shelf left empty. Ribbons protruded from some of the spines; others glowed with mysterious runes.

A comfortable-looking armchair, footstool, and side table beckoned from the right-hand end of this library. The side table was piled high with books; El took a step forward to get a better look at them and found himself striding hungrily into the room.

Spells of Athalantar, gilt lettering on one spine said clearly. El extended an eager hand and let it fall back to his side, muttering, "No. It breaks my soul to refuse such knowledge, but . . . where's the fun of finding new magic, mastering it phrase by guess, and deduction by spell trial?"

The room didn't fall away into darkness as all the previous apparitions had done. El blinked around at more spellbooks than he could hope to collect in a century or more of doing nothing but hunting down and seizing books of magic, and swallowed. Then, as if in a dream, he took a step toward the nearest shelf, reaching for a particularly fat volume that bore the title *Galagard's Compendium of Spells Netherese.* It was . . . inches from his fingertips when El whirled around and snarled, "No!"

In the echoes of that exclamation his world went dark and empty again, the dusty room swept away in an instant, and he was standing in darkness and on darkness, alone once more.

A light approached out of black velvet nothingness, and became a man in ornate, high-collared robes, standing on a floor of stone slabs with a spell staff winking and humming in his hand. Not seeing Elminster, the

man was staring grimly down at a dead woman
sprawled on the stones before him, gentle smokes rising from her body, her face frozen in an eternal scream
of fear.

"No," the man said wearily. "No more. I find that
'First among Her Chosen' has become an empty boast.
Find another fool to be your slave down the centuries,
lady. Everyone I loved—everyone I *knew*—is dead and
gone, my work is swept away by each new grasping gen-
eration of spell hurlers, Faerûn fades into a pale shadow of the glory I saw in my youth—and most of all, I'm
. . . so . . . damned . . . *tired.* . . ."

The man broke his staff with a sudden surge of
strength, the muscles of his arms rippling. Blue light
flared from the broken ends, swirling in the instant
before a mighty explosion of released magic coalesced
into a rushing wave. The despairing Chosen thrust one
spearlike broken shaft end into his chest. He threw
back his head in a soundless gasp or scream—and fell
away into swirling dust, that convulsing jaw last, an
instant before the outward rush of magic became
blinding.

El turned his gaze away from that flash—only to
find it mirrored in miniature elsewhere, in a hand-sized
scrying sphere that a bald man in red robes was
hunched over. The man shook his fist in triumph at
what he saw in the depths of the crystal, and hissed,
"Yes! *Yes!* Now I am First among Mystra's Chosen—and
if they thought Elthaeris was overbearing, they'll learn
well to kneel and quiver in fear beneath the spell-
seizing scepter of Uirkymbrand! *Hahahaha!* The weak
might just as well slay themselves right now, and yield
their power to one more fitted to wield it—*me!*"

That mad shout was still ringing in Elminster's ears
as that scene winked out, and a circle of light occurred
right beside the last prince of Athalantar. Floating with
it was a dagger—and as he recognized it, it slowly
turned and rose, offering its hilt to his hand.

El looked down at it, smiled, and shook his head. "No. That's a way out I'll never take," he said.

The dagger winked out of existence—and promptly reappeared off to Elminster's left, in the hand of a robed man, his back to El, who promptly drove it into the back of another robed man. The victim stiffened as his wound spat forth a blue radiance, and the blade of the murderer's dagger flared up into a blue flame that swiftly consumed it. The dying man turned, his wound leaking a trail of tiny stars, and El saw that it was Azuth. Face convulsed in pain, the god clawed with his bare hands at the face of the man who stabbed him— and the radiance leaking out of him showed El the face of the recoiling murderer. The slayer of Azuth was . . . Elminster.

"No!" El shouted, raking at the vision with his hands. "Away! *Awaaay!*" The two figures struggled with each other in the heart of a spreading cloud of blue stars, oblivious to him.

"Such ambitions are not mine," El snarled, "and shall never be, if Mystra grant it so. I am content to walk Faerûn, and know its ways more than I know the deep mysteries . . . for how can I truly appreciate the one without the other?"

The dying Azuth swirled away, and out of the stars that had been his blood strode a man El knew from memories not his own, spell-shared with him once in Myth Drannor. It was Raumark, a sorcerer-king of Netheril who'd survived the fall of that decadent realm to become one of the founders of Halruaa. Raumark the Mighty stood alone in a hall of stout white pillars and vast echoing spaces, at the top of a high dais, and his face was both pale and grim.

Carefully he cast a spinning whorl of disintegration, testing it by dragging it through one of the giant pillars. The ceiling sagged as the top of the sheered-off pillar fell away into heavy crashing shards to the unseen floor below. Raumark watched the collapse, stone-faced, and brought the whorl back to spin in front of him, just beyond the lip of the dais.

He nodded down at it, as if satisfied—and jumped through it.

The scene died with Raumark, to be replaced by a view of a dusty tomb. A man El did not recognize but somehow knew was a Chosen of Mystra was taking an old and tattered grimoire out of a shoulder sack and placing it into an opened casket, the same task El had done so often for the Lady of Mysteries.

This Chosen, however, was in the grip of a seething fury, his eyes blazing with near madness. He plucked a cobwebbed skull up out of the casket, gazed into its sightless eye sockets, and snarled at it, "Spell after spell I just *give away,* while my body crumbles and grows deaf and stumbling. I'll end up like you in a few winters! Why should others taste the rewards I dole out, while I do not? Eh?"

He flung the skull back into its resting place and shoved the stone lid closed violently, the stony grating so loud that El winced. The Chosen strode forward with red fire in his eyes and said, "To live forever—why not? Seize a healthy body, snuff out its mind, ride it to ruin, then take the next. I've had the spells for a long time—why not use them?"

He resumed his determined walk, fading like a ghost through Elminster—but when the Athalantan turned his head to watch what happened to the Chosen, the man was gone, and the tomb he'd left fast fading behind him.

"Such a waste," El murmured, unshed tears glimmering in his eyes. "Oh, Mystra, Lady Mine, must this go on? Torment me no more, but give me some sign. Am I worthy to serve you henceforth? Or are ye so displeased with me that I should ask ye for death? Lady, tell me!"

It was a shock to feel the sudden tingling of lips upon his—Mystra's lips, they must be, for at their touch the thrill of raw power surged through him, making him feel alert and vigorous and mighty.

Elminster opened his eyes, lifting his arms to embrace her—but the Lady of the Weave was no more than a dwindling face of light, beyond his reach and receding swiftly into the void. "Lady?" he gasped almost despairingly, stretching out beseeching arms to her.

Mystra smiled. "You must be patient," her calm voice came quietly into his ear. "I shall visit you properly in time to come, but I must set you a task for me, first: a long one, perhaps the most important you'll ever undertake."

Her face changed, looking sad, and she added, "Though I can foresee at least one other task that might be judged as important."

"What task?" El blurted out. Mystra was little more than a twinkling star now.

"Soon," she said soothingly. "You shall know very soon. Now return to Faerûn—and heal the first wounded being you meet."

The darkness melted away, and El found himself in his clothes again, standing in the woods outside the ruins. A few paces away, two men were talking with an elf, all three of them sitting with their backs against the trunks of gnarled old trees. They broke off their converse to look up at him rather anxiously.

One of the mages suddenly sprouted a wand in his hand. Leveling it at Elminster, he asked coolly, "And you would be—?"

El smiled and said, "Dead long ago, Tenthar Taerhamoos, save for the fact that Mystra had other plans."

The three mages blinked at him, and the elf asked rather hesitantly, "You're the one they call Elminster, aren't you?"

"I am," El replied, "and the mission laid upon me is to heal ye." Ignoring a suddenly displayed arsenal of wands and winking rings, he cast a healing spell upon Starsunder, then another on Umbregard.

He and Tenthar locked gazes as he finished his castings, and El inclined his head toward the ruins and
asked, " 'Tis all done, then?"

"All but the drinking," Tenthar replied—and there
was suddenly a dusty bottle of wine in his hand. He
rubbed its label, peered into it suspiciously, drew out its
cork, sniffed, and smiled.

"Magic seems to be reliable once more," he
announced, holding out his other hand and watching
four crystal goblets appear in it.

"Mystra's need is past, I think," El told him. "A testing is done, and many dark workers of magic have been
culled."

Tenthar frowned and said, "It is the way of the cruel
gods to take the best and brightest from us."

Umbregard shrugged as he accepted a glass and
watched several other bottles appear out of thin air.
"It is the way of gods to take us all," he added, "in
the end."

Starsunder said then, "My thanks for the healing,
Elminster. As to the way of gods, I believe none of us
were made to live long. Elf, dwarf, human . . . even, I
think, our gods themselves. The passage of too many
years does things to us, makes us mad . . . the losses—
friends, lovers, family, favorite places—and the loneliness. For my kind, a reward awaits, but that doesn't
make the tarrying here any less wrenching; it only
gives us something to look at, beyond present pain."

Elminster nodded slowly. "There may well be truth
in thy words." He looked at Starsunder sidelong then
and asked, "Did we meet, however briefly, in Myth
Drannor?"

The moon elf smiled. "I was one of those who dis-
agreed with the Coronal about admitting other races
into the Fair City," the elf admitted. "I still do. It hastened our passing and gained us nothing but all our
secrets stolen. And you were the one to break open
the gates. I hated you and wished you dead. Had

there been an easy, traceless way, I might have made things so."

"What stayed your hand?" El asked softly.

"I took your measure, several times, at revels and in the Mythal, and after. And you were as we—alone, and striving as best you knew how. I salute you, human. You resisted our goading, conducted yourself with dignity, and did well. Your good deeds will out-live you."

"My thanks," Elminster replied, his eyes bright with tears as he leaned over to embrace the elf. "To hear that means a lot."

* * * * *

The Fair Maid was elbow-to-elbow crowded. It seemed the High Duke's latest idea was to send huge armed caravans along the perilous road. Ripplestones looked like a drovers' yard, with beasts bawling and on the move everywhere. Inside, shielded a trifle from the dust if not the din, Beldrune, Tabarast, and Caladaster were sharing a table with a haughty mage from the Sword Coast, brimming tankards in every hand. The talk was of spells and fell monsters vanquished and wizards who would not die rising from their tombs, and folk were crowding around to listen.

"Why, that's *nothing!*" Beldrune was snarling. "Less than nothing! This very day, in the heart of the Dead Place, I stood beside the god *Azuth!*"

The mage from the Coast sneered in open disbelief, and thus goaded, Beldrune rushed on, "Oh, *yes*—Azuth, I tell you, an' . . ."

Caladaster and Tabarast exchanged silent looks, nodded, and with one accord rose and rummaged in Caladaster's pack while their comrade snarled on, jab-bing a finger in the Coast mage's startled nose. "He

needed our help, I tell you. *Our* spells saved the day—
he said that!—an' he gave us to understand—"

"That we'd earned these magical robes!" Tabarast
broke in triumphantly, holding up the daring black
gown for all to see.

The roar of laughter that followed threatened to
shake the very ceiling of the inn down on top of all the
table-slapping, hooting drinkers, but as their laughter
finally trailed away, a high-pitched chuckle joined in,
from the doorway. Those who turned to see its source
went very still.

"That almost looks as if it would fit me," Sharindala
the sorceress told the four gaping mages brightly. "And
I do need something to preserve my modesty, as you
can see."

The Lady of Scorchstone Hall wore only her long,
silken brown hair. It cloaked her breast and flanks as
she strode forward, but no man there could fail to notice
that aside from her tresses, she was bare to the world
from the top of her head down to her hips—where her
flesh ended, leaving bare bones from there to the floor.

"May I?" she asked, extending a hand for the garment. Around her, several folk slid down in their seats,
fainting dead away, and there was a rush of booted feet
for the door. Suddenly there was a small circle of empty
space in the Fair Maid, ringed by men who were mostly white-faced and staring.

"I've got to get through a few more spells before I'll
be able to eat or drink anything," Sharindala explained,
"and it's rather embarrassing. . . ."

Tabarast snatched the gown out of her reach with a
low growl of fear, but Caladaster stepped in front of
him, tugging on his own robe. He had it over his head
and off in a trice, to reveal a rotund and hairy body
clad in breeches and braces that were stiff and shiny
with age and dirt. "It's none too clean, lady," he said hesitantly, "and will probably hang on you as loose as any
tent, but . . . take it; 'tis freely given."

A long, slender white arm took it, and a smile was given in return. "Caladaster? You were just a lad when I—oh, gods, has it been so long?"

Caladaster swallowed, red faced, and licked lips that seemed suddenly very dry. "What happened to you, Lady Sharee?"

"I died," she replied simply, and utter silence fell in the Maid. Then the sorceress shrugged on the offered robe, and smiled at the man who'd given it to her. "But I've come back. Mystra showed me the way."

There arose a murmur from the crowd. Sharindala took Caladaster's arm in one hand and his tankard in the other—her touch was cool and smooth and normal-seeming enough. She said gently, "Come, walk with me; we've much to talk about."

As they moved toward the door together, the half-skeletal sorceress paused in front of the mage from the Coast and added, "By the way, sir: everything that's been said about Azuth here this night is true. Whether you believe it or not."

They went out the door in a silence so deep that people had to gasp for air by the time they remembered to breathe again.

*   *   *   *   *

He seemed to have lost his boots again and to be walking barefoot on moonlight, somewhere in Faerûn where the sun of late afternoon should still have reigned. A breath ago he'd been talking with three mages in a forest, and the cheese had begun to arrive, to go with their wine—and now he was here, left with but a glimpse of their startled faces at the manner of his going.

So where exactly *was* here?

"Mystra?" he asked aloud, hopefully.

The moonlight surged up around him into silver flames that did not burn but instead sent the thrill of power through him, and those flames shaped themselves into arms that embraced him.

"Lady mine," Elminster breathed as he felt the soft brush of a familiar body against his—there went his clothes again; how did she *do* that?—and the tingling touch of her lips.

He kissed her back, hungrily, and silver fire swept through him as their bodies trembled together. He tried to caress soft, shifting flames—only to find himself holding nothing and standing in darkness once more, with Mystra standing like a pillar of silver fire not far away.

"Mystra?" El asked her, letting a little of the loneliness he'd felt into his voice.

"Please," the goddess whispered pleadingly, "This is as hard for me as it has been for you—I must not tarry. And you tempt me, Elminster . . . you tempt me so."

Silver flames swirled, and a hungry mouth closed on El's own for one long, glorious moment, fires crashing and charging through him, rising into splendor that made him weep and roar and writhe all at once.

"Elminster," that musical voice told him, as he floated in hazy bliss, "I'm sending you now to Silverhand Tower to rear three Chosen."

"Rear?" El asked, startled, his bliss washed away into alert alarm.

There seemed to be a laugh struggling to break through the tones of the goddess as she said, "You'll find three little girls waiting in the Tower, alone and uncertain. Be as a kindly uncle and tutor to them; feed them, clothe them, and teach them how to be and who to be."

Elminster swallowed, watching Mystra dwindle once more into a distant star. "You are forbidden to control their minds, or compel them save in emergencies most dire," she added. "As they grow older, let them forge forth to make their own lives. Your task then will be to watch over them covertly, and to ride in and pick up the pieces to ensure their survival from time to time, not to guide them unless they seek your advice . . . and we both know how often willful Chosen seek out the advice of others, don't we?"

"Mystra!" El cried despairingly, reaching out his arms for her.

"Oh by the Weave, man, don't make this any harder for me," Mystra murmured, and the kiss and caress that set him afire then also whirled him end over end, away.

Epilogue

Perhaps the greatest service Elminster has ever done for Faerûn is to be father and mother to the daughters of Mystra. Holding almost all of Mystra's magic and keeping Toril together with his very fingertips during the Time of Troubles—that was easy. Rearing little girls of clever wits, much energy, bewitching beauty, and mighty magical powers, and doing it well—now that's hard.

Antarn the Sage
from **The High History of
Faerûnian Archmages Mighty**
published circa The Year of the Staff

Silverhand Tower, when he found himself standing a little way off from it, blinking in the sunlight, was a riven shell, little more than a cottage attached to an empty ring of battlements and the gutted stump of a keep. Deep woods surrounded it, cloaked it, and were in the patient process of overwhelming it, hewn back only from an oval vegetable garden. A small, dirty face was peering doubtfully at him from its leafy green heart—a face that vanished, leaving only dancing leaves behind, once he smiled at it.

Elminster peered at the garden to see if he could catch sight of a little body scuttling anywhere. He could not, and soon shrugged and strolled toward the cottage, its straw roof a mass of bright flowers and nodding herbs.

"Ambara?" he called gently as he approached. "Ethena?"

The door seemed to be stuck fast—off the latch, but refusing to open. He nudged it with his knee, mindful of the fact that little bodies might be crouched behind it, and heard the faint protest of wood splintering. It had been pegged closed, into a dirt floor. Someone had a mallet or mace or axe to hand.

"Ambara?" he asked the darkness within. "Ethena? Anamanué?"

The wand spat so close behind him that he heard the young, light voice murmur the command word quite clearly before the rain of magic missiles tore into him, hurling him against the door. His body was still shuddering as something snatched the peg away and hurled the door open, spilling him into the dim interior, and something else drove an axe at his head, hard.

It struck his spellshield with a shower of sparks and glanced away, numbing hands that were too small for it and making their owner sob with pain. Without thinking El reached out and placed a healing on the small, barefoot slip of a girl who was trying not to cry . . . and became aware that an utter silence had fallen.

He drew his hand slowly back from the one he'd healed, seeing an intent face above a tightly clutched and dusty dagger, close by his left ear—and an equally intent face, over the ready-held wand, just out of reach to his right. Long and tousled silver hair adorned all three heads, and all three of the faces, even in their dirty, alarmed, and childlike state, were breathtaking in their beauty.

"How is it you know our names?" the eldest one—with the wand—asked him fiercely. "Who are you?"

"Mystra told me," Elminster replied, giving her a grave smile, "and sent me to do for ye three what thy mother now cannot."

"Our mother's *dead!*" the girl with the wand told him fiercely.

Elminster nodded. "Ye're Ambara," he said, "aren't ye?"

"Nobody calls me *that*," the girl told him, tossing her head angrily. Gods, but she was beautiful.

"Ye're Ambara Dove, four summers old," El said gently. "What would ye like me to call ye?"

"Dove," the little girl told him. "And that's Storm. She can talk a little. Laer can't, yet—she just cries."

"She needs changing," El observed gravely.

"We all do," Dove told him severely, "after the fright you gave us. What we need most, though, is something to eat. I can't be wasting this precious thing"—she waved the wand with the air of a veteran battlemage—"blasting down any more little birds and beasts that make us sick to even look at them . . . and the things I know are safe to eat are *gone*."

"I'm not a great cook," El told her.

Dove sighed. "Why'd Mystra send *you*, then?" she asked rudely, then pointed with the wand. "We use *that* bit of the stream, below the stump, to wash, and drink from up here. You change Laer, and I'll go hunting. Storm'll be—"

"Watching you," Storm said suddenly, putting out a hand to take firm hold of Elminster's beard. "Shielding Laer. Be nice . . . like your beard. Nice."

Elminster grinned at her, found that he had a lump in his throat and tears threatening to burst forth. He swept them all into his arms and wept openly, knowing just a little of what a long, hard road lay before these three little ones, down the long years ahead.

Laeral gurgled with pleasure at being so close to the man who'd banished her pain, but Dove swatted him matter-of-factly on the side of the head and snapped, "Stop that cryin.' Night soon, and we've got to *eat*."

Elminster's tears turned to a chuckle, and suddenly he was rolling around on the dirt floor with three laughing, tumbling girls locked onto his hair and beard.

How many years was he going to be doing this?

* * * * *

The roast lizard was just bones and scorched scales and a pleasant smell, now. His crushed-berry sauce had been crude but a beginning, and he'd discovered that none of the girls had enough clothing to keep them warm as they slept, to say nothing of decent—but that his cloak would easily furnish three blankets just large enough to wrap them in. The sun was going down, and as El stared up at the twilit woods, he saw Mystra's dark eyes gazing down at him from among their tangled branches.

He stared into those eyes of deep mystery, as they sent him silent love and sympathy and fond admiration and sent back a silent prayer for guidance. He did not move until it was fully dark, and true night ruled the land.

A small hand captured one of his. Gods, but they could move silently, these three—or stealthily enough that an insect chorus could cloak their noises, at least.

Elminster looked down and whispered, "Shouldn't ye be getting off to sleep?"

Dove pulled at his hand.

"Uncle Weirdbeard," she said insistently, "it's dark time, and I can't sleep until I know you're on guard against the wolves and all—else I have to stay up with my stick. I'm tired. Hadn't we better go in?"

He stared at her, found tears swimming in his eyes again, and quickly looked up at the brightening stars overhead.

"Sir," she asked almost sternly, pulling on his hand again, "Hadn't we better go in?"

El sighed, gave the stars a last look, his heart full. He knelt down, gave her a gentle kiss and a smile, and said, "Yes, I suppose we should. Why don't ye lead the way?"